# BOARDING PASS

## A Novel

by

## PAUL CUMBO

*This is for Dad.*

# PROLOGUE: FIRE

*Heat squeezes him. Crushing. Suffocating. All around him, thunder that won't stop—thunder in stereo-surround. The hiss of his breathing. Static on the radio. Darkness envelops him. Ironic, really. So many flames, like a million candles, but always so dark. The ceiling and walls form an abstract kaleidoscope, a twisting mass of oily plumes and seething tongues. He can feel the fury of it. The hunger. It devours.*

*He sees the exit door below, a fuzzy rectangle of light. It's dim through the haze, the smoke, and the condensation in his mask. The unconscious man slung over his shoulder wasn't heavy at first, but that was almost two minutes ago. In fact, it's been one hundred and four seconds in the furnace since he found him on the floor, and now the weight pulls on him. The seal on his mask broke somehow, must have caught on something, and he tastes the poison leaking in. His eyes burn. Gripping the charred rail with his gloved hand, he takes one step down. Two. Testing the stairs. Praying they hold, doubting they will. The beam of his headlamp arcs ahead, lost after a few feet. His ankle is a twisting, white-hot spike of pain. He winces. His rapid breathing hisses weakly through the regulator, clean air mixing with hot, coppery smoke.*

*The rail collapses. He fights for balance, nearly falls. He braces himself, knees bent, and shrugs the man's dead weight back onto his shoulder. Six more steps down. Maybe seven. A last push. Outside, the chief is shouting, others already spraying him through the doorway with the low-pressure hose. He stumbles through the shattered detritus of the lobby. Room keys are strewn across the floor where the cabinet fell from the wall.*

*Outside. The thunder fades, replaced by ringing in his ears. Weight is lifted as the paramedics take the man from his shoulders. Blue and red lights pulse, dancing in tiny droplets inside his mask. He loses his balance again, falling to one knee. He's dizzy. The chief grips his arm, helps him to his feet, and tears away the mask. The air is cold and sweet, wet on his tongue. He heaves it in deeply, drinking its purity until he coughs hard and vomits. "Daniels, Jesus Christ…you pull a stunt like that again and I'll…" The chief breaks off to answer the radio, still glaring at him but distracted.*

*Now on a gurney, he breathes dry, cold oxygen. The chief holds his hand in one of his, speaking orders into the radio he holds with the other. He winces, still coughing, as another medic pulls his boot off and wraps the ankle in cold packs. "Probably just a sprain, minor injury," someone says. He turns on his side, resting his head on the pillow. Across the parking lot, he sees the figure he carried being lifted into an ambulance, notices now that the man is barefoot, in a bathrobe.*

*A bathrobe he's seen before. Green plaid. Ugly. Like the kind his mother had bought back when …*

*He sits up on the stretcher, pissing off the paramedic, and throws the mask aside. Swinging his legs down, he limps across the wet pavement to the open ambulance, catching the rear door before the driver can shut it. The chief is yelling after him, "Daniels! Get back here for Chrissake! Wouldja get back here an' siddown!" But he has to look. That stupid plaid bathrobe. He clambers aboard, craning his neck over the kneeling medic to get a better look at the man's face. Bewildered, he reaches for the oxygen mask obscuring his features. The naked light inside the ambulance removes all doubt, and he can already tell. He can already make out the scar above the left eyebrow from the fight the night he left them. Angular cheekbones, short-cropped platinum hair, wrinkle lines at the corners of closed eyes…*

*So dizzy. He can smell the ash, feel it burning his eyes as it mixes with sweat. Maybe it's just the smoke. He took in a lot of smoke. No. He's sure.*

*"Dad," he whispers, as much to himself as anyone.*

*The medic puts the mask back in place on the patient and shoots him an aggravated look. "That's my father?" he says. It comes out as a question. He coughs. His throat is burning. The siren kicks on, and the medic pushes him toward the door, shouting for the others, yelling, "Hey! Get this kid outta here! We gotta go!" They pull him from the ambulance. He doesn't resist. There's nausea now. Waves of smoke seem to billow from somewhere inside him. He feels expanding, spiraling, upward pressure, vertigo that twists and throws his guts. He vomits again, falls, and lets the others lift and ease him back onto the gurney.*

*But he watches. The doors are shut, and the ambulance carrying the man who used to be his father heaves into the street away from him, lights flashing and siren wailing. The chief points at him and yells something indecipherable to the paramedic. He can hear bits and pieces of their shouted conversation: "smoke inhalation…disorientation. Fatigue. Vertigo…possible hallucinations." He turns the other way and looks back at the hotel. Dizzy, confused. The flames tower into the sky, high above the collapsing roof. Smoke churns from windows, black like charcoal, an expanding mass against the cloudless blue-velvet sky. Stars shimmer behind the rising heat, and paper-white ashes fall gently as snowflakes.*

# PART I

# CHAPTER 1

I only cheated once in high school.

I was fifteen, and I did it to help my best friend. He didn't make me do it. He didn't even ask me to. It was entirely my idea, and it was rooted in the desperate, saccharine type of love and hate that exists simultaneously between boys growing up together, especially the embattled kind of growing up that happens in a boarding school. It's a sort of loyalty, but it isn't perfect. It's tainted with envy. That envy certainly existed between the two of us, and it fueled a sort of underlying, unspoken competition. The competition was overshadowed by affection, though, and for the first six months of my sophomore year, Trey Daniels was the best friend I could ask for.

Like any kids in tenth grade, we took a lot of tests. Some of them were multiple-choice—the kind with the bubble sheets where you mark your answers with a number-two pencil. During one of these tests, I didn't write my own name, Matthew Derby, on the answer sheet. Instead, I wrote, "Trey Daniels." And he wrote my name in place of his. The teacher never found out, so when she put our scores in the grade book, I failed and he passed. It was only one grade and I was a strong student, so it didn't affect my average much. On the other hand, it was enough to keep him afloat for a while.

But only for a while, as it turned out.

The ability of boys to accept each other despite our differences is remarkable. That's not to say we always do, but the truth is, in contrast to the men we eventually become, most boys are surprisingly unassuming, tolerant, and open. I imagine the same might be said about girls and women, but I wouldn't know half as well, never having been either. There's something about the warmth and vital intensity of the early friendships that form among boys, qualities that become increasingly elusive as the years go on. I'm surprised that I've noticed this already. In fact, a perspective like this might even sound a little bit ridiculous coming from me, since I'm only twenty-one. But it's true. I've noticed that friendships have changed. Those memories of boyhood are already taking on vague sepia tones.

Now those tones come in varying shades—mostly in the warm palette of trust, warmth, acceptance and joy. But there are colder, darker hues, too. There's anger and confusion and betrayal and sadness. There's the desolation and abandonment a kid feels when his father fails him, like Trey's did, or the way you feel when your best friend—that one guy who, for a while, is your confidant and your wingman and your backup—leaves you behind, intentionally or not, as mine did to me when he disappeared halfway through sophomore year.

This is the part where you might, understandably, think this is another sad story about a boy's untimely death—a reflective elegy shared years later in serious tones with nostalgic perspective. I'm afraid it isn't quite that dramatic. In fact, I'm not so sure that anything I'm about to tell you is all that dramatic. I just want to tell you about a friend who taught me about decisions, forgiveness, and courage. In the process, he helped me figure out some of the things that a twenty-one-year-old guy needs to figure out. You might say he gave me the kick-start I needed to face reality. To realize how much I'd been hesitating to grow up.

A quick disclaimer: If I'm going to write about decisions and courage, I should start by telling you that I haven't been all that decisive or courageous

4

lately. I'm lucky. I've got one year of college left. Everything looks great on paper. But the truth is, things haven't been too clear for the past year or so. A guy in my position is supposed to have things pretty well mapped out. He's supposed to have direction. Well, until recently, I had little. They say that's a thing about this generation: we have so many choices that we can't make decisions. Accurate. Well said. See, there's a difference between *choices* and *decisions*. You make a choice at the drive-through. Coke or Sprite. Extra pickles, maybe. Decisions, though. Shit. I've been having a lot of trouble in the Decisions Department.

But then this stuff happened last week—the last week of August 2002. That friend whose name went on my tenth-grade English test almost six years ago made his way into a burning building in a small western town. And when he fought his way out, he carried his father in his arms.

Fate got together with Circumstance, met up somewhere with Chance, and the three proceeded to tango. That's when everything changed.

■ ■ ■

My family has a small, modest cottage about sixty miles south of Buffalo, New York, deep in the woods of Cattaraugus County near Ellicottville, a tiny ski town in the Allegheny foothills not far from the Pennsylvania border. There are few lights, even fewer neighbors, and I like it that way. We have a pond in front of the house, certainly not big enough to be called a lake but sizeable enough, nestled in a three-acre meadow with tall pine trees surrounding it. A dock extends fifteen feet out over the water. Building it was a summer project my father undertook a few years ago, and it had kept him happily occupied in the fresh air on weekends.

I was perched at the end of that dock last week, bare feet dangling over the edge, wearing khaki shorts and a zip-up Georgetown sweatshirt. I sipped a cold bottle of Pabst. The sky had that pinkish blush you get with late August sunsets, and a breeze rippled the surface and danced through the dense pines on the banks of the lake, whispering that summer was almost over. Our tiny rowboat bumped against the dock where it was tied to the metal ladder. Dragonflies hummed, skirting the surface.

I nibbled on sunflower seeds, pinching tiny handfuls from the bowl I'd brought from the kitchen. After throwing a few in the water, I watched them float until little sunfish came up to eat them. I caught a glimpse of their mouths and reddish stripes for half a second before they slipped beneath the surface with a tiny plop. My reflection wavered in the glassy surface, a dark silhouette against the deepening pastels of the sky.

It was pretty peaceful.

I could hear Mom and Dad doing the dishes through the open windows several yards behind me, cheerful banter inspired by a full carafe of sauvignon blanc with dinner. It was grilled rainbow trout, my dad's idea of a celebration for our last night here. I turned around and saw warm light spill from the open window, steam rising from the sink as Mom dried a dish. She looked up and gave me a little wave and a smile.

Like she used to. I still feel like a kid there. My room still has the sailboat wallpaper and glow-in-the-dark stars on the ceiling. It is a world away from school, from DC, from the craziness of 9/11 just less than a year ago. And far away from Lynn, the girl who came into my life last year and fell away this spring. No, nothing changes at the cottage. Stasis. We've been going there for as long as I can remember. It used to be the whole month of July when I was little. Me, Mom and Dad, uncles, aunts, and cousins. Now it's just the three of us, and a few days in August is the most that jobs and schedules will allow.

Of course, the last time I was here, I didn't feel much like a little kid at all. Lynn and I had driven up one weekend last November, when the place was closed for the winter. I had to climb in through a window, and the water, power, and heat were shut off. We lit candles, got reasonably drunk, clumsily undressed each other the way that drunk college kids do, and fooled around in front of the fireplace before falling asleep in a down sleeping bag I use for camping. In the morning, we sat out here on the dock, drank coffee we boiled on a camping stove, and watched the snow fall on the nearly frozen lake. She held my hand. We both shivered, but we stayed out here for an hour, listening to the silence of the woods and each wondering what the next year would hold for us as we began to think about life after college.

That was last November.

The screen door slammed—I was supposed to fix it—and my dad headed across the little yard and stepped onto the dock. I could feel it shake as he walked. He sat down heavily next to me, handing me another bottle and opening one for himself.

"How's my kid?" Dad's voice was quiet, mellowed by the wine. He reeked of insect repellent.

I nodded, twisted the top off the beer, and quietly clinked bottles with him. "Nice out here tonight."

"It is," he replied. "Hey, I meant to tell you, I like the haircut. You look about sixteen again."

"Thanks, I think." I ran my hand through my short-cropped hair. It had been longer for the past couple years of college, sort of a dirty-blond mop.

We sat silently for a while. A sunfish nabbed another seed, sending ripples outward. Dad inhaled loudly through his nose, which is something he does before he asks a question bearing great significance.

"Any more thoughts?"

"On what?"

"Plans. You know. Last year of college. The great adventure in self-sufficiency starts in May, buddy. I stop paying bills. Behold, the real world is upon thee." He gave me a good-natured punch to the shoulder—the kind good-natured dads give their sons.

*It was so quiet out here a moment ago.*

I threw more seeds into the lake. They stuck together in a little triangle that spun slowly, and it took the sunfish a few tries to take them under. "Still trying to decide about law school." I stared at my rippling reflection.

"Hmm. When are applications due?"

I dodged the question. "I was thinking it might be good to do something else first." I took a long draw on the beer. "Just for a while." Dad was quiet for a moment. He sipped his own beer and then set it down on the dock.

"Something else like what?"

"Not sure. I was leaning toward looking for an internship on the Hill. Or I could teach for a while. There's always a lot of teaching jobs in the private schools down there, and you don't need state certification for most of them."

His brow furrowed. "Teaching is a real possibility. But you have to *want* to do that. Anyway, you have to start moving on something soon or you'll be like every other college grad waving a diploma around with no job."

"I know. But I've got a lot of connections. Georgetown's the biggest old boys' club down there. One of the professors has a few leads on the Hill. I could always talk to Brady about teaching at Ashford for a year or two. Pretty sure I could work that out." Lately, I'd thought more and more frequently about heading back to my alma mater to teach.

Dad picked the beer up. "Connections are good, but they aren't surefire." He took a sip, swallowed it, and raised his eyebrows. "Sounds like someone needs to make up his mind."

I cocked a smile and looked at my dad—platinum hair, tortoiseshell glasses, Buffalo Bills cap, and a flannel shirt. *Michael Derby, aged forty-seven. Father, Navy veteran, self-made businessman, and after-school special!*

"I'll have a history degree. Pretty open-ended," I mumbled. I studied one of the sunflower seeds up close, brushing the fine powdered salt with my thumb. "Maybe that's the problem, huh? Lots of options."

"I don't know if options are a problem at twenty-one. I didn't have…" Dad decided to let it rest. He clapped me on the back. "It'll come together."

"Yeah."

*Lord be praised. It is finished.*

"So, what's the deal with Lynn?"

*Goddamnit. It is not finished.*

"Not much of a deal at all." I slugged the rest of the beer down.

"Spoken to her at all over the summer?"

"Once. Well, not really. No."

"She seemed nice."

"She is nice, dad. It's not because she wasn't nice."

"Hmm." Dad finished the beer and set the bottle down, deliberately this time.

I detected advice coming on. It was the way he put the bottle down and, again, noisily drew in his breath. I wasn't in the mood for more advice. "I need to take a leak." I stood, brushed the salt from the sunflower seeds off my sweatshirt, and pointed to the beer. "Another one?"

"Sure." He handed me the empty bottle and gave a nod, apparently content to let the subject settle on the bottom of the pond. Part of me did want to get my dad's insights on the whole thing, but at the same time, I absolutely could not bring myself to talk about it right then. Lynn and I had broken up at the end of the second semester. It was a slow process of falling apart for a series of stupid, small reasons that seemed important. The tension between us had been growing since the weeks following Christmas and finally escalated into an embarrassing shouting match in the front hallway of her apartment in the middle of finals in May, essentially about whose fault it was that we weren't talking anymore. I was a mess and nearly bombed one of my exams because of it. Fortunately, one of the gifts bestowed by my expensive education is a remarkable knack for composing pretty convincing bullshit, the kind that's custom made for a 300-level philosophy final. So I passed the exam, and then went on not communicating with Lynn.

I padded across the lawn, the grass tickling my ankles, and slapped a mosquito on my neck. I opened the screen door and let it slam behind me. It was warmer inside and still smelled like dinner. Mom was humming as she pulled some clothes out of the dryer in the laundry room. I passed the tiny TV set on the kitchen counter, a serious-looking reporter detailing the weather for the coming week. "Dropping temperatures, and—can ya believe it, folks?—September's just around the corner!" I stepped into the bathroom, kicking the door halfway closed. I lifted the toilet seat and peed. I half-listened to the reporter rambling on while I washed my hands.

"And continuing our spotlight on hometown heroes from around the country, we bring you a heartwarming story of bravery and amazing coincidence from the small town of Jackson, Wyoming. Firefighter Thomas 'Trey' Daniels, twenty-two, is in stable condition at St. John's Medical Center..."

*Thomas Daniels.*

*Trey.*

I froze for a second and then shut the water off. I quickly dried my hands with the little towel hanging next to the sink and then stepped back into the kitchen. The reporter went on: "...after rescuing his own father from a raging hotel fire in the early hours of yesterday morning. The father, listed in critical condition at the same hospital, was visiting from out of town when the fire broke out." I leaned in close to the set. Footage played of a building engulfed in flames, the red lights of fire trucks spinning as medics carried a stretcher into an ambulance.

The reporter continued, "The blaze, which began around one o'clock this morning local time, is blamed on a faulty gas line running to the hotel's kitchen. Thomas Daniels, the first firefighter to enter the building, suffered minor injuries and smoke inhalation after pulling his unconscious father from the floor of his upstairs room. That's right, his own father." A flash of a photo, Trey in the department uniform. The face immediately familiar. Dark, narrow eyes. Upturned grin. "What makes this story truly amazing," continued the reporter, "are the coincidental circumstances. According to friends, Daniels Senior had been estranged from his wife and son for five years and had come to make a surprise visit, planning to try to make amends. His son, the firefighter, had no knowledge of the visit and did not recognize his father until *after* pulling him from the inferno."

My mind flashed back to sophomore year at boarding school. There was a storm that night. Trey had gotten in another fight. He was crying. He'd said, "I wish you were my brother."

The camera switched to the Jackson fire chief, his face smudged with ash. "This is an incredible coincidence. This young man saved his own father's life. But the father's in a rough way. So we just need to pray for both of them. Trey is a good firefighter and a good friend to many of us here in Jackson Hole. He's made us proud."

*You could go there and see him.*

I stared absently at the set as Trey's photo faded in again, "Hometown Heroes Series" appearing in stencil letters across the bottom of the screen.

*Go and see him.*

My mind raced. *A flight to Wyoming. When do classes start? Not until Monday. It's only Wednesday.*

*"I wish you were my brother."*

*I forgot about him.*

I turned off the sports report and opened the fridge for a couple more beers, staring at the brightly lit contents, feeling the wave of cold on my legs and face. Mom came out of the laundry room with her cup of coffee and headed outside. She called through the window. "Bring down those folding chairs, would you, honey?"

"Sure." I went outside, grabbing the chairs on the way. It felt cooler now on the dock. The three of us sat, staring out over the pond.

"It's so peaceful out here at night." Mom spread a plaid picnic blanket across her lap and brought it up to her shoulders. "Chilly, though."

"I just saw something on the news." My voice was flat. The explanation didn't take long.

Mom sipped her coffee while I finished the story. I picked up more seeds. Dad's voice was quiet. "Ah, Trey. Trey of the famous Bahamas vacation. He was expelled, right?"

"About a month after that trip. He was my best friend there for a while."

*"Stay in touch, man."*

Mom looked at me. "National news! Trey was such a nice boy. I remember when he stayed with us for that weekend after your rowing race. Why don't you go out there and see him?"

I threw her a sideways glance, pausing in midthrow with the seeds, while the words sank in. She looked at me, raised her narrow eyebrows, and shrugged. She turned her attention back to the darkening sky and started humming another nameless little tune.

"Go out there?" I repeated it to myself, not meaning to say it out loud. It sounded like a question when I did.

She laughed. "That's right, just go out there. Look up his address, give him a call, and fly out there. What's the big deal? I'm sure he would enjoy seeing an old friend. Shouldn't be hard to find. He's a local hero, right? I think it would be a nice gesture, to reconnect." Mom has a remarkable knack for simplifying things. It might be a product of working for so many years in complex scenarios as a nurse. She can boil situations down to their essential components quickly, and filter out the questions and complexities. A sort of triage process for life. And she was right. It really was that simple. I had a friend, we lost touch, he got hurt, and it would be nice to go visit him. Just that simple.

*No, it isn't,* I thought.

Yes, it was. I could head back to Georgetown tomorrow, get situated in the dorm, fly to Jackson on Friday, be back at school Sunday night. Could work. Wouldn't be hard at all, I thought. Wouldn't be hard at all except the part about seeing a friend I hadn't seen in almost six years. Truthfully, six years is not a very long time. But this was a little bit different. Trey was the first real friend I'd ever made, and he'd disappeared. It had hurt. I'd forgotten how much it had hurt.

"I didn't even know he was a firefighter," I said. "I don't know anything about him. Used to know a lot."

Dad stretched his arms. "It happens, son. People drift apart. Distance. Circumstance. You know."

"It was the wrong school for him."

*Distance. Circumstance.*

"I think your mom is right," said Dad. "It's the decent thing to do. You guys were close for a while, and people change a lot, right? And beyond that, you know, it's your last free weekend before school starts. That's a beautiful part of the country and it might be a good place to go clear your head. Certainly a better way to spend the last weekend than partying in Georgetown."

"I guess it would be."

"Well, I would go if I were you. We'll help you with the ticket. Not first class, though, okay?"

12

"Right."

I watched the sunflower seeds sail through the air, and as they settled on the inky darkness of the pond, I realized it that was exactly what I was going to do, because there are people who come into your life at times that matter. Sometimes it's just for a little while. But even for that little while, they are the friends you need, and they teach you the things you need to know about being a person. Six years ago, that's who Trey Daniels was to me.

# CHAPTER 2

The following night, I sat in boxers and a white T-shirt in the darkness of my bedroom back at Georgetown, tired from the seven-hour drive. Brian McNeal, one of my two roommates, was in the other room with his girlfriend, Tricia. From the muffled sounds I could hear, they were having a happy reunion.

I held a cell phone in one hand and a scrap of paper in the other. I couldn't find Trey's number, but I was able to find a listing for his mom in Jackson through an online search. I dialed the cell phone and stared at the glowing numbers before pushing send. No answer. A machine picked up, the voice clear and melodic, like a voice on soap commercials talking about nourishing moisturizers and revitalizing nutrients.

*Tracy Daniels.*

I pressed end right after the machine beeped, unable to think of what the hell to say. *Hi, Mrs. Daniels, this is Matt Derby, Trey's old roommate from the prep school he got kicked out of. So, I hear your ex-husband is in the hospital clinging to life after Trey rescued him in what amounts to a frighteningly uncanny twist of fate! Anyway, mind if I come visit? By the way, can I bring you anything?*

I decided to call again tomorrow and set the cell phone down on the desk. I woke my laptop from sleep mode. A few minutes later, I'd clicked my way through the online reservation process, and the printer turned out a confirmation page. Reagan National to Detroit, boarding at 10:02, connecting flight to Jackson.

The noises were louder through the wall now. *Christ, McNeal.* I turned on the stereo. Reaching for the switch, I glanced at the picture still tacked to the wall. I had my arm around Lynn at the middle-school swimming pool where she worked. Both of us were smiling. A splash of her chestnut hair lay on my shoulder. My hair was longer then, which Lynn had liked. She called it "sandy blond." The camera's flash lit up my eyes and gave them a supernatural shade of blue, much brighter than the dull gray-blue they really are. I took it down and thought for a second about throwing it away. *You're such a baby*, I thought. I put it in the desk drawer instead.

I remembered the last night before my foreign policy seminar paper was due last semester. She'd lain in the bed, propped up on her elbow, flinging pink elastic hair bands at me while I stood at the desk waiting for the paper to print. I turned around and glared after taking a shot to my left ear, but it faded to a smirk when I saw her sitting upright, eyes wide with surprise and guilt and hands cupped over her mouth. She wore the soft flannel pajama pants I'd bought her and a white tank top. I shook my head, smiled, and pulled off my T-shirt. I switched off the computer and shuffled over to the bed, climbing in with her, feeling the warmth of her body on mine, the downy softness of her cheek against my neck.

I remember lying with her later on, the insulated, serene sensation of physical exhaustion and fading excitement, an enveloping calm quietly taking its place. I felt a chill and shivered as tiny beads of sweat evaporated from my chest and face. I could smell my Old Spice and the lavender scent from her shampoo.

After she said something I didn't hear, she looked up at my eyes, poked me in the ribs, and said, "Hey, you there?" I smiled weakly. We talked for a while. I remember the closeness of the conversation, how I had felt as much as heard our voices with our bodies pressed together. I was also aware of the pauses, the way each silence seemed to float delicately between us in the darkness.

That was April, a few weeks before everything fell apart.

Explaining how and why everything fell apart is not something I'm sure I can do reliably. What I know is that there was a ten-month period when we were best friends. When I knew that I could tell anything to Lynn and that I would be understood, loved, and smiled upon, even if what I'd said was stupid. There was a ten-month period when I regularly envisioned our lives together in the future. Things like marriage and kids had been, up to that point, only abstractions that I suspected would one day be part of my life. It seemed like they began to take on an almost tangible possibility, maybe even probability, with Lynn. I had been proud to introduce her to my parents, and we'd had dinner together in Georgetown, laughing and trading stories for almost four hours until the manager nearly kicked us out of the restaurant. For ten months we were intimate, and for the first time in my life that intimacy took on a meaning that was more than adolescent; it was something shared and expressive. It left me feeling whole, rather than used and empty.

And then one day, almost out of nowhere, it began to feel like we were taking each other for granted. We spent just as much time together, but as time went on we were less and less *together*. There was proximity and conversation and laughter and sex, but each of these things began to take on a sort of mechanical, hollow quality. I don't really know why. And then we stopped talking as much. And when we stopped talking as much, we kept more from each other. And when we kept more from each other, it got easier and easier to take each other for granted. And the cycle continued until that argument in May when we both made fools of ourselves in front of her apartment, each saying things we didn't mean. The next afternoon, we sat at a coffee shop, both in tears, trading watered down clichés about taking time apart and getting a little distance. She said that maybe it would be better if we did, since we'd be graduating soon anyway and would probably have to split up. I found myself agreeing, because on one level, it made so much damned sense and it would end the weird, out of control spiral pattern that seemed to be tightening against us. What I don't understand is why something that hurt so much felt so necessary right then.

After she walked out, I stared at one of her teardrops that had landed on the varnished wooden table. It was a perfectly symmetrical splash pattern. I remember a distinct falling sensation after she left, as though the floor had dropped out from under me. Before we had walked into that coffee shop, she'd been my girlfriend; afterward, it was clear she wasn't. It was as though all the shared memories and experiences were cheap paper fragments, disjointed and scattered. I remember a couple of occasions when I'd walked home to my dorm after having a bit too much to drink. It wasn't so much that I couldn't walk straight—just a sense of being off balance with a sort of tunnel vision. Walking home from the coffee shop in the bright May afternoon sunshine had felt pretty much the same.

I took the photo out again and looked at it for a while. Her smile was always so warm. I thought about giving her a call. But I put the photo away and gave up on the idea. Not now. Maybe tomorrow from the airport. I threw what I needed into my duffel bag along with a book on free-trade policy, turned off the stereo, and climbed into bed.

Brian and Tricia finished in the other room, the thrusting and pounding rising to a peak before abruptly ceasing. I could hear their muffled voices talking low and then fading as they fell asleep. The silence got heavy. I thought again about calling Lynn, telling her all this stuff about Trey, and then decided against it. Too tired. Too random. Too late at night.

An ambulance passed, sending shafts of blue and red light through the window, the sounds of the siren rising and then fading. As it turned the corner, the room settled back into silence and my thoughts shifted. I stared up into the darkness of the bedroom, thinking about the friend I was going to see, about the contrast between us: *I go to college. He fights fires.*

McNeal and I sat in the tiny kitchen the next morning. Tricia had left. Brian was making instant oatmeal, which was the only thing we had in the apartment left over from last semester aside from a vast collection of empty beer bottles. No one had gone shopping yet. He wore gym shorts and his varsity sweatshirt. "MCNEAL," it read in block letters, and below, "LIGHTWEIGHT CAPTAIN." I, by comparison, was just another guy on the Georgetown rowing team. McNeal's dedication far surpassed my own.

"We don't have any damn sugar." Brian rifled through the empty cabinets. "Why don't we have any sugar?"

"Sorry, man."

He found a packet of cherry Jell-O mix in the back of the cupboard. "Aha! This stuff is pretty sweet, right?" He ripped open the foil packet and poured the contents on his oatmeal. I looked at him. The Jell-O formed a reddish lump on top of the steaming cereal, and Brian stirred it in.

"That looks very bad," I said.

"Whatever." He jumped up to sit on the counter and began eating. He stuffed a large spoonful into his mouth. "It's not that bad." Brian is a remarkable optimist.

"I see you're off to a running start with Tricia," I said, reaching into the fridge for the orange juice.

Brian grinned and nodded, his mouth full. "An energetic back-to-school night. And I expect you to be on par this semester, Mr. Derby. Time to say a fond farewell to the ghost of Lynn."

"I guess we'll see. For now, I've got enough on my mind with this trip to Wyoming."

His smile faded, and his voice became quieter. "I know you guys were close and all, but it's been a long time. Isn't it gonna be kind of awkward?"

"Yeah. I haven't seen him in almost six years."

"You don't have to go out there, you know."

*True.*

"Nah," I said, "I really do. I never talked to him after he left. And now, well, I don't know. With his dad and everything. I just feel like I should go out and see him. I mean, it was so random seeing it on the news," I finished my glass of juice. "Kind of freaky. I think I was meant to see it."

Brian rolled his eyes. "I think you're full of shit."

"Yeah."

"Look, I'd go with you if I could. I just can't swing it right now. I got a fifteen-page paper due at nine on Monday and a meeting for freshman recruits on Saturday. Besides, I didn't really know him as well as you did." He ate another spoonful. "I can't believe that dude became a firefighter. Not what I woulda thought." Brian winced, looking at the bowl in his hands. "I just got a clump of Jell-O. This is terrible. Why did you let me put Jell-O in my oatmeal? You want it?"

"No, thanks. Firefighter. It is pretty weird, isn't it?" I played with the shoulder strap on my duffel.

"Remember when he saved that little kid?"

"I do." Vivid but scattered memories raced through my mind: a rainy street, brakes and tires squealing, Trey rushing across the sidewalk, a scared kid.

"Even so, I never would have pictured him some kinda blue-collar hero. Wasn't his father a billionaire or something?" asked Brian.

"Well, I don't know about billionaire," I replied. "They were pretty loaded, though, yeah."

Brian dumped the rest of the oatmeal in the sink. "Anyway, when are apps due?"

"Apps?"

"Yeah. Applications. Law school. Future." He flicked the water off his hands at my face.

"Not 'til January. I've got time."

"What about the LSAT?"

"Soon enough."

"I've heard it's a bitch."

"Yeah. I've heard you're a bitch."

He laughed. "You finished with that trade policy thesis?" He laced up his sneakers.

"It's coming together."

"The enthusiasm is overwhelming, Derby. You shoulda stayed with me in finance." He nudged me in the ribs as he passed. "Numbers. Very precise. Free of troubling vagaries and philosophical struggles." He opened the door to go outside. "Give my best to Daniels." He put on his cap and picked up his keys. "Hey, by the way, I just thought of something. Remember how much he hated Rick Eldrin back at school? You should tell him Rick is exactly the Ivy League prick we all knew he'd become and that we kicked the shit out of him in not one but *two* races last year." He clapped me on the shoulder on his way out of the kitchen.

# CHAPTER 3

Morning sunbeams filtered through the glass walls at Reagan National Airport, glancing off the metallic tail of a United Airlines jet lumbering across the tarmac. It was a big plane, a 747, and the towering fin's gray stripe matched rain clouds moving in from the south. I glided along on the walkway toward the terminal, just standing there, hands in the pockets of my jeans, the canvas duffel bag on my shoulder. "The moving walkway is nearing its end. Please watch your step."

I could feel the rhythmic clicking of the metal track through the soles of my sneakers. A pair of businessmen in pin-striped suits rushed past me, leather briefcases swinging at their sides. One of them, heavyset and balding, was talking on a cell phone and wrestled with the jostling weight of his luggage to look at his watch. His face was flushed. I heard him say, "Exactly the same bullshit I was talking about before!" The track continued to click.

"The moving walkway is nearing its end."

I stepped off, shoes squeaking on the marble floor, and took a left into the terminal. I looked at the flight information monitors: Detroit,

Michigan—Gate 26, boarding at 10:02. On-time departure. It was only 9:45, so I decided to get a cup of coffee and pick up a magazine to read on the plane. The recording faded behind me.

"The moving walkway…"

I bought an overpriced cup of coffee at Starbucks. I asked for a large but in fact received a *grande*, according to the girl behind the counter. She just threw it in there with the rest of her sentence, like "I need a *grande* house to go."

I thanked her for the coffee and then put three packs of sugar in the cup and poured in some milk, making the same khaki-shaded, creamy mixture that my mom drinks. Lots of sugar, plenty of milk. My father, a purist, refers to this process as prostituting one's coffee.

The hollow voice droned on, "All passengers should monitor their luggage at all times. Any unattended bags will be removed for inspection and may be damaged or destroyed."

Moving along toward the gate, I stepped into the airport bookstore and stopped in front of the magazine rack, which covered an entire wall of the store. My eyes leaped from cover to cover, scanning the titles: *National Geographic*, *Time*, *Newsweek*, *Men's Health*, *Women's Day*, *Boating*, *Climbing*, *Flying*, *Backpacker*, *Outside*, *Inside*, *Vogue*, *Us*, *Me*, *Them*, and *Playboy* on the top rack, next to *Hustler* wrapped in plastic. I chuckled, suddenly remembering Trey's vast and sordid collection of smut.

I picked up a copy of *Car & Driver* with an article about the ten best sports coupes for under fifty thousand dollars. Of course, I didn't have fifty thousand dollars and I wouldn't anytime soon, but it was a nice fantasy and it was going to be a long flight. As I stood waiting for the change, I glanced at the tabloids. I thought of Lynn, and our afternoon last summer visiting the monuments in DC; we had laughed so hard reading a tabloid cover story about the "Rhinoceros Boy of Southern Colombia" that I almost choked on my peanut-butter-fudge ice-cream cone. I'd coughed for the next half hour, all the while getting concerned and bewildered stares from the public on the National Mall.

The coffee had the same effect upon me that it always does, creating within about ten minutes an immediate and pressing need to take a leak.

Canned music played as I stared at the tile above the urinal. The toilet flushed automatically. Someone is rich because he thought to mount infrared sensors on urinals and then had the balls to actually risk doing it as a business venture. Infrared technology and urinals—who knew these two things could ever be associated? People get rich in strange ways.

Rich. As I washed my hands, I thought about Trey's dad, the private island in the Bahamas, the condo, and the chartered plane. *Trust-fund baby.* I'd learned that phrase in the locker room the day after Trey got expelled. That's what Hasselwerdt had called him. "Don't worry, Derby. He'll be fine; he's a trust-fund baby."

*How do you go from trust-fund baby to firefighter?*

I walked toward the gate. They were already boarding. "Ladies and Gentlemen," the gate agent began, "welcome aboard Flight 334 with nonstop service to Detroit, Michigan. We'll begin boarding our first-class passengers and those passengers traveling with small children, or anyone needing assistance down the jetway..."

Looking out the floor-to-ceiling terminal windows, I could see that the clouds had moved in from the south, expanding and billowing outward in voluminous thunderheads. I was glad we were taking off ahead of the storm. I waited for first class to board and then got in line, taking a look at my boarding pass. I was in 18-A, a window seat. I sat down and peered out. Fat August raindrops began to fall. Shimmering rivulets reflected the silver, blue, and red of the 737.

I thought about the news report and saw the photo in my mind. Amazing how little he'd changed. Sixteen to twenty-two. Some formative years. He was older, definitely, but the eyes were the same. *"A four-year veteran of the department,"* the reporter had said. It occurred to me that Trey must not have finished college, if he'd joined the fire department at eighteen. Had he even started?

And his father. Daniels Advertising Company, International. Andrew Daniels had built a huge business and had meetings in Europe, DC and New York all the time. That was why they had the Georgetown house.

But now he was a firefighter in Jackson, Wyoming, in the middle of nowhere. He had nothing to do with his dad's business. Whose decision was that? And if he had nothing to do with the business, I thought, does he have anything to do with the money?

And if he didn't know his dad was visiting, well, what did that mean? *Distance. Circumstance.*

I remembered Trey telling me that his parents were on the road to divorce. Had they gotten there? If they did, maybe the money wasn't there anymore. Or if it was, maybe he just didn't want anything to do with it. Something came to mind, a conversation during a thunderstorm back before he got kicked out: *"We are the fucked-up rich people, Matt."*

As the jet backed heavily out of the gate, I watched the airline guys run around in their blue-and-green suits, driving little trucks around and loading suitcases onto the plane at the next gate. It was a big British Airways 777. I could just barely see the faces of the passengers through the tiny windows. The tail was painted with the Union Jack. My mind shot back to school again, reading *Lord of the Flies* that first October at the Ashford River School. As we took off, I thought about William Golding, a crashed plane, and English schoolboys stranded on a coral island.

# CHAPTER 4

Fall 1996. English Class.

Miss Dillon was hot.

There's really no other way to put it—not hot like a supermodel, but in more of the "hot-because-she-really-exists" way. As sophomores, our minds were so preoccupied with fantasies of centerfold beauties that the reality of a young, attractive woman right there in our midst was in some ways more than we could handle. It was fifth period on a Thursday in mid-October, and she was writing discussion questions for *Lord of the Flies* on the board. It had been mercilessly humid that week, and today was the first cool afternoon. The sun peeked through clouds and threw spots on the varnished floor and paneled walls. Specks of chalk glanced off the board as she wrote, and with every stroke of Miss Dillon's arm, I watched her quiver just a little bit inside the tight fabric of her lavender pants. All the guys were pretty sure she wore a thong, and we were pretty sure she did it knowing full well she was teaching at an all-boys school—not exactly conducive to focusing our attention on the academic topic of the day. Maybe our grades would have been better in her class if our brains had been adequately oxygenated, but as it stood, the blood was often flowing elsewhere, utterly beyond our control.

There were only ten women among the thirty teachers at the Ashford River School, and the others were nothing to write home about. Trey Daniels, my roommate and fellow transfer student, had offered his treatise on the comparative hotness of several female teachers and staff members during crew practice just the day before. Ranking first, of course, was Miss Stevenson, but she was the headmaster's secretary so she didn't technically count as a teacher. Miss Rodriguez was from Guatemala and had nice legs, but her face reminded Trey of the salamanders in the bio lab. Mrs. Leavenworth, the art teacher, while not entirely unattractive in a lonely housewife kind of way, was married to Mr. Leavenworth in the science department, which made her just plain weird. Mrs. Carrolton was the secretary to the dean, and there wasn't anything hot about her because she was on the hefty side and besides, she was someone's mom. Not that this in any way precluded a woman from hotness, Trey concluded (there were some very, very hot moms who came to watch our home games), but it usually didn't help. Miss Brenner in the chemistry department was widely suspected of being a lesbian, which was in theory wildly exciting, except that she was not attractive at all. Besides, she was somewhere around fifty-two.

Miss Dillon, on the other hand, was hot. It was good that she taught sophomores and seniors, I remember thinking, as she wrote the last discussion questions on the board. It was good first of all, of course, because we got to have her as a teacher. But secondly, it was good because if she had taught juniors, they would have gone crazy. Dr. Carlisle, the school counselor, had told us in health class a week ago that there was no creature on the planet more sexually charged than the adolescent male of the human species, *especially* during the junior year. This was a little scary, since it was hard to imagine becoming any more sexually charged than I already was as a sophomore. Whatever sheepishness or embarrassment most guys harbored about these feelings, myself included, was not shared by Trey. He was pretty shameless, and enjoyed making comical references to his own state of perpetual horniness. His stash of magazines was known throughout MacKerry Hall as the most extensive resource available to quench the raging hormonal fires that frequently prevented us from focusing on anything else. It was 1996, still a few years before the Internet became mainstream and well before it became the primary channel for everything pornographic. So every once in a while, a guy would show up at our door, knock softly, and peer in at Trey as he worked at his desk. You could always tell what he wanted from the look in his eye, that sort of desperate and pathetic expression that said, *"Just lemme borrow one. I'll bring it back."* No words were exchanged, just a rolled-up copy of something passed off with the understanding that it would make its way back when the world had calmed down a little bit. Rumor had it he even had a few videos, but if he did, I never saw them. We weren't allowed to have VCR's in our rooms, anyway. The fact that our dorm room, courtesy of Trey, had become an unofficial lending library made me a little nervous, but it was also pretty funny.

Back to Miss Dillon. "Okay. So, based on your reading, what do you guys think of question number one up there?" Miss Dillon always said "you guys," which made her sexier. It reminded us that she was fully aware she was in a room full of guys, and furthermore, she was probably fully aware that we couldn't stop looking at her. The question read: *What early indications does Golding give that Jack and Ralph will emerge as foil characters?*

I half-read the question and then glanced outside at the maple tree. The leaves burned red and orange with autumn, and the branches quivered in the breeze, brushing the windowpanes. I was in a bit of a quandary. The rapidly departing kid in me wanted to be outside throwing a football; however, I had a new fascination with Miss Dillon that I couldn't seem to suppress.

"Anyone?" Miss Dillon was perched, half sitting, half standing, against her desk. Her breasts were straining against the fabric of her vanilla-white blouse. She held the piece of chalk lightly, between two fingers like a cigarette, her elbow sort of resting against her ribs and the chalk waving around in the air. I looked over at Trey, smirking. He was staring at her shirt.

"Trey?" She looked at him expectantly.

He quickly sat up a little straighter in his chair and read the question on the board. He squinted his eyes, which was something Trey did when he wanted to make it look like he was thinking very hard. The truth, I knew, was that he had absolutely no idea where to begin, because he hadn't read the book and he definitely hadn't taken the time to define the list of literary terms we were supposed to, one of which was *"foil characters: characters who, because of significant contrasts, highlight each other's differences and usually influence each other in important ways."* I'd crammed to finish the assigned chapters and the notes the night before, staying up until about two. Trey had begun snoring somewhere around eleven, with the book on the floor next to his bed. So no, he hadn't read it. In fact, he didn't even have the book in class.

"Trey, have you read the book? Do you even have the book in class?" Miss Dillon was getting more aggravated by the second. She didn't know it, of course, but it made her even hotter. She walked over to his desk, her thick-heeled shoes clumping on the hardwood floor. His notebook was open and blank except for a doodle in the top right corner that resembled the Big Dipper.

"Um, no."

"*Trey.*" The name formed a complete sentence, somewhere between a declarative and an interrogative, with perhaps a slight hint of the imperative.

"But...but I can answer the question." Trey stopped squinting and looked over at me. The look in his eyes was sort of pathetic; his eyebrows arched and crumpled together. "See, when the fat kid—what's his name?"

"Piggy." Miss Dillon's voice was flat. "That *major* character's name is Piggy, Trey." She was standing in the aisle right next to him, her arms folded. Brian McNeal, who was seated one row over and one desk ahead, consequently had a fortunate position less than two feet from her butt. I noticed Brian's contentment with this situation. He was grinning. Evan McCarthy, the red-haired kid who was so short and young looking that I always thought of him as a sixth-grader, was trying to hide his laughter as he watched Brian.

Trey spoke. "Yeah. When Piggy says anything, it really pisses Jack off." I don't know if Trey actually intended to say, "Jack off," or if it just came out that way. But he grinned as he said the last two words, so I have a feeling he meant to. This is exactly the type of shameless malarkey he was best at. So whether he meant it or not, stifled laughter rumbled through the class.

Apparently, Miss Dillon either didn't get the joke—which I doubt—or was *really* good at ignoring it. She just made a disappointed face and said, "Trey, can you try to express yourself without using the phrase, 'pisses off'?"

*Very smooth, Miss Dillon. Nice dodge.*

Trey continued, trying hard to hold his composure after that brilliant little wordplay. "Um, yeah, sorry. And so that, uh, *bothers* Ralph, because originally, when they were swimming around and stuff in the first chapter, Ralph and Piggy got along okay. But Jack is so mean to Piggy, and that shows that maybe he and Ralph are really different."

Miss Dillon was willing to work with this, but you could tell she was annoyed. She'd probably rather Trey knew nothing at all than muddle his way to what was, in truth, a pretty insightful answer, even if he did have to make an inappropriate detour to entertain the class. This was typical Trey.

"Okay," she said in an energized voice, snapping the class's attention back to her, "so Trey's right about that. The dynamic among those three characters indicates a few things. Now, can anyone think of another more *specific* instance where this is particularly evident?" When she said the word *specific*, she glared at Trey. She *knew* he hadn't read this.

"Matt?" she said, calling on me.

I paged rapidly through the first chapters, looking for the place where I had underlined last night. "Oh yeah. Well, going off what Trey said. It's when they're gonna go explore the island. Piggy wants to go, but Ralph sort of betrays him and tells him to stay back and babysit the little kids."

Miss Dillon nodded. "Good, yes, that's a solid, specific example. And who *does* get invited to go explore the island instead?"

"Simon."

"Right. Good job." She smiled and made a note of the example on the board. Life was momentarily much better for me.

Brian McNeal raised his hand. He was wearing a bright-orange tie. It was free tie day every Thursday, so we didn't have to wear our navy-blue Ashford River School ties.

Miss Dillon gestured to him. "Brian?"

"I've got another example."

"Go ahead." She was waiting at the board, ready to list it below mine.

McNeal thought for a moment and then began speaking rapidly. "So Jack loses the election to be chief because all the other kids elect Ralph. Ralph could have just told Jack—err, *him* off…" Snickers erupted throughout the room again, which made both Brian and Trey smile. "…But instead he gives him a special duty." McNeal cracked his knuckles, which he always did when he was nervous. "Ralph puts him in charge of the hunters, so that's like Ralph's olive branch to Jack, and he's trying to maintain their friendship even though Jack is really beginning to hate him and be completely envious and whatever…so they're foil characters because they oppose each other even though they're trying to get along because they're so different."

I thought this was pretty good, even if it did involve the longest run-on sentence in history. "Olive branch" was a pretty nice touch. I'm not sure if Brian was trying to one-up me or not, but it worked. Miss Dillon was all over his answer, and we talked about it for the rest of the class. Later that week, when we took our first quiz on *Lord of the Flies*, I got a ninety-six, Brian got a perfect score, and Trey got a sixty. We compared our grades later on, but, of course, pretended not to care about them.

■ ■ ■

That was the way it was between Trey and me, Brian too, and probably a lot of other guys at the Ashford River School. Everything was a competition, even when it didn't need to be. There we were, three hundred and eighteen boys consigned to a regimented life of books, sports, and top-heavy spiritual guidance, all fighting to remain afloat in a veritable maelstrom of testosterone. Our days were divided neatly and regularly into uniform parcels of time, and the clock ruled all. As it does for anyone accustomed to routine, however, the tedium often escaped us, and instead, we jostled awkwardly but predictably from day to day in a blur of Latin quizzes, lectures, formal dinners, excruciating practices with demonic coaches, study halls, and communal showers, during which we bragged about the girls we'd gotten with—stories amounting to a truly comical level of libido-charged bullshit. Cram three-hundred-eighteen of us together in a few dormitories, and envy was bound to be a constant companion, like the chest colds and drippy-nose viruses that seemed to plague us ceaselessly from November until the break of spring, spreading through the building on slow currents of steam heat and cold drafts.

Envy snaked into every aspect of our young lives, because so much was enmeshed in competition. Class standing was an indicator of innate intelligence, not to mention a barometer for one's ability to manipulate "The System"—both essential qualities for the rising ruling class. Grades became our collective obsession. Even for the ostensibly nonchalant slackers, grades were a constant reminder of the Darwinian tendencies of the Ivy League and life beyond it. Only the fittest would survive, or at the very least, only the fittest would get the girl, get into the school, own the country house, and drive the Beemer. Our academic index was as much a measure of our self-worth as the weight on our bench press, the time on our quarter-mile runs in phys ed, or the size of our developing anatomies. What wasn't overtly quantifiable might as well have been, for we were so accustomed to measuring every aspect of our lives.

In a boarding school, everything is in fact relative.

If you didn't push ahead, you'd definitely get left behind. Guys who didn't measure up were terrorized, but not in the graphic ways you might imagine. There wasn't any hazing or the weird stuff you see in movies about boys' boarding schools. We didn't tremble in fear of creepy rituals passed down by secret societies or cloak-wearing fraternities. It just wasn't that kind of school. Maybe it wasn't old enough to have such deep-rooted conceits, as some very old schools maintain, all in the name of tradition. The prefects had us on a tight enough leash to prevent that sort of stuff. No, it was a silent sort of terror inflicted upon the weak, the worst kind for a teenager to endure. If a guy had no redeeming, quantifiable valor— grades, sports, or at least charismatic appeal—he'd simply be ostracized. It was not what the others would do *to* him; it was what they wouldn't do *for* him or *with* him. To disappear at the Ashford River School, one only had to be less-than-special. And even though we sometimes wished we could disappear, no one really wanted to. Disappearance would be an affirmation of that creeping suspicion that most every teenager ponders, especially on his darkest days: that ultimately, in the grand scheme of things, he really doesn't matter.

So there enters the loyalty. In this world of competition, we clung to each other like soldiers in trenches. Even as we pushed and shoved and elbowed our way through adolescence, we held to each other. We'd find a handful of brothers who'd recognize us for more than how we measured up. We'd find these kindred spirits who would forgive our inadequacies, with the understanding that we would in turn forgive their own. As students at a boarding school, we existed in a vacuum of sorts, condemned to an essentially monastic life at a time when, ironically, self-control was utterly outside our grasp. *Lord of the Flies* rang true. We were much like William Golding's boys stranded on the tropical island: savage, confused, and inno-cent all at once. We were all, like Jack and Ralph, very much "in love and hate."

Miss Dillon's personality worked for us. It was true that she was hot as hell—that hasn't changed in the six years since I sat in her class—but there was more to it than that. She knew how to ask the right questions, and she charged her inquiries with such force and weight that they bore a sort of significance that many teachers couldn't muster. I'm still amazed at her ability to relate to us. The truth is that despite the popular image of East Coast boarding schools as homogenous, Aryan proving grounds for the rich and famous, there's a certain sort of diversity within them. At

Ashford River, there were all kinds of kids. Yes, many—the majority, in fact—fit into a certain demographic (read "white" and "rich"). But in reality, it wasn't that simple. We came from every background, from billionaire to dirt poor, the common denominator being a basic level of potential and a desire—at least on our parents' part—to gain entrance to a selective college. For some, that was just a baseline expectation, a generational continuity from grandfather to father to son and so on. For others, it was the first foray into the upper American caste, and that was certainly true for me, a kid from Buffalo there on a three-quarter scholarship. So similar as we might have appeared in the pages of a yearbook, Miss Dillon obviously understood that we had many differences among us. So she leveled those differences. Her class was a proving ground, a place where how much your father made or what your last name was really didn't matter, because you damned well better have read the book.

She took no prisoners and abided no bullshit.

I think it was in Miss Dillon's class that I had my first flash of intuition that Trey could never survive at Ashford River, or, for that matter, anyplace remotely like it. It wasn't that he was inherently lazy—though in many ways he could be. Neither was it that he didn't have the brains; in fact, he was brighter than most guys in our class. He just genuinely didn't care. He didn't care about the Ivy League; he didn't care about his standing; and he didn't care about his image. Trey Daniels was possessed of a certain kind of courage, and I think that's why I admired him, though I definitely didn't understand this then. Other guys tried to imitate him. They appeared careless and free-spirited but in fact were desperately, pathetically enslaved to the expectations of their country-club, Fortune-Five-Hundred parents. They blew off classes, smoked cigarettes, did some pot, and sneaked into the maintenance closets with girls at our dances…they tried to be rebels. But come final exams or Monday mornings, they'd sharpen up enough to meet the deadlines, pass the course, and come out all right on parents' weekend. And if their mischief made enough ripples that Dad got word at his office, a single phone call would be enough to set them on the straight and narrow until the next time. A lot of guys pretended to rail against the system. A lot of guys appeared lost in occasional existential crises. But for most of them, it was never really a crisis. Because in the final analysis, these blue-blooded sons of American dynasties simply had to continue—or improve upon—the legacies their fathers or grandfathers or great-grandfathers had begun. Trey wouldn't do that. I guess I can only call it a kind of authenticity, looking back. He wouldn't play "The Game." In fact, I don't believe he *could*. Trey was, therefore, perhaps more an outsider at Ashford River than anyone else, far more so even than I was, the scholarship kid with middle-class parents from a rust belt city.

Part of it might have been that unlike most students at the school, he came from a small mountain town. He wasn't from a city like Philadelphia or New York or DC. No, Trey came from Lake Placid, a well known but relatively remote town set in the middle of New York's Adirondack Mountains, and that seemed to set him apart from most kids. On paper, he was as unlikely a student at the Ashford River School as I was. We were similar in two ways. First, we were both transfer sophomores. I came from a public school in Buffalo, and he from another boarding school in rural Connecticut. Second, neither of us had any legacy at the school; we were both there by chance. The difference was that for me, the place was a pretty enjoyable road to opportunity, whereas for Trey, it was a sort of prison—the third in a series of boarding schools he'd been sent to. He was an enigma to all of us, but mostly to me because I shared a room with him, and I actually wanted to understand him. I had met the kid six weeks before that day in Miss Dillon's class. And in the ways boys so often do when they make their first real friends, I wanted to be just like him.

# CHAPTER 5

"Ladies and Gentlemen, we've been cleared to land in Detroit. The captain has turned on the fasten seat-belt sign..." The flight attendant rambled on as the plane began to descend. I finished the plastic cup of ginger ale I'd been sipping and watched the clear skies outside turn dark and gray as we descended through the cloud cover.

Once on the ground, I followed as the passengers ahead of me shuffled off the plane. The terminal was alive with activity, and the remarkable system that is the modern airport amazed me yet again. Surrounding me was a mile-long stretch of architecture abuzz with the frenetic movements of thousands of people intersecting with only occasional collisions—a bumped elbow here, a spilled coffee there. As I glanced around the concourse, I took note of the variety of different people passing by each other, wondering where they were all headed.

Sitting in the departure gate, I began to wonder if Lynn would have come with me if I'd asked her to. She'd always said that getting back to traveling again was one of her dreams. She'd traveled all over the world as a child when her parents were together. After their divorce, money was a little tighter and travel moved down on the priority list. But her apartment's walls were adorned with photos, posters, and odd little knick-knacks from around the globe. Her favorite, tacky as it was, was a rhinestone-encrusted miniature Eiffel Tower she'd picked up outside the Louvre with her dad when she was five. We'd joked that someday when we were both rich we'd go back to Paris and make out under the Eiffel Tower. And when we were done, we'd be sure to buy another matching tacky miniature model, preferably rhinestone-encrusted, so we could each have one.

Of course, the longer I thought about this, the longer I put off taking my cell phone out of my pocket and dialing her number. When I finally did, I held my thumb over the send button like it was some kind of trigger. But I hesitated, because the image that was clearest of all was the sad way she'd looked at me the first time we'd argued in the spring. It was over something stupid, but I think it was the first time we both realized that things were on their way to getting messy. It was a look of disappointment, not anger.

So I didn't hit send. And when the gate agent came on to announce the boarding process, I tucked the phone back into my pocket. Before long, I was seated on the connecting flight to Jackson, again buckling my seat belt and looking out the window at the rain-soaked tarmac. The fat drops splattered on the window before cascading down the glass.

I thought of my first day at Ashford River School.

■ ■ ■

It had rained on Moving-In Day in 1996.

"Look, bud. There's some guys here to help you move in." My dad took a sip of black coffee from a Styrofoam cup, his other hand resting on the base of the steering wheel as we pulled into the circle in front of the main building. He looked like a federal agent in his gray suit and amber-tinted driving glasses. Salt-and-pepper hair. Close-cropped like mine. The sunglasses were the kind that got darker in bright sunlight and made things look brighter when it was overcast.

"Cool," I was sitting in the passenger seat of the huge silver Caprice. My voice sounded small, but I tried to sound casual. It wasn't working, though. Truth was I was nervous as hell. I sat up high on the edge of the seat, looking out the rain-spattered windshield at the scene in front of us. A bunch of older-looking boys in white polo shirts were carrying boxes from the trunks of cars up the steps and then inside through a set of double doors. They were soaking wet from the rain and shouted to each other across the steps, wrestling with the weight of the boxes. Over the entrance to the building was engraved an inscription:

## MACKERRY HALL
## GIFT OF THE CLASS OF 1927

The place was square and imposing, built out of red bricks topped with a copper cupola in the middle, three stories above. The cupola glistened in the rain, as though it had just been polished. The admissions brochure said MacKerry Hall was "a fine example of classic Georgian architecture."

The tie was too tight around my neck, and the sleeves of my blazer were itchy because I was wearing a short-sleeved shirt. I could smell the starch that my mom had sprayed on it yesterday before we left. My armpits were warm, and drops of sweat trickled down my biceps. I had tried to sleep in the motel we stayed at, but it didn't work. I was too wired, too anxious, rippling with the nervous energy a boy feels when he realizes he's a very small fish about to be tossed into a very large pond.

"Your mom would *love* this place. I wish she could have gotten off work this weekend." Dad sipped his coffee. We were idling at the outside of the circular driveway, waiting for a white Cadillac SUV to move. He absently tapped the wheel with his thumb and fingers, keeping with the rhythm of his Paul Simon tape.

"Yeah, she'd go nuts about the flowers," I said, my voice quiet. My mother is an emergency room nurse with a passionate love for gardening. The year before, she'd completely redone our front yard in Buffalo as a rock garden, and I'd spent the better part of two Saturdays hauling truckloads of forty-pound flagstones out of the creek near our cottage. It was a ton of fun. Literally.

A wispy-haired man in a suit was shaking hands with some other parents on the front step under an awning. Their son, a lanky kid with blond hair, stood between them looking around. Next to the older man stood a thickly built, red-haired priest wearing black clericals and a Roman collar. The polo shirts were taking boxes from the trunk of an open car behind them, and one of them shook the new kid's hand. The dad patted his son on the shoulder, and then the lanky kid went with the moving crew up the stairs inside, devoured by MacKerry's gaping front doors.

Dad pulled the Caprice around the front circle to an empty spot, and I could hear the tires on the wet pavement as we came to a stop. We got out of the car, and a polo-shirt immediately walked over. He shook my hand first. He had a crushing grip, and I figured he must be a senior or a junior the way his arms bulged out of his shirtsleeves. He had a five o' clock shadow, and it was only about eleven in the morning. *Small fish. Big pond.*

"Hi, I'm Steve Mallow. Welcome to Ashford River." Steve Mallow was tall, *really* tall. He had curly black hair that hung down around his ears and was sort of plastered to his forehead from the rain, almost like he had just climbed out of a pool. His voice was deep Manhattan, and a prominent Adam's apple worked under his chin as he talked. I noticed the veins in his forearms. The guy looked strong. *Really small fish.*

"Hey, I'm Matt. Matt Derby. I'm a transfer sophomore." I finally got my hand back from the older boy's grip. Steve Mallow and my dad seemed to hit it right off, and he began carrying boxes upstairs. We stopped on the way and met Dr. Winthrop, the headmaster, and Father Daley, the chaplain. Dr. Winthrop was tall, about the same height as Steve. I figured he was in his middle fifties, but his white hair made him look older.

"Welcome aboard, Matt." His voice had a deep Southern drawl, so that it became *welcome abawd*. "I'm Dr. Winthrop, the headmaster. We're very glad you decided to join us this year, all the way from Buffalo. It's always great to welcome one of our scholarship students." He spoke slowly and looked me directly in the eye. I shook Dr. Winthrop's hand, surprised he knew my name.

"Thank you, sir." I found myself averting my gaze and looking down at the ground. Dr. Winthrop's shoes were smooth, cream-colored leather, polished to a glistening sheen.

"Mr. Derby, it's a pleasure to meet you as well, sir. Evan Winthrop," he said, shaking my dad's hand. I noticed tiny, round cufflinks with the school seal. "I trust the drive down was uneventful, aside from this rather miserable rain we've had all morning?"

"Not too bad at all. We came halfway last night."

"Well, that's fortunate. Nothing like a long drive in rough weather to tire a man out." He smiled, his hands on his hips as he looked up at the sky, shaking his head. "Hmm. And have you gentlemen met our chaplain, Father Daley?"

"Uh, no, sir," I said as I shook the priest's hand. He looked a few years younger than Dr. Winthrop, maybe in his early forties, with just a few streaks of gray in his coarse red beard. He was built like a middleweight boxer, and his grip was powerful, like Mallow's.

"Good to have you, Matt. Welcome, Mr. Derby."

I forced a smile as my dad chatted a bit with Father Daley, but I was wondering how long this introduction needed to continue. I was hot in the sport coat, and it was itchy under my arms where I was still sweating like crazy. Fortunately, Steve Mallow came out through the door after carrying the last box upstairs.

"Excuse me, Dr. Winthrop, Father Daley. We're all set, Matt." He was slightly out of breath. "We can get you situated now."

Another round of handshakes, and we followed Steve over to the registration table. As we left Dr. Winthrop and Father Daley to greet another family, I was thinking that people there shook hands a lot more than they did back in Buffalo.

Mallow thumbed through a box of manila file folders. "Okay, let's see...Crane, Culaney, DaVinci...ah, Derby." He explained everything as we moved along. "This is your room key—room 211—and your mail key. Your mailbox is the same number as your room. We'll show you that later though. I just took your last box up, so everything should be in your room already. Just follow the signs upstairs and you can unpack." Mallow handed me the little envelope with the keys. He shook my dad's hand again and went outside to help another student.

We headed up the stairs. It was a broad, darkly varnished wooden staircase at the top of which was a stained-glass window displaying the school seal. There was a silver cross in the middle, with fields of navy and crimson and some words in Latin that I didn't understand. My dad looked at them. I could tell he wanted to explain what they meant, but instead, he just squinted at the inscription and nodded approvingly. I rolled my eyes. I knew he had no idea what the hell the words meant, but I wasn't going to say anything. He did stuff like that. Still does.

When we reached the top, we came to a lounge area with a hardwood floor, a fireplace, and shelves full of books on the walls. The light came from lamps like the ones in our living room at home. It felt warm. There was also a big-screen TV in a cabinet full of videos, and a couple of kids were playing Nintendo, sprawled on some well-used couches. A pizza box lay open on the coffee table in front of us, but all the pizza was gone, leaving only grease stains, a few shreds of cheese, and one lonely, hopeless-looking circle of abandoned pepperoni.

My dad laughed and nodded at the television. "Well, you've been asking me for a Nintendo for two years. I guess you've got one."

"Yeah."

The boys on the couch turned around. One of them sort of nodded and said, "Hey, whassup?" before going back to his game. We were about to walk toward the door that said "Dormitory Rooms 201–223" when a man in a sport coat walked up and extended a hand to my dad.

"Hi, I'm Patrick Brady. Welcome to Ashford River."

"Michael Derby. This is my son Matt." Dad patted me on the shoulder as I shook hands. Dad did that shoulder-pat thing a lot that day, in a

*Hey-that's-my-boy* kind of way. It was a little annoying, but looking back, I know he was caught up in the place, in the whole *I-never-had-an-opportunity-like-this* thing.

"Well, Matt, I guess we'll be seeing a lot of each other, since you're only a few doors down from me." This guy, Brady, confused the hell out of me for a few seconds, because I couldn't figure out if he was one of the polo shirts or a teacher or what. But his name tag cleared it up:

Mr. Patrick Brady
Sophomore Housemaster
English Department

"You mentioned an interest in rowing, right?" he asked. "The admissions office passed your name along."

"Uh, yes, sir." I wasn't sure if I had to call teachers sir, but I figured it couldn't hurt.

"I coach the junior varsity team. It's mostly sophomores, a few freshmen and new juniors, too. Practice starts after school on Monday. But for now, let's get you moved in."

Mr. Brady was a little taller than I was, though not by much, and stockier. He was obviously Irish and from somewhere north of here, maybe Vermont or New Hampshire. He had a dirty-blond crew cut like my own, but with a slightly receding hairline, and I guess that was what made him look a little older. Mr. Brady seemed to know how to talk to my dad. I listened as they talked about the academic curriculum and rules like curfew and formal dinner and all the interminable details that are of great interest to parents. Brady looked like he was in his mid-twenties, but I couldn't tell exactly how old. He knocked on Room 211. He was wearing a college ring, but I couldn't tell where from. Later on, I'd learn it was Georgetown, and that was one of the reasons why we stayed in touch, as I followed in his tracks three years later. "Matt," he asked me, "have you met your roommate yet?"

"No. It's Trey Daniels, right?" I had gotten a packet from the school that introduced me to various facts and figures, what I'd need, and the name of the kid I'd be rooming with. Just as I said the name, the door opened and Trey was standing there. He was wearing a pair of gym shorts and a faded, sky-blue T-shirt that said *"High Peaks Soccer"* and the number 7. He only had one sock on.

Mr. Brady made the introduction. "Matt, this is Trey Daniels from Lake Placid. Trey, Matt Derby from Buffalo. This is Matt's dad."

All I said was, "Hey."

"Hey back at ya." He did this sort of crazy grin thing, a bigger smile than I'd ever seen anybody make, narrowing his eyes to dark slits. He shook my hand and then my dad's. He was very tan.

My dad smiled as he and Mr. Brady stepped back into the hallway. "Hey, bud, we'll see you later at dinner. It was good to meet you, Trey. I'm sure you guys can get yourselves situated." I got another pat on the back as he turned to go.

After the door closed, Trey scampered back to his desk. He was hooking up his stereo to some speakers. I stood in front of the door, feeling generally awkward, looking at my boxes stacked in the middle of the room. The dorm was not big. It was about the same size as my room at home, maybe ten by twelve. There was a single rectangular window with raindrops splattering against it, a bunk bed, two bureaus, and a couple of desks, side by side against the wall.

"You like Bob Dylan?" Trey was filing through a CD wallet. He sat on the edge of his chair with his elbow on the desk, his fist under his chin.

Actually, I didn't know anything about Bob Dylan, and I wasn't sure if I liked him or not. For whatever reason, my parents didn't listen too much to him. Since my music collection was mostly limited to the tapes and CD's they'd purchased, it was Simon & Garfunkel, Johnny Cash, Hank Williams, Neil Diamond, Journey, Fleetwood Mac, or the Beatles at home. Bob Dylan hadn't made his mark yet. For some reason, though, I found myself lying. "Yeah. Sure. Dylan's cool."

"Sweet. He writes some good stuff. Half of it's completely about drug addictions, you know. I mean I don't know if he actually meant it that way, but it should be. Some of his stuff is really trippy. I read about the lyrics in *Rolling Stone*, and this one article says that's what he was talking about." Trey pressed a button, and "Shelter from the Storm" began to play, but the music sounded tinny. "I don't have the other speaker hooked up yet. Hold on." He ducked beneath the desk and messed with some wires. There was an electrical buzz, and suddenly the sound came to life in stereo.

"Sounds better." I sat down on the chair at the other desk. The reading lamp on Trey's desk lit the room dimly.

"Yeah. So, Buffalo, huh? What the hell do you do in Buffalo?" Trey was smiling and opening a bag of strawberry Twizzlers. He held the bag out toward me. "Man, you gotta relax. Take your tie off and unpack your crap."

"Uh, thanks." I took a Twizzler and loosened my tie, which had been way too tight all morning. I started to open boxes and put my clothes in the drawers, noticing how neatly my mom had folded everything. Dad and I had picked out a few posters the week before at a bookstore in Buffalo, and they were rolled up in cardboard tubes. Trey helped me hang them. One of them was John and Bobby Kennedy standing together on Martha's Vineyard, looking pensively out at the ocean. My dad was a fan of the Kennedy brothers.

"Kennedy was *the man*." Trey said between bites of his Twizzler. "Can't believe those assholes shot him. Could you imagine if he'd lived, how different stuff might have been, like with Vietnam and all that?" Trey had climbed up onto the top bunk, and he was leaning out and putting a tack in the upper corner of the poster, while I stood on a chair, holding the corners flat against the wall. "I think it was the government that shot him, like all those anti-Catholic morons who thought he'd take orders from the pope or something. This girl I know did a project about it once. And my mom's Catholic, and she agrees with me. I guess I am too, but I don't think I've been to church in months now. Not since my last school. My dad doesn't go." I was quickly discovering that Trey had a habit of speaking in rapid, rambling sentences with no apparent beginning, middle, or end. He looked at me. "You Catholic?"

"Yeah."

"That's probably why they put us together. Keep the faith and all that. You meet Father Daley?"

"Yeah, he seems okay," I said.

"I read the brochure. There's like fifty or so Catholic guys in the school. It's mostly Protestant. Everyone has to go to chapel, you know. Listen to Dr. Winthrop and Father Daley talk about our spiritual life and ethics and stuff. But us good Catholic boys have to do that *and* stay afterward for Mass," Trey said, biting the end off another Twizzler.

"I'm used to it," I said. "My parents are pretty old school about that."

"That's good. You can keep me awake. I got in a shit-ton of trouble at school in New York City because I fell asleep during some really important Mass for a retiring nun or something. They beat me with iron rods." He chuckled.

Now I was really confused, with this mention of New York City. "So where are you from? Lake Placid or New York?"

"Both. I sorta live in both places, mostly Lake Placid. My parents are sorta screwed up."

"Whaddya mean?"

"Kind of divorced but not really."

I didn't make much of this then, especially because of the way his comment just sort of rolled off the cuff. I knew a lot of kids with divorced parents, so it didn't seem all that significant. I brushed it aside and turned my attention back to sizing up this kid I'd be living with for a year. I could smell Trey's T-shirt when he leaned over to put another tack in the poster, and it was clear that he hadn't washed it in a few days. I looked over my shoulder at the lower bunk and saw his stuff, mostly still in boxes.

"So what time did you get here?" I asked.

Trey was holding a tack between his teeth so he couldn't really talk. "Umm...likth then-o-chlochk lasht nayhght." He took the tack out and put it in the poster, the final one. "About ten o' clock last night. My dad had to get to a meeting in London so I had to come early." He jumped down from the bunk bed and looked at the poster, squinting and touching his finger to his jaw. "Looks straight. Cool. I've got a Dylan poster. We should put it right next to Jack and Bobby." He began rummaging through the pile of stuff on the bed looking for the poster.

I was wondering what to talk about. "Your dad had to go to a meeting in London?"

"Yeah. He goes there a lot for work." That's all he said.

I changed the subject. "So how's that guy Mr. Brady?"

"Oh, him? He's real cool. Since I was the only kid here last night, him and the other dude, Mr. DiVincenzo—I think he's the other sophomore dorm guy, teaches math or something—took me to Burger King, which *sucks* by the way, 'cause it's like a twenty-five-minute drive. We're in the middle of goddamn *nowhere*. Nowhere, Maryland. That's us." He found the poster, and it had a tear in it. "Ah shit, my poster's messed up." He screwed up his face and glared at the poster, holding it up so I could see the tear.

"It's pretty cool they took you to Burger King." I was putting on a clean white T-shirt and a pair of navy gym shorts. I hung up my sport coat in the bureau and put my laundry in the hamper.

"Yeah. They let me order all this extra stuff because they said it was on the school."

"Sweet."

I pulled open the desk drawer. It was filled with scratched-in graffiti, names of past students, and several brief, profound reflections on life at the Ashford River School consisting primarily of four-letter words. One of the less creative examples was "Fuck Ashford." I noticed again that Trey's bed was completely covered with his stuff, so he couldn't have slept on it. "So, um, where did you sleep last night?" I hung the little portable tie-rack that my dad had bought me in the bureau.

"Oh..." Trey was laughing as he changed the song. "Actually, I slept in your bed on top 'cause mine was covered with all my shit. I hope you don't mind. I put my sheets up there. But I really want the bottom bunk. So why don't you just put your sheets on the bottom bunk, and I'll use them 'cause there's no point in redoing the sheets. So I mean we can just trade if you don't care."

I was trying to figure out what the hell he'd just said but decided it wasn't really that important. "Sure, yeah, whatever. By the way, dude, your T-shirt reeks."

Trey lifted his arm and smelled his shirt. "Holy shit, yeah, it does. In fact, I reek in general. Probably should shower. It's been about three days now." He grabbed a towel from somewhere in his bed full of stuff, along with a bottle of shampoo, and wandered off down the hall.

I was left by myself in the room with the music playing. I unpacked more of my belongings and looked at the stuff scattered on Trey's desk. In the open drawer, there were a few pictures of him with a couple I assumed must be his mom and dad. There was also one with a cute girl kissing him on the cheek on a chairlift at some ski resort. There was a mail key, a room key, and a wallet, which lay unfolded. Curious, I hesitated but looked at it. A State of New York learner's permit. Trey had turned sixteen a month ago, I was surprised to see, which made him almost exactly a year older than I. That meant that he had probably repeated a year somewhere down the line. I picked up the wallet to take a closer look at the photo, which was when I noticed the thick stack of cash. There had to be twenty-five or thirty one-hundred-dollar bills.

*Holy...*

My heart jumped a little when I saw the money, and I put the wallet down quickly, looking over my shoulder again at the closed door. I might have realized right then that Trey and I were from different planets, and maybe part of me did. Either way, I felt guilty and filed my discovery away in a place where it wouldn't bother me.

■ ■ ■

A few hours later, it was time for the arrival ceremonies and reception dinner. I too had taken a shower by this time, stumbling through an awkward conversation with a kid named Rick Eldrin, realizing how strange it was to introduce oneself in the shower to someone you've never met. In a way, that was the first thing that really brought home the truth that I was going to boarding school. There's something sort of humbling when you realize that you probably won't do *anything* alone, even take a shower, for the next few years. You were just another guy there.

Back in the room, I put on a dress shirt and my sport coat again. Trey and I managed our Ashford River School ties with a little bit of effort. It took me three attempts to get it right, trying to remember the steps my dad had taught me at home. Trey seemed a little better at it than I was, which made sense. This wasn't his first boarding school. He looked older dressed up. He kept his collar button loose and didn't tuck in the back of his shirt. He needed to borrow some of my deodorant because he said he forgot to pack it.

Packing. Christ. I remember my mom helping me pack a couple days before so that I couldn't possibly forget anything. *Anything.* I mean this had been a major family enterprise, executed in the orchestrated way characteristic of anything directed by my mother.

I'd been finishing up a bowl of macaroni and cheese, which I'd made myself before Mom got home from work. She sat across from me at the kitchen table in her hospital scrubs, wearing reading glasses low on her nose, dark-green eyes peering up at me through loose bangs as we put items on the list. My mother has a kind face, with a light complexion and barely visible auburn freckles that match the color of her wavy hair. When she smiles, the corners of her eyes form little wrinkles. She always looks tired, probably from the stress at work.

There was a list of stuff to bring in the entrance packet the school had sent along with the other rules and regulations, but my mother errs on the side of thoroughness, so she added "a few things here and there." She wrote in pencil on a yellow legal pad in big, loopy script, a cup of coffee steaming in her United Nurses' Association mug. Her hospital ID badge flopped back and forth, dangling from a lanyard, making little clicking noises as it tapped against the table while she wrote. She drinks a lot of coffee. Coffee makes me think of her.

After we finished the list, we went out shopping and bought everything on it: paper, pens, pencils, two highlighters (yellow and blue), colored pencils, notebooks and folders, five three-hole one-inch binders, a scientific calculator, a stapler, three-hole puncher, index cards, loose-leaf paper, a Scotch tape dispenser, eight each of undershirts and boxers, a new pair of dress shoes, five pairs of flat-front khakis (pleats, according to my mother, are for businessmen), three white and three light-blue oxfords, a brown leather belt, six pairs each of white socks and navy socks, the sport coat, a gray V-neck sweater, soap, shampoo, three sticks of deodorant, a bottle of Gold Bond body powder (which I had never heard of but was apparently, my dad had said in a knowing, *man-to-man* kind of way, "something that guys learn to appreciate as they get older"), Q-tips, three big tubes of toothpaste, an extra toothbrush, three towels, a washcloth—I'd never used a washcloth before and wondered why I needed one now—nail clippers, a razor, and shaving cream. My dad had insisted on this and bought a triple-bladed Gillette and a can of aloe gel formula shaving cream, even though I didn't have a hair on my face. Then there were two pairs of navy-blue mesh gym shorts, running shoes, a combination lock, swimming suit, goggles, a bulletin board and a little box of a hundred tacks, a bathrobe and shower shoes, and a whole bunch of other stuff, too.

But that wasn't it.

Mom insisted on laying everything out in neat little piles organized by category: dress clothes, athletic clothes, school supplies, et cetera, in the living room the night before we left, and then she checked each item off the list as I put it in the bag. Dad had been watching a game on TV and occasionally looked over his shoulder, raising his eyebrows and chuckling when he saw me methodically putting things in the duffel bag one by one while Mom checked them off her legal pad.

I was trying to watch the game from across the room and occasionally forgot to put a particular item in the bag. I remember sitting there on the edge of the ottoman, staring absently at the TV as a package of Fruit-of-the-Loom T-shirts dangled from my hand above the bag. My mother looked up at me above the black-rimmed glasses, again sipping a cup of coffee, and got my attention, saying, "Hey. Matty. Back to me, kiddo." I smiled and snapped back to the job at hand, stuffing the T-shirts deep into the duffel and listening for the next item on the list, the sound of the game fading as Dad lowered the volume. I remember the way he laughed after my mother said, "Socks, athletic, six pairs."

Dad turned around in his chair, took a sip of his beer, and said, "Are you going to itemize his underwear, too?"

We laughed again, decided to take a break, and watched the rest of the game together in the small living room. I sat between them like I had when I was a little kid. Mom played absently with my hair and looked at me more than the television. I could smell her coffee and feel the heat of the mug where my arm brushed it.

"*Fifteen*," she had said, smiling and shaking her head. "Wow."

■ ■ ■

Trey and I headed down together now, meeting up with my dad at the bottom of the stairs. There were lots of other parents and boys. Dads straightened out ties while moms brushed lint from sport coats. Classical music floated on the air from somewhere down the corridor. Dad smiled when he saw us and clapped us both on the shoulder.

"So, here are the men of MacKerry 211! You guys look pretty sharp."

Trey sort of grinned, and I rolled my eyes. At least Dad didn't look like a federal agent anymore. Fortunately, he had left the tinted glasses in the car.

As we walked down the corridor, my eyes wandered over the class portraits hanging on the walls, hundreds of black-and-white photos arranged in neat columns, some of the older ones yellowed with age. The crowd filed into the dining hall through the glass doors at the end of the corridor, and the music came to life. This was another moment when I realized I'd stepped into a different world. This was *not* a high school cafeteria. *The Hampshire Room*, the campus map called it.

My dad raised his eyebrows and elbowed me. "Looks like you've landed your ass in a tub full of butter, tiger." He leaned in close. "You better hang on to that scholarship."

"I guess I better."

Trey, on the other hand, seemed relatively unimpressed and busied himself with a loose thread on his sleeve.

No matter how many hours I spent there over the next three years, The Hampshire Room never failed to impress me. Named for some long-dead very wealthy alumnus, it was a long, rectangular dining hall, with leaded glass windows that stretched from the polished hardwood floor to a high ceiling. Elaborate plaster molding framed the windows, with intricate, sculpted designs painstakingly detailed in crimson and navy. Dark pine paneling, varnished over the years to a lacquered sheen, extended from the floor to the chair rail, and two immense, complicated crystal chandeliers illuminated the place with warm light. A quartet of violins played along with a bassist in the far corner. I think it was Vivaldi, maybe part of *The Four Seasons*. The players were wearing the same uniform as the rest of us: navy sport coats, white shirts, khakis, and blue ties with emblazoned crests. A buffet table lined the south wall, covered with warming platters, heaped baskets of bread, and plates of cut fruit arranged in symmetrical patterns. The pineapples were sliced in half, forming oblong bowls filled with strawberries and orange wedges. There were oak tables arranged in two rows, at the end of which was situated a larger head table, set up on a platform, almost like a stage. It was all very hierarchical, I'd later learn, with sets of tables reserved for the differing classes—one achieved closer proximity to the head table as he got older. The tables were covered with alternating gray and navy runners, and the places were set with glassware and plates bearing the school seal. A banner with the same seal hung behind the high table, and recessed lights shone, illuminating it from below. The windows looked out on the east quad on one side and a tree-lined hill on the other. The hill sloped down steeply at first and then more gradually to the rowing lake about a quarter mile away. French doors led to a flagstone terrace overlooking the hill. The doors were open tonight, and brass lamps glowed outside in the dusk. From time to time, I could smell the air from outside. It was humid, fresh, and earthy from the afternoon rain, which had stopped while we were upstairs.

Father Daley approached the three of us, sort of sauntering up in a casual way I didn't associate with priests. He held a glass of wine. "Mr. Derby, Matt, Trey, feel free to sit wherever you'd like except for the back two tables; that's where the student prefects are stuck tonight. There are some other sophomore families right over there." He gestured behind us to the third table, where two couples and their sons were mingling. We shook hands, and Father Daley headed off to greet the next family.

"I guess there's no assigned seats, gents." My dad gestured toward the tables Father Daley had indicated. "Why don't we head over there? You guys might as well get to know people right away." He led us over to the third table.

My father was incredibly into this, and getting in deeper by the moment. I liken it now to the way a man acts when entering a Mercedes dealership in the throes of his midlife crisis, sheepishly aware that the extravagance around him *should* be out of reach, always has been out of reach, but suddenly isn't. Of course, my dad was happier that the extravagance was for me rather than himself. To him, this was better than a Mercedes. I smiled, thinking back to the afternoon I came home from swimming practice in mid-January of that year. Dad had been standing on the front porch, shivering in the snow, a big letter-sized envelope in his hand. He was beaming as he handed it to me. I remember holding it for a moment, feeling the weight of it. *"Dear Matthew,"* it read. *"On behalf of the Administration, Faculty, and Trustees of the Ashford River School, I'm happy to offer you admission as a transfer sophomore to the class of 1999..."* Dad had read it out loud. *"Furthermore, based on your outstanding achievements in ninth grade and our belief in your academic potential, we are pleased to offer you a substantial scholarship equal to three-quarters' tuition and fees..."* The offer was more generous than anything we'd expected. We'd made a family decision midway through my first semester at the local public high school that I should apply to the private schools in the area. Before that time, when I was in middle school, money had been so tight that it just wasn't really part of our thinking. But then things had begun to turn a corner for Dad's business, and I found myself pulling all A's in school. We put in my transfer application to two private Catholic schools in Buffalo and, more or less on a whim, to a couple of mid-Atlantic boarding schools with reputations for awarding generous merit scholarships, including the Ashford River School. I was admitted to the local schools quickly, and their admissions officers countered each other's scholarship offers. But when the opportunity came from Ashford River, a much smaller, exclusive school, it was too good to refuse. With tuition more than double that of the more expensive local alternative—and a scholarship package that would make it more affordable than anything in Buffalo—it was an amazing offer. We went out to dinner that night to celebrate. My admission to Ashford River marked something for my father, something that I understand now more than I did then. He didn't go to prep school, and college only happened courtesy of the US Navy, in exchange for six years of service following high school.

After five minutes of handshakes and introductions, I had met Brian McNeal, Rick Eldrin (again, but thankfully with clothes on this time), Dave Culaney, and Jimmy Speers. Brian, Rick, and Jimmy had both their parents there, but Dave had only his mom with him. Trey sat between my dad and me. Just as I was about to ask Trey what his dad was doing in London, Father Daley's voice boomed over a microphone.

"Good evening, everyone. I know we're all hungry, but I think it's a fitting start to this occasion of welcome that we take a moment for a brief prayer before dinner." Silence descended upon the room, and Father Daley lowered his head. Everyone in the room followed suit. I glanced over at Trey and noticed him staring absently at a spot on the floor.

"In the name of the Father, and of the Son, and of the Holy Spirit. Almighty God and Father of all good things, we thank you this evening for the blessing of this meal and each other's company. We ask for your safe-keeping of our community, especially these newest members as they begin this new stage of their life. And so bless us, O Lord, and these thy gifts, which we are about to receive..." He finished the prayer with the sign of the cross and sat down with the rest of the faculty at the head table.

Soon, the room was filled with the din of loud conversation, and the waitstaff went busily to work. They were not like the lunch ladies at my last school. Four of them were young, unsmiling men, probably not much older than twenty. They might have been Mexican. The other two were older black women, which even then struck me as interesting, because there weren't too many black kids or Mexican kids sitting at the tables. I watched as they served and cleared plates, thinking they seemed like professional waiters at fancy restaurants I'd been to. One of the women smiled broadly when Trey said, "Thank you, ma'am."

The parents talked a lot during dinner, with Brian's and Jimmy's moms dominating most of the conversation, along with the Eldrin family. I just did my best to concentrate on eating, which seemed to be what the other guys were doing while our parents talked. There was carved roast beef and garlic mashed potatoes, waffle-cut carrots and peas, and salad made with iceberg lettuce, which, because of my mother's lectures, I knew had "absolutely no nutritional value," but I liked it better than the leafy kind anyway.

Dr. and Mrs. Eldrin were an older couple. According to the name-tags they wore, they were *Sophomore Parents' Committee Chair Couple*, and Dr. Eldrin was a proud graduate of the *Class of 1961*. His wife wore a satin evening gown that seemed way too formal. Her voice was smooth and Southern, similar to Dr. Winthrop's. "So, boys, I hope you're ready to get to work this fall! That reading list looks quite extensive."

None of us seemed to know exactly whether this comment required a response or not. We looked at each other blankly until Trey spoke up. This was the first of many instances in which I was to be amazed at Trey's ability to endear himself to women of any age.

"Well, yes, ma'am. I understand the humanities are very strong here." He smirked slightly, and I smiled, looking down at my dinner plate.

Dr. Eldrin chimed in with a similar Southern drawl. "Oh, Marlene, let's let the boys think about something other than *books*. Hell, they haven't even finished unpacking!"

This invigorating conversation carried on for another fifteen minutes, rambling through the realms of academia, the school's Episcopal roots but current ecumenical Christian identity ("And not just a *Catholic*, but a *Jesuit* chaplain, *for goodness sake*," remarked Mrs. Eldrin with some not-so-inconspicuous skepticism), athletics, the football season to come, the origins and symbolism of the school seal. The Latin was borrowed from Yale, *Lux et veritas*, "light and truth." The motto's tragic unoriginality but fitting metaphoric significance was explained at nauseating length by Dr. Eldrin, who'd already had four sons graduate from the school and, he reminded us again, was himself a product of the class of 1961, one of the most active alumni years in the school's history. "Yes, Rick is the sixth Ashford River man in our family!" Rick himself seemed far less enthusiastic about this legacy than his father. There was talk about the nearby girls' schools, which was a topic of interest to us but an awkward one in the company of parents, until, like an answer to our collective prayers, Dr. Winthrop tapped his wineglass with a spoon and stood in the center of the raised platform.

The room quickly hushed to a silence. Behind him, a row of teachers sat casually, leaning toward each other and whispering indecipherable comments, sometimes smirking and chuckling, watching the headmaster from their perch and taking occasional sips of their drinks as he spoke. His deep Alabama baritone resonated in the large room. Glassware clinked as places were cleared for dessert.

"Well now, I think it goes without saying that Mr. Radcliff and the dining staff have again outdone themselves," he said, gesturing to a short, stocky man with rolled-up sleeves and an apron, who stood at the service door to the kitchen. Dr. Winthrop prompted applause and continued after it died down.

"Tonight is always a particularly special night for me, and I think I can say the same for my colleagues on the faculty." He paused, looking pensively at his shoes. "You see, tonight I have the privilege to welcome our eighty-two incoming freshmen and transfers and to welcome back our returning students. It's not every day a family gains eighty-two sons." Parents laughed. I noticed an older teacher rolling his eyes.

"In all seriousness, you new boys, tonight you are entering a family. A *rich* family. But that richness lies not just with a beautiful campus and a wonderful meal. We are blessed with an incredible academic and athletic tradition here at Ashford River. However, the very foundation of those traditions lies in the strength of our community."

I watched Trey play with the dessertspoon, spinning it around on the tablecloth. He raised his eyebrows and grinned when he caught my eye. He mouthed the word *bullshit* in slow motion, exaggerating his facial movements, and I laughed and looked at the ground, trying to conceal it. Dad glared at me.

Dr. Winthrop went on.

And on.

"The majority of the faculty you see behind me," he made a sweeping gesture, "live right here at school. They will be not only your teachers, but also your mentors and your guides. They'll be the people who will help you meet the challenges that they themselves put forth. That's a truly wonderful family dynamic, and we're very proud of it. It's what strong families do." Another pause. Holding the microphone, he approached the string quartet, putting his hand on the shoulder of one of the violin players. The boy seemed to shrink a bit into the shoulders of his sport coat, and his face flushed, bright red against his blond crew cut.

"These young men providing this music, for example, are products of that family—a community that encourages each man here to develop his mind, heart, and soul. We want you to be men of diverse knowledge. You'll learn many practical things here, but you'll also learn about art, poetry, and music."

Trey had moved on to the sugar bowl, sculpting the white crystals into a symmetrical mound that looked vaguely like a breast, complete with a nipple. I'd later learn that he would do this on occasion in various media—clay in art class, Jell-O at dinner, snow in the winter. Nipples seemed to be one of his artistic specialties.

"I won't belabor you with much more talk. I know you all have moving in to finish, and your housemasters will give you more information tonight. I simply want to close with my warmest welcome to each of you and my hope that you might aspire to the truly excellent potential within you. Thank you again for coming to Ashford River."

There was more applause, not some small portion of which came enthusiastically from the Eldrins, and then another half hour of mingling over dessert. It was a fudge brownie with caramel and whipped cream. The dining hall staff must have spent hours working on the presentation. Three strawberry slices formed a triangular pyramid nestled in a circle of whipped cream on top of each brownie, and carefully poured lines of caramel and butterscotch sauce formed the cursive letters *ARS* on the plates. This was yet another example of the school's sometimes ridiculous culture of extravagance, something I would grow only more aware of throughout my three years.

The adults drank coffee. So did Trey. Dave, Brian, Rick, and I sipped Coca-Cola and talked about rowing. Rick Eldrin had rowed last year, and two of his older brothers rowed at Ashford and had a great time at it. One of them was currently in the top lightweight eight at Princeton. Brian McNeal wanted to do it because he was sick of riding the bench on the football team and he'd heard that rowing scholarships were abundant. I just thought it looked interesting. Trey had rowed before at a previous school. Jimmy Speers was only about five feet tall and already a coxswain. Dave Culaney, like McNeal, didn't even know what a rowing shell looked like, but he was also sick of football. Somewhere in the midst of the conversation, he decided to try it out for a week. Dr. Eldrin had lots to say about how it was a solid cardiovascular workout but cautioned that young men needed to be careful about repetitive exertion of the back and take care with plenty of stretching. Dr. Eldrin had lots to say about pretty much everything.

My dad played football at his public high school in Buffalo, so he didn't really have too much to say. I wasn't sophisticated enough at fifteen to understand how awkward the conversation was becoming for my father or how admirable was his genuine happiness for me in its midst. Despite his pride in me, the enormity of the place must have made him feel very ordinary and maybe even small, but Dad's character is such that it really didn't matter. This would become a more and more admirable quality to me as my years at Ashford River rolled on. He listened to the conversation, nodding. "Mr. Brady seems like he'll be a good coach," he added.

Dr. Eldrin mentioned that he thought Mr. Brady looked rather young for a teacher, though he was quite sure the man was competent or the likewise competent headmaster wouldn't have seen fit to hire him.

Ms. Culaney, recently divorced, made a point to mention that he looked *just fine*, much to the amusement of Mrs. Eldrin and Mrs. McNeal.

It went on like this for a while.

■ ■ ■

An hour later, I was standing on the front steps of MacKerry Hall with my dad and Trey. The rain had started again. The Caprice's engine rumbled, and I could smell the exhaust. Little beads of water dripped from the tailpipe, mixing with the puddles on the ground.

"Guess this is where I let you go." It was like a scene from some old black-and-white movie with the parents waving good-bye to their son as he leans out of a train car, bound for a new life. It seemed melodramatic. I laughed a little, but then the reality of my dad's departure began to take on real weight.

"I'll see you really soon. There's a rowing race in Pittsburgh in October. Maybe you guys could come down and pick me up. Could come home for a night," I suggested.

"That might work out. Well, make sure you give your mom a call tonight. Let her know you're okay and everything. You have that calling card number, and there's a pay phone in the hall outside your room. Or just call collect." He reached into his wallet and pulled out a few twenty-dollar bills. He leaned in close and gave me a hug, putting the bills in my shirt pocket. Just for a second, I hugged him tight. I heard him say, "Good luck, chief," right into my ear. There was a little strain, like he was trying to lift up a heavy box and talk at the same time. I could smell his aftershave, and the wool suit felt scratchy on my face. He let go, and I stood up tall, straightening out my jacket. Dad stared at the ground for a few seconds and then turned to Trey. His voice seemed suddenly loud and upbeat.

"Trey. Great to meet you. I'm sure you guys are gonna have a great time this year. Keep him out of trouble, okay?" He shook Trey's hand.

"Sure will, Mr. Derby. I'll try." Trey thrust his hands deep in his pockets after the handshake.

Dad turned, clapped me on the shoulder one more time, and hurried down the steps through the rain to the car. He opened the door, gave us a little salute, and then ducked inside. We heard the sound of the tires on the wet asphalt as he drove off. The same scene was happening on the other side of the steps, and I saw a kid hugging his mom as we headed upstairs, both loosening our ties as soon as we reached the landing.

After a half hour of wandering from room to room, making more introductions, we went back to our own to get changed. Trey put the stereo back on. It was The Rolling Stones this time. As I put my T-shirts into a drawer, I saw Trey unrolling another poster. I couldn't see what it was because of the glare from the lamp.

"What's this one?" I asked.

Trey was grinning. "Saved this one for last." He held up the poster. "*Sports Illustrated* series. I love this one." The poster featured a well-tanned brunette in a white two-piece, standing knee deep in the aquamarine surf of a tropical beach. She held a mask and snorkel in her hand, and she was soaking wet like she'd just come out of the water. The bikini clung to her body. Tightly. The wet fabric looked smooth, like the ivory keys on a piano, and I sort of reflexively imagined what it would feel like—supple but firm, warm from the sun and the salt water. The girl was smirking at the camera, like she'd just whispered the world's best-kept secret. There was a caption in bright-pink script that matched the color of the snorkel. It read, *"Tanya—exploring the world down under."* Trey held it at arm's length, his head cocked in admiration.

"Whaddya think?"

"I think I like it," I said. I could make out a line between Tanya's legs, a barely visible patch of darkness underneath the wet bikini bottom. This was the first of many visual aids, courtesy of Trey Daniels, that would educate me about the details of the female anatomy over the next few months. "Brady gonna let us keep it up, though?"

"We'll put it on the inside of the door. He won't ever see it that way unless he closes the door behind him. And teachers don't do that. They're too afraid of lawsuits."

"Yeah."

"Besides, if he does see it," continued Trey, centering it on the door, "I think he'll kinda like it."

Trey seemed to have this (and many other things) all figured out, and I held the poster up as he tacked it to the door. Just as we finished and stood back to admire it, there was a knock. A few seconds later, Mr. Brady's face appeared.

"Gentlemen." He looked surprised to see both of us standing so close to the door and hesitated, seeming to think about something for a second. "I need you to get together out in the hall in about five minutes. There's a meeting for all the sophomores with Mr. Wagner. Make sure you're out here in five. Dress code is casual." The door closed halfway, and then Brady poked his head back in.

"Oh. Incidentally...you guys wouldn't happen to be hanging something on the back of your door, would you?"

We exchanged glances.

"Because," Brady continued, "I'd rather you didn't." He paused for a bit. "I've been doing this for a little while, guys." He smiled, nodded, and closed the door.

"Can't get away with much around here, can you?" I looked at Trey.

"Eh." Trey shrugged, admiring the poster. "I think we'll keep it up."

"So we have to meet with Mr. Wagner. Who's he?"

"He's the new dean of discipline—the guy that throws people outta here." Trey was playing with a rubber band, making it into a gun. He pointed it at my chest, squinting to take aim before he let it go. It flew over my shoulder and hit the door, not far from Tanya Down Under's left nipple.

"Good shot. So whaddya know about him?" Trey seemed to have some intelligence about most things at Ashford River. Where he'd gotten it from, I had no idea.

"I heard he was in the army for about twenty years. Some big shot back in Desert Storm. Flew helicopters, I think; then he retired. He was a dean at some other prep school in the Midwest for a few years, but he's new here."

"So he's only been out of the army a little while. Probably a badass." I pictured Bruce Willis dressed as a teacher.

"Mallow said the guy they had last year was a pushover. I think they fired him."

"This guy doesn't sound like a pushover."

"Prob'ly not. But seriously, I know the drill," Trey said as we walked out into the hallway. "He'll probably just walk back and forth and look tough and talk about how much of a badass he is but also how he's there for us at any time, blah, blah, blah."

The second floor of MacKerry—Mr. Brady and Mr. DiVincenzo's floor—had twenty-two of us sophomores. Another twenty-two lived on the third floor, and the rest among different dormitories. Our group joined up with them downstairs in the foyer, and we all followed the teachers outside.

The quad had the smell of earth and grass after rain. Overhead, the clear sky was indigo, and floodlights illuminated the facades of the classroom buildings on either side. Maple trees, lit from below with tiny floodlights, lined the angular walkways. I followed the line of boys to a circular brick terrace at the middle of the quad, where we filed into the benches arranged around its perimeter. There was only room for about half the group on the benches, so the rest of us clustered around them, sitting on the ground. The terrace was damp from the rain, and I felt it seeping through my gym shorts. In the middle, arms behind his back, stood a stocky man with short-cropped, platinum-gray hair. He stood so still and looked so solid that for a minute he seemed like a statue. He looked to me to be around Dad's age, but there was something about him that seemed older.

The chatter stopped as the man began to walk the perimeter of the circle, just a few feet inside the ring of boys. I could hear crickets chirping and the sound of a plane somewhere overhead. The stocky man looked at each of us, pausing for a second, without expression. His barrel chest filled a navy-blue polo shirt. He wore khakis and polished leather dress shoes that reflected tiny points of light from the flood lamps. His square jaw barely moved when he spoke; his voice was Southern like Dr. Winthrop's but quieter and softer. The words came out slowly.

"Good evening, Gentlemen. My name is Kurt Wagner. I am your new dean. Each of you is here because when you applied to come here as freshmen—or as transfers this year—the admissions committee recognized your potential." He stopped pacing and scanned the faces of the boys. "I expect you to continue lending credibility to their decision."

Mr. Wagner cocked his head to the side and resumed his pacing. "Some of you might have heard that I spent a long time in the army. Some of you might worry that I'll run the school like the army. Don't worry. I may be new to Ashford River, but I'm not new to education. I spent the past four years at another school. This isn't the army, and I won't treat you like soldiers. I'll treat you like fifteen- and sixteen-year-olds, albeit ostensibly gifted, intelligent, capable, and potentially responsible fifteen- and sixteen-year-olds. The army did teach me to be reasonable and fair. And I am." His voice was absolutely level.

I remember wondering what the hell "albeit" and "ostensibly" meant.

"You ought to know the rules by now. You're not freshmen anymore, and most of you have been here a full year longer than I have. So there's no excuse for you not to know them. If there's any ambiguity, you have your student handbook, a copy of which I placed in each of your mailboxes this afternoon." He pulled a copy of the navy-blue booklet from his back pocket and held it up next to his head. "My understanding, based on the academic standards of this school, is that you are all capable of reading. So refresh yourselves on the rules and follow them." He slowly rolled the booklet into a tube and put it in his back pocket.

"You should be familiar with the disciplinary process here. If you break a minor rule, you'll serve detention, doing work around campus or in the kitchen. For serious infractions, you will meet with a disciplinary committee made up of five faculty members, one of whom will be yours truly. We will review your situation. We will then make a recommendation to the headmaster, who will in turn make the final decision regarding consequences. Remember that your first responsibility here is integrity. Next in line are your academics. The rest will sort itself out. If there is any ambiguity in the rules, or if there is a point on which you would like clarification, please feel free to bring it to my attention. As I said, it's my job to be reasonable and fair."

He pointed a thumb behind him at Mr. Brady and Mr. DiVincenzo. "These two men are assets to you. I have heard good things about their commitment and their professionalism. Get to know them and show them respect by keeping to the high road. They will help you stay there and raise the proverbial red flag when you are in danger of taking an undesirable detour. I can tell you from experience that sophomore year is fraught with potential detours. It's what we refer to in the army as a minefield."

He *was* an older Bruce Willis. I imagined him in desert fatigues, giving a similar speech, the sands of the Middle East swirling as he readied his company to invade Baghdad.

Mr. Wagner turned, shook Brady's and DiVincenzo's hands in a ceremonial sort of way, and nodded. He turned back to the circle of boys. "Good night, Gentlemen. I would encourage you to get some sleep." He walked down the sidewalk and disappeared around the corner. The circle stayed quiet. I looked at the faces around me. Most stared, stone-faced, at the ground. I noticed Trey on the bench across from me, just barely smiling.

"Okay, guys." Brady sounded loud and energetic after the menacing softness of Mr. Wagner's voice. "Now that Mr. Wagner has officially scared the hell out of you, I want to emphasize a few points." There was a general rumble of laughter, and the entire circle seemed to breathe a sigh of relief. Shoulders relaxed, and weight was shifted. "Mr. DiVincenzo and I are also very reasonable guys. We'll treat you according to how you act. Act like kids; we'll treat you like kids. Act with maturity; we'll treat you with maturity. You're not freshmen anymore, and we don't expect freshman behavior. I'd like to think you worked your way through that stuff last year." He nodded at the other teacher.

Mr. DiVincenzo was a heavyset man around Brady's age, with a dense beard and hairy arms. He had thick jowls, narrow eyes, and the lowest voice

I think I'd ever heard. "You guys are getting older now, and you're gonna have to learn how to deal with each other. This is a very different year from last year. We're not going to hold your hands as much, and we'll leave a lot to you. But we're around for you, and if you need anything, our doors are always open, even when they're not."

Mr. Brady took off his watch and held it in the air. "Anyone know what this is?"

Trey spoke up. "That's a watch, Mr. Brady. We use it to tell time." He was grinning, slouched on the bench now, his left arm dangling off the side and his right arm extended along the back of the bench behind McNeal's shoulders. His legs were stretched out, crossed at the ankle. He looked like he was watching a football game. The rest of the guys exchanged glances and chuckled, clearly amused by the new kid.

"Thank you, Mr. Daniels." Brady eyed Trey. "Yes, guys, this is a watch. Please utilize it. If there's one thing that aggravates me more than anything else, it's lateness. Lights-out, for example. Eleven o' clock on school nights. Big step up from last year: You've gained a whole hour. That means you are in your room, ready for bed, at eleven, eastern standard time—not brushing your teeth, not discussing politics in the shower, not on the phone with your mom and dad or whispering sweet nothings to honey-love from St. Amelia's. You're *in* your room, got it?"

I laughed along with the rest of them. A hand shot up from across the circle. I didn't know the kid's name at the time. He was really short with a freckled face and a mop of red curls on his head. "Mr. Brady?"

"Yes, Evan?" Brady was smiling.

The short kid pointed at his own watch. "Um, it's a school night tonight, and it's 10:56 right now."

Brady and DiVincenzo grinned at each other.

"Well then," Brady said, looking in the direction of MacKerry Hall and raising his eyebrows, "I guess you guys better haul ass."

# CHAPTER 6

September is always the best time to be in a school. Everything is new. A general optimism pervades the place, even among the most prehistoric faculty and seniors on lingering probation for some idiotic stunt they'd pulled as underclassmen. The inevitable tedium hasn't settled in yet. And even though everyone knows it's coming—feels its subtle approach—the sheen of a fresh start is enough to illuminate things. It's a time of renewal. Everyone is likeable—or at least tolerable—in September, even the jack-asses. And there are many of those in a residential community like Ashford River.

My first September at boarding school was invigorating, if challenging. It was filled with awkwardness and lessons sometimes learned at the expense of personal dignity. I learned the ins and outs of private school etiquette, where to sit in The Hampshire Room, how to deal with upperclassmen and which upperclassmen simply not to deal with at all. I figured out how to coexist with a roommate, and my tolerance for the lack of privacy grew. I got to know the campus, all four hundred sprawling acres of it. I slowly became attuned to the rhythms and patterns of institutionalized life and how to play the games so essential to happiness and survival. I began to learn the expectations of the teachers and that Latin is always the toughest subject. We figured things out as a class, too. The title "sophomore" implies both wisdom and foolishness, and we embodied both. We figured out how to get away with our collars unbuttoned, with the knots in our tie cinched just high enough to cover the fact. We began to figure out whom we could trust and whom we despised, though the dislike could still be subdued and controlled. Unlike the more jaded upperclassmen, for us, it was still a shiny new place with too much opportunity and not enough time. The teachers were cool, except the ones who weren't. The work wasn't easy but wasn't too heavy yet either. One could get away with stuff in September. There was leeway. A lot of that leeway came courtesy of Steve Mallow.

He was the student prefect assigned to our floor of MacKerry. It took a couple weeks to figure Mallow out, but I think I began to understand him sooner than the other guys did. Mallow was a senior from Philadelphia, but not a nice part of Philadelphia. I think we had a certain similarity in our backgrounds, in that we didn't come from the same kind of wealth that so many of the students at Ashford River did. Steve knew the terrain of the dorms. He'd been appointed student prefect because of a good—though not flawless—disciplinary record, an aptitude for leadership, and a willingness to extend himself to underclassmen in ways that most seniors simply didn't. He was the quintessential scholar-athlete and was all but assured entrance to Yale, his ambitions having turned toward New Haven ever since he visited the campus as a sophomore. Most of us on the floor considered Mallow an ally, a sort of counsel in gray areas, an advisor to be trusted, and an ambassador to the faculty when necessary. Of course, he had his own peers, and we weren't his buddies per se. He was a year older than most seniors, having been kept back a grade somewhere early on, clearly for athletic reasons. It wasn't uncommon for the feeder schools of the mid-Atlantic preps to hold kids back strategically so they'd be bigger, faster, and stronger candidates in the competitive world of admissions. So quite a few of them were eighteen, but Mallow was nineteen, actually close to twenty. As such, he maintained an almost professional distance from us, which in retrospect was pretty damned impressive. In fact, he was only a few years younger than our youngest teachers.

What earned Mallow more respect than anything else was his girl-friend, Adriana Stiles. Adriana Stiles and her incredible body occupied the majority of Steve's social life when he was allowed to drive off-campus, and it's safe to say that Adriana Stiles and her incredible body occupied a respectable portion of private fantasies in the sophomore dorm. Steve made a point of showing her off whenever possible. They'd hold hands conspicuously at football games, and sometimes they'd study together outside in the quad when she came to visit on a Saturday. She had a habit of wearing short skirts and snug-fitting blouses when the weather was warm. There was a lot of chatter about Adriana and how hot she was, and it was pretty well known that Mallow was doing it with her on a regular basis, so I doubt there was a sophomore in the hall who hadn't eased nocturnal tensions to the mental image of Adriana getting it in the back of Steve's Jeep. That created a brand of respect among us for him, which I think he sort of thrived on, whether consciously or not. Adriana Stiles afforded Mallow the right to study endlessly and still be cool. Actually, Adriana Stiles afforded Mallow the right to do pretty much whatever the hell he wanted and still be cool, even when he angered a guy by calling him out on a discipline issue. When Steve stepped into the shower, every other guy in there understood that the equipment dangling just a few feet away was intimately acquainted with the lesser-known parts of Adriana Stiles, and that earned Steve some serious props. And if that sounds awkward, it was equally amusing when Steve—a fellow Catholic—would serve Mass for Father Daley on Sunday mornings after we knew he'd been banging Adriana Stiles in the back of his Jeep the night before. Such are the contradictions of a Catholic adolescence.

Needless to say, Mallow held a lot of power on the second floor of MacKerry. It was in part because he was a genuinely good guy, even if some of the respect came only from the fact that he was sleeping with Adriana on a regular basis. I remember wondering what would happen to his authority if they broke up. Lucky for Mallow, the relationship and its ancillary benefits package lasted well into the summer following his graduation, fading conveniently to a pleasant memory just in time for them to go their separate collegiate ways.

It was midway through September when the inevitable collision occurred between Mallow and Trey. It wasn't a violent confrontation, but it reverberated through the dorms with the sort of quiet intensity of a low-level seismic tremor. It didn't do much damage, but everyone knew it had happened. The details were sketchy, but it involved a Latin take-home quiz, Trey's failure to complete said quiz, and his arrangement to copy the answers from Dave Buckley, a junior who (not surprisingly) was repeating the course. There were whispers about the arrangement between Dave and Trey, some of which implied payment in the form of cigarettes. I found this entirely believable, because I'd discovered that Trey kept a generous stash of Marlboro Reds in the space behind his sock drawer. There would be times when Trey would appear after a conspicuous absence following study hall, eagerly chewing spearmint gum and wiping some mud from his shoes. He never invited me on these escapades, and I never asked him about them. It was sort of a silent understanding—one of many that exist in any dormitory. Boarding schools depend on such unspoken understandings. (I've heard the same is true of prisons, but it wouldn't be fair to make too many comparisons.)

We had study hall each school night in the library after dinner, from seven to nine thirty. There was a little bit of downtime between dinner and the start of the study period, and we'd all head upstairs to get changed into sweatpants and T-shirts and pick up our books. Trey and I were walking down the hallway with Speers and McNeal, Brian bitching about Brady's crew practice that day (more on rowing later), when Mallow stuck his head out of his room and waved Trey over. The conversation took place inside Mallow's room, and we couldn't hear the details. The part that made news, however, was Trey shaking his head two minutes later as he emerged from the room, rolling his eyes. Halfway out the door, we heard Mallow say to him, voice raised enough to tell us he was pissed: "Keep it up, Daniels, and you'll figure out what I mean."

Trey stopped, looked at me for a second, and turned back to face Steve through the still-open door. "Mallow," he said, his voice even and calm, "go fuck yourself and your Ivy-clad morality. You're a goddamn hypocrite anyway." With that, he let the door swing shut, picked up the backpack he'd left in the corridor, and strode down the hall to meet up with us. It was a turning point for Trey and me, even though it was only a few weeks into school. I'd never seen him so much as flinch at anything, and clearly something had snapped that night. He wasn't red in the face or fuming the way most of us would be, but the flush in his cheeks was visible, and a film of sweat glistened on his forehead. Maybe what surprised me the most was the *eloquence* of his verbal assault. Trey was becoming known for easy conversation that ambled, apparently without aim or purpose, from topic to topic. "Go fuck yourself and your Ivy-clad morality" was simply not Trey speaking. At least, I didn't think it was. It was something we were more likely to overhear coming from a heated faculty meeting, not from this seemingly lackadaisical sophomore from a small town in the Adirondack mountains. But it was one of the first indications I had of just how smart the kid really was.

I think it took Mallow similarly by surprise, because Trey's infraction never came to light, and Steve was pretty quiet for the next couple of weeks. He settled into a more subdued pattern of schoolwork, practices, and Adriana Stiles and seemed to relax his grip on us as a whole. Trey was quietly earning a special sort of notoriety, not only among us, but among the upperclassmen too. It was a dangerous notoriety though, the kind that makes people look for ways to ruin you.

# CHAPTER 7

It was a little past three in the afternoon in the last week of September. Sun shone through the red-gold oak leaves outside the window, throwing amber squares on the hardwood floor. It was a Wednesday, and that meant a slightly different schedule and a later start to practices. Wednesday was supposed to be a day for catching up on your homework and meeting with teachers, who had to stay in their offices until four, and no practices or activities could start until four thirty. Of course, every guy knew that this was an inept strategy on the school's part because most teachers were also dorm supervisors, which meant that nobody was watching the dorms except the maintenance workers. This is just one example of many odd things one will find at any old private school, and Ashford was no exception. Some rules and practices managed to intersect with others at just the right angle, such that the two would quietly render each other completely ineffective. So if a guy wanted to do anything at the Ashford River School that did not fit into the "Prescribed Regimen of Spiritual, Intellectual, and Physical Education (Forming Young Men of High Caliber Since 1887)," he did it in the dorms on Wednesday between three and four thirty in the afternoon. Chances were the enterprising young man wouldn't get caught. A lot went down that never got noticed. It's when most of the various types of contraband—cigarettes, cheat sheets, dirty magazines, et cetera—were traded. Occasionally, when kids got carried away, they did get noticed and had to face the music.

Two weeks prior, a group of freshmen had been caught using an over-sized slingshot to send water balloons on long-range ballistic paths directly over the football field out the window of their dorm room. They probably would have gotten away with it had a balloon not exploded on the ground directly in front of the athletic director and a visiting college coach as they strolled the perimeter of the field. A week later, four seniors were dragged to the Dean's office after it was discovered that they had smuggled a cage full of white mice into their dorm room for the express purpose of spray painting them crimson, silver, and navy in a misguided surge of school spirit. What they had intended to do with the mice was never revealed, but rumor had it they were to be set loose in the faculty lounge.

On this particular Wednesday, Trey was showing off the latest addition to his ever-expanding library of smut. "Where the hell did you get it?" Chase Alexander asked, throwing his backpack on the floor. Dust particles swirled in the sunbeams. Our room smelled like socks. I was sitting at my desk finishing my geometry problems—odd numbers, one to thirty-three. I turned around and looked at the two of them. Trey sat at his desk chair, his eyes glued to the *Hustler* he had just opened. Chase stood behind him, his top shirt button loose and his Ashford River School tie, navy blue with the crest emblazoned boldly in the center, dangling moronically from his neck as he peered over Trey's shoulder. Trey was smirking, reveling in his latest acquisition.

"I ripped it off from Mallow. Captain Boy Scout had it in his backpack in the locker room, kind of sticking halfway out. I had to take a leak during gym class, and it was just sitting there, so I grabbed it."

"Yeah, I thought you were gone for a long time just to take a leak," Chase said, laughing.

"Shut up."

"Mallow is gonna flip *out*!" Chase Alexander had this crazy lacrosse hair that hung over his eyes and made him look a little canine, like one of those long-haired sheepdogs. He had an oddly gravelly voice. It was widely rumored that Chase was supposed to be a junior.

The geometry was almost finished. I was on number 31. Since this was about the ninth magazine that Trey had accumulated in our room, the thrill of this particular escapade was getting old, and I was trying to finish my homework before we had to head to crew practice. I was no innocent angel, and certainly found time to peruse his collection occasionally, but at this moment I wasn't interested.

Trey was flipping the pages slowly. He wore a navy blazer, which was hopelessly wrinkled because he never hung it up. He had taken his tie off a while ago, though, and with the blazer over his white oxford, he looked like he belonged in a catalog, the kind that feature preppy-looking kids hanging out in places like Vail or Fifth Avenue or Nantucket and striking poses, staring off with intense, almost painful seriousness at some indiscernible but obviously captivating point in the distance as a slight breeze ripples their carefully tousled hair. He was smirking the way he always did, not showing any teeth, and his eyes narrowed. His dark-brown hair was a mess. He had stubble on his face, the vague beginnings of an adolescent beard, hardly heavy enough to absolutely require an immediate shave but not light enough to completely escape notice. His real name was Thomas William Daniels, but he was Trey to the whole world except his mom. At least he was Trey to the whole population of MacKerry Hall, which was, for a sophomore at the Ashford River School, pretty much the whole world.

He stood up and handed the magazine to Chase, who grinned and quickly ran out of the room with it stuffed under his sport coat. I wondered if he'd be late to practice.

Trey tapped me on the shoulder. "Hey, you finished with your homework yet? Almost time to go."

"Yeah. Close enough," I said, as I stood up and started to get changed.

"You think today's set will be tough?" He threw his blazer on the ground and got into his workout clothes. "Eldrin's been talking about it all day."

I tied my sneakers. "When is Eldrin not talking?" I asked, rolling my eyes.

"Good point. Well, I guess we'll find out," he said. "Couldn't be as bad as the first day, right?"

■ ■ ■

Twenty-eight freshmen and sophomores had shown up for the first day of junior varsity crew practice a few weeks back. Unlike in other sports, one's particular class year didn't necessarily define him as a JV or varsity rower, so the tradition at Ashford was to train all first- and second-year rowers together. The more experienced guys trained with the varsity coach, Mr. Williams. Those of us who were new had no idea what the hell was going on. Trey knew the basics. But Rick Eldrin, having rowed the year before, seemed to have appointed himself captain, eager to dispense his vast knowledge to us novices at a moment's notice. I can't say it was my first intuition that Eldrin was a dick, but the day helped confirm the idea in my mind.

You might think that the first day of crew practice would have been remotely associated with boats or at least with water, but that was not what Mr. Brady had in store. Instead, it was a grueling two hours of running, sprinting, push-ups, and a particularly demonic abdominal exercise innocuously called the "seated row."

Brady had us gather on the well-packed dirt surface behind the boathouse, where he had set up a table with a notebook and pencil. Next to the table was a scale and a two-by-four post driven into the ground. A measuring tape was tacked to the post. One at a time, we signed in, stepped on the scale to weigh in, and stood, back against the post, to be measured. This took a good ten minutes, and we watched the varsity guys launch their shells while we waited. They moved in unison with a practiced efficiency, coxswains barking commands and the long, narrow shells swinging overhead in sweeping arcs as the rowers carried them from the boathouse and placed them in the water. Eldrin narrated the process, explaining the approximate dimensions of the craft and the strategy behind weight distribution of different sized rowers. The heavier guys went in the middle, in what Eldrin referred to as "the engine room." The stroke man sat in the back of the shell closest to the coxswain, setting the pace for the other seven (since rowers sat facing the stern) and had to have good technique, excellent oar control, and a solid sense of rhythm and timing. Eldrin informed us that he, therefore, would probably serve as stroke.

Trey, grinning, muttered under his breath that he had no doubt Eldrin was good at stroking something, all right. Eldrin may or may not have heard this remark, but McNeal and I chuckled.

When the weigh-ins were finished, Brady called us over, and we gathered near the table.

"Siddown," he said, looking over the list of names on his clipboard. He wore a whistle around his neck and a Georgetown cap pulled low over his face.

We sat down on the dirt. The sun was warm. McNeal picked at a scab on his knee next to me. Eldrin stretched his hamstrings. "We're gonna run for sure," he whispered, asserting his prophetic knowledge for the third time in ten minutes. I rolled my eyes.

Brady looked up from his clipboard. "Over the course of the practice, we'll do a complete Ashford River run, which is four and a half miles. Returning guys, you know the drill, but I'll review the basics for our new guys. You'll be in two columns of fourteen, doing what's called an 'Indian run.' That means you're all jogging in a single-file line a few feet apart. The guy at the back of the line sprints up to the front. When he gets there, the next guy goes. Get it?"

Various groans and nods.

"I'll be up in front, running between the two columns, setting the pace. It'll be a moderate pace, but when it's your turn to sprint, I want you really sprinting. Run up to where I am and jump back into line, slowing down to my pace. In other words, don't pass me. If anyone has to stop, get out of the way and start walking back to the boathouse, because we're not stopping with you. Some upperclassmen will be patrolling the course in case you have a problem."

It seemed a little over the top for the first day, but I'd done Indian runs before and I knew that the pace was slow on the jogging part. It started out okay, but soon guys began to drop out of the line. Once we got about two miles into it, we were down by a few. All the sophomores were hanging on. Every minute or so, Brady would turn around and jog backward, inspecting the groups and yelling at us to straighten up the columns. It had a sort of boot-camp feel to it. By the third mile, we'd lost a couple more freshmen. Eldrin was behind me, and I could hear exaggerated sounds marking the rhythmic, strategic breathing pattern about which he'd told us that morning. The jogging wasn't bad—Brady kept it purposely slow—but the sprinting was excruciating. In the end, only one of the returning sophomores quit, but he didn't seem to want to be there anyway. Twenty-two of us—nine sophomores and thirteen freshmen—came limping to the boathouse in the end, and that was when the real fun began.

Brady (who, by the way, seemed to have hardly broken a sweat, the bastard) showed us how to do a "seated row," a sort of modified crunch that included a sculling motion with the arms and legs. We did about seven million. My quads burned like never before, and that was when we began the adventure in push-ups—not just any push-ups, but special Brady push-ups. We'd have to hold ourselves in a perversely painful plank position, elbows bent halfway between up and down, for a few seconds between every push-up. This is a great deal more painful than you might imagine. Eldrin bitched a lot. Brady told him to save the commentary and to get his back flat and butt out of the air. There was one particularly memorable juncture, holding said position, all of us nearly in tears and our arms shaking, when

Trey glanced over at me with a maniacal grin, his face beet-red, and said, "This is fun."

Two more freshmen quit before the practice ended. All in all, the eighteen rowers and two coxswains who were still there at five thirty made the team. It was a simple selection process. A little mercenary perhaps, but definitely clear and simple.

# CHAPTER 8

By the first of October, routine had settled in.

The alarm went off at seven thirty. I groped until I hit the snooze bar and then dozed off, my arm dangling over the side of the bunk bed. Five minutes later, I jolted awake as the alarm sounded again. I clambered down the ladder to the cold floor. In the lower bunk, Trey grumbled beneath a heap of blankets. One of his feet protruded off the side of the bed, a graying sock hanging on loosely. Trey always slept in his socks. I reached for my towel from the hook on the door and shuffled into my shower shoes. When I opened the door to the corridor, I squinted and rubbed my eyes. The air felt cool and light after the sleepy heaviness of the room. I ran into Brian McNeal and Jimmy Speers coming out of 208, and we acknowledged each other with a silent nod, three bedraggled, half-asleep figures shuffling down the hallway in boxers and T-shirts, towels draped over shoulders or dragged along the carpet. I could hear other alarm clocks coming from behind closed doors. Someone groaned.

Mr. Brady's apartment door—212—was always open in the morning, and I could hear the morning news on his TV and smell coffee as we approached. Brian and I would usually stop by, leaning on the door frame, dazedly looking at the oddly awake and colorful images on the screen, the sound of the traffic helicopter whooshing behind the static voice giving the beltway commuter report. Mr. Brady sat on his couch with his feet resting on the coffee table, sipping a cup of steaming coffee. He woke up around six every morning and ran four miles, so by the time we shuffled down the hallway, he was already revved up for the day. He'd be sitting there in his khakis and a white crew neck undershirt, look up from the TV or the papers that he was grading, and throw out some chipper morning comment like, "Welcome to the new day there, Matt!" or "I think you should keep your hair like that all day, McNealyman!" or "Ready to hit that Latin quiz today?" or sometimes, if he was distracted by what was on the news, just, "Morning, chief." Of course, even if he seemed distracted, I knew he was checking each of us off his mental list, and he'd wander from room to room to check on anyone he didn't see up and moving before eight. He knew each of our rooms and seemed to know who the late risers were, who needed motivating words, and who just needed a friendly kick to the mattress. Trey, for example, usually just needed the kick.

I headed down to the shower. From out in the hallway, I could hear the raised voices and running water. As I opened the door, the sounds grew suddenly louder, and I felt the steamy warmth of the room. The smell of shampoo and the fluorescent light finished the process of waking me up as I hung my towel on the hook, shimmied out of my T-shirt and boxers, and stepped into the brightly lit, white-tiled showers. Like every morning, five or six of the other guys were in there, none of them really awake, trying their best to deal with each other's still-awkward presence, carrying on with casual conversation, an entirely different stream of thoughts coursing through our heads: *I'm-in-the-shower-with-you-guys-and-we're-all-guys-here-so-this-is-perfectly-normal-so-let's-ignore-the-fact-that-we're-all-naked-and-just-talk-because-I-mean-really-no-big-deal-I'm-secure-aren't-you-secure-too?* The voices were loud and magnified in the white-tiled room. Six sets of eyes doing their best to stay in bounds, avoiding eye contact and keeping up the banter, dutifully attending to the business of showering. Shampoo, soap, rinse. Every once in a while there was the inevitable furtive glance, a quick, almost reflexive darting of the eyes and an instantaneous round of measurement and calculated comparisons. All of this occurred in between more chatter, loud enough to be heard over the sound of the water. It was hard to tell who was talking. The elevated voices sounded the same.

"You going to that dance at Holy Child?"

"Yeah, but I don't have a ride."

"I'm getting a lift with a junior."

"Who, Dave Buckley? He's an asshole."

"Yeah, but he's got a car."

"He's still a shithead."

"You're a shithead."

"Buckley has a date? What's wrong with this world?"

"Gimme that shampoo."

"Get your own damn shampoo."

"Just gimme the goddamn shampoo. When's the Latin quiz?"

"Today."

"The ablative one?"

"Fourth period, just like Daley said yesterday and the day before."

"Seriously?"

*"Would you please give me the fucking shampoo?"*

"Christ, here it is. Ask your mom to send some!"

"Maybe I'll ask *your* mom to bring some when she—"

"Fuck off."

"Did you hear about Miss Dillon?"

"No. What?"

"Rumors abound."

"Oooh, mysterious."

"Long story, tell you later."

"Are you going to the game?"

"Who's it against?"

"St. Alban's, I think."

"Maybe. Depends on homework."

"Gimme back the shampoo."

This never took long, because there were only eight showerheads for the twenty-two sophomores on the hall along with Mallow, so the process had to be quick. By quarter to eight, there'd be a line of late arrivals leaning against the wall outside the stall, arms crossed as they stood there waiting in their towels, staring at the floor, some with their eyes closed, half asleep. I stepped out, dried off, brushed my teeth, and trekked back down the hallway, my flip-flops making squishing sounds. I hated this walk. It was always cold in the corridor after the steam heat of the shower room.

Brady called out at me after I passed his apartment door. "Derby!" His New England voice sounded like some half-serious imitation of a drill ser-geant. "Kick Trey for me, will you? Tell him if I don't see him in two minutes he's getting rinsed." We'd learned that Mr. Brady was not a man of idle threats. Just last week, he'd followed up on his promise, pouring a glass of cold water on Chase Alexander's head after he refused to get out of bed, dozing past eight. Chase had shrieked, darting upright in his bed, his long hair flopping around like a madman's as he looked around the room to see eight other sophomores standing, fully dressed in their shirts and ties, laughing their asses off. Brady had loomed over him at the foot of the bed, his arms crossed, and simply said, "Up." Then he'd walked out of the room, picked up his briefcase from the floor, and headed down to The Hampshire Room for breakfast, whistling.

Chase made it a point to set his alarm earlier from then on.

I leaned against the weighted door of my room as I turned the knob, pushed it open, and stepped in. The blinds were still drawn, and the room had a sleepy darkness to it after the bright lights of the hallway. I grim-aced. The air had the earthy smell of a room where guys have slept in the company of a week's worth of dirty laundry and closed windows. I stood for a minute, drying myself off, letting my eyes adjust to the darkness of the room. The clock read 7:52. We had to be downstairs in The Hampshire Room for breakfast assembly by 8:05.

Trey's foot still stuck out from the blanket. The sock dangled loosely. I grabbed the end of it, pulled it off, and pitched it at the mound of blankets, just about where I figured Trey's head was. A groan. The foot retracted into the tangle of sheets and blankets, like a snail into its shell.

"It's almost eight," I said, pulling open the blinds. The room was filled with whitish sunlight, making me squint.

"You took my sock," mumbled Trey from under the covers.

"Get up." I found a pair of boxers, rolled on my deodorant, and put on a clean undershirt.

"Why'd you take my sock?" Trey pulled the covers down below his chin. His hair was matted down over his forehead. He was smiling now, lying there with his arms crossed behind his head, like he had all the time in the world.

"Dude, it's really almost eight. Brady's gonna kick your ass."

"I live with a sock thief," Trey said as he rolled out of the bed. He stood up, stretching. His voice was high and tight while he stretched and yawned. "A kleptomaniac."

I tucked my shirt into my khakis and buckled my belt. This was my fourth day on this pair of pants, and they still looked clean. Amazing how long you can wear a pair of pants, I was finding. There used to be a jewelry commercial that claimed, "Diamonds are forever." Well, in the schoolboy world, khakis are like diamonds. Khakis are forever. "You're gonna be late." I did my tie, getting the length right on the second try.

Trey clapped me on the shoulder. "'Sup, klepto." He grabbed my towel from the floor and made for the door.

"That's wet."

"Yeah. Well, mine's worse than wet." The door closed behind him.

I glanced at the lumpy heap of Trey's laundry in the corner near the door. The orange towel was crumpled under the pile, a small fold of it visible under an inside-out pair of plaid boxers. It didn't look clean. I picked up my blazer and stepped out the door, my hair still dripping. *Kid brings enough cash to fly first class to Hawaii but only brings one towel.*

"Breakfast Assembly" sounds a lot more formal than it really was. All three hundred eighteen students at the Ashford River School were supposed to be there, but without exception, ten or fifteen weren't, for various reasons. Most excuses generally ranged from slightly to completely illegitimate, such as Anthony Politano's infamous claim that a bat had flown into his room during the early hours of the morning, landed on the buttons of his alarm clock, and consequently reset his alarm for three hours later. Unfortunately for Anthony, his story lacked credibility on various fronts. Not only did the screen on his window appear intact, but the knowledgeable Mr. David Novette of the biology department insisted that bats had exhibited no behavioral precedent for landing on an electronic device, the magnetic components of which would doubtlessly interfere with their echolocation processes. Perhaps most damning of all, however, was the discovery upon inspection that Anthony Politano did not, in fact, possess an alarm clock at all.

The Hampshire Room was a lively place in the morning, with the energetic air of a place awakening. A breakfast buffet lined the north wall, and clusters of students sat together, blazers strewn over the backs of chairs, sleeves rolled up, ties in various states of looseness around their collars. The room was a sea of khaki, white, and navy, with bobbing heads of chestnut, black, red, and blond hair. The teachers were scattered about the room, some in pairs, some alone, chatting with students or colleagues or reading the paper, most drinking coffee. Each teacher served as an academic adviser to a group of twelve or fourteen students of various years, and they checked each name off on a morning attendance sheet, which was then submitted to Mrs. Carrolton, Mr. Wagner's secretary.

Dean Wagner wandered from table to table, straightening collars and offering gentle reminders to button top buttons and tuck in shirts. From time to time, he locked eyes with a surprised-looking upperclassman, raising his eyebrows with a look of seriousness as he formed his fingers into a pair of scissors, delivering a silent but clear message: *Get a haircut, son.*

I sat with Brian McNeal and Kyung Lee, a sophomore from South Korea. There was a Korean community at Ashford River, a sort of fraternity of international students from wealthier families around Seoul. Kyung's grandfather was the first from his country to attend, in the years following the Korean War, when the school was reaching out to increase the size of its international contingent. When I was there, there were nine of them, but Kyung was the only sophomore that year. They usually ate lunch as a group, and I had observed a certain formality when they were seated together, sitting oldest to youngest with the seniors at the heads of the table and the underclassmen fetching bottles of ketchup, refilling drinks, and clearing plates for the older kids.

Kyung, like most of the other Korean students at the school, took on an American name, bestowed upon him by the upperclassmen. For some reason unknown to anyone except the inner circle, the name Robert was chosen for Kyung. But Tim Anderson, a senior prefect living on the junior hall, had remarked on the first night in the dorms last year that Robert in fact looked a little like "a Korean Robert Redford," and since that time, he'd been called Redford by just about everyone. I didn't think Kyung looked too much like Robert Redford, but the name stuck. His English wasn't perfect yet, and since the things he'd say were always entertaining, he'd taken on a sort of mascot-like popularity.

"I am today *soooo* scared of math class," said Redford, taking a bite out of a chocolate-covered doughnut. He had longish hair that hung down on either side of his face. "We have quiz."

"*A* quiz," I said. I'd noticed that our international classmates collectively had a lot of trouble with the proper use of articles.

"Whatever. We have *a* quiz," repeated Kyung/Redford.

"Really? Ours isn't till tomorrow," McNeal said as he looked up from the world history notes he was studying. His notes were written in a tiny, barely-slanted script on graph paper, with perfectly straight underlining (in red) and asterisks marking the major points. McNeal was an obsessive freak about that sort of thing. He also organized his socks by color and, as he proudly informed us one day during crew practice, had made a solemn moral resolution to utilize Trey's magazines for personal reasons only on

Tuesdays and Fridays, and only after 9:00 p.m. I'm still not sure exactly what his logic was on that, but it probably wasn't true anyway.

"Yes," continued Redford, "but you, McNeal, are in the different class. *We* have quiz *today*."

"That sucks." Brian underlined something in his notes. Twice.

"It sucks *big-times!*" exclaimed Redford, digging into his bowl of cereal.

I was leaning with my elbow on the table, using a coffee stirrer to etch a face into the chocolate frosting on top of my doughnut. "Yeah, but we've got that Latin quiz after lunch. At least you don't have to take friggin' *Latin*, Redford."

"At least you speak friggin' *English*, Derby." Redford thought this was very funny and laughed loudly. He was a funny kid. I remember one day in geometry class during the first week of school when Mr. Tabler was taking attendance. The only guy missing was Evan McCarthy, who everyone knew was laid up in the bathroom with a nasty case of the runs, no doubt due to the entire quart of prune juice that he'd downed on a dare from Rick Eldrin the night before. When Mr. Tabler had asked if anyone knew where Evan was, Redford volunteered, "Umm, sir, Evan is not here because he is upstairs *making super big shit!*" The room had erupted with laughter, including Mr. Tabler after a few stunned moments. Since that time, Mr. Brady had encouraged Redford's peers to enlighten him on the proper and improper use of the vernacular. The truth is, Redford probably knew exactly what he was saying but knew he could get away with it. Being an international student, for all its difficulties, had its perks.

The 8:25 bell rang and the room erupted with the noise of a couple hundred chairs being pushed back, books thrown into backpacks, and conversations ending loudly. As I shouldered my backpack, I looked around for Trey. No sign at first, but then I spotted him at the buffet table, his tie loose and the collar of his blazer upturned crazily, helping himself to a powdered doughnut. He spotted me looking at him and sort of nodded his head; grinning and pointing at the doughnut, he gave an approving thumbs-up as he walked over to meet us.

"These are really stupendous doughnuts," he said, his mouth full and a smear of the white powder on his face.

"You ready for that history quiz, Trey?" asked Brian.

"Nope. You want a doughnut, McNeal?"

# CHAPTER 9

Later that afternoon, we were on our way to crew practice. We were excited because the Head of the Ohio Regatta in Pittsburgh was next week, and our junior lightweight boat was coming together nicely. I was surprised we'd travel as far as Pittsburgh, but as it turned out, Brady had a college buddy coaching for one of the schools there, so the connection worked out. Pittsburgh is only about three hours from Buffalo, so my parents would be coming down for the race. I'd invited Trey to spend Saturday night at my house and drive back to school on Sunday evening with us. It was a lot of driving for a short trip, but it would be a good break from the dorms for both of us. I found myself really looking forward to seeing Mom and Dad, especially since Brady was working the hell out of us to get us ready for the race.

I looked around as we walked to practice. The hill sloped gently from The Hampshire Room terrace, steep in some parts, and flattened out at the brick boathouse a quarter mile away. The slope was broad and covered in grass, dotted with clumps of small pine trees clustered around some very tall old ones. The October air was chilly and carried the smell of the pond with it. I'd just gotten a crew cut from Rob Dwyer, a junior on the team. It was a leap of faith, but even Mr. DiVincenzo vouched for Rob's skill with a set of clippers. I could feel the chill of the breeze on my head now, giving me goose bumps. Ahead and below, I could see the tiny forms of guys milling around the boathouse, carrying oars down to the docks. There was only the slightest breeze and the pond was flat that day. The water looked silver and glassy. Of course, it was a lot bigger than a pond. The rowing lake had been formed fifty years before when they dammed up the tiny Ashford Creek at the south end of campus. It was a little less than a mile and a half long north to south but no wider than a few hundred yards at any point, shaped roughly like an elongated kidney bean. On the other side of the pond, the school's land continued for a narrow bit, climbing uphill before running into a row of pines that marked the property line. A wheat field belonging to a farm lay on the other side. The whole four hundred acres formed a bowl, with the pond at the base and the campus buildings nestled on the sloping west side.

A V-line of geese honked above us, heading off to the south, the sound of their calls growing louder and then fading as they passed. Trey wore running pants and a sweatshirt with the hood pulled low over his forehead. The nylon pants made swooshing noises as he walked. "You think Brady is gonna keep me in the boat?" He wiped some snot from his nose.

"Probably."

"My grades suck."

"Yeah, but you pulled a really good score last week." I was referring to his score on the ergometer, an indoor rowing machine used to measure power and endurance.

Trey pulled back his hood and squinted at the gray afternoon sky. "True. But McNeal and Eldrin were saying that they think he's gonna take me out and make me an alternate."

"When did they say that?" I asked.

"Heard 'em yesterday in the bathroom. They didn't know I was in there taking a crap. Eldrin sounded *happy* about it. He's a prick." Somehow, over the previous few weeks, Eldrin and Trey had managed to develop a silent but deepening mutual hatred, and we all wondered when it would come to a head.

"But who would he put in? Culaney's been sick the past week, so he can't get in there, and what's-his-name, the freshman from Connecticut…"

"Howard."

"Yeah. Howard. He's gotta fly home for his brother's wedding."

Trey let out a little laugh that sounded more like a snort. "So I'm still in the boat only because they can't be." He kicked a clod of dirt a good ways down the hill. "That's really encouraging."

I threw my hands in the air. "I dunno, man. You're good. You pull a good score, you know how to row, and, well, even if your grades do suck right now, Brady knows that you pull your weight in a race. Think about Saratoga."

■ ■ ■

The regatta at Saratoga Springs in New York had been two weeks prior. It was mostly just the varsity crews that went, but the top JV guys raced as well. Instead of rowing an eight, Brady had decided to split us up into two fours, the "blue crew" and the "red crew." The blue four (which really meant "the faster four") included Rick Eldrin in the stroke seat, followed by me, Brian McNeal, and Trey in the bow. Jimmy Speers was the coxswain. The red crew, which everyone knew was second string, had Dave Culaney, Chase Alexander, Mike Hasselwerdt, and Andy DaVinci, with Evan McCarthy in the cox seat. The interesting thing was, though, that Trey had been a last-minute switch on Brady's part. Chase Alexander was bigger and stronger and had been rowing with the crew for three practices before the race. The fallout hadn't been pretty.

We'd driven up on Friday after leaving school early, all ten of us crammed into one of the school's fifteen-passenger vans with Mr. Brady at the wheel. Normally, we drove in the school's Chevy Suburbans, which were a lot more comfortable, but Brady couldn't get a second driver and there wasn't room for eleven (eight oarsmen, two coxswains, and a coach) in a Suburban. It had been a long drive, and we stayed at a cruddy motel outside of Saratoga Springs, but I hardly cared. This was my first trip with the team.

Before we went to bed, we got together in Mr. Brady's room for a meeting. The ten of us, dressed in sweatpants and T-shirts, found spots around the room, seating ourselves on the bed and on the floor. Jimmy Speers wore the ridiculous red-and-blue ski hat that had become his lucky racing hat for reasons no one understood, since he hadn't worn it in any races he'd won last year. It had a loose thread that dangled over his left ear. The room smelled like the Chinese takeout Brady had picked up from across the street, which sat there, half eaten, a few stray noodles hanging out of the paper carton like they were trying to escape. A can of Lipton iced tea stood sweating next to the carton. I eyed the food hungrily and noticed some of the others doing the same. We'd stopped for dinner, of course, but I found myself, since beginning my rowing career and high school in general, in a near constant state of hunger.

Brady sat at the small motel table, his feet up on the bed, a pair of reading glasses low on the bridge of his nose, looking at his clipboard and scribbling some notes. I thought he looked kind of funny. I'd never seen the reading glasses before, and they made him look older. He was wearing a beat-up pair of navy-blue school-issue sweatpants, like most of us. But on top of that, he had on this stupid emerald-green T-shirt, faded and threadbare from too many wash cycles, which said, *"My Better Half Is Irish"* across the chest in white cursive letters. A cartoonish shamrock with a grinning face dotted the second "i" in "Irish." After we settled down and got quiet, he looked up from the clipboard and spoke.

"First of all, no, you can't have Chinese tonight." Brian groaned, and Trey reached up to steal the carton, which Brady grabbed and put on the floor behind his chair. "That's all we need. Pork lo mien heaving through your guts halfway through the race tomorrow." We laughed.

"Secondly, I've made a decision about the boats." His voice grew more serious. "Chase, you'll be moving to three-seat in the red boat. Daniels, to bow in the blue." He set his clipboard facedown on the bed next to him and took a sip of the iced tea. He set the can back down on the table with a *clunk*, which seemed loud in the now-silent room.

An electric ripple jolted through the group. Rick Eldrin, stroke man in the blue boat, just about gasped out loud and looked straight at Brady with wide eyes. Chase stared at the shaggy rug on the motel room floor, with a look on his face that said he'd expected this. His face was flushed. I figured later that he must have known before the rest of us, and it made sense as I recalled Mr. Brady talking to him alone outside the van as we stopped for a bathroom break in Pennsylvania. Trey, sitting right next to Eldrin, just sort of looked up with a confused expression on his face, halfway between a grin and a frown, the way he looked in class when he didn't know how to answer a question. I felt a strange twisting in my stomach. I was happy for Trey making the boat—it had been putting some awkward distance between us that week—but at the same time, I knew Chase was stronger. McNeal didn't say a word.

Eldrin launched the first protest. "Um, *Coach?*"

"Yes, Rick?" Brady took another sip of the iced tea and then held the can in his lap.

"Um, I don't wanna sound like, you know…" he faltered.

"Like what?"

Eldrin raised his hands. "Well, I just don't know if it's such a great idea to make this change at the last minute." He looked around the room, avoiding Trey, who stared at the floor. "I mean, we've been practicing together for a *week* now."

Brady took another slow sip of the tea and set the can down on the table. "Yes, you have. And I've been coaching this sport for six *years* now. The decision is made, and the reasons are valid. That doesn't mean I have to explain them to you. I want you guys in bed within a half hour."

Eldrin stood up, his hands waving in the air again. "But you can't just do that!"

The coach ignored him. "I'll get you guys up at six thirty. Keep the noise down."

We filed out of the room into the cold night air and back to our rooms. I clapped Trey's shoulder as we walked outside. Trey kept walking, looking at the ground, his hands in his pockets. We heard Rick continue to argue with Mr. Brady. I heard their muffled voices rise for a minute, but I couldn't tell what they were saying.

McNeal, Trey, Speers, and I shared a room. We'd just climbed into the beds and turned out the light when we heard a soft knocking on the door.

McNeal sat up. "Who the hell is that?"

Trey murmured from under his pillow. "Eldrin. I guarantee it. I'm sure he wants to come in here and blame me for original sin."

"Just ignore him," Speers said. The knocking came again, a little louder this time. "Let Brady catch the prick outside his room after lights-out. He'll put him in the goddamned *purple* boat." Chuckles all around, but then more knocking.

Trey climbed out of bed and opened the door. Eldrin stood there in a T-shirt and boxers. "I wanna talk to you," he hissed.

Trey put on his sweatshirt, rolling his eyes, and went outside, pulling the door closed behind them. Brian, Jimmy, and I leaped to the window and peered outside through the curtain. I couldn't see them very well, because they were down in the parking lot, standing on the other side of the rental van near a pine tree. Eldrin was talking, pointing his finger at Trey's chest, stabbing the air. It didn't last long. I couldn't tell if Trey had said anything or not; he just came ambling back across the lot with his hood over his head. I opened the door, feeling the cold air billow in as the hooded figure walked in. I shivered. Jimmy and McNeal stood, leaning against the wall, all of us expecting a report. Trey climbed into the bed, pulled the covers tight around his shoulders, and closed his eyes.

"Early race, guys," he said, pulling the covers higher, up to his chin. "Get some sleep."

The rest of us climbed into the beds. I lay there for a long time, watching the tiny red blinking light on the smoke detector and wondering what Eldrin had said to him.

By early the next morning, we were buzzing with excitement as we warmed up with a jog along the racecourse in the cool Upstate New York air. Eldrin was silent and didn't look at Trey at all. Mr. Brady ran with us, without talking, our steps falling together like a group of marines. We stretched and reviewed the race plan. Most fall events are headraces, in which boats chase each other down a long course and race for time. However, the Saratoga Invite was a 1500-meter sprint, like most spring-season regattas. I liked those more than the headraces. A sprint required a different kind of explosive intensity that seemed more suited to our crew.

We got together, said an *Our Father* with our hands joined together, and launched the shell. The race began and went by in a flash. After we cruised across the finish line in first place, I lay down in the boat, my head resting on McNeal's knees behind me, gasping for breath and trying to hold back the vomit that threatened in the back of my throat from the exertion. My heart had been beating wildly, so hard that I could feel the pumping through the sides of the carbon fiber shell where I gripped the gunwales. There'd been high fives back and forth across the boat, though we were all so exhausted that the slaps were weak and elastic. Even Eldrin seemed content.

It had been a good race, and Trey and I hung our medals together over the window in our room.

■ ■ ■

"Saratoga was before," Trey said, kicking another clod of dirt down the hill as we continued toward the boathouse two weeks later. "This is now, man, and my math grade dropped like eight points when I failed that test."

"You talk to Mr. Tabler?"

"No makeup. Told me I had to 'get my act together.'"

"Probably good advice," I said, patting Trey on the shoulder. I was developing a remarkable capacity for sarcasm.

"Yeah. Thanks. You're such a pal."

Brian McNeal came jogging down the hill behind us. He stopped between us and put an arm around each of our shoulders, out of breath. He was holding his Latin notebook.

"Whassup, boys? Just came from Daley's Latin review. You shoulda gone. Told us what's gonna be on the test."

"Good. You can fill us in later, ace," said Trey.

McNeal rolled his eyes. "What else is new? So, you guys ready for another *invigorating* crew practice? I hear Brady's all jacked up on some new workout he heard about from his old coach at Georgetown."

"Great," mumbled Trey, kicking the clod far down the hill. "This oughta improve my week."

"Eh, it'll be great," Brian said. "Might fix up our balance. It could be cleaner."

"McNeal, why're you always in such a good mood?" I asked.

"Because you light up my life, Derby!" He slapped me on the butt with his Latin book and sprinted ahead down the hill to the boathouse.

■ ■ ■

I was riding in the coach boat because there was a new transfer from Kentucky, and Brady wanted to give him a try and get a look at his technique. I also had a feeling that this was about a little one-on-one conversation. Actually, I could detect it a mile off. It's tough to have a private conversation in a boarding school, and everyone knew that Brady used the coaching launch as a conference room.

It was a warm afternoon for October. The coach was wearing Oakley sunglasses and a *Georgetown Crew* T-shirt.

"Mike, you need to tighten up that finish. Bring the handle right into that spot, all the way to your chest…That's right. Good, yeah." He coached through a megaphone rigged up to the console, speaking into a handset on the end of a coiled cord. His voice sounded metallic through the speaker. Mr. Brady kicked the throttle up, and the pontoon boat heaved forward, leaving a muck-brown wake behind. The coaching launches had a flat deck but no bench, so we sat in plastic lawn chairs.

"Okay, Jimmy, I've gotcha at twenty-six; let's build 'em up to thirty." Brady was talking about the stroke-rate, the number of strokes the crew took per minute. I was amazed at the technicality of rowing, the numbers involved. For a sport that seemed so simple and repetitive, there really was quite a bit of strategy involved—lots to do with rates and intensity. But I'd started to pick up most of the terminology as the season went on.

Jimmy Speers was the coxswain, a word that, for sophomores, was always entertaining to say. He gave the call, and the shell cut faster through the water. I was no expert rower, but I could tell that Chase was rushing up his slide, throwing the timing off, and that it was driving Brian McNeal crazy. It didn't take much of anything to drive McNeal crazy, mildly obsessive-compulsive as he was, so something like this guaranteed an explosive reaction before long. He was sitting behind Chase in three-seat. He couldn't stand rowing behind Chase and had bitched about it for a good ten minutes at dinner the previous night. I just waited for the fireworks, enjoying the warm sun on my arms and neck as I rode in the launch.

Speers called it first. The coxswain spoke into a headset connected to speakers in the boat, so he didn't have to shout. The device is called, appropriately and amusingly enough, a "cox-box." Speers's voice was deep and authoritative. "Four-man, you're rushing it."

Brady decided to chime in too: "Chase, keep it down. We're looking for thirty. Just watch the rush at the end. That's a little better…"

McNeal, however, didn't think it was getting any better. The frustration built like water in a kettle and suddenly boiled over. "Chase, will you slow the fuck down!" McNeal's voice cracked on "down," and everyone laughed, especially Chase. The crew faltered and glided to a stop, oars trailing on the water. Dragonflies danced near the surface as Brady slowed the engine to an idle, pulling the launch alongside the shell.

I heard Trey say, "Not in such a good mood now, are we, McNealy?"

Brady didn't like this in the least. "McNeal, Daniels, shut up. How many times have I told you that you keep your mouth shut in the boat? Let me do the coaching. Otherwise, I'll find a replacement for you in about two seconds, you got me?"

Silence.

"And by the way," the coach continued, "you don't *stop* unless I tell you to stop." Brady had a way of yelling at you without actually yelling. His voice was level through all of this, but it was clear and loud through the megaphone. I heard "stop" echo from the far embankment. He slammed the handset back into its holder and muttered to himself, "Goddamn *babies*."

McNeal rolled his eyes and muttered something under his breath but knew better than to talk back. His face was red from frustration and embarrassment. I felt bad for McNeal, because he was a good kid, and he was right. Chase was strong, but his technique left a lot to be desired. It was now clear to us why Coach had made the last-minute change at Saratoga.

I noticed that Mike Dean, the new freshman transfer from Kentucky in two-seat, was missing a lot of water, not making the oar reach as far as he should. It happened, I had learned, when you started pulling before the oar was really locked in the water. "Hey, Coach, looks like Mike's missing some water." I moved from the bow of the skiff over next to Mr. Brady and pointed.

"Good eye." He picked up the handset. "Two, you're missing some water. Let's lock it in at the catch before you drive the legs. Straight arms, Mike, right from the finish. Down and right away, full extension right to the catch. That's it, kid." Mike looked contented, having fixed the problem. "Okay, Jimmy, they're all yours. One more minute easy; then build 'em up for four minutes at a twenty-eight, full pressure. To the dam and back to cool off, and I'll see you on the dock. Take her in slow and easy. I don't need another cracked-up boat, right?"

The previous fall, apparently, a senior coxswain named Phil McGroarty managed to destroy a four. He'd rammed it squarely into the dock after being distracted at the last minute by the discovery of an evidently used Trojan floating in the pond, not far off the starboard side. Rumor had it that it belonged to Steve Mallow and had been used, not twelve hours prior, in carnal endeavors with Adriana Stiles.

Brady put the handset back in its holder. I waited for the words that would start our "little chat." I knew when one of these was coming on. It wasn't the first one we'd had, and they invariably wound up focusing on Trey and his ongoing disciplinary saga, general lack of effort, and apparently nonexistent motivation for doing any work in school.

"So, Matt—oh, hold on a second." He picked the handset up. "Jimmy, I want everyone weighed when you get back in and then a river run." Brady was hitting us hard today, and I was actually happy to be in the coaching launch instead. Maybe I could even get out of the four-and-a-half-mile run. We all thought it was pretty lame that he called it an "Ashford River run." It didn't really go anywhere near the Ashford River for more than a tenth of a mile, and that was just where it crossed the footbridge behind the headmaster's house. It went around Ashford *Lake*. In fact, the word *river* itself was kind of a joke. It was really called Ashford Creek and was just some little tributary of a slightly larger creek flowing out of the Blue Ridge, but "the Ashford Creek School" doesn't sound all that prestigious, and sophisticated old-money families from East Hampton for damn sure wouldn't want to send their kids to a school named for a seasonal drainage ditch.

Mr. Brady grabbed a water bottle out of the small cooler on the skiff and threw one to me.

"Anyway. So how's things?"

*Here we go!*

This was a typical Brady opener. I used to think that he started every conversation like this because he didn't really know what to say. But after a couple of months of living with him, I realized that he was pretty sharp and he did this on purpose. I once asked Dr. Carlisle, the school psychologist, what it was like to be a counselor. He told me it was mostly about listening, about knowing what to listen for. Someone who spends enough time listening to other people's problems becomes really good at picking up on things. He said something about allowing the student to reveal what's really on his mind without projecting too much into the conversation. It makes sense to me now, but it was beyond me then. In any case, I often felt like I was being psychoanalyzed when I talked to Brady. It was a little disquieting, but at the same time, it made the guy intriguing. I remember thinking that I wanted to be in his English honors class junior year. But then, later, while preparing for the man's demonic final exam, I cursed the day I made that choice.

"Things are okay. I'm doing pretty good in school." I was playing with the quick-release buckle on my lifejacket.

"Pretty well," corrected Brady.

"Pretty *well*."

"Are you going home this semester, besides Thanksgiving?" he asked.

"I'll probably stay there the night after the Pittsburgh regatta, if I can. My dad'll drive me back on Sunday."

"How long a drive is that?" Brady took another swig from his water bottle. We were trailing the crew, sort of buzzing along at low throttle. They were fifty yards away now, about to start the workout.

"It's about seven hours, give or take. Sometimes he does it in under six, though. Drives like a maniac."

He upped the throttle as the crew began to accelerate. "So, tell me about Trey."

"Uh, what about him?" I snapped the lifejacket buckle shut and let it go, my eyes rising to meet Brady's.

He continued to watch the crew as he spoke. "Miss Dillon tells me that he's doing hardly anything with *Lord of the Flies* and that he failed the test."

"Because he never read it," I said.

"Does he just screw around during study hall?"

"No, he doesn't mess around that much. He just doesn't really do much of anything," I replied. "I mean, he'll do worksheets and stuff, but only for about a half hour. Then he's done." I found myself wanting to continue, which I didn't really understand. Here I was, talking to our teacher and our dorm supervisor about my best friend's academic habits. I felt traitorous but justified. It was weird. I continued.

"I mean, it kinda sucks because he's smart. He talks about pretty sophisticated stuff, and he's traveled a lot. He was telling me about this café in Brussels and the conversation he had in French with the waitress about the French Revolution or something." It occurred to me then that I'd never heard Trey actually say anything in French, and I filed this away as something to ask him about later.

"I knew a guy like that in college," replied Brady. "His name was Mitchell Porter. This guy didn't do jack except talk about all the girls he got with. And I believed him most of the time. Mitch was really smart though and always managed to pull things out of somewhere at the last minute, and he coasted his way through. He was always on the brink of crashing and burning. That remind you of Trey?"

"Yeah, I guess it does."

"So what do you think we should do?"

*We?*

This had suddenly become a team effort.

"I dunno. It's not like he doesn't understand stuff, so I don't think he needs a tutor or anything. He just needs something to motivate him. Sometimes I think he's kind of depressed or something about his parents having problems. But I dunno if that's it. The kid just doesn't do *any* work."

"I've considered suspending him from the team. Do you think that would motivate him?"

"Mr. Brady, no offense, but I don't think that'd work. He's really into crew and…to be honest with you, it would just give him more free time to get into trouble." This might have been bullshit, but I was feeling more traitorous by the second and was getting defensive in spite of myself.

"Do you think he'd talk to me?" he asked.

"He'd talk, but I don't know if he'd like, really, *talk*."

"Well, does he *talk* to you?" The crew had turned around and was heading into the dock. The skiff was idling, and Brady was staring me down through his Oakleys, which reflected the bare tree branches on the opposite shore.

"Yeah. Yeah, he talks to me."

"So I guess you're our guy."

"Yeah. I guess so. I guess I am."

I looked at Trey as the shell drifted into the dock. He waved and gave me a thumbs-up. I didn't feel very good that day.

# CHAPTER 10

Everyone at Ashford River had to go to chapel at nine o'clock on Sunday mornings in jacket and tie, but the fifty or so Catholic guys had it especially rough. Most weeks, we had to go to chapel, listen first to a sermon by Dr. Winthrop, followed by some typically rambling speech by a member of the senior class, and then stick around the extra hour for Mass while the rest of the school was set free to enjoy the last few hours of the weekend. But once a month, there was a night Mass instead. On these Sundays, we got to sleep in while the other guys rose early, putting on jackets and ties for regular morning chapel. It was Father Daley's arrangement, a way of rewarding our patience with our non-Catholic brethren, or so he said.

The reality, which I've come to understand since my time at Ashford River, is that the school remained in the midst of a century-old spiritual identity crisis. It was opened as an independent school (loosely) affiliated with the Episcopal Church and then somehow fell into poor standing with the hierarchy. It spent a few years as essentially secular in the late sixties before being spiritually rescued—another loose term in the opinion of many alumni—by an unlikely duo: an Episcopal priest and a forward-thinking Jesuit from Georgetown. Together they revived some of the school's faith-based foundations, and the Jesuit ushered in the school's growing Catholic population in the seventies and eighties. Even the skeptics among the old guard alumni seemed happy with the arrangement because of the increased enrollment and reliable tuition income it provided. So despite the sort of schizophrenic religious identity of the school, somehow, it all hummed along without more than an occasional murmur of discontent among various curmudgeons. It was—and still is—a peculiar arrangement. Daley was a Catholic priest, but chaplain for the whole school, and Dr. Winthrop was an Anglican deacon who'd pursued advanced studies in theology along with his doctoral degree in education. The end result of all of this is that most graduates of Ashford River emerge thoroughly confused when it comes to anything theological. But then again, that's probably true at any high school, prestigious or religious or not. There were lots of gray areas, but the general idea was clear enough: be honest and be nice. I guess that served well enough.

We were in the chapel for night Mass. These Masses were casual and therefore popular, even though they were held at nine-thirty. Daley wanted us to be relaxed. We showed up in sweatshirts, warm-ups, even some plaid flannel pajama pants. Lights-out would be shortly after Mass. Many of us were ready to sleep, and it was sometimes hard to stay awake in the dim light.

We sat clustered around the altar, a few loose benches and pews formed into a rough half circle, our faces bathed in candlelight. Daley really did a job creating atmosphere. No lights, just candles, and only a few. The hymns were just Steve Mallow playing his guitar. (The irony of this was not lost on any of us.) The environment did, admittedly, set me at ease. *It must be the same for the rest of them,* I thought, looking around at calm faces and normally tense shoulders relaxed. Our hands were folded, eyes fixed on candle flames, or at some point in the darkness of the ceiling. The tall, stained-glass windows were black and dark gray, the images they displayed in sunlight barely perceptible. The chapel had a unique smell from years of incense, lacquered pews, and candles.

The red-bearded priest sat on a folding chair, wearing jeans, a gray sweatshirt, and sneakers. Even Daley kept it casual for this. No vestments, just the stole, a plain green and blue strip of fabric that looked like a scarf, hanging loosely from his shoulders. He'd just finished reading the Gospel. He sat with his legs outstretched and crossed at the ankle, arms folded, holding the lectionary against his chest. His eyes were closed; reading glasses set low on his nose. After a moment, he set the book on the table next to him. The motion made the candles flicker. Soft light danced on our faces.

"You've all heard that one before," he began, his voice soft. "The Prodigal Son. A story about two brothers and their dad." He looked up at the faces around him.

"And you've probably heard lots of homilies about it, too." He pointed at a sophomore. "McMann, do you think the story is more about the dad, the older son, or the younger son?" He looked at Billy McMann over his reading glasses.

The boy's voice was loud and seemed to jar the silence. "Umm, all three?"

Daley laughed. "Safe answer, Billy. But noncommittal. Daniels, how 'bout you?"

I turned my head to look at Trey, who was sitting on the floor, elbows hooked around his knees. "I think it's about the dad."

Daley nodded. "Interesting. Why do you say that?"

"'Cause the little brother messes up, but I think it's really about the dad forgiving him. And I guess the big brother too."

"Good, Trey. Anyone else?"

Dave Halsworth, a junior, spoke from the bench to my left. His voice was low. "Definitely the little brother. Because he's the one that changes the most. He messes up and then changes."

Daley nodded thoughtfully and leaned forward in his chair, elbows on his knees. "I think, guys, that this is a story about many things, and there is much to learn from it. But one of the key things it's about is how we make decisions. Each of the men in this story—the father, the two brothers—comes to a place where he has to make a decision. Some of the decisions in the story are good; some aren't."

I nudged Speers, who was dozing off next to me.

Daley continued, "What we need to look at is what *guides* their decisions. When the younger brother decides to blow all his money on sex, drugs, and rock 'n' roll..." Chuckling could be heard throughout the room. "...he's making decisions based purely upon himself and what he wants at any given moment. And the older brother, when he challenges the father about welcoming his reckless brother home, seems to be thinking primarily about himself—and how it doesn't seem fair to him."

"When the younger son decides to come home, he's struggling. But I think he's struggling in the right direction and for the right reason: He knows he messed up badly, and he wants to be forgiven. When the father forgives without hesitation, that's a selfless, loving decision. The kind we'd hope a father would make. And the older brother—well, he might be the one who struggles the most. That's what I like about the older brother. Maybe he's the most like a lot of us. The Big Man tells us that, 'we are our brother's keeper.' But we aren't always so good at keeping our brother, are we? Or forgiving our brother? So what's the bottom line here?" He raised his arms and looked around the group.

No answer.

"Oh, come on. I know it's late. That doesn't make you *ignorami*, does it?" Father Daley never missed an opportunity to slip in a little Latin.

McNeal chimed in from the back. "Good decisions usually happen when we're thinking about other people and not just ourselves."

"Bingo. Thank you, Brian. Good decisions usually happen when we're thinking about other people. Nicely, simply put. And I'm sure you can relate. We all take paths every day. When we come to a juncture, we have to make a decision. Handle it one way or the other." He scratched his beard, looking at the ceiling. "Do I do the homework...or do I copy McNeal's? Do I study for the test, or do I cheat on it? Do I drink at the party...or do I behave? The girl at the party is pretty hot, she's had a few drinks, and she's all over me. Do I take advantage, or do I think of her and make a good decision?"

This last one got a peal of loud laughter. We were awake now.

"I thought that might wake you up. Even you, Speers."

"So," he continued, leaning back in his chair, "what I'm talking about is coming to these little decision-making junctures—DMJ's, if you will—and thinking outside the self. That's a big part of human life. Whom else am I affecting with this decision? And I assure you, if we have the humility to think outside ourselves, like the young man in the story finally began to do, we'll probably make the better decision. Of course, it will probably, then, affect *us* for the better as well. The kicker, though, is that it's usually the tougher choice. We have to struggle just like the big brother, guys. We have to, in fact, be our brother's keeper."

He paused for a moment, letting the words resonate in the quiet chapel. I watched the candle flame dance. "And to truly do that well," the priest said, his voice nearly a whisper, "is probably the toughest struggle I can think of."

# CHAPTER 11

We lived for "out-weekends."

The administrative powers that controlled our lives had decided long ago that, for reasons of camaraderie and spiritual unity, it was essential that most weekends be spent on campus. The intention was admirable. But like many policies in education, this one had mixed results. The "in-weekend" was one of the many ways they tortured us, right along with the food in the dining hall (again, a good intention with a questionable result). The dining services had, you see, put their best foot forward for Moving-In Day. It was a scam. They impressed the parents and then did so again for the annual fundraiser. The rest of the year, they fed us the same rotating schedule of questionable material from week to week. I guess I shouldn't complain. Kids are starving in other countries. But still, it was comical.

The greatest irony of all was that in-weekends usually began with the worst meal possible—fried haddock with collard greens—on Friday night. Normally, this would be a good thing, perhaps something you'd like to take your family to have while on vacation in the Old Deep South. At

Ashford River, however, it meant pasty, overcooked fish with a sort of wet fried breading that literally dripped with grease. And then there were collard greens, which they doused in salt and butter. After this wonderful experience in table fellowship, the in-weekend festivities would begin. Options usually included riding the school van to see a movie in Bethesda or DC with the same guys you hung out with all week, watching a rented movie with the same guys you hung out with all week, working out in the gym or horsing around in the pool with the same guys you hung out with all week, or, most exciting of all, tromping over to Dr. Winthrop's house to put on an obsequious show of gratitude for his wife's latest failed attempt at chocolate-chip cookies. This was done with—you guessed it—the same guys you hung out with all week.

Sometimes, we had fun. There were van trips we'd sign up for that took us into downtown DC to wander around with relative freedom for a few hours or the rare excursion to see the Redskins play. Sometimes, it was just simple stuff—playing football or baseball under the lights on the well-groomed fields, passing lacrosse balls or Frisbees around, watching home games, or participating in violent tournaments of "manhunt." This was a sort of full-contact hide-and-seek that took advantage of the sprawling campus and lasted well into the night. We'd return to the dorms in the vicinity of 1:00 a.m., exhausted and high on nothing more than endorphins and the company of our friends. Some, including Trey, were also high on other things from time to time. One time, Dr. Winthrop had a stack of sheet pizzas and four gallons of Ben and Jerry's waiting for us when we came inside. We sat out in the quad, covered in grass stains and mud, and wolfed it down in minutes before heading back up to the dorms. I'm sure this kind of healthy, energetic fun was what our administrative benefactors had in mind when they designed the in-weekend. In a way, I guess we were grateful for being forced to hang out with each other. As least it gave us a good excuse for not having girlfriends.

But whatever fun we had on in-weekends was usually at someone's expense. It might be a fantastic practical joke that took all week to assemble or a spontaneous project of some illegal nature. There was the time we tore all the pages out of one of Trey's *Playboy* magazines and used them to wallpaper Mr. DiVincenzo's door. And the time we hung all of Rick Eldrin's clothes from tree branches near the boathouse using a stepladder, so they were all just out of his reach.

In-weekends meant long naps on Saturdays and maybe even studying a little bit too, doing things like desperately needed laundry and cleaning our rooms for the weekly Monday room inspection. So in-weekends were a mixed bag. Of course, out-weekends brought their own social challenges. If you were lucky enough to live within driving distance of the school, your parents might pick you up and you might spend some time at home living like a normal kid. "Normal" was, of course, a relative term for some guys who went to Ashford River. For some of my classmates, "normal" meant being picked up by Mom or Dad—rarely both—in the Mercedes or the Escalade, spending some downtime at a country club, skiing in the winter, or maybe hanging out at the beach house on the Chesapeake. There were various shades of normality at the Ashford River School.

If you lived out of range like most guys, you had to figure something out. We had an out-weekend coming up in October, and I didn't have any plans as of Thursday. So I asked Trey what he was up to.

"Not much. Just going to the Georgetown house. My mom's there."

It was like Trey to do this, just casually drop this significant piece of his family life randomly into a conversation. So now I knew there was a house in Georgetown in addition to the two residences I'd counted up already—one each in Lake Placid and Manhattan.

"Oh."

"Hey, why don't you come for the weekend?" He was trying to stuff enough clothes to last him a few days into a duffel bag, grabbing assorted toiletries like deodorant and toothpaste from the bureau, most of which were mine. "My mom is totally cool. She'd probably like to meet you. And she'll be playing tennis all weekend so we can get out a little bit. Visit some ladies."

And so this nonchalant invitation into another part of Trey Daniels's life was passed along, and I took it. Getting out of the dorms was a major priority, and girls were an intriguing prospect for the weekend. It wasn't lost on me that I was apparently an afterthought to the whole scheme. If I hadn't asked what he was doing, I don't know if the invitation would have come. But that mattered little compared to the prospect of a weekend stuck in MacKerry Hall again.

■ ■ ■

Trey's mom had just come home from playing tennis and was drinking a glass of lemonade in the doorway to the living room. I noticed the very short shorts she was wearing, made of the same material as my sweatpants. They stopped just a few inches down her long, lean thighs. She had on a sports bra, and a small semicircle of sweat at the top of it ran parallel to a necklace that accented her bronzed skin. I had met her when she came to pick us up in an immense Lexus SUV, and at first, I thought maybe she was Trey's sister or a cousin.

"Do you guys want some sodas?" she asked.

We were playing a football video game on the Nintendo at her townhouse in Georgetown. It was Saturday afternoon, and we were signed out until Sunday, when we had to be back by 5:30 for dinner. The television was huge, one of those big-screen deals at least four feet across. There were glass cabinets on either side of it with china plates inside. French doors looked out on a cobblestone alley full of sunflowers. Sun glinting off the hood of the Lexus threw rainbow prisms on the white walls, making a glare on the screen.

"Sure, Mom," said Trey, "Ginger ale. Do we have any?" He scored a touchdown and dropped the controller, standing up to do his end-zone dance. His not-so-clean socks left tracks in the thick carpet.

"Yeah, we've got ginger ale. Matt?"

"Um, I'll have ginger ale too." I hadn't had ginger ale since having it at my grandmother's house when I was little. It was the only kind of soda she would buy.

So Mrs. Daniels went back into the kitchen, and I wondered how come Mr. Daniels—or anyone, for that matter—would even consider leaving such a beautiful wife. She called in from the kitchen: "If you guys want to order a pizza, go ahead. I'm not cooking tonight."

"Pizza is *clutch* right now," said Trey. That was one of his latest expressions of choice. He had a constantly shifting vernacular. He'd pick words and phrases up from somewhere and use them incessantly for about a week and then move on to something else. The previous week, it had been *whack*; this week, it was *clutch*. Funny thing was, they all seemed to mean approximately the same thing.

"What do you want on it?" he asked. "I like everything except peppers. They suck."

"Yeah, peppers do kind of suck. Let's just get pepperoni," I said.

"Clutch." Trey had both hands back on the controller, and he scored a field goal, further widening his lead.

Mrs. Daniels came back carrying two glasses of ginger ale and ice cubes. She put them down and asked, "So, who's winning?" Trey didn't answer, and I told her that Trey was kicking my butt. I almost said, "kicking my ass," but managed to slip "butt" in there at the last minute.

"Well, I hope it turns around for you. Okay, Trey. I'm going up to take a shower. Be down in a little while."

I dedicated a few moments of my life to picturing that shower, missing a touchdown pass in the process. Distractions were everywhere.

Trey took the ice cubes out of his ginger ale and put them in the potted plant next to the television. "I always like it better with no ice. It's sweeter. The ice makes it taste weird, and you can't really drink it 'cause the cubes get in the way...Did you ever notice that?"

I never had come close to noticing that. I took my ice cubes out, too.

"My dad drinks ginger ale with whisky," continued Trey. "I don't really like whisky, but ginger ale is awesome. It's kind of a classy drink. Just try it at your next party. When everyone else is drinking rum and Coke or something, get a Jack and ginger and see what people say." Trey played the video game, his eyes narrowed with concentration as he explained all of this. He was still winning.

I had never had a rum and Coke or a Jack and ginger or pretty much any other drink except for one beer at our family reunion last year, and I probably wouldn't know the difference.

We heard the water start to run upstairs, and Trey went to order the pizza. I paused the game and looked around the room while I waited. There was a mahogany end table behind the leather couch, and Mrs. Daniels had put about four thousand framed pictures of various sizes there. I saw one of Trey and his dad. It looked like they were on one of those big deep-sea fishing boats. Trey was a lot younger in that picture, maybe eight or nine, with a poofy yellow lifejacket that was way too big for him. His dad was wearing tinted aviator sunglasses and looked like Tom Cruise in *Top Gun*. The deck of the boat was bright white and the seawater deep cobalt behind them, hardly discernible from an equally blue sky. Mr. Daniels had his arm around Trey's narrow shoulders. They were both smiling. I could see where Trey got his signature smirk.

Despite the number of pictures, there weren't any of Mr. and Mrs. Daniels together.

When I turned around, the smirk was right there. Trey was standing not two feet behind me, holding the cordless phone. I jumped a little bit, startled. His voice was quiet. "My mom loves that picture of me. That was when I was eight. We were in the Bahamas."

"Did you catch anything?" I looked back at the photo.

"Nope. Nothin'. We were out there for about six hours though. I got sunburned like hell. My mom was so pissed at him." He chuckled a little bit.

"Does your dad fish a lot?"

"Used to, I guess. When I was little. Not so much anymore though. He's working more now." Trey walked back over to the TV and sat down on the carpet. He toyed with the video game controller. An offensive lineman was frozen in midplay on the screen, the pixels wavering in a static hum.

"My dad and I go fishing sometimes." I sat down next to Trey. "We have this cottage on a little lake south of the city. We just go out in a rowboat or off the dock. Sunfish and stuff. Always throw 'em back because it's never anything big."

"Huh. That sounds cool. My dad wouldn't fish like that. He'd want to catch something exotic and freeze-dry it to hang above his fireplace or something." He laughed. "I think that's why he and my mom can't stand each other. Stuff like that."

"So are they, like, officially divorced, or what?" I wasn't sure if two people could be unofficially divorced, but it seemed like a reasonable question.

"No. Sort of. I dunno. I gave up trying to figure it out a few months ago."

Silence reigned for a little while. I wound the controller wire around my index finger and took another sip of the ginger ale, looking for something else to say. "Hey, did you get your math grade up at all?"

"Not really. Still sucks."

"Not as much as practice this morning," I said.

"That was bullshit. I swear that guy's on crack sometimes."

It had been too windy to row, and Brady had made us run an Ashford River run, plus some added detours, winding among the jogging trails all over campus—almost seven miles by the time we finished, just before lunch. Brady ran with us, hardly breaking a sweat, chirping away incessantly about the beautiful autumn weather and cracking incredibly corny jokes.

"Yeah, but he sure was happy today," said Trey. "Maybe he saw his girlfriend last night."

"You'd be happy, too. Guy's twenty-five years old, and he lives like a monk with us." Brady's social life, or the lack thereof, was an occasional topic of conversation among guys on the floor. We knew he had a girlfriend, but she was in graduate school in New York City and only visited occasionally.

"True. Hey, how about *Eldrin*," said Trey, shaking his head.

I laughed, doing a high-pitched impression of a whining Rick Eldrin: "But, Coach, I've got *shin splints!*"

"That kid's a joke."

"You're a joke," I said, laughing and punching him in the shoulder.

"Thanks, dipshit." Trey took a drink of his ginger ale. "Hey, did you see how fast McNeal ran that second lap?"

"Brian's a maniac. You shoulda invited him over."

"I did. His little sister had some championship soccer game this weekend. Parents made him go home for it."

Mrs. Daniels called from upstairs. "Trey, hon, did you order the pizza?" She came down, wearing a pair of jeans and a blouse. She had a towel wrapped around her hair.

"Yeah, Mom."

"Okay. I'll be on the phone for a while. I put the money on the counter." She went back upstairs.

"So, does your mom live here all the time?" I asked.

"Nope. Most of the time, she's in Lake Placid. But my dad's here and in New York a lot for business, so they have this place too." He laughed. "They don't like to be here together, though."

"Your dad around this weekend?"

"He's at a conference in Amsterdam or something."

"Amsterdam, like, in Europe again?"

"Yep."

"What does he do again?"

"He owns an advertising company. Let's finish this game." He hit the pause button to restart the game, and simulated applause filled the room. I saw Trey glance back at the photo.

# CHAPTER 12

Just a few hours later, as a result of a complicated matrix of phone calls on Trey's part, we were on our way to a mixer (that's Mid-Atlantic jargon for "dance") at St. Amelia's, one of several Northern Virginia prep schools for our female counterparts. This was ostensibly an invitation-only event, and Ashford River School students were not on the invitation list. But fortunately for us, Trey was, in his own inimitable way, somehow very well connected. After convincing his mother that this was an open dance and securing a ride from her, we met up with his St. Amelia's contact (apparently the ex-girlfriend of his second cousin), and she ushered us into the gym.

The bass was deafening, and I could feel it as much as hear it pulsing through the floor. It was dark, with colored lights aimed haphazardly at the walls, some of them spinning and flashing. A sea of kids writhed, spun, humped, bounced, and gyrated on the floor in front of us, while scattered teachers paced the perimeter, looking bored and occasionally checking their watches. A fog machine spat out clouds that hovered over the crowd and gave substance to the shafts of light. The air was warm and humid, charged with an intoxicating, pheromone-rich blend of sweat, cologne, perfume, and raw hormonal energy.

Trey elbowed me in the ribs and nodded approvingly. He pointed across the mass of writhing bodies and shouted over the music, "Come on; let's go." I wasn't sure where we were going, but he seemed to know. I followed him as he pushed his way into the edge of the crowd, making his way with singular purpose toward some spot on the far side of the room. As we got closer, I realized we were heading for a trio of girls clustered around one of the pillars near an exit sign. He sure didn't hesitate.

It would be worth stopping at this point to describe the sort of panic that was rising in my chest. Girls. I had no experience. None. Well, that's not really true. At one point, I discovered that I had a crush on a girl named Melissa Crane back in seventh grade, but beyond giving her a chocolate heart on Valentine's Day and talking awkwardly with her on the phone a few times, I'd had no contact. Girls were a foreign entity to most of the younger guys at Ashford River, wonderful and mysterious and exciting in theory but painfully distant, obscure, and intimidating in reality. The glossy pages of magazines and occasional whispered accounts of some guy's lucky score revealed the carnal basics. But when it came to this living, breathing reality, most of us were clueless.

So as Trey ambled confidently toward the girls, I hovered closely behind him, hands buried in my pockets, grinning stupidly and trying to look cool. I had absolutely no idea what the hell he was up to. The one sensation I remember more clearly than anything was the feeling of sweat dripping down my arms, more sweat than I'd noticed during a crew practice.

The girls, who had been huddled closely, talking the way teenage girls do—in rapid waves of intense gossip punctuated by bursts of laughter—now paused in midsentence as they looked at Trey and me. One of them, shorter with brownish pigtails and wearing a tight pink polo shirt, blushed so quickly and darkly that I thought she might have something wrong with her. She hid behind the other two, who seemed infinitely more worldly and confident. Almost as quickly as she had blushed, she sneaked away, leaving the four of us.

"Hello, Ladies," Trey said this with a sort of comic suaveness, which was exactly what kept him from being intimidated in this sort of situation. He managed to make something as ridiculous as "Hello, Ladies," sound smooth and funny, as though he knew it was ridiculous and that was the whole point. It worked. They smiled, raising their eyebrows, aiming for a look of skepticism and disinterest, but there was definitely a spark there. Trey fed off the energy, building momentum. I continued to sweat in the background.

"I'm Trey. This is Matt." He nodded at me, flashing a winning smile. The girls exchanged quick glances, and then the taller of the two stepped forward and extended her hand.

"Hey, I'm Nicole. This is Natalie."

Nicole wore jeans so tight she must have painted them on that morning and a short white tank top that exposed a perfect strip of midriff. She had on flip-flops, which was sort of funny, since most of the girls were wearing dressier shoes. Her voice had a strained tone to it, as though she were always stretching when she talked. She had big brown eyes and short-cropped dark hair that sort of arced around her ears. Natalie was shorter. Her hair was longer and blond, braided in a complicated ponytail. She toyed with it as it rested on her shoulder. She wore the same white tank top. I noticed, probably at the same time Trey did, the subtle crest printed on each: *St. Amelia's Swimming.*

Trey pointed at the crest on Natalie's shirt. "See, Matt? You were right." He smiled at me, winking.

*I was?*

Natalie took the bait. "What was he right about?"

"Matt saw you girls from across the room and knew you were swimmers right away."

*I did?*

"Really?" The girls flashed each other a look. "How?"

I realized the question was being directed at me.

"Um. From your legs. Definitely from your legs. You just look like swimmers. With legs. Of swimmers." I thought it sounded okay.

Trey jumped in on cue. "It takes one to know one. We both swim for Ashford River. I'm all over the fifty freestyle."

"No kidding," replied Nicole. "Me too. What about you, Matt?"

"Breaststroke." For some reason, this was the first thing that came to mind. "But I'm not that great."

Trey cut me off. "Aw, he's too humble. He's got the one hundred down below one-oh-eight, and it's his first year." He clapped me on the shoulder for good measure. Apparently, Trey was familiar with swimming jargon. Thought it was true I had been on the swim team at my old school, I was nowhere near competitive.

Natalie nodded. "That's pretty good. We're half of our top relay team. I swim fly, and she's our freestyler. The other two aren't here."

There was a bit of silence, and then Nicole shifted the nature of our evening. "You guys dance?"

I don't know exactly how long we were out there in the mix of grinding bodies. Before I knew what was going on, Nicole had grabbed Trey's arm and Natalie mine, and they pulled us into the crowd. She wore perfume that smelled like citrus, and her hair tickled my neck as she leaned in close, wrapping her arms around my back. I saw Trey and Nicole in the middle of a similar embrace.

"So," Natalie half-shouted into my ear, "do you swim better than you dance?" She was giggling and squeezed me tighter, her hands slipping lower on my back. I was getting excited, and I knew she felt it as she rubbed against me in rhythm with the music. To call this dancing would have been a real reach.

"I guess I don't get much dancing practice. Trey and I tried once in our room, but that got pretty awkward." I laughed at my own joke and adjusted our movement as the song switched to an R.E.M. track.

She laughed too and put her head against my neck. "So how'd you guys escape the dorms and get in here tonight? This was supposed to just be for guys from St. John's."

"Trey's a resourceful guy."

"Hmm." She slid her hands down into the back pockets of my jeans and pulled me tighter against her. "Well, I'm glad you guys decided to come."

*Wow.*

It was the first time I'd been that physical with anyone, and I felt like I was out of myself, watching from some outside perspective. Life at fifteen is full of firsts, and this was certainly one of them. She had me excited, and she knew it. Up to that point, my state of arousal had been entirely a private affair. So it wasn't just the physical sensation. It was the fact that she *knew* what was going on down there, she *knew* what I was feeling, she *knew* that she was causing it, and she was doing everything possible to keep it that way.

It was surreal how quickly all this had happened, how we had just met these girls and within a half hour, I had one of them pressed up against me, her hands in my back pockets, my own hands pressed firmly against the small of her back, music pushing us closer together, noise thunderous around us as I just let these strange, dazzling new forces ricochet like sparks from a striking hammer. I'd still never been drunk at that point in my life, but this was my first taste of intoxication. I drank it all in. The music, the friction, the smell of her hair, the nearness of her, the warmth of her skin against my neck and hands, the distinct pressure of her fingers through the fabric of my back pockets, heat rising off of me, the sense that she craved that heat, and more than anything, a sort of primal, almost carnal urge to share it with her.

Suddenly, it made sense, this girl thing, and like a switch that was flipped, I was into it in a very real way. In that moment, the world expanded. Up until then, these feelings and these impulses were muted and blurry, and that whole strange forbidden world was nothing more than a distant, obscure *something*. Right there, right then, in this space, with this music, with this girl, the blur sharpened into crystal clarity, just like that. I was shaking with the intensity of it.

We kept this up until the end of the next song, when Natalie and Nicole decided they needed to freshen up. I was covered in sweat, and as she pulled away from me, I shook my head, trying to clear it from the haze of sensations that threatened to knock me to the ground. Trey threw an arm around my shoulders and led me over to the corner where we both leaned against the wall, catching our breath.

"Holy shit," he said. "Holy *shit*." He giggled, elbowing me in the ribs for about the twelfth time that night. "Is this happening?"

I shook my head, smiling. "Oh, it's happening all right."

"These girls are *crazy* into us, Matt."

"The swimming thing..."

"So *what*? Dude, that's a minor detail. Here they come."

The girls shared furtive glances and giggled as they approached us. Nicole leaned in between us and shouted over the booming music. "You guys up for racing?"

"Huh?" was all I managed.

"You heard me. Racing. In the pool."

This was too much, even for Trey. "You're serious? In the pool?"

"Best place to swim," said Natalie, her eyebrows raised.

"We don't have anything to swim in," I started to say.

"Don't you wear boxers?"

"Yeah, but..."

"Good enough."

I looked at Trey. *Holy shit.*

■ ■ ■

A few minutes later, we were outside, crouched low and creeping alongside the building behind a row of hedges. Nicole led the way, motioning us to hurry up and stay quiet. After we rounded the corner, she came to a fire exit that had been propped. She pulled it open and ushered us inside. The four of us squeezed through, looking nervously over our shoulders, and then collapsed inside in the darkness of a corridor; the red glow of an exit sign reflected off the freshly waxed floor.

"Come on," whispered Nicole as she took off down the length of the hall, rounding another corner. We followed, still crouching low as we skulked along the rows of lockers. We stopped at a door labeled *"Locker Room,"* and at that moment, I felt a new rush of dizzying excitement as I realized that given the nature of the school, this was a girls' locker room. My heart was pounding with the sheer stupidity and risk of this, the danger of the whole thing absolutely delicious.

We walked through the dim locker room, Trey and I looking around us in utter amazement at where we were. It was nothing like ours—clean, organized, nothing on the floor. Pink tile and long, varnished wooden benches gleamed in the red glow of smoke alarm indicators and exit signs.

Showers. *Where girls shower.* Trey elbowed me again as we passed them. "I know," I mumbled. We came to a heavy door labeled *"Pool."*

"Wait, isn't it locked?" Trey asked. "Pools are always locked."

Nicole pulled a key on a lanyard from her pocket. "There are benefits to being a lifeguard," she whispered, smirking as she put the key in the lock, twisted it with a satisfying click, and pushed open the door.

It shut behind us, and we stood in the warm darkness. I could smell chlorine and hear the low murmur of the filter running. Again, it was the dim green light of an exit sign that illuminated the space, but our eyes were accustomed to the dark now. The light gleamed off the glassy surface of the pool, with just the most subtle ripples near the filter jets. The girls whispered something to each other and let out low, conspiratorial giggles. Then, in a single, fluid motion, they simultaneously lifted off their tank tops and flung them on the bench along the wall. Trey and I stood there frozen, watching this play out, each trying to figure out again if this was some sort of dream. They wore similar bras, sporty little deals with wide straps over their shoulders, the sort of thing a girl might wear running.

"So are we gonna race or not?" asked Nicole, as she unbuttoned her jeans and slowly unzipped them, revealing underwear that matched the bra.

By this time, I was breathing hard, my heart beating rapidly, and I felt dizzy. The combination of chlorine and testosterone at such a dosage is probably not a healthy thing, and I actually felt myself waver, my knees shaking, and reached out for the wall behind me to steady myself. Trey had already hurriedly pulled his T-shirt over his head and was undoing his belt.

The girls, now wearing very little at all, scampered over to the starting blocks at the far end of the pool.

"Matt!"

"Huh?" I snapped my attention to Trey, who stood next to me in his boxers.

"Come on!"

Again, feeling like I was watching myself through a movie camera, I took off my shirt, jeans, shoes, and socks. The pool deck was cold. I was happy for the darkness as I hurried across the room to the starting blocks, given that boxers do a lousy job of containing a young man's excitement.

"Okay, what are we swimming?" rasped Natalie, as loudly as a whisper can get.

"Fifty free, with a dive." Nicole stepped onto the block in her lane. "Swimmers, take your marks."

The state of my anatomy was the only reason my boxers didn't fly off when I dove into the water. Of course, the girls killed both of us in the race, reaching the far end before we were halfway there. They were laughing and pointing as we reached the edge, trying to be quiet but not doing a very good job. The water was chilly.

"Oh my God, you guys are *so* not swimmers!" Natalie whipped her arm across the surface, sending a wave of water into my face. "I knew it!"

We were about to respond with a counterattack when we saw the flicker of lights under the door leading to the locker room. We froze, exchanging panicked looks all around. Moments later, we heard the jingle of keys.

In what seemed like a single motion, Nicole jumped out of the pool, sprinted across the deck to where Trey and I had dumped our clothes, and stashed them behind a bin of kickboards. Then she grabbed a stopwatch hanging from the wall. She mouthed, gesturing, "Natalie! Swim! You two, get underwater!"

I turned to look at Trey, but he was already under. I took a deep breath and plunged under the surface as Natalie took off swimming. Moments later, I heard the muffled sounds of shouting over the roaring in my ears. Trey and I pressed against the rough tile at the bottom of the shallow end. I clung to the ladder to hold myself down, and Trey held onto my leg to keep from floating to the surface. My heart pounded, and we did our best to squeeze into the corner, where we'd be out of sight of anyone standing on the deck just a few feet away. Twenty seconds passed. The talking continued, but the volume went down. I thought my heart was going to explode, and I winced in pain as I fought the impulse to shoot to the surface. My ankle was numb where Trey was holding on. Finally, after what had to be a full minute, the noise stopped.

As quietly as I could, I slipped above the surface and drank in the air, gasping. The room was empty, and the girls were gone. Trey's head popped up out of the water next to me, coughing and sputtering. Once we regained our senses, we could hear voices from the locker room, just on the other side of the door.

"…and so you ladies decided it was just a *fine* idea for you to be down here in the middle of the night doing time trials with no supervision?" It was an older woman's voice, clearly a teacher, or maybe worse, the dean.

"We just wanted to work on her stroke with the race coming up, and I'm a lifeguard, and—"

"Ten thirty at night, in the dark! No, it is not okay! And in your *underwear* no less! *Completely* inappropriate! What were you girls thinking?"

Two muted voices responded, "Sorry, ma'am."

We caught only bits of the exchange huddled in the dark pool, shivering, our hearts still pounding, but it seemed like Nicole had it covered. Impossibly, she actually had it covered. This teacher must have been as dumb as bricks. After a few more minutes of heated conversation, the lights flipped off in the locker room and the voices faded away into the corridor. All I could hear was the filter running, and the quiet lap of the water against the side of the pool—that, and my teeth chattering.

Trey and I looked at each other, still catching our breath.

His eyes were wide. We simultaneously burst out laughing, doing our best to stifle the noise. After a good full minute of laughing our butts off, we climbed out of the pool and found our clothes where Nicole had stashed them. Losing the soaked boxers, we toweled off as best we could with our T-shirts before getting dressed. Still half soaked, carrying our dripping boxers and reeking of chlorine, we tiptoed back to the fire exit and crept outside. It was cold, and our damp clothes weren't helping.

Trey looked alarmed. "What time is it?"

"Ten forty-five." Trey's mom was supposed to pick us up at eleven. I held up the soaking boxers. "What the hell are we supposed to do with these?"

"Umm…" He looked around, shivering. "Uh, I think we'll have to cut our losses." With that, he jogged over to the dumpster and threw his in. I did the same, and we scampered around to the front of the gym, where we found Mrs. Daniels's Lexus already idling in the parking lot.

"Hey." I tugged at his shirt as we approached the car.

"What?"

"What about the girls?"

"The girls," he said, with a look of mock seriousness and his hand on my shoulder, "will find us. For now, we have other issues."

By other issues, of course, he was referring to the obvious reek of chlorine rising off of us. But in a fit of signature Trey Daniels ingenuity, he explained to his mother that it was because of the fog machine at the dance.

Back at his mom's townhouse, I felt much better after a hot shower, for a variety of reasons. After a bowl of ice cream and another round of football on the Nintendo, we went to bed. Trey went to his room, and I slept on the pullout sofa in the living room. I looked out the window at the passing lights until I fell asleep, replaying the incredibly vivid mental footage of the girls pulling the tank tops over their heads.

# CHAPTER 13

A few days later, Trey and I had still not heard from Nicole or Natalie, though he had gone to great lengths to get ahold of their full names and phone numbers from his second cousin's ex-girlfriend. He was confident she'd come through. As for me, thoughts of Natalie were a regular and welcome distraction. I wrote her a ridiculous letter trying, in all seriousness, to capture the way I'd felt that night while I was with her. Unfortunately, it turned out sounding ridiculous, not to mention mildly pornographic, so I gave up on that idea, tore it into about seventy-eight pieces, and stashed them so deep in three different garbage bins that no one could ever find them. That letter was the sort of thing that—if ever found—could be your undoing at a boarding school. In fact, I had thought about burning it, but reconsidered this when I imagined the dorm going up in flames all because of a stupid love letter.

On Wednesday evening, Mr. Brady gathered the whole floor in his living room. The twenty-two of us hardly fit in the small space. It was bigger than any of the student rooms, but not by much. Brady was wearing a hooded sweatshirt and a pair of warm-up pants, holding a bottle of orange Gatorade. He stood in the doorway to talk with us. He looked a lot more like a normal guy than he did in his shirt and tie during the school day. Everyone quieted down after we noticed that he was ready to talk.

His voice was serious. "I brought all of you in here because there's something we need to address."

I stopped breathing, my eyes involuntarily darting to Trey, who stared straight ahead. I was waiting for the hammer to drop. *Apparently, somebody in this room decided it was a good idea to go skinny-dipping with the JV swim team from St. Amelia's in the middle of the night last weekend.*

Fortunately, this was not the case. Brady continued, "Jeff on the maintenance staff has been finding a lot of cigarette butts lately down near the boathouse." He took a sip of his Gatorade.

"Now, I know this is not exactly a matter of national security. I'm not here to create an inquisition." He took another sip and looked around the room. "But," he continued, "I do want to gently remind you that smoking is a pretty terrible thing to do to your lungs and, moreover, it's obviously not allowed. The other teachers and I are going to have our eyes open for this more than usual. Please don't put me in a position where I have to punish any of you. It's a pain in butt for me, for you, and for everyone involved. Is that understood?"

I was sitting on the couch between Trey and Chase. Rick Eldrin was on the floor in front of us, playing with a loose thread on his sock. He glared at Chase and then Trey. They stared straight ahead at the poster of Ernest Hemingway hanging on Brady's wall. Hemingway looked pissed off, staring straight back at them, brow furrowed and pipe protruding.

McNeal raised his hand. "Uh, Mr. Brady?" I was watching Trey, and I saw his shoulders tense.

"What's up, Brian?"

"I'm pretty sure that it's..." He paused, glancing sideways at Trey. "...that it's the seniors going out there. I mean it's kind of hard for us to sneak outside since we have to be in our rooms by eleven."

Mr. Brady was nodding his head, but his rapid glance at Trey didn't escape me. "McNeal, you make a valid point, and again, I want you guys to understand: I'm not pointing fingers, and I just want to get the message out there. If you're doing it, stop, because we're going to catch you sooner or later, and it's not gonna be pretty when we do. You'll be dealing with Mr. Wagner, and I'm not bailing you out. If you're *not* doing it...well, good. End of discussion." He stood up and looked at his watch. "Okay, it's almost lights-out, but I'll give you a few extra minutes. Everyone in their rooms by ten after, got it?"

After my shower, I put on sweatpants and sat at my desk, putting books in my backpack for tomorrow. Trey was leaning against his dresser, his face close to the mirror as he inspected a zit on his forehead.

"I love when Brady tries to give a scary speech. He loves trying to sound tough, but he sucks at it. Besides, he's not actually going to do anything about it."

"Whaddya mean?"

"I mean he doesn't *want* to do anything about it. That's how it works at these places. Trust me." Trey took off his T-shirt and threw it into his pile of laundry in the corner. Tanya from Down Under gazed down from the door. "They don't like catching us at stuff because then they have to deal with it."

This hadn't really occurred to me. It was another time when I realized that Trey was a lot more street smart than I was, despite his affect of consistent cluelessness. "So you think Brady knows who's smoking?"

"Of course he does. He's not stupid. Didn't you see him looking straight at me? He just knows it's not really hurting anyone, and it looks bad when the school has to make an issue out of it. Like there's a problem with their supervision. Besides, he doesn't like to be the bad guy. He was talking directly to me. He just needed you guys there to hide it."

"Huh."

"Dude," Trey lowered his voice to a whisper, "me and Chase have been sneaking out after lights-out at least once a week."

I really did feel like an idiot. I knew he had snuck out to smoke from time to time, but I didn't think it was that frequent, and I sure as hell never noticed him going after lights-out. *Sneaky bastard.* "You have?"

"Yeah. I mean, no offense, man, but you sleep like a rock. One time, I even slipped while I was climbing down the bunk and slammed my leg against your bed, and you didn't wake up." Trey climbed up onto the top bunk and got under the covers. We'd switched bunks a while ago.

"Really?"

"Really. Of course, the funniest thing about it…the *ironic* part," he said with his voice lowered, "is that we aren't the ones smoking the *cigarettes*."

I didn't get it. "Whaddya mean?"

Trey narrowed his eyes in his conspiratorial way and whispered, "McNeal was right. The cigarettes are from the seniors."

"So what do you…" I started to ask. Then it clicked. They *were* smoking. Just not cigarettes. I looked at him, eyebrows raised. "Really?"

"Yessir."

"Are you crazy?"

"Am I?"

"You'll get nailed."

"Haven't been nailed yet. There's seniors who've been getting away with it for four years."

I turned the light off and got into my bed. It was quiet for a minute before I spoke. "Don't you ever feel bad?"

"About what?"

"I dunno. Like, about smoking. Or what we pulled at the dance? Lying to Brady?"

"No, not really. I love Brady. He's my man." Trey's voice sounded more distant now.

"Well, yeah, but that's what I mean. It doesn't bother you that you lie to him?"

Trey laughed. "No, I don't *really* lie. It's not like he asks me if I'm sneaking out and I say no."

"You know what I mean."

"Yeah. I guess I just don't see how it really matters. I mean I don't cheat on tests and stuff like other guys do. And I'm not mean to anyone. To be honest, the stuff I do is really pretty harmless."

I thought about a Saturday back in Buffalo the year before. I was supposed to come home early from soccer practice to help Dad move our old washing machine, but the whole team went to Burger King for dinner after practice, and I really didn't want to be the only guy who didn't go. So I came home later and told Dad that I completely forgot about coming home early and that I was really sorry. The washer got moved. It just got moved the next day. No harm done, really, and Dad wasn't even mad about it. But I felt lousy for the next few days, especially standing in church between my parents. I never told the truth on that one. Maybe I would have felt better if Dad *had* been mad.

The fact that Trey had kept his smoking a secret from me created a feeling that was hard to explain. Looking back, I suppose it was a mild sense of betrayal, just a twinge of mistrust. I wouldn't have called it as much at the moment, but whatever it was, it felt lousy. I decided to change the subject. I remembered Brady's words in the coach boat: *"So I guess you're our guy."*

"Hey, I got a hundred on that reading quiz on the Hawthorne stories. Man, I thought I bombed it."

"I *did* bomb it," Trey muttered.

"Well, maybe that's 'cause you didn't read it." I put my feet up against the bottom of the upper mattress and messed with a scab on my knee. I could see Trey's arm dangling over the side of the top bunk.

"Yeah, that could be part of it," he mumbled.

"So why don't you just read it? It's actually pretty cool stuff."

"Yeah. I know. I will. Hey, do you know if we have another Latin quiz tomorrow?"

"Yeah. It's on the vocab."

"Shit."

"Hey, Trey, who's the girl with you on the ski lift in that picture? The one taped up on your desk." I meant to ask him this when we first moved in. I had also meant to ask him why he had three thousand dollars in his wallet.

Trey leaned over the side of the bunk, and his head appeared, the ridiculous grin upside down and hair dangling over his eyes. "Oh, that's Katrina. She's this girl I've known my whole life. She used to be my best friend when we were little kids. Our families used to go skiing all the time at Whiteface. Then we made out last year when we were drunk at this party and that kind of screwed things up. Haven't talked to her in a while."

"She's cute."

"Yeah, she is. I screwed that up. She was mad at me."

"Why? What did you do?"

"Ha. You want the details?"

"Um. I dunno." I wanted the details, but I didn't want to ask for them. There's usually nothing fun about someone else's details. They leave you feeling sort of inadequate and pathetic. So of course I got the details, which involved some intense fooling around in a hot tub after the mutual consumption of a bottle of cheap wine. Okay, so it was established and on the table: Trey, while still fairly innocent himself, was nonetheless light years ahead of me in the field of sexual experience.

He smiled absently after he finished the story. His face was flushed from leaning over the bed.

"Did you drink a lot at your last school?" I asked.

"Not any more than anyone else. Just a couple times, at parties and stuff. And down in the Bahamas at my dad's condo last winter with these kids from Manhattan. You should come down there this year." Trey's head disappeared as he lifted himself back up onto the bunk.

"You have a condo in the Bahamas?" Just another twist in the ever-complex and unfolding Daniels family story.

"Yep. Seriously, I'll ask my dad if you can come down over winter break."

"Wow. I've never traveled anywhere like that. And I've never been drunk," I said, as much to myself as to him.

"Never?"

"Nah. My dad would kill me. I drank a beer once at a family party, but that's it. My mom's a nurse. She'd be able to tell, no problem."

"Aw, Matty, you're such a good kid. So innocent! I should tell Natalie." Trey was laughing.

"Shut up." There were times when I really wanted to punch him.

There was a knock on the door, and a few seconds later, Brady opened it and stuck his head in. Tanya from Down Under swung out of view.

"Guys, get some sleep." Brady was wearing his *My Better Half Is Irish* T-shirt again.

"That's a helluva T-shirt, sir," said Trey.

"Thanks, Trey."

"Think I could get one somehow?"

"You're not Irish, Trey."

"My better half is." He leaned over the bed again and smirked.

"All right, get to bed. You have a Latin quiz tomorrow. I expect to see you at breakfast on time, reviewing your notes. You too, Matt."

We both said, "Okay."

"Jesus, kid. Stop leaning out of your bed like that or you're gonna fall out." Brady chuckled and shook his head as Trey pretended to fall out of the bunk.

"Good night, guys."

The door clicked shut.

# CHAPTER 14

"Put your seat belt on, Brian." Mr. Brady peered back at Brian in the rearview mirror. He looked a little ticked off because it was the third time he'd told him. McNeal was kneeling on the bench of the Chevy Suburban, leaning over the back of it and looking at the *Sports Illustrated* that Trey was reading. He rolled his eyes, turned around, and buckled the belt.

We were hightailing it west through Central Pennsylvania, about half-way to Pittsburgh. The Head of the Ohio boat race began early the next morning. It was already twenty past six. The traffic was rough coming up through Maryland, and Pennsylvania was, as usual, in a state of perpetual roadwork. We were headed for a motel outside the city. We'd been arguing for the past twenty minutes about who would share a room with whom, even though chances were Brady was just going to assign them anyway.

The six sophomores in the Suburban made up the majority of the light-weight eight that would race. It was Trey, Chase, Brian, Rick Eldrin, Mike Hasselwerdt, me, and Jimmy Speers, the coxswain. The other two, Mike Dean and Dave Dwyer, were freshmen and were riding in the other van with

Mr. Mackey, the new assistant coach. Mr. Mackey was a graduate student at Georgetown and a college pal of Brady, who got him the job. He used to be a coxswain in high school, and he seemed to know his stuff, but he sure didn't look much like an athlete now. He was only five foot two and had a huge beer gut and a voice just like Rodney Dangerfield. He wasn't, according to Mr. Brady, "aging well." But the heavyweight four he'd coached had medaled in their first two races of the year, so everyone was taking Mackey's coaching seriously. Mr. Brady had a white T-shirt made for him that read "Heavyweight Coach" in navy block letters and had the whole team sign it with a Sharpie marker. I was growing to appreciate Brady's subtle sense of humor.

I was sitting on the rear bench with Mike Hasselwerdt, who was passed out with his headphones on. My forehead leaned against the window as I watched the ground rush by, the concrete shoulder and long grass beyond it blurred with motion. The sky was fading to dusk, and I yawned before fading off to sleep.

Two hours later, I woke to the jolt of the Suburban coming to a stop. It was dark, and I could hear Mr. Brady's U2 playing quietly. It was all he listened to other than classical music and the occasional country song. It sounded distant and tinny from the front speakers. The rest of the guys were still asleep. I sat up, stretching my arms and working the crick out of my neck, stiff from sleeping at an odd angle. We were in the parking lot of Denny's. Mercury vapor lamps illuminated the damp asphalt, making the white lines glow. The highway was just twenty yards or so away, and headlight beams arced through the windows. I could hear the *whoosh* as trucks sped past. Brady stretched in the front seat, his arms behind the headrest. He caught my eye in the rearview mirror.

"Hey, buddy." His voice was tired, and the words got lost in the beginning of a yawn.

"Hey, Coach. How far we gotta go still?" I took off my seat belt and arched my back. Chase Alexander's head popped up from the seat in front, his hair in its usual state of chaos as he stretched.

"We're here, kid. The hotel's just across the driveway, over there." He pointed as he opened the driver's-side door. The overhead lamps came on. At once, there was a general stir in the Suburban, and Chase groaned, squinting.

"But," Brady said, leaning in over the driver's seat, "I thought you guys might like some dinner."

A few minutes later, we were sitting in Denny's. We were an odd-looking group, and we got stares from some of the other patrons. We were all still wearing khakis and school shoes—all, that is, except Trey, who had made quite a point of changing into his mesh soccer shorts on the road, attempting to moon a passing busload of senior citizens in the process until Mr. Brady, trying hard to hold back laughter, threatened to bench him for the race. Chase, Jimmy, Rick, Mike, and I still wore our white oxfords, untucked and wrinkled, with our uniform ties dangling at various angles from the collars. Brian chose a tank top in an effort to show off his biceps to any interested ladies, but there didn't seem to be any ladies at all. Mr. Brady somehow fit into the motley crew, still wearing his shirt and tie, now loosened at the collar as well. The day's growth of beard, road-weary eyes, and the receding hairline set him apart.

Trey, Chase, Rick, and Mike sat at a booth on the other side of the room. Jimmy, Brian, Mr. Brady, and I were at a table near the window. I could hear Chase and Trey going back and forth at the other table, recounting the story about the time they ordered fifteen pizzas on the science department's credit card.

The waitress came over to our table. Her name tag read "Erica." Erica was probably about nineteen. I noticed the curve of her butt, the way the tight uniform slacks hugged her. She wasn't exactly a model up top, no Tanya from Down Under. She had about fourteen rings on her fingers and big, loopy silver earrings.

"How you boys doin' tonight?" she said, with a vague mid-Pennsylvania twang. She was chewing gum the way only girls can, sort of hiding it in a corner of her mouth. She was standing there, steaming coffeepot at her side and elbow perched against her hip.

"We're doin' all right," Brady said. "How 'bout you?" He looked up from his menu.

"Oh, okay. Tired. Coffee?"

"Sure." She poured some coffee for Brady, smiling at him as she leaned over his shoulder, closer than she needed to be. I kicked McNeal under the table, nodding at Brady's slightly blushing face. Trey, Rick, Chase, and Mike were watching from the other table behind her, grinning. Trey leaned closer to Chase, whispering something. Chase's head went down to the table, as he tried to hide his laughter. I knew immediately that Trey was up to something.

"So. You guys a school group or something?"

"Rowing team," Jimmy said. "Gotta race tomorrow."

"Y'all are a *rowing* team?"

"Yep."

"You the *coach*?" she asked Brady.

He took a sip of his coffee, the corners of his mouth in a smirk. "How'd you guess?" The man had a way of mocking people without them knowing it.

"Well, ya don't look much older than these guys. How old *are* you anyway?"

Brady raised his eyebrows and gave her an annoyed look. "Twenty-five."

"Huh," Erica said, giving her gum a particularly loud smack as she put down the coffeepot and pulled out her pad and pen. "What can I get you guys tonight?"

We ordered, and when Erica went to the other table, I caught Brady rolling his eyes. The teacher shook his head, smiling, and poured some milk into his coffee.

Jimmy whistled. "Mr. Brady, you want me to take over supervising the guys the rest of the night? You can stay and drink more coffee." We were all laughing. Brady grunted as he took a sip, trying not to spill it.

"Thanks, Jimmy. She's nice. Just maybe a little…young."

"I bet she's twenty," Brian said, narrowing his eyes and looking at Erica from across the room as she disappeared into the kitchen.

"I don't think so, Brian."

"Hey," I said, "the man's taken, Brian." I remembered the picture of Emily on the bookcase next to Brady's TV. She was pretty. I had asked him about her once while we watched a Redskins game. But the phone rang, then the Skins scored, and that was the end of that conversation.

"You wanna tell us about Emily?" asked Brian. He was building a pyramid out of coffee creamers.

"Well, not really," said Brady.

"Come on," pleaded Brian.

"She's going to grad school in New York City."

He'd already told us that. We tried unsuccessfully to get more details out of him about Emily, but he didn't budge. Eventually, our conversation returned, as it inevitably always does among students, to making fun of various teachers and doing impressions of the more eccentric ones. Brady tried to be professional and stay out of the fray, but I could see him chuckling at some of our remarks.

Erica came back with the orders after a little while. She took a long time putting Brady's plate down. He thanked her. She said, "No problem," and strutted away back to the kitchen.

"Gotta be tough," said Speers, taking a bite of a French fry. "Long-distance relationships *suck*. My older brother dated this girl over the summer, but she lived like an hour away." He shook his head thoughtfully as he sipped his Coke. "I'm not gonna make that mistake."

Brady smiled. "It's not easy. But we deal. We see each other about once a month. It's only for the rest of this year, and then she'll be moving to DC." He paused, staring at the table for a moment before taking a bite. A small blob of ketchup landed on his shirt. "Ah, damn." He got most of the ketchup off with a napkin and a little bit of his Sprite.

Speers talked with his mouth full. "You guys gonna get married?"

Brady laughed. "Well, we'd have to get engaged first."

"So, are ya gonna ask her?"

"Probably. There's a lot to think about, but probably. She's a special woman." He took a bite of his burger.

"Think we have a good chance tomorrow?" I asked. I figured maybe Brady wanted to change the subject. Over at the other table, the four of them were leaning in close, looking serious now. I couldn't make out what they were saying.

"Yeah. Yeah, I do." The teacher's voice sounded livelier. "Hopefully you guys will get set up with a nice tailwind. Headwind on this course makes for a very tough row. It's pretty exposed if it's windy."

Erica came back. I think she'd done something different with her hair. And her apron was gone. "How is everything, guys?"

"It's great, Erica. Really. Thanks." Brady was smiling politely at her, sort of the same way he smiled at his students when he was annoyed with them. His voice was flat.

"Mr. Mackey was saying there's bridges to steer through," said Speers, continuing the conversation. Erica rolled her eyes and went away.

"There are. But the course is wide," said Brady, watching the waitress out of the corner of his eye. "We'll look at the course map tomorrow. It's not too tough. You'll be fine. The key is to stay tight and pass close. Don't go wide; you'll add too much distance." Brady demonstrated with two French fries on the table, one behind the other. "They'll send crews off from the start at thirty-second intervals, so in a headrace you're basically racing in a single file down the course. If you're overtaking a crew, they have to give way and let you pass."

Brian pointed at the lead French fry. "And if that's us..." He shifted the fry over to the right, leaving a grease stain on the table. "...then we have to give way, too. Just like on the highway." Brian was getting ready for his road test over Christmas break.

"Right," said Brady, "but you guys aren't gonna let that happen, right? Not with McNeal's biceps on our side. You'll be passing everyone." He reached across the table and clapped Brian on the shoulder. "Just keep the turns tight, Jimmy. It's easy to go wide, and that adds seconds to the clock. This'll be good practice for Regionals at the end of the season."

Brian looked up from his food. "Are we all gonna race there?"

"Don't know yet. We'll enter an eight and a four if they're both competitive enough."

"What if they're not?"

"Then it'll just be an eight, or maybe just a four."

"I think we could have a really fast four," I said. "Me, Brian, Trey, Mike..."

"Maybe Eldrin," added Speers.

"Yeah, maybe Eldrin, too," I said.

McNeal yawned. "I'm tired, Coach."

"Yeah. Me too. Matt, you want to go ask our friend Erica for the check?"

I got up, wiped my mouth with my napkin, and walked over toward the kitchen. I saw Trey standing next to Erica, writing something down on a napkin, grinning and talking in a hushed voice.

"Hey."

Trey turned around. "'Sup, Matt?"

"Umm, Erica, could we have the check?"

She punched a few keys on the register. She was smiling. "Coming right up."

I gave Trey a look, and he just grinned, raising his eyebrows. I rolled my eyes and went back to the table.

Brady left cash for the bill, and a five-dollar tip for Erica. She waved at us from the kitchen door as we stepped outside and piled into the Suburban. Trey and Chase were giggling like girls. I got in the backseat next to them.

"What'd you guys do now?"

Trey was laughing hard but trying to keep quiet, glancing at Brady's reflection in the rearview mirror. He lowered his head below the seat and pulled me closer. "Dude, this is gonna be hilarious."

"What?"

"I gave her Brady's cell phone number."

"That was kind of ballsy."

Trey elbowed Chase, who was laughing a little too loud. "I also told her that he just broke up with his girlfriend and that tonight is his birthday."

"And?" Chase said, motioning for him to continue.

"And that he's got no one to celebrate with tonight."

"*And?*" encouraged Chase.

"And I think I threw in..." Trey was really cracking up now "...that he's not only a teacher, but a swimsuit model for Speedo."

At this, I burst out laughing. It was so, well, Trey.

Speers and Brady were talking more about the race up in the front of the truck as we pulled into the motel parking lot. Brady glanced back in the mirror. "What's so funny back there, guys?"

"Dirty joke, Coach. Not really appropriate for teachers," Trey said.

"Okay, then." Brady rolled his eyes.

Chase was still cackling.

By ten, we were in our rooms. Brady had done a bed check, and everyone was settled in. I was in a room with McNeal, Speers, and Chase. Speers brushed his teeth and played with the remote on the TV. He spoke with a mouthful of toothbrush. "You guys wanna watch TV?"

Chase came out of the bathroom drying off. "Only if you can find something with naked chicks."

Speers spit out the toothpaste in the sink. "Sorry, Chase, all we got is NBC, ABC, the History Channel, and HBO. And I already checked HBO. They're playing *Ghostbusters*."

"We gotta get up at five," I said. "I wanna get some sleep."

"Me too," said Brian. He closed the *Rolling Stone* he was reading and threw it on the floor next to the bed.

Chase climbed into the bed with Brian, laughing. "So glad we get to sleep together, McNeal."

"Yeah. It's just magical. Now shut the hell up, will ya?"

"Sure there's nothing on? Did you check Cinemax?"

"We don't get Cinemax. Come on, man. We gotta race in the morning," Brian muttered.

"Jesus Christ," grumbled Chase. "How does Brady pick these places? No Cinemax. Damn."

"Chase," said McNeal, his face buried in a pillow, "what does it take for you to shut the hell up?"

"Maybe a few hours with Erica," replied Chase, giggling.

"Trey could probably arrange that," said Speers.

"Brady's gonna kill him if she calls."

"Brady might *thank* him if she calls."

We all laughed at that one. Speers's unnaturally deep voice rumbled from the other bed. "Go to sleep, guys."

A few more stifled laughs, and we lay there in the darkness. I was just about asleep when I heard the loud knocking on the next door. *Trey's room.* I punched Speers, waking him up, and scampered over to the window.

"Yo, McNeal!" I hissed.

"Huh?"

"Get over here! I think she called."

McNeal leaped from the bed and crouched down. Our faces were near the windowsill, and we moved the curtain aside a few inches.

Because of the angle, I could just barely see Brady, standing in front of the door of the other room, barefoot in his sweatpants. He wasn't smiling, and his arms were crossed over his *Irish* T-shirt. He leaned forward, knocking again. We could hear the sound through the thin walls. Brady was muttering something under his breath. Chase giggled. I gave him a punch to the shoulder. "*Shut up*, man!"

A few seconds later, Trey was standing out on the sidewalk in his gym shorts and a sweatshirt, looking half asleep, rubbing his eyes as Brady grabbed him by the collar with both hands and pulled his face just inches from his own. For a second, it looked like our coach was actually going to throw our teammate up against the wall, but then we saw that he was smirking, trying hard not to burst into a laugh. He let go and said something in a whisper, stabbing at Trey's chest with his finger. We could hear clearly the last thing he said, shaking his head, before he turned to walk away: "*Speedo?*"

Trey smiled triumphantly and waved to us before going back inside.

# CHAPTER 15

I was vaguely aware of the looming shadow of the bridge overhead, but my attention was focused on Rick Eldrin's shoulders in front of me as the shell cut through the water. Everything was in motion around me. The crowd roared onshore, a couple hundred meters off to my left, so the finish line had to be close, but I was only vaguely aware of that, too. Instead, I focused on the sounds of the crew, the whoosh of the slides and the clunk of oars turning in their locks.

Drive. Finish. Recover. *Breathe!*

Speers's voice crackled over the cox-box speakers, punctuated by the rhythmic percussion of the strokes. He was shouting at us now, what little was left of his voice haggard and heavy.

"That's it, guys! Drive 'em long... we've got less... than five hundred meters!"

The familiar ache was radiating through my entire body; my heart was pounding in my chest, the desire on all fronts to *stop this torture*. But the adrenaline was pumping too, the rhythm of the crew pushing me to push back, my legs driving hard against the footboards, shoulders tensing with each stroke.

"Pump it up for ten now! Gimme ten, boys…*one!* Pound'em down! Two! *Movin' on 'em!* Three! *Bring it up! Four!"*

The count continued, and I closed my eyes, the pain in my chest tightening and burning. I heard Eldrin growl in front of me, a sort of grunt of pain, and his voice came through clenched teeth. "Friggin' *pressit, guys!*" Opening my eyes, I could see the crew we were passing, and I stole a quick look out of the boat, something I knew Brady would kill me for later. But we were creeping past the other crew, the opposing oars swinging broadly and diving into the water less than a foot from our own on the starboard side. Water was flying. Speers was screaming now, as much at the other crew as to us.

*"We…are…passing…you!"*

The roar of the crowd was louder now. Speers kicked us into the final thirty. My lungs were exploding, heaving, as I drove the final strokes, legs shaking. The pain became unbearable. My mind cleared except for the constant streams of agony rising from my quads. My view of the periphery faded to black, and my focus blurred. The sounds of the crowd, of the other crews, of Jimmy's voice, even the *clunk* of the oarlocks, became muffled and faded away. The stroke became automatic, my body seemingly out of my control. The catch and recovery were just reflexes now. The only thing left to feel, to focus on, was the drive and the hurt that came with it. *Drive.* The last thirty strokes felt like they took longer than the entire race before; only one thing echoed in my mind: *Make it hurt…don't stop.* For a few moments, I thought to myself, *I can't do this.* It was not until the last stroke and the sound of the horn at the finish line that my perception returned, and it returned with a vengeance. I felt a new pain, no longer the screaming of quads and back and calves, but the thumping of my heart, pounding like it would burst in my chest and throat, my starved lungs gasping for air. It was like a dam had opened, and the waters poured in; the sights and the sounds of the crowd, of Eldrin in front of me and Anderson in front of him, gripping the gunwales, bent over oar handles, McNeal up in stroke seat trailing his hands in the water to cool them off.

It turns out that among the fourteen crews in the event, we were the only junior lightweight eight registered with a majority of sophomore rowers, and that made our second-place finish that much more impressive. And the fact that the crew from Ashford River hadn't placed anywhere near that last year helped out, too. But I wasn't thinking about that after the race as we posed for a photo with our medals. I wasn't thinking about much.

I was just *there*, and it was a good place to be.

My legs were still shaking as we stood in the sun, the smell of river water and sweat rising from us, arms interlocked over shoulders. Brady stood beside us. Multiple flashes erupted from parents' cameras, and I was beaming. Mom and Dad waved. I saw Dr. Eldrin next to Dad, giving a big thumbs-up. Mrs. Speers was there too, and so was McNeal's mom, and the Andersons. My shoulders ached, the film of sweat on the back of my neck cooling in the breeze. After the shots were taken, there were hugs all around and slaps on the back and handshakes from Brady.

It wasn't first place, but that hardly mattered. Because, I realized, as we stood there together, we weren't Eldrin and Daniels and Speers, Derby and Alexander, McNeal, Anderson, Hasselwerdt, and Dwyer. We were a crew. The moment was solid. For a little while, I felt the glowing warmth of being very much a part of something bigger than myself.

■ ■ ■

We helped de-rig and load the boats onto the trailer, said good-bye to the crew, and exchanged handshakes with Brady, who shook his head and grinned at Trey, calling him "a real piece of work" and clapping him on the back. A few hours later, Trey and I were in the backseat of Dad's Caprice, headed for Buffalo. The sun was pale in the afternoon sky as we climbed onto the freeway, the river and the racecourse far below.

"We'll take you guys home first," Dad said, lowering the radio volume. "You can get cleaned up, and then I say this occasion warrants dinner out!"

"Sounds great, Mr. Derby." Trey was playing with the drawstring on his sweatshirt.

Mom turned around and looked at us. I could see the passing lane lines reflected in her glasses. "You guys did really great out there." She smiled. "Trey, it must be hard for your dad, being so far away. I bet he'd love to be able to see you race."

"Oh. Yeah. It would be tough for him to get off work anyway, I'm sure." He twirled the drawstring tight around his thumb. A semi passed, the high-pitched whine of its engine deafening for a moment.

"Well, we're happy to have you with us to celebrate. You guys will eat well tonight." She turned back around in her seat. "And you," she said, poking Dad in the gut, "hardly *need* to."

Dad threw me a look in the mirror, rolling his eyes. "She's got me pegged for a heart attack next Tuesday, bud."

"Your father's cholesterol is not exactly stellar."

"Sharon, I'm sure the boys are interested in *all* aspects of my health. Aren't you, guys? Shall we discuss my erectile functions next?"

"*Michael!*" snapped Mom, holding back a laugh.

"What? They're big boys."

I shook my head, looking out the window.

Trey was laughing. "My mom became a vegetarian last year after she read some article about heart attacks."

"That's probably not a bad idea for this guy, Trey," Mom said.

Dad turned around, looking at Trey with a grave expression. "Please don't give her any ideas."

"Would you mind looking at the road while you drive?" Her voice was flat.

"She helps me with my driving, too, as you can see."

I rolled my eyes. They always did this when I had friends around. *The Mom and Dad Show.* I used to imagine theme music. "So, Dad, what time are we leaving to go back to school tomorrow?"

"Oh. Your mom's gonna take you guys, champ. I have to go to this thing for work. 'Professional Day,' they call it. Mostly a bunch of us listening to speakers and acting unprofessional." He turned on the blinker and glanced over his shoulder, and we headed down an off-ramp.

"Hmm. So anyway, what time we leaving, Mom?"

"What time do you guys have to be back?"

"Supposed to be there by four. But we can be late."

"We should leave by nine or so. Traffic might be bad tomorrow."

Dad glared at her. "*Nine?* Are you planning on the scenic route? It is *not* a seven-hour drive, hon."

"I'm planning on driving at a legal speed."

"I drive at legal speeds."

"You drive at speeds legal in *Montana*, Michael."

Eyes in the mirror, brows raised. I smiled at my dad. Then I fell asleep.

# CHAPTER 16

"Here we are, guys." We pulled into the driveway.

I opened the door and looked up at my house, feeling something hard to describe. It looked different somehow, smaller maybe. *Tired.* I'd only been gone a couple months, but it *felt* different, too. The house was a squat, two-story colonial with a wide front lawn, nestled in between two similar homes on either side. The siding was good, but it needed a coat of paint—the off-white was chipped away in places, and the graying wood underneath was exposed near the eaves. Forest-green shutters framed the windows, sagging just a little on their hinges, and the concrete steps leading up to the porch were still cracked on the side where the railing was attached. A rusting push lawnmower leaned against the rail on the porch. Looking down past the corner toward Delaware Park, I could see rows of houses in the distance and the sunset burning red. A dog barked somewhere across the street. I saw Trey looking around, the faintest hint of a smile on his face.

Dad lifted our duffel bags out of the trunk while Mom climbed the steps, picking up the newspaper off the porch and opening up the front door. "Hon," she called, "make sure you bring in that cooler."

"Got it. Trey, this one's yours," he said, handing him the bag. "Here ya go, tiger," he said as he threw my bag to me. We climbed the steps, Dad between us with a hand on each of our shoulders.

Inside, my first impression was of the smell, which was weird, because I'd never been gone long enough before to notice it. I can't tell you what it was, but it was unmistakably *home*. I heard the creak of the heavy front door on its hinges, and the *clink* when Mom put the car keys in the little dish on the table in the foyer. Her shoes made a familiar clacking sound on the kitchen tile as she walked in. The grandfather clock in the living room struck six. Some kids were shouting as they played kickball down the street. These sounds had once been such a part of the daily rhythms of my life that I'd hardly heard them. Now, each was distinct and memorable. It struck me how quickly that had happened.

Trey, looking a little lost, stood close to me, the duffel bag dangling at his side.

"Matt, we set the cot up in your room for Trey," Mom called from the kitchen above the noise of the sink. She stepped out into the hall, drying her hands with a dish towel. "I turned the guest room into an office, so I'm afraid it's the cot tonight, Trey."

"That's fine, Mrs. Derby. Really."

"Good," said Dad. "Why don't you guys get settled in, and we'll plan on leaving at, say..." He looked at his watch. "...six thirty? That enough time?"

"Yeah. Come on." I climbed the stairs two at a time like I always had, switched on the light at the top, and led Trey through the narrow hallway to my room.

The neon sign glowed red: *The Buffalo River Pub*. I could read the letters, backward now, from our table against the wall. The place was dimly lit, and the reddish glow reflected off our glasses and silverware. The Goo Goo Dolls crooned from a stereo, and the exposed brick walls were covered with local paraphernalia, pictures of various mayors and Bills quarterbacks, line drawings of turn-of-the-century grain elevators, and sepia-toned images of War of 1812 regiments over the fireplace in the corner. Bills and Sabres pennants dangled from the ceiling, and a few signed jerseys hung on the walls. The place had a decent crowd, the bar across the room loud with clinking glasses and lively conversations. It was one of my parents' favorite hangouts, mostly because the food was great and it never got too loud. It was the kind of place you could have dinner and sit at a table in the early evening—even with your fifteen-year-old kid—before the bar crowd took over later at night. My dad said it was a "no bullshit kind of place."

*Home.*

Dad sipped a pint of Labatt's and mom a cup of coffee. Trey and I slouched in our chairs, empty plates in front of us, glasses of Coca-Cola fizzing with an occasional bubble.

"I'm just an old JV running back who barely made it through my sophomore season, guys," said Dad, leaning back in his chair, one hand holding the pint and the other extended around Mom's shoulder. "Never did anything like rowing. So tell me, what's the toughest part about it?"

Trey played with his fork, sliding it around on the empty plate as he squinted, thinking. "Honestly, probably Saturday practices. They're at seven."

"Seven on Saturday mornings," I repeated, recalling the day of the seven-mile run. *Super seven at seven on Saturday,* Brady had called it.

Mom smiled, sipping her cup of coffee. "Oh, come on. Seven's not *that* early."

"Your mother's halfway through kicking all the doctors around by seven most Saturdays," Dad said, giving her a peck on the cheek.

Trey continued, "As far as racing, it's the last minute or so. I've never hurt that much in my life. It's like your whole body just wants to explode."

"It really does use every muscle group," Mom added, "from what I can see."

I stirred my Coke with the straw, sending a flurry of carbonation to the surface. "The toughest part's the middle. By the end of it, I can hardly feel it. I kind of go into a zone. But the middle. Ouch."

"How competitive is it? I mean with you guys, to make the boat?" Mom asked.

"Well, with Regionals coming up it's gonna get tighter. It depends on who Brady decides to take up there," I said. "I think our fastest boat is a four."

"Your eight seemed pretty fast today, hon."

"Yeah, but there's some people in there that…well, we'd be more competitive if we took the fastest four guys and put them in a boat to row in that event, instead. Me, Trey, this kid Hasselwerdt, and McNeal."

Trey smiled, shrugging his shoulders. "That is, if I can keep my grades up. Brady's pretty strict about that."

"Well, I'm sure a bright kid like you can give it the old college try, right?" Mom smiled. I knew she was about to change the subject. The conspicuous sideways glance gave it away, the sharp inhalation. "Trey, will you go back to Lake Placid for Christmas?"

Trey continued his fork-on-the-plate game for a second, sliding a single remaining pea around the perimeter. He looked deep in thought or maybe just tired. "You know, I'm really not sure. Either there or at the place in Georgetown. Or it could be New York City. Guess I just don't know yet. It depends on my dad. But we always go to his place in the Bahamas for New Year's."

My eyes darted to my parents. I could feel the slight shift in their position on the seat, the tension in Dad's shoulders and the glance into the depths of his amber beer even as his expression remained fixed. I felt an odd heat between my shoulder blades, and Trey seemed to shrink a little into his seat. He set the fork down and stared at the pea. Mom reached for her coffee. *Another topic, please.*

"It must have been nice growing up in Lake Placid. I took a trip there once in college. Do you ski, Trey?"

He nodded. "Um, yeah. I used to a lot, with my dad. I snowboard more now." He stretched his shoulder, twisting around in the chair. "Hey, Mr.

Derby, Mrs. Derby, thanks so much for dinner. It was really good. I really like this place. It reminds me of a restaurant in Lake Placid I used to go to. It's off the main street and away from the touristy stuff." He smiled as he looked around at the brick walls and pictures hanging on them. "I get tired of all the hotshot restaurants in New York and Georgetown sometimes. They try too hard. This place is just real."

Dad put down the beer, sat up straight in his chair, and straightened out his jacket. "No problem. Glad to have you here. It's just an old local hangout. Matt's mom and I have been coming here for years."

"*Years*," I said in my best redneck voice, grinning at my mom. "We don't like change 'round these parts."

"Oh *stop it*, Matthew David. Trey, we should tell you about the time when Matt dumped a bowl of soup on his head. Right over there at that corner table. He was two."

Trey raised his eyebrows. I looked at the ceiling, humming the theme song in my head: *The...Mom and Dad...Show!*

"He didn't like the carrots," Mom continued.

"They were mushy carrots, Sharon. I don't blame him." Dad raised his arms, stretching. "So who's up for dessert?"

■ ■ ■

Back at home, The Rolling Stones sang about wild horses, the song drifting up from the speakers in the living room. Mom and Dad were reading the paper. Trey stood in front of my bedroom window, staring out at the dark street. The same dog barked again somewhere. I was putting some extra clothes into my duffel for tomorrow.

"Your parents are awesome." Trey's voice sounded strange, bouncing off of the window. He made a foggy patch on the glass. "They're so...I dunno, nice."

I paused, holding the T-shirt above the bag. "They're pretty cool."

"Nah, but seriously, Matt. Like, the way they talk, joke with each other and stuff."

I kept packing.

"What's your dad do?" he asked. "I forgot."

"Software company. He does regional sales for Western New York."

"How'd they meet?" Trey traced a line through the foggy cloud on the window. Drips trickled from his finger.

"They met in the navy."

"Really?"

"Yeah. Then they didn't see each other for a few years, and then they both went to Syracuse University. Just don't ask them about it or my dad will go on talking forever. Once he gets started about the navy, he never shuts the hell up."

"They don't seem like the military type. Especially your mom." Trey was playing with his silver medal from the race, swinging it around by the ribbon.

"Oh, they are, though. In a lot of ways, actually. Dad says Mom used to terrorize the officers down in Bethesda. She was stationed at the hospital down there. That's one of the reasons they liked the idea of me going to Ashford River. She knows the area." I zipped up the duffel bag and got into bed. "I don't know about you, man, but I'm beat."

"Yeah. I didn't even realize how tired I am." Trey put the medal on the floor next to his bag and climbed into the cot. "You think we have a chance at Regionals?"

"Uh-huh. Better if he prioritizes the four instead of the eight, though."

"That'd be pretty cool." I heard him shifting on the cot.

"Sorry, I know that thing's not too comfortable."

"It's okay. I could sleep on a rock after that race."

I turned out the light and lay there, staring at the ceiling for a while. It felt good to be in my own bed. I could hear the faint, indiscernible rumble of city sounds that was absent at school.

Trey's voice was quiet. "You guys always stay here for Christmas?"

"Yep. Every year. My grandparents and cousins come." I yawned, rolled over in the bed, and pulled the covers up tight.

The dog barked again.

"I bet it's really nice here at Christmas." Trey yawned too, his voice trailing off.

# CHAPTER 17

I sat on a bench in the field house locker room on a Wednesday afternoon, tying my sneakers and waiting for Brian, Mike, and Trey. We'd just finished up a test review in Miss Dillon's class. Brady had cancelled practice that day. The weather was terrible, and he had what he described as "an interminable stack of papers" to grade, so the four of us decided to do a weight-room workout. If we had understood anything about physiology, we would have known that a day off would have benefited us more, but try telling that to a sophomore in high school.

The locker room smelled like sweat, menthol, and dirty socks. A pair of khakis with a leather belt lay crumpled in the corner, and a stick of deodorant, missing its cap, sat on the oak bench. A few odd shoes were scattered around, and the single fluorescent tube sent a flat light over the navy-blue lockers and concrete floor. A few seniors came in and started to get changed. They talked loudly about their plans for the summer after graduation. One of them was Ralph Bradley. He was headed to Princeton in the fall; he'd been recruited for football and held the Ashford River record for rushing yards that season. I remember the Friday morning assembly when the assistant coach from Princeton came and spoke to the student body about the university and gave Bradley a wood-framed certificate of recruitment. Ralph had walked around the rest of the week acting like he was king of the school, but everyone said he'd been doing that for about four years, so it was no big deal.

He slapped me on the back as he headed toward the weight room.

"Hittin' the weights there, Derby?" He knew my name because we took the same Latin class. Bradley didn't do much work in Latin.

"Yeah. Just waiting for McNeal and Daniels. Hey, when does your training camp start for Princeton?" I stood up and stretched my arm, pulling my right elbow behind my neck.

"Too soon, man. Too soon. Starts up in mid-July. Gotta be ready, or they're gonna kick my Ashford River ass, if you know what I mean." Ralph chuckled as he turned the corner and disappeared.

"I guess so," I said to no one, rolling my eyes. I could hear Mike, Trey, and Brian coming down the hall toward the locker room, their voices growing louder and then suddenly clear as they stepped through the door.

"I still can't believe you got away with that, man," Trey was saying to Brian as they walked in. McNeal walked with a certain swagger. He had loosened his tie, and his shirt was un-tucked. He'd actually gotten in some trouble for the first time two weeks before, and he'd been wearing a Trey-esque, shit-eating grin ever since. It must have been a liberating experience for Brian to break a rule. It flipped some sort of switch in him. What he'd gotten away with—and the way he got away with it—was pretty funny.

It took all of us by surprise, and we were impressed by how ballsy it was. Apparently, McNeal had snuck out of his room over the course of a couple of nights. He'd run across the darkened quad to the junior hall and climbed onto the fire escape. His idea had been to get access to the roof. Why exactly he wanted to get to the roof remained a mystery for a while, until everyone realized what he had discovered while rescuing an errant Frisbee from up there: that from the roof, you could look through a vent cover and see directly into Mr. Pulaski's apartment. This would probably be of little interest except that Mr. Pulaski had started seeing Caitlin. She was a PhD student doing an internship with the school's finance office. Any guy at Ashford would agree that she was pretty attractive, but McNeal, for some reason, had taken a sort of obsessive interest in her. Rumor had it that she'd been seen leaving Mr. Pulaski's place—on more than one occasion—very quietly around four in the morning. So McNeal had done the math and figured out that there was a good chance of seeing Caitlin at a compromising moment (which carried with it the unfortunate possibility of also catching Mr. Pulaski at the same compromising moment, but there are, Brian explained later, risks to every endeavor). Sadly for McNeal, the moment never came. He did, however, manage to slip on a loose roof tile, which caused him both to cry out and knock a bunch of leaves from the gutter down so that they fell directly in front of Pulaski's window. This was well after midnight.

Now, Brian must have cried out loudly with the shock of slipping, and Pulaski must have been near the window at that particular moment. The teacher stuck his head out and caught McNeal—literally, by the leg—trying to climb back down the fire escape. But the story McNeal concocted in front of Dr. Winthrop and Mr. Wagner, after being dragged down to the dean's office the following morning, was brilliant. He'd been trying, he explained in his most penitent voice, to get to a place where he could try smoking a cigarette without getting caught by the teachers or made fun of by the other guys. You see, he'd never smoked before and didn't want to cough or look stupid.

This was a risky explanation, but the sheer brilliance of it soon became apparent.

Brian had gone on about how he was actually *glad* he got caught and how it would keep him from developing a stupid and dangerous habit like smoking. And, of course, the teachers were so distracted by the whole ongoing smoking issue that they didn't think to question this crock of absolute bullshit or to question why McNeal didn't have any cigarettes or matches on him. Beyond that, they were so happy to salvage the good judgment of a "good kid" like Brian McNeal that he really got nothing more than a slap on the wrist. McNeal wound up writing an essay about the addictive qualities of nicotine and had to pay for the damage he did to the roof tile. As if on cue, though, after-hours sightings of Caitlin ceased, which was a real disappointment all around, especially for Mr. Pulaski. As for him and Brian, they seemed to settle into a sort of amicable, unspoken truce. Brian hadn't mentioned Caitlin spending the night during his time in the disciplinary hot seat, and Pulaski left well enough alone, not giving Brian too much of a hard time about the rooftop incident. It was the sort of thing that happens at a boarding school. Every once in a while, the personal lives of students and teachers glance off one other, intersecting in awkward moments of mutual human weakness. Sometimes, the result is a student getting expelled; sometimes, it's a teacher getting fired. Sometimes, it's both. In this case, the Fates smiled on both teacher and student, and life continued on as though nothing had ever happened. Pulaski somehow managed to avoid Brian for the next two years, though. Brian never lived in his dorm, and he was never in his class. This was probably not coincidence.

I walked over to where they had thrown their bags on the floor of the locker room. Brian was laughing. "It could have been bad," he said. "Look what happened to Billy Mailer."

"That was bullshit," Trey said. "I still don't think they shoulda kicked him out without at least hearing his side of the story." I had no idea what they were talking about.

McNeal stood there in his khakis, unbuttoning his shirt. "What other side of the story is there to tell? He took the answer key right off Belknap's desk in his office the night before the test." He pulled his tie off as he continued. "He got ahold of the maintenance guy's keys, got in the office, and took it!"

"Whoa, when was this?" I asked.

"Just last night," Trey said, kicking off his school shoes.

"Pretty criminal," said McNeal as he put on a bright-orange *Virginia Beach* T-shirt.

"Pretty gutsy," I muttered.

"Pretty stupid," Trey said.

"No shit," said McNeal, tying his sneakers. "Makes my story seem innocent." He chuckled.

"I still can't believe they kicked him out," Trey said.

"Yeah, but that wasn't his first strike. He got caught with weed earlier in the year." McNeal looked up from his sneakers at Trey, his eyebrows raised. "I figured you'd have known about that."

Trey shrugged his shoulders. "Yeah, okay, maybe he did." This was the third expulsion so far this year. The first two were a couple of maladjusted freshmen who'd been sipping vodka out of Sprite bottles at a football game. They probably wouldn't have gotten caught, since they weren't really bringing much attention to themselves at first. Unfortunately, one of them got drunk enough to start shouting expletives at the opposing team, which raised some suspicions, as this was not normal for freshmen. The suspicions were confirmed as soon as one of them threw up all over the stands during a particularly exciting sixty-two-yard rush into the end zone. They might not have been expelled except that they then proceeded to get into a fight, during the course of which they threw enough drunken punches—at both fellow students and teachers—to seal their fate.

I threw my stuff into a locker and kicked it shut. "You guys ready?"

We headed into the weight room, Trey pulling on his T-shirt as we walked. Inside, the radio blared Nirvana. The room normally wasn't big enough for all the guys at school who wanted to use it, but today the only other people down here were Ralph Bradley and a couple of other seniors. Because it was in the basement of the field house, the only windows were narrow strips of glass block along the ceiling. They were dirty with early winter mud. The walls were painted navy to waist height and white above that, with a badly stenciled school seal on the middle of the back wall. The floor was rubberized tile, the weight benches and other equipment smudged and dented with age. Lifting belts and loose dumbbells lay scattered around the floor, looking neglected, despite Mr. Sharp's best efforts to keep them racked and organized.

"You guys want to start with benches this time?" I asked. This was sort of funny, since, like most guys, we put an inordinate amount of focus on bench presses.

"Sure." McNeal picked up a weight and slid it onto the bar. Trey did the same on the other side. "Whaddya wanna start at?"

Trey picked up another disk. "We started at one-fifteen last time, and then we worked down." He put the weights on the bar. "Let's do the same. You wanna go first?"

McNeal got down on the floor and did a quick ten push-ups to warm up. He stood up, stretching his arms and chest for a few moments, and then lay back on the bench, reaching up to grip the bar. "Spot me."

Trey stood behind him, his hands just below the bar. "Go ahead." He nodded.

Brian took a couple of deep breaths and pushed the bar up. His arms shook just a bit as he lowered it to his chest and then pressed it up. Trey counted for him. By the eighth one, McNeal's forearms were shaking, and the veins were visible. He winced and grimaced as he pushed his tenth lift. "That's it," he managed in a whisper as Trey helped him put the bar back on the rack.

"You only did eight of those last time," I said.

McNeal was taking a drink from his water bottle. "Yeah. Getting a little easier, I guess."

I got on the bench and pushed out eight, and Trey did the same. We took a break to stretch and get some water. We rotated like this for a while.

"Dillon's test is gonna be a bitch," McNeal said, taking a sip from his water bottle.

Trey stared at the ground. "Think it'll be bad?"

"It's all that grammar stuff. I screwed up the last two quizzes," said McNeal.

Rick Eldrin came in from the locker room, a Walkman clipped to the waistband of his shorts and headphones on. He was soaking wet and must have been out running in the rain. He put the headphones around his neck. "Hey, guys."

166

"'Sup, Rick," I said. Trey was doing a set of crunches on the ground while I spotted Brian doing dumbbell raises.

"I wouldn't be lifting today if I were you guys."

Trey finished his set. "Why's that, Rick?"

Eldrin shook some water out of his hair. "Cause we're erg testing tomorrow."

"Testing?" McNeal put the dumbbells on the ground.

"Yeah. I guarantee it. Brady's gonna test us tomorrow. Twenty minutes. Wants to figure out the top scores so he can put them in the four. So I don't think burning it today with a lift is a good idea if you wanna do well tomorrow."

McNeal looked at the rest of us. "Bullshit. He told us it'd be Saturday morning. Why would he do it tomorrow?"

"Because he just decided he's going to New York to visit his girl-friend—what's her name, Emily—for the weekend, and he wants to set the boats before he leaves. Coach Mackey'll be running practice on Friday and Saturday."

Trey began his second set of crunches, and his voice was strained. "How do you know that?"

"I heard him talking to Mackey this morning. He said he wants to set the boats so they can train together all weekend. Makes sense he'd do it tomorrow, too, since today was a day off."

■ ■ ■

Eldrin was right. The following day in the boathouse, Brady was looking at his clipboard when we came back from our warm-up jog.

"It's gotta be today, guys," he said. "I know I told you Saturday earlier in the week, but things have changed." We all knew about it by then, of course, thanks to Eldrin's announcement, so it wasn't a surprise. "Set 'em up for twenty minutes. This'll be the last test before Regionals." The room went quiet as we took our places on the rowing machines. Brady's last words before we started were, "Show me what you want."

Since rowing is not the most popular sport, most people have little appreciation for the intensity of it. It's hard enough on the water, but the ergometer brings a whole new measure of agony. Every muscle group is taxed. It hurts like nothing else I've ever done. I've gotten a lot better at it over the past six years, but it's never gotten easy. I have buddies at Georgetown—top athletes in different sports—who've tried to finish an erg workout, just to see what all the talk is about. One of two things invariably happens when they try. Most quit halfway through, claiming that it bothers their back. The ones who finish swear they'll never touch the damn thing again. And I'm talking about top athletes, including runners, swimmers, and gymnasts. There's something uniquely demonic about rowing. Why I've stuck with it is, sometimes, completely beyond me. That first twenty-minute test was a hurdle I will never forget. The pain of it was one thing. The duration, on the other hand, was what nearly shut me down. We'd done long rows on the water and even ten-minute pieces on the erg. But this was a new level of pain. This went on and on and on. It became a mental battle as much as a physical one—a constant effort to resist the powerful urge to stop. I honestly consider it one of the milestones of my life, finishing that first twenty-minute test at age fifteen. I'd never been pushed like that before.

Twenty minutes later, the group lay scattered around the room. It looked like the aftermath of an explosion. Some guys were on the floor panting; others were crumpled over the garbage can, puking up their lunch. Steam rose from our backs into the cool air. Brady walked around, reading the scores off the ergometers and marking down the numbers on his clipboard. He squinted at the tiny screens, his face responding to each score, either raising his eyebrows with approval or shaking his head. As we slowly got up and struggled over to the drinking fountain, starting to recover, he sat at the desk in the corner and tabulated the scores. After a few minutes, he tacked the rank sheet to the wall.

The list was penciled in his tiny, all-capitals print:

NAME (GRADE) / METERS

1. MCNEAL (10) / 5350
2. HASSELWERDT (10) / 5294
3. DERBY (10) / 5120
4. DANIELS (10) / 5108
5. ELDRIN (10) / 5087
6. ANDERSON (9) / 5014
7. ALEXANDER (10) / 5007
8. DWYER (10) / 5003
9. MARCHINSKY (9) / 4993
10. SMITH (10) / 4964
11. ELLIS (10) / 4933
12. GELDERMAN (9) / 4873
13. RUSSO (9) / 4722
14. LEONARD (9) / 4652
15. PITTS (9) / 4533
16. SCHWARTZ (9) / 4530
17. BRADY (9) / 4507
18. DEMARCO (9) / 4487

We crowded around the list. Brady spoke from the desk where he was seated.

"As of today, we'll be practicing a four and an eight. That's what we'll be rowing at Regionals. Final boat assignments won't be made until the end of the week, but for today, I'm going purely by erg score. That puts McNeal, Derby, Hasselwerdt, and Daniels in the four. Hasselwerdt, you'll be in stroke seat. We'll fill the eight from there. Eldrin, you stroke the eight. The bottom four on the list, as of now, will be alternates. Speers, you take the top four out."

Eldrin stared at the floor, his jaw muscles clenched.

Brady focused on the four during practice. He sent the eight off with Coach Mackey, and we all knew that meant it was second priority. The coaching launch idled next to us as we drifted to a stop after the warm-up. Brady brought it close so he didn't have to speak through the megaphone.

"Gents, remember that you're not locked into these positions. You're the strongest four guys on the erg, and I also think you row well together. Trey, you've come a long way technically, but you're only a few meters ahead of Eldrin, which is not necessarily enough to make a definitive difference. So I'll say it again: nothing is set. You guys will have to stay on top of your game if you want to stay in the boat. I don't want to see any elitist bullshit. And the grades, guys—the grades have to stay up." He looked directly at Trey when he said that. "Okay, Jimmy. Let's get them up to speed, and we'll go six minutes at race pace."

The rest of practice went well. We rowed together, and the balance and timing were good. We did a total of five full-intensity pieces, six minutes each. At the end of the last one, we finished "on the fly," which meant we stopped rowing and locked our handles against the gunwales. When we did this, the boat cruised along with blades raised in the air like the wings of a dragonfly, perfectly balanced. We held the position for almost a full minute, which isn't easy to do in a four. By the end of just one practice, the five of us in the boat realized that we'd struck on something unusual in rowing: a lineup that had true chemistry. We had a natural sense of timing and rhythm that just clicked. After several more years of rowing, I've learned not to underestimate this intangible quality, and now I understand why Brady wanted to keep the lineup as it was, even though Rick Eldrin might have been the more logical choice. We had discovered the elusive element that makes a boat move faster than the sum of its rowers. Brady understood this. And while I can't say that we *understood* it as sophomores in high school, there was no question that we *felt* it that day on the water, and we didn't want to change a thing.

The guys in the eight were not so happy—especially Rick Eldrin.

"How was the four?" he asked, turning on the shower in the boathouse locker room after practice.

I rinsed the shampoo out of my hair, turning to Rick. "It was pretty solid." Our voices were raised over the sound of the water, and they echoed on the tile.

"The eight is a complete joke."

"Hey, Eldrin," said Dwyer, one of the other sophomores in the eight, "maybe if you'd stop messing around and take it seriously, it wouldn't be such a joke."

Eldrin glared at Dwyer. "Jesus Christ! You think I'm the problem? Marchinsky's only been rowing for two weeks, and Smith can't even put his blade in the water without fucking us up. It's a waste of my time."

Hasselwerdt had been quiet up until then. "Sure, Rick. Blame the freshmen." This got some chuckles from the rest of us.

Dwyer followed that, saying, "You're not exactly an Olympian yourself, Eldrin."

"I'm at least as good as the stoner in their bow seat," he shot back at Dwyer, glaring at Trey.

Trey squinted and turned to face him. "You got a problem with me, Rick?"

"Yeah, Trey, I do. We all have a problem with you. You can't be relied on." Rick slammed the knob on his shower off and then turned as he ripped his towel off the hook and wrapped it around his waist. He stabbed the air with his finger, pointing at Trey, his voice acid. "Brady's wasting that spot on him, and you guys know it. He's close to failing two classes. He isn't gonna last. What are you guys gonna do when you've practiced that lineup for weeks, and then he suddenly gets pulled off the team for failing in school? You want stability in a boat! He isn't stable! You notice his parents never come to any races? You notice his parents weren't even here when he moved in?" He looked directly at Trey. "You're just not gonna last here, man. Watch and see. You're a short-term investment. A fucking bad one."

Trey stood under the shower unmoving, his eyes closed. No one said anything else. Part of me wanted to deck Eldrin right then and there, but I decided it wasn't worth it. Besides, all I could think about was what he'd said about Trey's parents. We did our best to ignore what he'd said, got dressed, and trudged up the hill to dinner.

# CHAPTER 18

The team began to refer to the group of us as "the sophomore four." This is an oddity of rowing parlance, since including the coxswain and rowers, a "four" is actually a crew of five. And, as often happens among rowers who have discovered that elusive chemistry I mentioned, we began doing things together as a boat. This included studying, since we now realized that each other's grades were as much a factor in sticking together as our performance on the water. One morning, we were up extra early, studying in our room before school for Miss Dillon's English test. Alarm clocks were going off down the hall.

"I'm screwed," said Trey, slamming his pen down.

Mike turned around in the desk chair. "It's not gonna be that hard."

"If I fail this test, I'll be failing my second subject. That'd knock me off the team." He stood up and paced back and forth, swinging a lacrosse stick through the air.

"Yeah, but it's not gonna be that hard," repeated McNeal.

Trey stopped and leaned in close to him. "I don't know *any* of this shit, Brian."

I closed my book, stood up, and leaned against the window looking out. The grounds crew was already well into their work outside, raking leaves and mowing the wide expanse of lawn on the hill. The sound of the lawnmower faded as they moved away.

Trey continued, "If I fail this, Brady's gonna kick my ass out and stick Eldrin in. You guys know it."

"It's gonna be multiple choice, right?" asked Mike. "How hard can it be?"

"I still don't know *any* of it." He slammed the lacrosse stick against his mattress.

"It's one of those bubble sheets," I said. My voice was low. They all turned to me.

"So *what?*" Trey shot back.

"So it's graded by a machine." Something criminal had just clicked in my head. It both thrilled and scared me. It took me by surprise, and I felt a certain rush of energy. Maybe it was the mental equivalent of adrenaline. I'm not sure, but there was something thrilling about how clearly the details coalesced and lined themselves up, the intricacies and contingencies. It all just flowed together.

Trey looked up, squinting. McNeal cocked his head. Hasselwerdt looked at a spot on his book.

I stared at the floor, my voice lower. "There won't be any handwriting on it. All you write is your name on the bubble sheet." I paused. "I could... put Trey's name on my test."

"Huh?"

I looked at Trey, and the words came out fast. "I just put your name on my test, and you put my name on your test, and Dillon won't ever know."

Trey clenched his jaw.

"But...that'd mean you'd fail," said Mike.

"No way, man. You'll be screwed," added Brian.

"Wouldn't matter. My grade's high enough already. I'll still get almost a ninety for the semester, even if I fail it." As I said this, I realized that this would keep me off of first honors for the semester. This was something I'd worked hard to accomplish, more so for mom and dad than for myself.

"She'd never believe it. If Trey does well and you fail, she'll know something's up," Mike said.

"Not if we make it believable."

"Whaddya mean?" asked Trey.

"I mean I'd have to make it just passing. Not too high. High seventies, low eighties."

"But what about you?" Trey's voice came out loud, probably louder than he meant it to. He looked over his shoulder at the door. He whispered, "There's no way she'll believe that you messed it up that badly! Oh yeah, Matt Derby with the ninety average suddenly lands a sixty on a test. That'll really fly." He threw the lacrosse stick to the corner.

I picked it up, spinning it in my hands as the deceptive plan kept forming in my mind. "I'll just tell her I felt sick this morning. And that I haven't really studied much. I'll blame all the rowing we're doing lately. I'll just mess up for a change. Is it really *that* hard to believe?"

"What if she looks at the names? We still have to write each other's names."

"But she won't be looking for anything, Trey. You think she's gonna catch on and do a handwriting analysis?" I asked.

"She might," said Brian.

"No, she won't. Think about it. As long as we don't make his grade too high, she's gonna have no reason to suspect anything."

Trey sat down on the floor and pulled his knees to his chest. "No. No way. It won't work."

"Derby, this isn't like you," said Mike, laughing nervously. "It's goddamn *criminal*, man."

I exhaled loudly. "It'll work. She won't notice it. She teaches seniors, too. And their thesis papers were due yesterday. Believe me, she's got her hands full with those."

"It's stupid." Brian shook his head.

"It won't work," said Trey. "And what about first honors? That doesn't matter to you all the sudden?"

I slammed the stick against the door. "No, it does matter. I'm trying to help you out! You say it won't work? Well, it has to! Jesus Christ, do you want to be in the boat with us or not?" My face was flushed. "Look, I don't like it either, but there's not much choice."

"Otherwise, Eldrin's in," muttered Mike. "Matt's right. Trey and Rick are basically dead even on the erg and on the water. Brady's only keeping us together because he knows it clicked, but chemistry only goes so far. He won't have a choice if Trey's knocked out."

"We're all screwed if you get caught. All *four* of us, not just you two," said McNeal.

Mike's voice was low. "But that's exactly what this is about, Brian, the *four* of us." He cracked his knuckles. "It's a decision-making juncture."

Silence. We looked at the floor.

My heartbeat felt like a series of dropkicks to the stomach.

Trey looked up at us. His jaw was clenched tight. "It is just one test, right?" His eyes darted among the group.

"Just one test versus Regionals. What we've worked for all season." Hasselwerdt's voice became a whisper. "McNeal, you know how fast that boat is moving right now. We were flying out there yesterday. Brady's psyched. If we change anything now, we'll lose that."

"Especially if he puts Eldrin in," I said. "I don't want to pull hard for that prick."

"Me neither," said Brian. Hasselwerdt nodded. "It'll screw everything up."

We were quiet for a minute; we could hear the traffic report on Brady's TV down the hall.

"We should practice writing each other's names a couple times," said Trey. "Just in case."

Whatever criminal gears had leveraged this plan kept turning in my mind. "We have to be sure that we mix up the order of the tests when we hand them in."

"Whaddya mean?" asked Brian.

"There's only eighteen of us in the class. Miss Dillon might notice who hands his test in last. What if it's Trey or me? We have to be sure she can't notice the names not matching. We have to 'accidentally' knock the stack of answer sheets to the ground, so they get mixed up."

"Do we tell Speers?" asked Mike.

"Christ, no." Brian hissed. "This is already screwed up enough with four of us involved. We need him thinking straight to steer straight."

■ ■ ■

I could feel heat rising from my chest and sweat trickling down my arms as I filled in the small circles with the pencil. Miss Dillon sat at the desk at the front of the room, hands folded, watching us. I looked down at the space marked "Name." It was still blank. The pencil made a dull scratching noise as I filled in the bubbles.

*Careful. Make it believable. Not too high. God, this test is easy.*

I stole a glance at Trey, two rows over to my left and ahead. He was hunched over the paper, his toes tapping quietly on the floor. Someone coughed. A chair creaked. Outside, a groundskeeper ran a leaf-blower on the other side of the quad. Hasselwerdt was behind me, McNeal in the far corner. Eldrin sat in the front row.

Twenty minutes passed. One minute to the bell. Frantic scribbling around the room. I finished and quickly wrote Trey's name in the box the way I had practiced. My hand covered it casually as I stared at the eraser on my pencil.

The bell rang, and with it erupted the cacophony of chairs being pushed back and papers rustled. Eighteen students stood up, a few bending to put their names on at the last minute. I got in the line that formed at her desk. Each guy put his answer sheet down and shuffled out the door. Trey and McNeal were ahead of me.

*Mix up the order.*

I put my test down, and with a subtle flick of the wrist, caught the stack of papers with my watch. The whole pile fell, scattering, to the floor.

I muttered an apology, and three other kids helped me pick them up. I handed the stack to Miss Dillon.

"Are you all right, Matt?" She put a hand on my arm, pulling me aside. Her touch felt cool on my burning skin. I saw Trey out of the corner of my eye, filing out of the room with the rest. He paled as he noticed Dillon talking to me. McNeal looked over his shoulder as he walked out the door.

"Yeah, I..." My knees felt weak. "I just don't think I did very well. I'm really not feeling too good today. I threw up last night."

*I'm gonna throw up right now.*

She pursed her lips. "Get some rest. I'm sure you did okay. You know this stuff. You're just doing too much lately, Matt. I bet things will be easier on you guys when the crew season is over."

I nodded quickly, smiling weakly as I headed out the door. "Hope so."

*Get me the hell out of here.*

■ ■ ■

That really was the only time I cheated in high school. The raw simplicity of the plan still amazes me, as does the irony that I did it to raise someone else's grade. I remember times later on when the opportunity was there, when I easily could have raised my grades and saved myself hours of work. But I could never bring myself to do it again.

It wasn't out of some valiant sense of honor; I think it was more out of pure shame—not for the act itself, but more because it reminded me of Trey, and I realized this was a significant turn of events leading to his downfall. I learned in the weeks following that day that a conscience was a potent thing, able to torture a guy more than most anything else. This may have set me apart from some of my classmates, and it might be the reason why I didn't have too many close friends at Ashford River. Of course, a lot of guys there really didn't cheat, either. It was and remains a good school full of mostly honest, hardworking students. But for a good number of guys, cheating simply became ubiquitous, a sort of cultural norm. By the time we were juniors, it took on a sort of comical insignificance in the quest for marketable grades. There were occasional crackdowns, and from time to time, one of the more honorable students in the class would stand up and make some noise about it. Nothing really changed in the long term, though. The real irony of it is that most of those who did cheat were smart enough to pull it off, which meant they were smart enough not to need to in the first place. So when you do the math, you realize it equated to pure and utter laziness. They did it instead of doing their work because they *could*.

I never cheated again, though. It made me feel cheap and hollow, even if I did it thinking I was helping someone. Of course, I know now that a single test grade hardly would have made any difference for Trey. Yes, he would have been taken out of the boat if he'd failed that test, sure. But considering the changes he faced in the next few months and years, it probably wouldn't have mattered.

■ ■ ■

As it turns out, the Sophomore Four won gold at Regionals by 1.8 seconds in the final after a pretty tough push in the last two-fifty. The eight had a good race but finished fourth in the six-boat final. They'd raced earlier in the morning and then headed back to school. Our race was one of the last ones of the day, so we had the good fortune of a trip home without the brooding company of the other crew. The only race later than ours was the varsity eight, and they came away with a third-place finish, which was a major accomplishment given the tough competition in that event. We stayed to watch the older guys race, cheering them on at the finish line. Then we de-rigged and loaded the boats onto the trailer.

Now we were on our way, quiet and exhausted in the back of the school's Suburban, gold medals around our necks. I watched the sun set behind the hills as we headed south on 95. I turned the medal over in my hands, feeling the weight of it. Brady tapped out the rhythm of a lame country song on the steering wheel; Speers rode shotgun with his feet up on the dashboard. Mike was passed out next to me, and Trey and Brian lay sleeping, each stretched across a row of seats. I looked at the regatta program and saw our names listed: "Speers, McNeal, Derby, Hasselwerdt, Daniels." We were the Junior Varsity Four with Coxswain. Capital Area Regional Champions.

I smiled, watching the sky turn to dusk, not thinking about English tests, Miss Dillon, decision-making junctures, or even Rick Eldrin. In fact, all I thought about was seeing Natalie that night.

# CHAPTER 19

Before leaving for the regatta, Trey and I had signed up for the van trip to Bethesda on Saturday night. Since it was an "out-weekend," most students had left, and this was just about the only activity planned. That was fine with us. The van was scheduled to depart from the steps of MacKerry Hall at six thirty, right after dinner. It would drop us off in downtown Bethesda in front of the movie theater and would be back for a pickup at eleven. The general idea was, of course, to see a movie, and that was what the other guys planned to do.

Trey and I were there to see a movie, yes, but we had a higher priority. We were there to meet our swimming partners.

Crew and school had dominated most of our free time over the previous two weeks, but the memory of our escapade with Nicole and Natalie remained vivid, and we'd tried on a couple of occasions to get out to see them. The closest we came was almost getting a ride from Steve Mallow to a St. Amelia's swim meet. That fell through. But finally, through his networking prowess, Trey was able to find Nicole's home number and make arrangements for us to meet her and Natalie in front of the movie theater in Bethesda at 7:30 on Saturday.

I looked at my watch as we stood outside the theater. The other guys had long since bought their tickets and headed inside. It was quarter to eight. It was a surprisingly cold night, and I shivered in my sweatshirt. "I think we got stood up."

"You are a pessimist," he said.

"I'm a cold pessimist."

"We just won Regionals. Girls are on their way. These facts should warm your soul."

I rolled my eyes and wrapped my jacket tighter around me.

Just then, Nicole and Natalie hurried toward us from the metro station across the street. They ran up and gave us big hugs. "Oh my God, guys! We haven't seen you in, like, *so* long!" As Natalie gave me a kiss on the cheek, all the sensations from the dance came rushing back and made me a little bit dizzy. She was wearing the same citrus-scented perfume, and it washed over me, even out there on the breezy sidewalk. Trey smiled and winked at me.

We wound up going to the movie, which was funny but not particularly memorable. What was memorable was holding Natalie's hand. But what was even more memorable was what happened while I was drinking a chocolate milkshake afterward.

There was a soda bar across from the movie theater, a sort of gourmet ice-cream shop with wood-paneled walls, a jukebox, and an old-fashioned counter with upholstered metal bar stools. It was packed with people, mostly kids. Smashing Pumpkins blared on the radio. There were round tables with high-backed chairs along the front windows, and that was where the four of us sat. We each had a malted shake in a tall glass. Trey had put M&M's in his peanut-butter shake, and the girls both had vanilla with a cherry. It had gotten windier outside and had begun to pour. The wind was buffeting the windows with sheets of rain. They were steamy from the warmth inside, and the bluish glow from a neon ice-cream cone glistened in the tiny droplets.

Nicole was in the middle of recounting the moment when her teacher opened the door to the pool that night, when Rick Eldrin and a few guys from the eight came sauntering in. They hadn't come to Bethesda with us, but the soda bar was a popular spot after the movies. Eldrin saw us immediately. He came up and put a hand on each of our shoulders. Trey and I both stood up.

"It's the big champs," he said. It seemed to me he might have been drinking. I thought there was just a little bit of slur in his speech, but I couldn't say for sure. "What's up, boys?"

"Hey, Rick. This is Nicole and Natalie," said Trey. "Ladies, this is Rick Eldrin. We were just on our way out."

"These guys tell you they just won a big, big, big race?" Rick asked. The "big, big, big" assured me he was, in fact, at least a little drunk.

"No," said Natalie, turning to me. "You had a race this weekend?"

I looked out the window. "Yeah, we won Regionals in the JV four."

"That's awesome," replied Nicole. "Are you a rower, too, Rick?"

"Yeah. I've actually been doing it for a couple years now. I—"

"Well, we should get going," Trey said, cutting Rick off as we worked our way to the door.

Eldrin looked surprised. "Why don't you guys stick around with us? We can all—"

"Nah," said Trey, stepping closer to the door.

More kids flew past us on their bikes outside. We were walking out the door, and I was just thinking about how nice it would have been if Rick Eldrin hadn't shown up. Then it happened.

One of the kids riding by must have caught a pothole in the sidewalk. His bike swerved into the street, skidded, and then crashed to the ground a few feet from the curb. The boy was sprawled next to it, dazed. The headlights from the approaching truck lit up his wide eyes. He was frozen. The headlights grew brighter and glinted on the chrome of the bike's wheels. They illuminated a jagged red cut on his forehead. One second, Trey had been pushing open the door; the next, he was outside in the street, the rest of his milkshake splattering on the sidewalk where he dropped it. Then the blur that was Trey scooped the kid up by his midsection, twisted, and half pushed, half threw him out of the street. Trey, almost in midair, caught a glancing blow to the elbow from the truck's side mirror. In the same instant, the truck's front passenger wheel crushed the bike frame, grinding it hard into the wet asphalt, throwing sparks as it lurched to a stop.

I rushed outside ahead of Rick, the girls, and a few other kids from the soda bar. Trey had landed, peculiarly, in a seated position on the curb next to the boy, as though both of them were just sitting there, waiting for the next bus. The driver came around the front of the pickup, running. He was a young man in an army dress uniform. He looked panicked. The boy's head was bleeding, but the scariest thing was his breathing. He took quick, shallow breaths that sounded labored, and his eyes were open wide.

"...Inhaler..." he managed, frantically feeling in his pockets and looking nervously at Trey. "...Asthma...need my..."

Trey padded the kid's pockets then looked up. "It's not here." There was urgency in his voice, but he was oddly calm. He looked around for a few seconds. "Matt. There, in the street."

I spotted the inhaler where he pointed, and grabbed it, handing it to Trey. Trey lifted it to the boy's mouth, and he took a deep puff. The kid's breathing slowed as Trey sat, holding him, his arm around his shoulders. Meanwhile, the staff of the shop had called for an ambulance, and before long, a police car's red and blue lights illuminated the scene. The officer called the boy's mother, and the soldier, visibly shaken, backed his truck off of the crushed bike. The ambulance arrived a few minutes later and EMT's examined both the boy and Trey. Amidst all of the confusion, there's one image that remains perfectly clear in my mind: Trey, his wet hair plastered down his forehead, sitting in the back of the ambulance next to the frightened boy, holding his hand. When he glanced up at me, standing outside, his eyes looked perfectly calm. He smiled for a moment and then whispered something in the boy's ear. When the kid's panicked mother arrived, Trey clambered quietly out of the ambulance and stood next to us. Nicole gave him a hug. I stood there with my arms hanging at my sides, not knowing what to say.

After a few minutes, Mr. Wagner arrived with the school Suburban for the scheduled pickup, the situation obviously taking him completely by surprise. He spoke briefly with the cop and the medics before approaching the group of us huddled in the rain.

"Trey! Are you all right?"

"Yeah. Fine. Just banged my elbow."

"You realize you just saved that kid's life, son?"

As if on cue, the boy's mother rushed over to Trey. Her eyeliner was streaked down her face. "I don't know how to thank you. He...sometimes he can't breathe, and..." She kissed his forehead, shook her head with a desperate expression, and then quickly turned and went back to her boy. We all just sort of stood there looking at Trey as the ambulance drove away. He put his hands in his pockets, said good night to the girls, and walked quietly toward the Suburban. I was left standing there with Natalie and Nicole. I said a hurried good-bye to both of them and followed Trey to the truck. Eldrin and the rest of the guys he was with scattered, avoiding Mr. Wagner.

When we got back to the dorms, Trey used Dean Wagner's office phone to call his mom. I didn't hear their conversation. After a little while, he came up to our room.

I stood up when he came in. "I can't believe what you did."

He looked at me. "Why? I mean, really, why?"

"It's just...I dunno, Trey. You *saved* that kid!"

"Anyone would've," he said as he got undressed.

"But no one else did. *You* did. Did you tell your mom?" I asked.

"Yeah." He threw his jeans into the pile of laundry in the corner. "That elbow's gonna be sore. Shit."

"What about your dad?"

"Couldn't get him. He's in Europe or something. She'll tell him when she talks to him." He threw his socks on the pile. "Man, we gotta do laundry soon."

"Huh?"

"I'm tired," he said and climbed up to his bunk. "Mind hitting the light?"

"Yeah. Um, sure."

I lay in bed for a long time that night, staring out the window, still hearing the sound of the truck tires crushing the bike. Trey snored in the bunk above me.

■ ■ ■

His actions didn't go unnoticed.

First of all, the parents made a point of visiting the school with their son early the following day. Trey met them downstairs before the start of chapel. They wanted to thank him personally. Their boy, Nick, was ten and had been on his way home from the movies with his friends. Aside from a deep cut on his forehead, a bruised knee, and a sprained wrist, he was unhurt. He handed Trey an envelope, and I saw later that it contained a short note written in the boy's awkward script. It said, "Dear Trey: Thank you for saving me. I probably would have been smooshed by that truck. And then I couldn't breathe until you helped. I will be a lot more careful now on my bike. You are a really good guy. —Nick."

Dr. Winthrop made a point of addressing the heroics at chapel, commenting on Trey's lack of hesitation in the face of a crisis situation. There was a lot of applause. Trey squirmed through the whole thing. He hated this. I could tell. Father Daley avoided heaping more praise on Trey at Mass, though he couldn't resist giving an extra-approving smile when he came up for Communion. Brady pulled him aside that same evening during study hall and spoke in hushed tones. At the end of the conversation, he shook his hand and squeezed his shoulder. Trey walked back to his desk and buried his head in his Latin book.

There was a small article in Monday's local paper, which I cut out and pinned to the bulletin board above his desk. He took it down and put it in his drawer when he thought I wasn't looking. Nicole called him on the hall phone, but he didn't talk much. I overheard the conversation from our room. He said he needed some time to get caught up with school and that maybe he'd see her soon. I talked with Natalie once after that, but we didn't see each other again. Trey's dad also mailed him another copy of the newspaper article, which a work acquaintance had apparently sent to him over the wires. Underneath the photocopy he'd written, "Great job, son!" Nothing more. Trey stuffed that one in the desk drawer as well.

Things were strange for a few days that week. Both teachers and students noticed when Trey walked by. They said hello to the celebrity. Eldrin left him alone, and Steve Mallow seemed to have a new respect for him. He didn't want to talk about it with me, and I avoided bringing it up when we were in our room. Eventually, the distractions of classes and routines of school took over. The buzz died down. Trey seemed relieved. The only constant reminder of the whole thing was Nick's thank-you note, which he kept tacked on his bunk. He never did talk to his father about it, at least not as far as I knew.

I kept wondering what he'd whispered in that little kid's ear in the ambulance, but for some reason I'm not sure of, I didn't ask him.

# CHAPTER 20

After a few weeks, as we neared the end of November and entered the tedious, dark days that preceded winter, hardly anything was exciting at all. The days blurred together as they got progressively shorter, and a general sort of boredom settled on the campus after the end of fall sports. The excitement surrounding Trey's heroics had long since subsided.

Library study hall eventually became the bane of our existence at Ashford River. It wouldn't have been so bad if it weren't so long, but part of the school's "Commitment to a Strong Foundational Work Ethic" demanded the nightly academic equivalent of a forced march. The juniors and seniors had the privilege of in-room study hall, but underclassmen needed closer supervision. The freshmen were in The Hampshire Room each night, and we sophomores had the library. But no matter where you were, by late November, two hours of study hall was really damn long. We got a fifteen-minute break at eight o'clock, the halfway mark. I had just finished my Latin, and now I was hanging tough, glancing at the clock hanging on the far wall.

7:52.

*Come on.*

I sat at the end of the ancient study table, absently tracing my pencil eraser across a deep scratch in the varnished surface, listening to the wind whipping the branches outside. It was just starting to rain, and a few fat drops splattered against the window. The library had its own smell: the mustiness of old books mixed with the coppery, static air of a room full of computers. Brady had us at the end of a whip during study hall tonight, two weeks after mid-semester progress reports, or *regress reports*, as he liked to call them, and the library was as silent as it could be with sophomores in it—coughs, sneezes, sniffles, the zippers on backpacks, shuffling papers, but no talking, not even whispers. Usually, there was a pretty consistent hum of commotion, but Brady and DiVincenzo really let loose on us after dinner, talking in grave, no-bullshit voices about mediocrity, potential, and expectations.

I leaned back in my chair, stretching my arms overhead until I heard my shoulders and back crack and looked around. The library was not that big, maybe about the size of five or six classrooms put together. But it seemed larger in the dimness of study hall. The walls and ceiling were paneled with dark oak, and area rugs covered most of the pine floor, varnished over the years to a dull sheen. Long tables were arranged kind of like the ones in The Hampshire Room, and we sat spread out, five or six to a table. There were fluorescent lights in the ceiling, but Mr. Brady always turned them off in favor of the small desk lamps at each table. They were old-fashioned banker's lamps with translucent green shades. Small halos of bright but confined light hovered under each. We wore comfortable clothes like sweats and rugby shirts, hunched over history texts and math workbooks. I'd often find myself leaning back, staring at the ceiling. The lacquered wooden paneling looked black in the greenish glow from the lampshades. The place had the feel of a vast subterranean chamber at night.

Along the far wall, banks of computer carrels held machines, most of them in power-save mode, indicator lights glowing in the dark. Jimmy Speers was sitting at one of them typing a paper, his spiky hair silhouetted against the bluish screen. The fireplace in the corner had a gas flame insert, but it *looked* real and it reminded me of home at Christmas, which was still five weeks away. Five weeks. More than a month. Almost forty days. A vast expanse of time. Biblical proportions.

7:57.

*Jesus Christ.*

Brady sat in one of the leather recliners by the fireplace reading the *Washington Post*. I couldn't see his face, but I knew he'd be peering over the top of the paper periodically, keeping an eye on things. He was probably confident that we wouldn't mess with him too much tonight after the stern talking-to he'd given us. Brady shifted his forearm to look at his watch, undoubtedly synchronized precisely with the school clocks. The man wouldn't call break even a minute early. It was a Brady thing. Not 7:58. Not 7:59.

*Eight-o-clock is eight-o-fucking-clock.*

Rick Eldrin and Mike Hasselwerdt were scribbling furiously in their math workbooks.

Jimmy Speers leaned in close to the computer screen, squinting, his face just inches from the monitor.

McNeal leaned back in his chair wearing a threadbare Redskins T-shirt, flexing and unflexing his biceps, examining them, a pencil held between his teeth.

Redford colored in his diagram of the tectonic plates for science class.

7:59.

Trey, at the next table with his back to me, sat on the edge of his seat, his neck craned to look out the window at the rain. He was nibbling on the drawstring of his sweatshirt.

The minute hand on the clock shifted with a *click*, and I let my chair rock forward, slamming my feet back on to the ground. Brady said, "Take a break, gents. Back by quarter after eight. Don't be late." But the "don't be late" got lost in the noise of the roomful of guys standing up, slamming books shut, and making for the doors of the library. I set my pencil down on the table and headed for the bathroom.

The window was cracked a few inches, and I could hear the rain falling on the bushes outside as I stood at the urinal. When I was finished,

I stepped back into the hall outside the library. Rick Eldrin was tossing a tennis ball back and forth with Chase, bouncing it once on the floor between them.

"'Sup, Rick?" We had something of an uneasy truce following the events of a few weeks ago.

"Nothing. Hey, your pal the hero must be in trouble or something," he said, pitching the ball against the wall. Chase ran to catch it on the rebound.

"Whaddya mean?" A quick series of possibilities shot through my mind.

"Check it out." He caught the ball with a loud *thwap*. "Brady's got him in a little conference or something. Maybe he finally got nailed for the weed, huh? Had to happen sooner or later."

I left Eldrin in the hall, opened the glass door, and stepped back into the dim light of the library. It was empty except for a few kids still sitting at their desks, heads buried in books or craned over homework. Trey, however, was standing over by the fireplace with Mr. Brady, both of them leaning against the mantel and talking closely in hushed voices. Trey had his hands shoved deep in the pockets of his sweatshirt and was staring at the blue and orange flames dancing behind the protective glass. Brady was holding a steaming coffee mug. His other hand made gestures in the air, his wide eyes and raised eyebrows seeming to say something like, *"So, where does this leave us?"* I couldn't hear what they were saying, but Brady was doing most of the talking. Trey, his shoulders visibly tensing, shifted uncomfortably on his feet and nodded. After a minute, Brady pulled a small envelope from his back pocket and handed it to Trey.

Trey walked over to his table and sat down, opening the envelope. I watched as he ripped little pieces of the flap off, tossing them on the table. He pulled out a single piece of paper with a short paragraph of typed text, but I couldn't see what it said. He seemed to read it a few times and then looked up at the window before stuffing it into his pocket. He got up to walk out of the library.

I glanced at the clock on the wall. 8:11.

"Trey." I tugged on his sleeve as he passed me.

"Huh. Oh. I didn't even see you." His voice sounded tight.

"What's goin' on?"

Trey grinned. "I'll tell ya what's goin' on. I have gotta *piss*. Back in a sec." He broke into a little jog and scampered out the door into the hallway.

Brady yelled from behind his paper, "Three minutes, guys. Tell your pals in the hallway to get back in here on time."

I stood up and walked over to the door.

"Derby, make sure everyone is getting back in here. I've got no patience for bullshit tonight," Brady said, not looking up from the newspaper.

"Okay."

Eldrin and Chase had moved the tennis ball game outside, and I could see their blurred figures through the patterned glass window at the end of the hallway. Redford, Speers, McCarthy, and Dan had joined in too. Muffled shouts and laughter. I opened the door to the bathroom. Trey was standing in the corner, leaning against the windowsill.

"Hey."

He lifted the arm of his sweatshirt, using it to wipe his nose and eyes before he turned his head around. His eyes were wet and bloodshot, and he took in a few sharp breaths.

"Hey."

"What's goin on?"

"Nothing." He walked over to the sink and splashed water on his face. "Just the usual shit."

"Whaddya mean? Here." I grabbed a crumpled handful of paper towels from the dispenser and handed them to him. "What was the deal with Brady?"

Trey took a deep breath, closed his eyes, and exhaled, leaning heavily on the sink with both hands. The running water sent steam up past his face, clouding the mirror. "My father wants to know why I'm not applying myself."

The steam billowed.

"Oh. Is that it?" Some cowardly part of me was relieved. I thought it might have been about the cheating.

Trey let out a stifled laugh that sounded more like a snort. "Well, no, that's not the good part. My dad really wanted to have a good father-son chat about this, you know?"

"Huh."

"So he sent Mr. Brady a fax to give to me."

"Oh."

"A *fax*, Matt," Trey said, his voice rising through almost-clenched teeth. "He can't call me. He sends a damn fax instead." The tears came again, and Trey squeezed the sides of the white porcelain sink hard enough to turn his knuckles the same color. He looked over at me, his eyes wet. "Here. My second highly personal communication from my father this year." He handed me the piece of folded paper from his sweatshirt pocket. It read:

===

**FACSIMILE**

**DANIELS ADVERTISING CO. INTERNATIONAL**

**To: Patrick Brady, Sophomore Housemaster**
**From: Andrew Daniels, Founder/CEO**
**Re: Msg for Trey Daniels, Grade 10**

**Dear Mr. Brady:**
**Please pass this note along to my son.**
**Thanks,**
**Andrew Daniels**

**TREY—You might recall a conversation we had before you left for school. It was about you holding up your end of our bargain. So far, from what I can see on your grade reports, this isn't happening. I'm still amazed by what you did to save that little boy. But your grades aren't cutting it. Let's do what we need to do. I know you are going to mom's for Thanksgiving so I will see you at Christmas. —DAD**
===

I read the text and then read it again. I could hear the water in the sink, Trey splashing his face. *Let's do what we need to do.* Somehow, it sounded like something my own dad might say—but maybe up at the lake cottage or while we were driving to the grocery store to pick up stuff for dinner or sitting in the Caprice waiting to pick up Mom from work.

Not in a fax.

"A real pick-me-up for the dark days of November, huh, man?" He gave me sort of a half-grin, sniffling, eyes bloodshot. "The best part is the cute, fatherly pat on the fucking back *again* about saving the kid."

Rick Eldrin stepped into the bathroom. "Brady wants both of you guys back in the library right now." He glared at Trey, who was drying his hands off.

Eldrin leaned in close to Trey as he stepped through the doorway into the corridor. "You finally get caught or what? Big hero."

Trey stopped in midstride. He stared at the floor. I could sense the tension, and I saw Trey's fist clench, the knuckles going white and the veins of his forearm bulging. He walked abruptly to the end of the hallway and out the door. Eldrin followed him out. I hesitated for a moment, glancing through the library doors at Brady. He had his head buried in the *Post*, so I went outside.

The fight was brief and loud. It began with Rick shoving Trey. The counterattack was ferocious. Trey moved as quickly as he had rescuing Nick that night, and his fist made a solid, gut-wrenching sound when it connected with Eldrin's face. Blood exploded from his nose, arcing across the sidewalk. I tried to pull them apart. The crowd gathered quickly. The door swung open, and kids rushed out, encircling us. Trey pushed me aside with surprising strength, and, stunned, I hesitated. It took both Brady and Steve Mallow to pry the two of them apart. By that time, Eldrin's forehead was bleeding, and Trey had the makings of a pretty good shiner under his left eye. Both of them were cut up and covered with grass stains and grit from the concrete walk.

It's hard to say who won. But it's safe to say they both lost as Mr. Wagner arrived on the scene, spoke briefly with Mr. Brady, then led both boys across the dimly lit quad to the dean's office, one hand firmly gripping each of their arms. Mallow stood, breathing hard, brushing his hands on his sweatpants. "All right, guys, back inside," he said. Nobody talked for the rest of study hall.

# CHAPTER 21

"November sucks." Trey lay on his bed two nights later, arms folded behind his head. In addition to the disciplinary probation, he bore physical signs of the fight. His left eye was a bloodshot, black-and-blue mess from Eldrin's one decent right hook. He hadn't had a haircut since September, and he needed to shave. It was just after midnight, and Pink Floyd played low on the stereo. The small fluorescent tube over my desk, the only light in the room, flickered from time to time and made a low hum.

I was reading *The Great Gatsby*, scribbling notes into the margins like Miss Dillon taught us. I was at the part where Daisy Buchanan drives Jay's yellow car down the highway, killing Myrtle Wilson. F. Scott Fitzgerald impressed me. Bob Dylan hung above Trey's desk, slightly skewed, looking pensively down at his guitar. The poster was torn at the bottom right corner, as though some giant with a six-inch-wide mouth had taken a bite out of it. The Kennedy brothers were still there too, but there was a splotch on Jack's shoulder where McNeal's soda can had exploded and sent grape soda in ballistic patterns all over our stuff. I lost a halfway decent wool sweater to the incident. Now the sweater was tacked up to the window frame, where the dangling sleeves served as makeshift curtains, stopping the strongest of morning sunbeams from piercing a broken section of blinds. The bent blinds were a good example, according to Brady, of the perils of indoor lacrosse.

Our mutual act of academic subterfuge had salvaged Trey's English grade, at least temporarily. But he was failing world history and was on the line in Latin. He probably should have been failing that, too, but Father Daley was pretty lenient these days. Right now, his books lay on the floor as he stared up at the patterns of wood grain in the bunk bed.

"I can't remember if that marks a weak spot or a really hard spot in a piece of lumber. I'm pretty sure you're not supposed to put a nail there if you're building something," he said.

I looked up from the book. "Huh?"

"That mark in the board. I think it's called an eye. My dad told me that when we were building a tree house in Lake Placid. He was wearing this stupid John Deere hat."

I went over and looked at the mark in the wood.

"Kind of looks like a big raindrop."

Outside, there was a thunderstorm approaching, and the window was lit pale blue with lightning.

Trey suddenly sat up, bracing himself up on his elbows so that his bony shoulders protruded. "I just thought of the coolest place to watch a storm." He sprang up from his bed with surprising energy and put on a sweatshirt. He grabbed his Redskins cap from the closet, along with a lighter and a pack of Camels that he had hidden inside a rolled-up sock in the back of his underwear drawer. He tugged on my shoulder. "Come on. You can read later."

A few minutes later, we were climbing out the window of the bathroom onto a sort of ledge supported by the back entrance, overlooking the quad. It was kind of like a fire escape. An overhang covered it so it stayed dry. Trey closed the window, and we sat against the brick wall with our knees hunched up under our elbows. Rain was falling hard now, slanted a little, and thunder rolled a couple miles away. I was cold in my gym shorts and sweatshirt, even though it was a pretty warm night for this time of year. The rain was loud, and I could hear it hitting the copper gutters and the sidewalk below.

Trey took out a cigarette and cupped it in his mouth. He lit it and offered me one. A number of thoughts raced around at that moment. First, I wondered how the hell he never got caught. Second, I figured I shouldn't do this. Third, I realized that this moment was right out of the *Male-Bonding Handbook*. Fourth, I thought about Dad and how he would kill me if he knew I was smoking. But Dad wasn't there.

Trey knew how to smoke, and he took long drags. I sort of puffed on the cigarette and then tried to inhale. I felt like I would cough up a lung, so I didn't try it anymore and sort of just faked it. Anyway, this was pretty damn cool, perched on this secret spot at the Ashford River School smoking Camels with Trey Daniels. Lightning illuminated our faces as Trey elbowed me in the ribs.

"It's really cool, the storm, huh?" Trey's voice sounded strange. Far away or something.

"Um, yeah."

"No, I mean, seriously. Like the way the rain hits the trees and makes the leaves heavy so they bend toward the ground. And the thunder. And the sound the rain makes. Makes you feel really, I dunno…like *safe* if you're in a dry place, like here, outta the rain. You can see it, and you know it's right out there, but you're not in it." He took a long drag on his cigarette. "I used to watch storms in Lake Placid with my dad." His voice was quiet.

*I guess you're our guy.*

"Doesn't talk to you much, does he?" My smoke was only half burned down, but Trey was lighting a second.

"No. It's the traveling, I guess. I don't even really know exactly what he does. Except send encouraging faxes."

"Huh."

"My mom and dad are two of the weirdest people around. Gotta be the money. We're really rich, Matt. Makes them crazy." He chuckled and exhaled a long stream of smoke through his nose. "It's such a cliché, right? You know, the fucked-up rich people? Well, that's my family. We *are* the fucked-up rich people."

With a twinge of guilt, I remembered looking in Trey's wallet and seeing the stack of money.

"Um, how rich?"

"Rich. I dunno. I told you about the whole advertising company thing and all the houses. Our house in Lake Placid isn't some cute little log cabin in the mountains. It's a huge old wilderness lodge about a hundred years old, but totally renovated. Used to belong to some industrial hotshot from New York City. We own about six hundred acres of forest. He's got like four million dollars in the bank, and God only knows how much in mutual funds and real estate and bonds and equities and all that kinda shit. I saw my dad's taxes once, and he owed close to a million in taxes. I don't know what that means, but I know it means he's loaded."

"Yeah." It occurred to me at that moment that I'd never been friends with anyone really rich before.

"Maybe that's why I don't work hard in school," Trey went on, his voice soft. "That can be my new excuse, huh? It's all my dad's fault. He worked really hard, and he built this clutch business. Now he's got more money than God, but my family is all screwed up." He flicked some ashes to the concrete floor. "What the hell is an equity anyway?"

The cigarette made an orange glow on Trey's face as he inhaled. He stood up and leaned against the railing, reaching out to catch the rain. Drops splattered against his hand, and he rubbed the water off on his sweatshirt. He was staring out at the clouds. The sky flashed blue, and he was silhouetted against it. A few seconds later, a long roll of thunder echoed through the quad. The storm was moving further off to the south.

"Mr. Wagner gave me the usual 'you're on thin ice, mister' crap tonight. Dr. Carlisle keeps talking to me about my family, and I think he's trying to get me to admit that I have a drug problem or something or that I'm depressed because of my dysfunctional parents." Trey was talking fast, louder now. "I swear he gets off on probing into that shit. I think he wants me to match one of the fucking case studies in his teenage psychology books or something." He flicked the Camel over the railing down onto the sidewalk and leaned over to watch it fall. "The other day, he asked me if I felt like I was alone."

"What did you tell him?" I stared at the smoldering tip of my cigarette.

"Sometimes. That sometimes I feel alone." Trey put the hood of his gray sweatshirt over his head, sat back down next to me, and punched me lightly in the shoulder. "You know what?"

"What?"

"I wish you were my brother."

I stopped puffing on the cigarette and looked at him. When he said that last thing, it made me sort of want to cry, but I didn't. The two of us sat out there in silence, smoking a couple more cigarettes and passing the last one back and forth. The rain stopped. We listened to the thunder fade, until the only sound was water dripping from trees to the cement below.

# CHAPTER 22

Things seemed to settle into an uneventful routine for the next couple of weeks, and the conclusion of the rowing season brought a new kind of normalcy to my life. Brady ran winter workouts four days per week, but they didn't have the intensity or the duration of our on-water training. Classes found a rhythm, and there was even relative peace between Eldrin and the rest of the world. Natalie and Nicole were so busy with swimming that we'd pretty much given up on them altogether.

The most exciting part of December, other than the end of classes for Christmas, was Trey inviting me to the Bahamas for winter break. His dad owned a timeshare on a semiprivate island not too far from Nassau. It was a push for me to get my parents on board, but they finally agreed—probably against their better judgment, and I'm sure my mother fought it all the way. They decided that it would be my Christmas present. A few years later, during college, we talked about it, and they admitted that they couldn't believe they'd let me go. It might have been the last-minute nature of the invitation, or their happiness that I had "found a good friend" in Trey. I guess the fact that they had met him in person made it easier, even if it was clear to them that he lived in a different universe. Either way, they took the risk and let me go after my dad talked briefly to Mr. Daniels on the phone.

Maybe it's the sort of risk parents figure they need to take to let their teenage kids learn responsibility. Well, I can't exactly say I was completely responsible. The trip was a turning point in a number of ways. First of all, in the way that sophomores tend to do, I broke some fundamental rules that my parents had tried to instill in me for years. And I did this, it seemed, before I even realized what was happening. Second, the trip also showed me a great deal more about the strange world Trey lived in—one where those fundamental rules were far less clear.

Trey had passed along the invitation during a Saturday-morning practice run just before break. He explained in short bursts as we ran, pausing to catch his breath. "We've been going there for a few years now. My dad's company and some other companies pretty much own the island. It's sweet because there aren't too many people. Just a handful of families. Usually about twenty kids there. All the parents go out on this huge sailboat every night, get hammered, and do God-knows-what. Don't even wanna know what's going on below decks." He paused for a minute as we climbed the last stretch to MacKerry, getting winded, the cold air painful to inhale. "What I'm saying," he continued, breathing hard as we climbed the last stretch, "is that it's easy to get away with stuff while they're out sailing the high seas."

"Easier than here?" I asked, laughing. We stopped, arms overhead, walking off the run and catching our breath.

"Even easier," Trey said with a cough. He laughed and punched me in the shoulder.

■ ■ ■

On the day before New Year's Eve, Dad drove me to the airport in Buffalo. He helped me check my luggage and pick up my boarding pass at the ticket counter. Just before I got into the security line, he looked me directly in the eye and said, "Call when you get to Miami, and call again when you get to the island. Have fun and be careful. Use your head." I told him I would. We hugged, and then he left.

I caught a flight to Miami—the first time I'd ever flown by myself. I met Trey in the Miami airport at the designated spot, called dad collect from a payphone, and then the two of us boarded the connecting flight to Nassau. I gazed out the window, watching as we flew over tiny islands amidst the vast cobalt sea. Closer to land, the shallower waters took on countless shades of blue and green before washing up on white strips of beach. Once on the ground in Nassau, I felt the intense Caribbean heat for the first time. I followed Trey across the sunlit tarmac to a single-engine plane that was waiting for us. The pilot was a broad-shouldered, smiling islander with tightly braided, jet-black hair. I looked out the windows as the Cessna lifted off the runway and climbed steeply over azure waters, afternoon sun glinting on breaking waves. We landed a half hour later on a gravel strip, coming to a bumpy halt at the smallest airport I had ever seen. It was nothing more than a shed with a radar tower and a chain-link fence around it.

Mr. Daniels was waiting at the end of the small runway, leaning against the hood of a topless yellow Jeep Wrangler. The scene made me think of a TV commercial. Andrew Daniels was tall and heavily built, wearing an unbuttoned linen shirt, khaki shorts, and sandals. Above reflective Ray-Bans, his hair was a tousled chestnut mop a lot like Trey's. He leaned against the hood of the Jeep, arms crossed casually, smoking a cigar.

He didn't move, just held the pose, smiling as we walked across the sandy tarmac to the Jeep. When we approached, he held the cigar in the corner of his mouth and raised his arms. The linen shirt flapped in the breeze. Chest hair. Gold chain.

*Daniels Advertising Company, International.*

"Eagle has landed," Mr. Daniels said with a smirk as he gave Trey a hug, slapping him hard on the back. "Matt. Welcome to paradise." Big handshake. He might have been in his forties, but his voice was still twenty.

"Thanks, Mr. Daniels. Great to meet you." I couldn't see his eyes. Just cool, reflective, mercury lenses.

"Well, limo's ready to roll, boys. Toss your gear in the back, and let's go."

The Wrangler's top was off, and there were no doors. I rode in front. Trey lounged in the back, sprawled across the seat, leaning against the side. Mr. Daniels pushed in a CD and turned up the volume. Steve Miller. The cigar smoke swirled over the dashboard as we pulled onto a dirt road, leaving the airstrip behind. I watched as the Cessna took off behind us and faded into the bright sky.

He worked through the gears quickly, driving the Jeep hard on the rough road. Wind whipped through, a hot breeze. We passed grape trees on the side of the road, and I caught glimpses of white sand and cobalt blue beyond. Mr. Daniels skidded into a sharp left turn that nearly threw me out of the Jeep. All three of us laughed at the wide-eyed panic on my face, but I gripped the seat a little tighter after that. The road now ran parallel to the coast. There wasn't a cloud in the sky, and the sun glinted off the yellow hood. "Solid trip down, boys?"

"It was really cool. I've never been in a small plane like that," I said.

Mr. Daniels reached for the volume knob. "What was that? Gotta speak up!" he shouted. The Jeep bounced as we clambered over a series of deep ruts.

"Never been in a small plane like that!" I shouted.

"Yeah. Little Cessna deal. Sorry about the pilot. Doesn't talk much. Damn cool approach, flying to this island. I woulda flown you guys myself, but I didn't get enough hours in this year to keep up my license. Trey, you ready for dinner with Barney tonight?" His dad grinned in the rearview mirror.

"Hell yeah. Grouper?"

"The usual. Said he's got conch stew. He's bringing it over and we'll eat at our place."

"What about that dessert? Remember that thing with the coconuts?"

"The pie! Absolutely!" The cigar burned down and got flicked out the window. "Matt, wait'll you try this pie. It's something."

Trey leaned in from the back. "Are the WaveRunners working?"

Mr. Daniels shifted into second as we slogged through some wet sand. "Had them tuned up just this morning. The blue one's running a little noisy, but they're both clippin' along. Barney and I tested 'em both out just after lunch."

The ride went on like this for another few minutes. WaveRunners. Dinner plans. Which families were "down" this year. The plan for the week. Mr. Daniels had a meeting to go to in Nassau on Tuesday; he'd be there overnight. Then an overnight cruise with friends. We'd be okay on our own. Crucita would be around.

"Who's Crucita?" I asked.

"She's the maid."

*Of course she is.*

"Who's Barney?"

"Longtime friend. Partner at the company. Used to be a professional chef before he found the brains to invest with me. Still makes the best seafood meal you'll ever taste. Whoa," he said with a chuckle, "hold on!" The Jeep plunged into a puddle that had overrun the road, sending a spray of water high into the air and throwing us forward in our seats. Mr. Daniels put it in first, and we plowed through, the engine growling.

"Thing's a tank, eh, Matt?"

"Sure is. My uncle has one."

"You ever drive it?" Mr. Daniels asked as he upshifted out of the pool, the tires kicking up gravel and wet sand.

"Nah."

"Can you work a clutch?"

"Sure. My dad taught me this summer."

He slammed on the brakes, threw the transmission in neutral, and undid his seat belt. The engine rumbled. "Well," he said as he jumped out, "it's all yours!"

"Seriously?"

"I'm always serious! Right, Trey? Come on, give it a spin. Nothing like a Jeep off-road. We'll take it onto the beach for a while!"

I looked back at Trey, who smiled, shrugged his shoulders, and took his shirt off. "I'm gonna get some sun back here. Just don't kill us, Derby." He made a show of putting on his seat belt with exaggerated urgency.

The transmission handle rattled as I tested the clutch, easing the Jeep into first like Dad had taught me. It felt different from Mom's Volkswagen, though, and it took some getting used to.

"Gotta give it a little more gas. Thirsty little sucker…that's it." Mr. Daniels was in the process of lighting another cigar, motioning with his elbow as he held the lit match. "Easy, there she is."

The Jeep lurched forward, threatening to stall as I shifted into second, but then I got a feel for it, moving smoothly into third on a straight section of road. Mr. Daniels turned up the volume on the radio and then pointed with his cigar at a path leading over some sand dunes to the right. "Let's put it in four and take it up there."

I slowed down, shifted to neutral, and he showed me how to throw the transfer case into four-wheel drive. I turned the wheel, steering us across the roadside ditch. It *looked* shallow, but the tires made a loud *thwump* and I felt a hard jolt as the suspension bottomed out. I glanced at Trey in the mirror. His eyebrows were raised, the corners of his mouth forming his signature smirk. Mr. Daniels just kept smiling, drumming out the beat of the Steve Miller on the dash, not fazed at all by the jolt. Cigar smoke swirled behind the windshield. As we reached the crest of the small grassy dune on the other side of the ditch, the view opened up. A smooth line of white extended along the shore, and surf lapped the beach, leaving a glimmering sheen in the early evening sun. The foam looked pinkish in the fading light.

"Okay, hold it there," he said. "Gotta let some air out of the tires, or we'll get stuck in the sand." I stopped the truck and shut off the engine. We hopped out and watched him release the air from each tire until it looked like they were nearly empty. "I know," he said. "Looks too low, right? But believe me, you have to do it or this bad boy will sink right into the sand."

"How do you fill them again?"

"We have a compressor at the condo." He reattached the inlet covers. We hopped back in, and I started the engine.

"Okay. Easy down onto the beach, then swing a left. Right there along the water. Gotta go where the sand is solid. Not into the surf. That's it." Mr. Daniels fumbled through the glove compartment, mumbling through the cigar. "Where the hell is my Tom Petty?"

We cruised along the beach as Tom Petty sang about the great wide open. I had the hang of the Jeep now and slid it gently into third as we got up around twenty-five. The tires hummed on the smooth white sand. I finally relaxed enough to take my left hand off the wheel and reached out, feeling air rush through my fingers. A breeze whipped through the jeep. Evening rays of sun were warm on my face, and I could see the orange ball dipping low on the horizon directly in front of us, silhouetting the broad trunks of palm trees arcing over the beach. Trey took off his seat belt and stood up on the backseat, holding on to the roll bar.

"Welcome to the island, Matt my man." Mr. Daniels smiled.

"It's incredible. Your company owns it?"

"Ha! Well, not all of it. But a good portion of the land. We invested in some offshore accounts in the late eighties, and this just sort of presented itself as part of the deal."

"Wild," I said, slowing a little bit as we rumbled over some driftwood.

"In business, it's referred to as 'a substantial ancillary benefit.'" Mr. Daniels laughed, sounding a lot like Trey. As we rounded a bend, a low stone pier came into view, extending fifty yards into the surf. "Hey, pull it over here. Sun's about to go down. You guys should see the sunset from out there."

We stopped, the engine rumbling to a halt as I turned the key. The surf seemed to grow louder. Mr. Daniels pulled a cooler from the back of the Wrangler and clambered over some rocks onto the pier. "Come on out here."

We walked out along the pier, Trey stopping at one point to pick up a small black crab and toss it far out into the water. Occasional gaps in the stones revealed rushing water underneath, and the warm spray shot up like a geyser with each incoming wave. At the end of the pier, Mr. Daniels sat down, his legs dangling over the edge. He opened the cooler.

"For me, a cold Corona." He pulled the beer out of the ice, using the opener on his keychain to flip the top off. "And for you two…" he said, reaching for two bottles, "a couple of Cokes."

"Dad!"

"What?"

"Come on!"

Mr. Daniels smiled as he put his sunglasses up on his forehead. I did a double take at the likeness to Trey. Same eyes. Dark and narrow. "Pulling your chain. Different rules down here, right?" He put the Cokes back in the cooler and pulled out two more Coronas. He cranked them open and handed one to each of us. The bottles sweated with condensation, and I felt the cold drops run down my arm. Mr. Daniels took a lime from the cooler.

"I almost forgot!" He opened a pocketknife and cut the fruit into narrow wedges, pushed one into his beer, and quickly placed his thumb over the top. "Now you flip it upside down; let the lime float up…" We followed suit, Trey trying hard to make it look like he knew this already. "And then slowly turn it back over, like this. Take your thumb off, real slow. I watched as the beer foamed in the neck of the bottle, a little spraying out as I removed my thumb. I could smell the lime.

"Cheers." Mr. Daniels tipped his bottle toward us, and we did the same, clinking the necks. The beer was very cold. It had been snowing particularly hard in Buffalo just that morning. I thought about my dad—somewhat guiltily—brushing the windshield off while the engine warmed up in our driveway.

The surf got stronger now as the tide moved in. We sat silently, listening to the smaller rocks being rolled around as waves broke against the pier.

"The bottom out here is made of little pieces of dead coral, and if you lean in real close, you can hear it. Sounds like glass bottles." Mr. Daniels lowered an ear over the edge. "Kind of hard to hear, but there's a little bit of a *clink*, kinda like this." He tapped his beer against the stone. "Listen."

"That's very interesting, Dad, but we're starving." Trey rolled his eyes as he took a deep chug.

"Hey! Slow down! Can't have you getting plowed before dinner."

Again, I found myself wondering if this man was really Trey's father or some scripted stand-in from a movie. I took another sip of the beer, rolling a bit of lime around my tongue. The sun was a burning red ball now, halfway below the horizon. The sky blushed, and the foam was deep pink, the deeper water a lavender gray. Seabirds cruised low over the waves. We watched the red disc slip beneath the horizon, and the breeze seemed a little cooler. Trey hugged himself and then pulled on his T-shirt.

"I'd say that alone was worth the flight, eh?" Mr. Daniels stood up and collected the bottles. We ambled back to the Jeep. He held out his hand for the keys. "I think I'll drive now, Matt." This was probably a good thing, because I could feel a little lightness in my head from the beer. I was not a heavyweight drinker at age fifteen, as I would learn all the more clearly later in the week.

Just a few minutes later, we drove up the bank to a gravel driveway, where I had another glimpse of Trey's strange world. The condo was huge, surrounded by palms. There was a swimming pool in back, which seemed odd given the beach and ocean just a hundred feet away. Inside, it was hotel-room cool, with granite countertops and coral decor on the walls. There was thick white carpet in the living room, with a fifty-two-inch widescreen theater system, pool table, and lounge chairs made out of bamboo. The guest room for me and Trey was in the loft. There were two twin beds and a huge triangular window overlooking the ocean. Sliding glass doors opened onto a second-story deck. Outside, a perfect stretch of beach extended in either direction, with two shiny WaveRunners parked on the sand. Further out, a good-sized Bayliner tugged at its mooring. We unpacked and threw our bags in the corner.

■ ■ ■

Dinner with Barney Hallihan was an event.

The businessman, at fifty-five a good ten years older than Mr. Daniels, made the most delicious meal I had ever tasted. In fact, I was pretty bewildered by every aspect of this white-haired, scruffy-bearded Jimmy Buffett look-alike. His wife looked about twenty and was definitely in the hotness league with Miss Dillon. To round out the picture, the man had an endless stock of the dirtiest jokes I'd ever heard, along with a willing desire to tell all of them over dinner. We sat on the back deck overlooking the pool, the stars bright overhead in an indigo sky. Tiki torches stood around the perimeter of the deck, their flames fluttering in the evening breeze.

It was the one about the two cheerleaders and the bottlenose dolphin that literally just about killed both of us, as Trey and I laughed, nearly choking on cilantro-seasoned grouper steak. Mr. Daniels stood up, doubled over with laughter, and barely avoided spitting a half-chewed mouthful rather unceremoniously into the garden before reminding Barney that, "For Chrissake, the boys don't even know what that *is!*" Of course, we did know, because we were sophomores in high school. After dinner, Barney mixed everyone a large margarita, watching with amusement the mouth-puckering effects of the salted glass on his youngest guests.

It wasn't late before the day's travel (along with the margarita) caught up with us. We went inside, leaving Mr. Daniels, Barney, and his wife to finish off the drinks. Mr. Daniels called from the deck as we opened the door.

"Crucita will have breakfast at nine, gents. Sleep on in till then, and we'll take a cruise in the morning. There's a sandbar and a pretty good reef around the eastern tip. Maybe a little snorkeling?"

"Sounds good, Dad."

"Thanks for everything, Mr. Daniels," I said.

Trey pushed the sliding glass door shut, and we climbed the stairs to the loft. Trey dug his toothbrush out of a bag and began brushing. "So whaddya think 'a this place?" He talked through the toothpaste, the words garbled. He did that a lot.

"Don't even know what to say, man. It's incredible." I put my money and passport, stored in the zippered pouch Mom bought, in the inside pocket of my duffel bag. Her advice. "So what about your mom? Is she coming down?"

Trey laughed, spitting toothpaste in tiny white flecks on the mirror. "You know, she was supposed to. She even had a ticket."

"So what happened?" I joined him at the sink.

"*Allegedly*," he said the word with gusto, having heard it on CNN in the airport, "allegedly, she had to go to her college roommate's wedding shower, which she allegedly forgot about at the time of ticket purchase." Trey shook his head, smiling. "I guess they're at it again. He's such a dick to her." He chuckled again.

"Doesn't bother you?"

"Ah, man, I dunno. Maybe it does; maybe it doesn't." He rinsed the toothbrush in the sink.

"Huh."

"To be honest with you, I'm sick of thinking about it. Besides, my dad's a lot more fun to be with when they're not together. They just bitch at each other all the time."

He flipped out the bathroom light, fell heavily onto his bed, and buried his head under the pillow. "Tomorrow," the muffled voice pronounced, "is New Year's Eve. Tomorrow, we find girls."

"Think this'll go any better than the last time we found girls?"

"I'd say that went pretty well."

"Didn't end well. As far as I remember, it ended with you and I half-naked in a dark swimming pool freezing our asses off."

"I think things will end better down here."

I slept well and dreamed about the girls we'd find.

# CHAPTER 23

At around nine 'o clock the next morning, I was sitting on the beach in the shade of a palm tree, drinking a glass of passion fruit juice and eating a breakfast sandwich that Crucita had ready and waiting on the counter downstairs. The drink had an umbrella in it, and she had cut some melon in an elaborate star pattern. A silk napkin with a coral napkin ring had been placed at a precise angle next to the plate. Trey was down along the shore, putting gasoline in the WaveRunners. Crucita came out of the kitchen and joined me. She was a thin woman, about fifty, with long black hair she wore tied in a ponytail. Her skin was dark and freckled. She smiled, saying, "Buenos dias, Señor Derby." I grinned and thanked her for making breakfast.

"You like here?" she asked, clearly struggling with English. She smiled after taking a sip of coffee.

"Yes. It's beautiful."

"I like it here very much also. I'm from Dominican Republic. I'm here now two years with my daughter and my grandbaby boy. He has just five years. His daddy he was killed in motorbike accident three years 'go. Hard to live with no daddy! We came for the job, my daughter and me, so we can learn English. Maybe we go to New York someday. But is very beautiful here."

"Where do you live?" I asked.

"We live cross-ways down the road." She nodded. "Little casita there. You like the sandwich?"

"It's good. Thank you."

"Your daddy friends with Mr. Daniels?" she asked.

"No. I just met him. I go to school with Trey."

"Mr. Daniels is very important man, I think. Muy importante. Always on telefono! Always business! You know where is Mrs. Daniels?"

"I don't think she could come."

"No this time, eh? Okay. Bien. You enjoy the sandwich." She headed back to the house, humming a tune.

I felt the sun in acute spots where it patched through the tree branches and hit my legs and chest, though the sand was still cool underneath. I squinted, looking out over the bright strip of beach. It arced around and formed a sort of bay, and the green-brown shapes of coral reefs rippled under the aquamarine surface twenty or thirty yards out. It brought to mind the word *archipelago*, even though I wasn't sure if this was one or not. I was thinking about the lagoon in *Lord of the Flies*. Trey had finished eating and left his crumb-covered plate and half-empty glass in the sand next to mine. The umbrella looked sort of dejected.

He was about twenty yards away wrestling with the weight of a WaveRunner, dragging it down into the surf, and I heard the rumble and sputter as he started the engine. "Hey!" He motioned to me. "Get the other one!"

"Coming." I got up and then looked at the plates and glasses. "What about the plates?" I shouted.

"She'll get 'em. Don't worry. Come on."

I shrugged, jogged down the beach, and dragged the second WaveRunner into the surf. I hopped on the back. Trey gave me about a nine-second tutorial, muttering something about throttle and choke, and then took off into the bay in a spray of exhaust, whooping and hollering. After I figured out the controls, I gunned the throttle and was nearly thrown from the back, but I eventually got a feel for it.

Maybe that first experience on a WaveRunner was a good analogy for the way I felt that morning. There was a momentum building, a sort of muscular acceleration that exhilarated and frightened me all at once. As I sped along the surf, feeling the cool breeze and sun on my back, I looked out at the deepening blue of the Caribbean, and it hit me for the first time exactly where I was. Buffalo was a long way off. A lot of things were a long way off.

■ ■ ■

An hour later, we lay on oversized towels in a little cove about a quarter mile down the beach, the WaveRunners parked on the sand. Ted from Manhattan was with us. I never got his full name. Ted from Manhattan sort of just appeared out of nowhere on his own WaveRunner, apparently coming from another condo a ways further down the beach. He seemed to know Trey, their paths having crossed there on the island and once or twice up in New York. It was around noon now, and the water was a different shade of aquamarine beyond the ivory beach. Our towels, which Trey had pulled from a compartment in the WaveRunner, were bright red, and the whole scene looked a lot like a postcard. There was a queasiness in my stomach. Might have been the margaritas combined with the waves. I don't think it was a hangover, but maybe it was. Ted from Manhattan, on the other hand, was *very* hungover. He was wearing Oakleys, and they reflected the glare of the sun, so I had to squint when I looked at him.

He lay on his side, hunched up on one elbow. He turned to Trey. "Mandy's having a party tonight," he said, tracing a finger in the sand.

217

"Her parents are taking their yacht to the other island for an overnight cruise. She's got some stuff."

I thought back to Dr. Carlisle's health class and the statistic that one out of every three high school students tries marijuana before his junior year, or something like that. I stared out at the water. Despite the sunny skies on the beach, a giant thunderhead was visible far off. It must have been at least a hundred miles away.

Trey was very interested in the party. "Mandy. I remember Mandy from last year. What time?"

"I dunno, like nine or something. We gotta go. Mandy's *completely* smokin', and she has this friend, Christina. From what I hear dude, she wants it *bad*." Ted lay back down and adjusted himself through his board shorts, smiling reminiscently. Even though I lived in the world of charged sexual energy that existed in the dorms, there was something jolting about his comment. Ted was another exhibit in this strange tour of Trey's life.

Trey smiled. "We'll see how bad she wants it. As for stuff, I've got enough for like one joint, but that's all I have left," he chimed in, flipping over onto his back. My eyes shot in his direction.

*You couldn't have brought it with you on the flight. Could you?*

I'd never actually seen him smoke up, but I remembered the time we'd had no study hall because of the homecoming game. Chase and Trey disappeared for a while after dinner. Trey came back and lay on the floor of our room for about a half hour, staring at the ceiling and listening to R.E.M. He'd rolled a lacrosse ball back and forth on the floor, bouncing it off his dresser until Mr. DiVincenzo stuck his head in the door and told him to knock it off because he could hear it down the hall. So far, for whatever reason, Trey hadn't invited me into that corner of his life, and it was something that remained pretty much unspoken between us. I guess he considered it a sort of innocence of mine, something that he didn't want to force upon me. On the other hand, he didn't take any excessive measures to hide references to his habit. I had no idea where he kept it if he had it, but I knew it was going on. Still, the idea of bringing it on an international flight struck me as simultaneously ballsy, remarkably stupid, and nearly impossible, so I had to assume that he already had some down here. And I guess he'd decided that he no longer needed to keep it a secret from me.

"You smoke, Matt?" Ted asked.

"Nah. Not really." *Your mom an ER nurse, Ted?*

"You should. No pressure, man, but this is like the *best* place to do it 'cause you're absolutely *not* gonna get caught. I mean, I remember being nervous doing it at school, but there's nothing to worry about here." Ted talked a little like he belonged on MTV. His favorite word was *like*.

He shrugged his shoulders. "Seriously. The nearest cop is, like, on another *island*. In fact, you can get away with pretty much anything here, brother."

Trey said he was hot and wanted to get in the water. He sat up, brushed some sand off his arm, and shuffled down into the surf.

"You guys, like, good friends?" Ted asked. "Trey said you were roommates. Dude, I hate my roommate." Ted went to a boarding school in Connecticut, one that cost a lot more than Ashford. I found it odd that he would ask if Trey and I were good friends. Apparently, in his world, you might invite just any old acquaintance to spend a week with you on your private island in the Caribbean.

"Yeah," I replied, "we're pretty tight. We're different though. I guess I work harder in school, but Trey definitely has more fun." As I said this, Trey was mooning us from the water.

"Matt, seriously, like, no pressure about the weed. I, like, totally respect if you don't want to smoke. That's totally chill. There's this one girl, Laurie, who doesn't smoke at all. And she's, like, cool as hell. She'll be there tonight. Besides, you can always just drink and still get pretty messed up, right?"

*Ted, the All-American Good Guy.*

"Right."

Trey was back from his swim, and he shook his head like a dog, sending water droplets flying. As we got ready for the party later, I felt a lot like I had going into the St. Amelia's dance.

Mandy's New Year's Eve party started out pretty tame. The whole thing was on the front deck of her parents' condo, about a mile down the beach from Trey's. It was on another little private bay, which Trey said was ideal because there were no other houses around. There was a screened-in gazebo at the end of a pier that went out about twenty yards over the water. A couple of girls were down in the gazebo when we got there, but most of the sixteen kids at the party were on the deck right in front of the house, sitting on lounge chairs and drinking from plastic cups. Bob Marley played low on the stereo. It was a clear night, and the stars were incredible. Tiki torches illuminated faces with flickering orange light. One of the girls jumped up when she saw us. I assumed this had to be Mandy.

"Trey! I haven't seen you since, like, *last year*! I am so completely psyched that you came. Is this Matt?" Mandy was wearing a black tank top and some *really* short shorts. Her legs were tan. Her voice was lower than I expected it to be, sort of the teenage version of a cigarette voice, and her teeth were brilliantly white. They glowed against her tan face. She gave Trey a hug and then hugged me, too.

*Oh. Hi!*

I looked around at the small crowd seated on the deck, wondering which one of the girls was Christina-Who-Wanted-It-Bad. Ted from Manhattan wandered over. He was wearing a pair of khakis, cuffs rolled up above his ankles, with a turquoise ribbon belt and no shirt. The finishing touch was the string of shells he wore around his neck on a tight-fitting leather cord. He set his drink down and threw an arm around each of our shoulders.

"Happy New Year, gentlemen of the Ashford River School! Let's get you guys a beverage!" Years later, one of the things I remember most clearly about Ted is the way he said the word *beverage*, which, for whatever reason, annoyed the hell out of me.

We followed Ted to a table laden with two bottles of extra-high-proof rum, a cooler of ice, and some soda. "We figured we'd go all out with the heavy artillery. Don't need much of this little mixture to get crazy." Ted grabbed a scoop of ice for each cup, and then he was pouring rum, kind of like a professional bartender, I thought, because he didn't stop pouring as he went from cup to cup.

"Do you have any ginger ale?" Trey was looking through the bottles of soda.

"Ginger ale? Umm, no. Coke and…Coke." Ted held the bottles in either hand, grinning.

"Coke's fine."

We had our drinks now. It occurred to me then that this was the first of my parents' major rules I was breaking on the trip. I followed Trey around, meeting people and getting high fives from some guys and hugs from some girls, none of whom I'd ever met before. In the middle of some conversation about skiing in Vail, Ted from Manhattan came over and put his arm around my shoulder again.

*My old buddy Ted.*

"Dude, that's Laurie over there," he said, pointing with his drink. His *beverage*. His voice was low and hummed with electric promise. "Come on and I'll introduce you."

When he did, my opinion of Ted suddenly climbed a few notches, despite his continued use of the word *beverage*.

Laurie had hair the same color as her rust-red T-shirt, which fit tightly over breasts that drew attention to themselves with no effort from her. She wore blue mesh shorts with white stripes, the short kind that girls wear. She had these flip-flops with plastic daisies on the toe straps. Laurie was buzzed already, and, I realized, I was too. I grinned as she extended her hand for a girl-style handshake, looking me up and down.

"So, you're Trey's friend." She said this, I thought, the way my mom said, "So, let's have a look at this report card." She had a nice smile, though, kind of a smirk not entirely unlike Trey's. She seemed older, maybe a junior or even a senior.

"Yeah, hi. I'm Matt Derby. Ted told me a lot about you." *Hi, I'm Matt. I go to an all-boys boarding school, and I don't really talk to girls much. I'm awkward and adorable all at once!*

"Oh really? Did he, now? Well, I hope he told you something nice." She reached down and pinched Ted's butt through his khakis.

"Only good stuff, babe, only good stuff." Ted laughed, slapped me on the shoulder, and flashed a conspiratorial grin. He wandered back to Trey in the far corner.

"I mean, he didn't really tell me anything," I said. "Actually, all he told me is that you didn't smoke. And that we should meet." I sat down next to her on a bench. "'Cause, umm, I don't either, really."

"Well, I guess that makes two of us. There they go now, to the carcinoma factory." She nodded toward the pier.

Trey and Ted were walking down to the gazebo with a few other kids. I felt a certain panic at being left there with Laurie. I could feel my heart beat faster and a sudden sensation of having been abandoned. She put her hand on my arm. I can't exactly say her touch calmed me down, but it sure as hell felt good. I looked at her hand. It was a deep, tanned bronze but cold from holding the drink. Her fingernails were unpainted. *What were we talking about? Oh yeah. Weed.*

"I dunno, I don't really have a problem with it," I was saying. "It's just that I've never done it, and, well, I dunno." *Smooth.* I looked at the little bubbles in my cup.

"Yeah," she said, drawing a deep breath and sort of sighing. "I'm the same way. Smoking sucks, and it messes up your hair. I get messed up enough drinking this stuff! Ha, if I smoked too, God knows what I'd do— probably kill someone at this party!" She let out a little laugh before she finished her drink. The image of Laurie wielding a knife and smoking a joint ran through my mind. I giggled nervously.

"So. An all-boys boarding school, huh? What's it like living without girls?"

"Um, it's okay, I guess."

*Oh yeah sure, it's okay. After all, who needs girls with all my roommate's magazines?*

"I hear you there. I like boarding, but I think I'd go crazy if I went to an all-girls school. I like coed life. I think it's more well-rounded."

"You could probably say that." The drinks were kicking in. I swirled the cola around in the plastic cup. "Some guys say it's better without the distractions. Academically, I mean."

Laurie laughed. "Am I distracting you, Matt Derby?" She touched my arm again.

*Heat.*

I looked up at her. She was smirking as she took another sip of her drink.

"No. No, I meant..."

"It's okay. I know what you meant." She pulled on a loose thread dangling from the collar of my shirt, still smiling. I watched her fingers play with the thread below my chin, wrapping it around the tip of her index finger, making little white lines from the pressure. *Say something intelligent, Desperado.*

"So, do you go to school with Ted?"

She pulled sharply on the thread, and I felt the collar tighten around my neck until the thread snapped. "Yep. He's a year ahead of me, though. He's a senior."

"You're a junior?"

"You have something against older girls?" She flashed an amused grin.

"What? No, I just...."

"You don't sound too convincing." She crossed one leg over the other and played with the daisy on her flip-flop, her eyes focused on it. She was smirking now. "I'm just kidding, Matt. Relax."

I looked down at her flip-flop, too. The drink was making me dizzy, and I heard a *whoosh* in my ears. "Sorry. I just amn't too good at it. I mean talking. To girls, I mean." *Damn!*

"Amn't? I think you might be drunk, Matt Derby from Buffalo!" She reached up and lifted my chin until our eyes met. Her fingertips were still cold from holding the drink. "You, my fellow boarding school friend, are good and buzzed."

"Might be, yep." I chuckled happily, looking down at the empty cup.

"Well, so am I!" she said.

We ambled around a bit, having scattered conversations, getting progressively more inebriated. At one point, I caught myself telling the story of the girls and the pool, but Trey managed to shut me up and change the topic, lest it be perceived that we had girlfriends back home. After an hour or so, Laurie said, "Matt Derby, I've decided that I like you, and I think it's about time we went for a walk."

"Um…okay."

Blood was pumping rapidly. It was the first moment in my life when I had the shock of realization that something was *really* about to happen, that I was set on a course toward it and it was nearly inevitable. I'd had the beginnings of that feeling with Natalie, but for some reason—maybe it was the alcohol—this was far stronger and more certain. I knew for sure when Laurie stood up and extended her very tan hand, her mouth slightly open in a little pout, eyes looking deeply into mine.

We walked a ways down the beach, stumbling a little bit. Laurie was giggling. She held my hand, which was good because I was feeling pretty dizzy. This rum was no joke, and Ted must have gone light on the Coca-Cola. She kicked off her flip-flops and said she was pretty sure that no one would steal them. They landed with a *thup* in the sand. I found her comment phenomenally amusing and laughed, hard. I could hear the music from the deck, tinny and distant over the sound of the breakers. It was Dave Matthews singing about satellites, which I remember thinking was sort of fitting in a metaphoric way since we were looking at the stars at that very moment. A wave crashed onshore.

After a while, we sort of half fell down onto a sand dune. Laurie decided to make the first move, which was probably the way it had to be if anything were going to happen, considering how nervous I was. She kissed me, pressing her body against mine, and I realized, in much the same way I had with Natalie at the dance, that there was no way to disguise the physical effect she was having on me. Dad's words played in my mind, telling me to behave and not to do anything stupid.

*This is definitely a decision-making juncture.*

Despite fifteen-and-a-half years of cautionary advice, Catholic education, and parental guidance to support them, my father's words of wisdom were no match for this intoxicating blend of testosterone, high-proof rum, and the seductive overtures of a very pretty girl. And so, liberated from irksome thoughts of consequences, I smiled to myself as Laurie lifted my T-shirt, helped me pull it up over my head, and then took off her own. Her breasts were pale in the moonlight, the same color as the sand. I felt her shoulder blades as I pulled her tightly against me, and we kissed again. The sky was black, and the stars seemed very, very close. Her hand traced the hard-earned six-pack on my stomach, going still lower. I inhaled sharply, shivering a little bit—she laughed—as she reached into my shorts, awkwardly undoing the button and zipper. My heart was pounding.

As it turned out, things didn't get completely out of control, and the rest of Laurie's own clothes stayed on. We did share, however, a very hands-on experience, which was more than intense enough. Had things progressed any further, I would hardly have known what to do anyway. And so, too dizzy and drunk to do much else, I gave in and lay back on the cool, soft sand. I closed my eyes, which made my head spin, and then opened them to find Laurie smiling, her face just inches from my own. I looked up at the sky as a familiar, rhythmic, yet more-intense-than-ever warmth surrounded, enveloped, and overcame me.

*Oh.*

*Wow.*

*Those.*

*Stars.*

*Are.*

*Bright!*

Just seconds later, I lay next to her, shaking a bit from an electric mixture of nerves and something else. I was still dizzy from the drinks. I could hear the surf, closer now as the tide came in. Her hair smelled clean. I was covered in tiny beads of sweat. She giggled. It was musical. She kissed me again, and I shivered.

Then, over the noise of the surf, we heard the kids back at the condo counting down the seconds to midnight. They cheered when the hour struck.

"Happy New Year, Matt Derby. I'm glad we met!" She hiccupped and laughed again.

"Me too." I felt a swimming mixture of exhilaration, a little bit of nausea, which I fought back, and something on the periphery of guilt. A part of me knew the guilt would kick in later in a much stronger form. But more than anything else at that particular moment, I was thinking it was pretty clutch, as Trey would say, that all this had happened on the beach on a tiny island in the Bahamas under the stars with a really cool girl like Laurie.

■ ■ ■

I woke up early, and the sky was just starting to get light. I was lying exactly where, apparently, we'd both passed out last night on the beach. I panicked for a second but then remembered that Mr. Daniels and Mandy's parents would still be out on the yacht until later that evening. The night before came back to me vaguely, but I definitely did remember Laurie and, well, *that*. And she was still there, just sort of waking up and rubbing the sand from her eyes. I expected it to be more awkward than it was. But she just sat up and said, "Man, what time is it? I have got to drink some water. Drinking completely dehydrates you." She turned and looked at me. My hair was kind of crazy, and I had sand crusted to my face. She burst out laughing as she rubbed it off.

"Eww! You drooled!" Her hand was very soft.

I felt stuck to my shorts and decided to go jump in the ocean. My head hurt. A lot.

The morning good-byes were brief, because everyone was hung over. Laurie gave me an awkward little hug, and said casually, as though nothing had happened at all, "See ya!" Then we all just sort of scattered, leaving Mandy's deck a mess of plastic cups, scattered patio furniture, depleted bowls of tortilla chips, and a couple of empty liquor bottles. There was no sign of Ted; apparently, he'd made his way into the house at some point.

Trey and I walked back along the path to his condo. It ran along the beach, and we could hear the rollers coming in. He had tied his T-shirt around his waist and was using the sleeve to clean off his sunglasses. The sun was bright and hot at nine a.m. He spoke first. "Kind of crazy last night, huh?" His voice sounded deep and half-asleep, the way it did early in the morning back at school.

"Yeah. Yeah, it was." I remembered how crazy it *was*, feeling a little bit of an electrical shiver go down my spine. I felt nauseous and shaky.

"Saw you wander off with Laurie," he said.

"Yeah," I muttered.

"How'd that go?"

"She's pretty cool."

Trey laughed. "You guys *do* anything?"

"Um, yeah, she…uh…" I said, kicking a round, white stone a few paces ahead.

"She *what*?" Apparently, he did in fact want the details.

"We had a good time." I left it at that.

"Me too. With Mandy." Trey nodded, squinting his eyes and stretching his arms. We walked silently for a while. He stopped and punched me in the shoulder, grinning. "Okay. Look. I just want to get this straight. You're still a virgin, right?"

"Yeah."

"Okay." He laughed. "Me too. But just barely."

"Yeah, just barely." I didn't know if my just-barely was the same as his just-barely, and I had a feeling it wasn't. But I didn't ask.

"So, Ted tried to hook up with Christina, and she punched him in the balls," he said.

"Seriously?"

"Yep. Punched. Closed fist."

"Ouch."

"Yeah. He puked right then and there, all over the gazebo. Dropped the joint he was smoking and almost lit a wicker chair on fire."

We both laughed at this, at which point I fell down in the sand, feeling suddenly dizzy. After rinsing off in the ocean, we continued along the sandy road, kicking the stone ahead of us, not saying much, thinking. The sun felt hot on my shoulders, and I knew it was the beginning of a burn.

# CHAPTER 24

 

The rest of the week was relatively tame by contrast, with most of our time spent exploring the island, swimming, hanging out on the beach, and cruising along on WaveRunners. There was one more evening party, but nothing intriguing went down. The guilt I'd been afraid of did, in fact, kick in, and it continued to nag me at a constant, low level. I avoided Laurie for the most part. When we did see each other, we stuck to some light, casual banter about our respective boarding school experiences. She seemed content to let it stay this way, as though nothing had happened between us, and that made the whole interaction all the more confusing. Trey seemed to be in the same place, and we kept ourselves busy with more innocent pursuits at night, like playing pool, which kept us from seeing much of the girls. Fortunately, most of the other families took off just a couple days after we arrived, leaving the island much more serene. Ted from Manhattan left with his parents to spend some time at home in the city, and most of the girls flew out as well. Laurie stopped to say good-bye on her way to the airstrip and gave me a polite little hug that seemed oddly innocent given the rawness of our night on the beach. I blushed, shoved my hands into the pockets of my shorts, and walked down to the water after she left. I stood there looking at the ground, idly drawing designs in the sand with my big toe.

I didn't notice Trey approaching until he was standing right next to me.

"Hey."

"Hey," I answered.

He bent down and picked up a shell. "You know, I was thinking."

"Careful."

He chuckled. "No, seriously. I was thinking. Girls are really crazy."

I paused in my sand drawing and looked at him. I had expected him to say something deep and philosophical. Instead, he smirked and tossed the shell into the water. "Do you think they're all as crazy as the ones we seem to find?"

"No, I think you just attract the crazy ones," I said.

"Maybe," he replied.

"Yeah, I think so," I said. "I think there are probably nice, normal girls out there that don't drag people down to their swimming pool or get drunk and hook up with guys they just met." I sat down next to him.

"Derby, you almost sound ashamed." His voice was mockingly serious. "Am I ruining your moral integrity?"

"Come on, it's all great and everything, but you can't tell me you don't ever feel guilty."

"We're Catholic. We were born guilty. That won't change no matter what we do or don't. If I let myself feel guilty every time I did or thought something questionable, I'd go nuts."

"True."

"Hmm." He picked up a pebble. "I dunno, Matt. I guess if anyone's going to hell for all this, it's me, 'cause I always drag you into stuff."

"Not really. I know what I'm doing." I knew this was bullshit, that he did drag me into things, but it sounded good.

He laughed and tossed the rock into the surf. "Really? I'm glad somebody does."

"Right."

"So how about this." He extended his hand in an official-looking way. "Let's shake on this. A New Year's resolution."

"Oh yeah? What's that?"

"Let's keep each other out of hell this year." He smirked.

I shook his hand, laughing. "Sure, Trey." The sun moved out from behind a cloud, and I squinted. It was hot. "So, it's our last night here. What's the plan?" I asked.

"Dinner with Barry and my dad again, then nothing much. Early morning tomorrow. The plane's supposed to pick us up at six, 'cause the flight from Nassau's at eight thirty."

"That is early."

"Yeah. Dinner's in a couple hours. Meantime, I wanna work on this killer tan while the sun's still strong."

We grabbed a couple of towels and spent the rest of the afternoon lying on the beach, not doing much. And even though I wouldn't have minded another spin on the WaveRunners, just relaxing and enjoying the sun was good enough for me. I was already pretty tan, but a little while to round things off wouldn't hurt. Besides, I knew that in twenty-four hours, I'd be back in the snow.

■ ■ ■

Barry Hallihan wasn't as wound up as he had been the first night we arrived, but he was still at his best when it came to dinner. This time, it was steaks and conch chowder. His wife was more subdued as well. They were leaving in the morning, too, and seemed distracted by the thoughts of real life back home. Trey's dad was friendly but quiet; more than once, I caught him absently staring off at the ocean. The conversation among the five of us hovered in the safe territory of home, school, and rowing, focused squarely on Trey and me. I think there was a mutual understanding with the adults that our respective New Year's Eve festivities didn't warrant discussion, and they avoided any talk about their own homes or work.

It was after the Hallihans left when the evening turned weird. Trey and I had just loaded the dishwasher (apparently Crucita had the evening off), and Mr. Daniels was scrubbing a pot in the sink. He was wearing a plaid bathrobe.

I hadn't detected much tension between Trey and his dad all week. In fact, it was the opposite. It seemed like there was a lack of *anything* between them, sort of a willful avoidance of anything that could tip the balance. But the absence of Mrs. Daniels had somehow become a nearly palpable presence. If their conversations had even steered anywhere near the topic, one or both of them had nudged things quickly back into the mundane. They seemed to cooperate on this, but I sensed Trey was more willing to go there than his father was. So, all things considered, I think Trey said what he said very deliberately. And when he did, the rest of the evening became anything but mundane.

"So, have you called Mom even once this week?" He shut the dishwasher and wiped his hands off on a rag. His voice sounded smaller than it usually did.

Mr. Daniels paused in his pan scrubbing and looked at Trey. He glanced at me and then back to his son. "Excuse me?"

"You could have at least wished her a Happy New Year." Trey crossed his arms. His shoulders seemed to shrink.

"I don't think right now is the time for this conversation," said Mr. Daniels, his voice quiet.

"When is the time for this conversation?"

"Trey..." He set the pan down, paused, and turned to me. "Matt, would you excuse us for a few minutes?"

I nodded and started to head upstairs but then realized that outside would be a better idea. I stared at the floor as I walked out, sliding the glass door shut behind me. I could hear the ocean down below and ambled down the stone pathway to where the sand began. Looking back, I could see that things had quickly escalated into a shouting match. It must have been loud, but the expensive double-paned sliding doors did their job, and I couldn't hear a thing from inside. Just the waves. It was like watching something on TV with the volume muted. Mr. Daniels stabbed the air with his finger, and Trey's arms were outstretched, his face red as he shouted back. I turned away, sat down against the trunk of the tall palm tree, and looked up at it. The long leaves rustled in the evening breeze, blotching out the stars as they moved, so it looked like the stars were blinking. Moonlight reflected on the breakers.

After a few minutes, I heard the screen door slide open, and Trey's voice shattered the quiet.

"Because it *does* matter, Dad! We don't ever talk about *anything* that matters! And *this* fucking matters! *She matters!*" He slammed the door shut and sprinted across the patio, past me, and out onto the beach. I stood up and called after him, but he kept running down the beach. Sprinting.

Moments later, Mr. Daniels came outside and sat down on the step. He left the door open behind him. He looked pathetic in the bathrobe. His elbows were on his knees, and he had his face buried in his hands. He rocked quietly back and forth, and I crept away down the beach as silently as I could in the direction Trey had gone.

I found him a few hundred yards away, sitting on the sand the same way his father was. He was weeping—not just crying, but absolutely weeping, with deep, desperate heaves. I sat down next to him and put my arm around his shoulders, and he leaned into me like a little kid. He tried to say something, but nothing came out except sobs. He was shaking like crazy. It took a while for it to subside, and he wiped his nose with the sleeve of his T-shirt. We got up and walked back to the house, both staring at the sand, not saying anything. The lights were off, and Mr. Daniels had gone to bed. I went to get us a couple of glasses of water. Trey drank his slowly, wiping his eyes. He clapped me on the back, said, "Thanks," and trudged up the stairs. I sat in the kitchen, listening to the rhythmic hum of the dishwasher.

After a minute, I saw movement out on the deck. It was Crucita. She was in a nightgown, and held a dog on a leash. I opened the sliding door. "Hi, Crucita."

The moonlight was blue on her white nightgown, and her eyes seemed to sparkle. She spoke quietly. "I walk the dog and hear commotion. Todo esta bien? Everything okay?" The dog pulled at the leash, nuzzling me. I knelt down to pet it.

"It's okay," I said.

"Bueno. Who shoutin'? Who make all that noise? That Mr. Daniels an' the boy?"

"Yes. It was. But it's okay now."

She shook her head, her voice low. "Dios mio. Not a good thing, a boy and his father to shout one another. My grandbaby, he have no father. And my husband he die fifteen years 'go. You love your father, Mateo. You miss him soon enough."

I nodded, not sure what to say. She went on, petting the dog, and looked up at the dark condo. Her voice was low. "They good people, but angry. I can tell. I know. Sometimes before, too, when his momma she was here? They real quiet, but angry. But I mind my business. Okay. So long everybody okay, I'm mind my business and go back home. You get some sleep now Matt." She turned, dragging the dog back toward the road. "Vamanos."

■ ■ ■

Trey was already awake and in the shower when the alarm clock went off at five. There was no elaborate breakfast from Crucita in the morning, but Mr. Daniels had gotten up early and cooked eggs and bacon. I could hear CNN on the TV. I showered and went downstairs to find him watching the news.

"Morning, Matt. You want some coffee?" Mr. Daniels passed me a cup.

"Oh, uh, no thanks. Thanks for cooking, though."

"Sure." He spooned some eggs onto my plate. "Bacon?"

"Thanks."

Trey came in from outside. "Morning," he said, and poured himself some coffee. He nodded at the TV. "It's cold back at school. Snow."

"Not as much as Buffalo," I replied.

Mr. Daniels looked relieved as the conversation turned to the weather. "How much do you think is on the ground there now?"

"I bet there's a couple feet."

It went on like that until we packed up the Jeep. We listened to Tom Petty again, not talking, and watched the sky brighten as the sun began to rise. It felt strange to be wearing jeans and shoes for the first time in a week. As we drove away, I saw Crucita with a young woman and a little boy who I assumed must be her daughter and grandson. They were walking on the side of the road toward the house. They waved. "Adios!" she said, smiling.

We didn't talk much on the way to the airstrip. After we pulled into the driveway, Mr. Daniels walked with us to the tiny plane and exchanged small talk with the pilot as we loaded our bags. He turned to shake my hand.

"Great meeting you, Matt. Thanks so much for coming down. Hope to see you next year again."

"That'd be great. Thanks for having me."

He turned to Trey. "Hey." He spread his arms for a hug. Trey stepped closer, and they embraced for an awkward few seconds. "I have meetings in Nassau for a couple days, but I'll be back in New York by the end of the week."

"Okay."

"Mom will pick you up at Reagan."

"Okay. Thanks. See you soon."

"Hey." Mr. Daniels gripped Trey's shoulder.

"Huh?"

"Good luck with school. Get to work up there, okay?"

"I will. Bye."

"Bye."

We climbed into the plane and buckled in. Mr. Daniels waved at us from the Jeep as we lifted off. I waved back. Trey didn't.

After we landed in Miami, we read car magazines and drank Cokes while we waited for our connections. His flight to DC left first, and I punched him in the shoulder as he picked up his bags to board. "See you in a few days," I said.

"Yeah, dude. Enjoy Buffalo. Don't freeze your balls off."

"I'll survive. Thanks again, man. It was fun."

"Sorry for the drama." He looked around him at the crowd in the airport. He was uncomfortable, distracted, and clearly waiting for me to leave.

"Whatever. No big deal," I said and turned to walk to my gate.

My flight left about an hour later, and when we landed, it was snowing so hard I couldn't see the terminal.

■ ■ ■

Dad was waiting when I arrived. His eyes lit up when he saw me. "Holy smokes, are you tan! What'd you do? Spend all week lying on the beach?"

I smiled and gave him a hug. "Pretty much."

"Your mother's gonna test you for skin cancer."

We picked up my luggage and fought the snow walking through the parking lot.

"God, it's so freezing here." I laughed. "Feels even colder now after being down there."

"Ah, this isn't bad. You should have been here last week."

"How much worse can it get?" I looked around as he unlocked the car. Visibility was maybe a hundred feet.

"It was freezing rain for two days," he said, slamming the door and starting the engine. "That was worse. More accidents than I've seen in years. Mom worked three shifts in a row." He smiled and handed me a snowbrush. "Welcome home. You can do the honors."

"Ah, crap," I muttered as I got out and brushed the car off, wincing as the snow landed on my neck and hands. I did it as quickly as I could and then got back inside and slammed the door. I stomped my feet to get the snow off my shoes. "I think we should move to the Bahamas."

"You and me both, tiger. So tell me about it." He fished for the parking stub, which he had stashed above the sun visor, where he always put stuff like that.

"Well, where do I start?" *I know, how about the New Year's party?* "Their condo is unreal."

"Yeah? And how's Mr. Daniels? Nice guy?"

"He's a good guy. Definitely weird, though. Rich, Dad. Really, really rich."

"Too much money makes people weird. Don't get me wrong; I'd like some more of it. But seriously, not too much more. Makes people nuts." He rolled the window down and paid the parking attendant.

"We really had a good time, though. Didn't do too much, mostly just hung out and rode WaveRunners. It's an awesome island."

Dad looked at me. "Hmm. I assume you had a few drinks down there. Were you careful?"

"What? Dad, watch the road."

"Come on; it's all right. I'm not an idiot; I'm your father. New Year's in the Bahamas with your best pal? I'm sure you had a drink or two. You were careful, right?"

"Yeah. Just a little bit. I didn't drink too much."

*Except when I did.*

"So, meet any ladies?" He grinned.

I clenched my jaw and wiped some frost from the windshield. *What the hell, were you having me tracked or something?* "Some, yeah."

"And?"

"And what? Gees."

"Any one in particular?" He eyed the rearview mirror as he shifted lanes.

"One in particular, yes, if you gotta know."

"American or some native hottie?"

I glared at him. "Native hottie? Really, Dad? It was the Bahamas, not the jungle."

"Come on, who was she?"

"She was an Amazon priestess with diamonds on her nipples, Dad, and we did the whole *Kama Sutra* in the temple of the coconut goddess while her naked servants fanned us with palm branches. You can expect a grandchild in nine months."

He laughed. "Don't worry. I won't tell your mother. It'll ruin dinner."

After he finished with the interrogation, we listened to his Paul Simon album for the rest of the ride. I watched the snowflakes rush past the window. Christmas lights glowed under blankets of snow on rooftops. I glanced at my dad as he stared intently ahead, muttering occasionally at other drivers. It occurred to me that despite the questions, he wasn't really asking me anything about the trip, and he didn't press me. He knew it was my experience and he couldn't fully share it. He must have known that I wasn't so innocent anymore. He must have known that there was a part of me that was growing apart, branching away from him and Mom, on a new trajectory determined by other people, places, and circumstances that had nothing to do with them. And he knew that was how it always would be between fathers and sons. He must have known all of this before I left for boarding school, and certainly before he let me go to the Bahamas. He knew it long before I figured it out.

I smiled, and in a way I hadn't before, I admired my dad.

# CHAPTER 25

It was six p.m. on a Tuesday in early February, just a month or so after the trip to the Bahamas, and a steady snow was falling on campus. I don't know exactly why, but I had been in a dark mood for a week. A blanket of snow three inches thick had already collected since noon, and the forecast called for two inches more by morning. By Buffalo standards, this was nothing, but it was enough to paralyze anyplace south of the Mason-Dixon line. The county cancelled school, and Ashford River always followed the decisions of the county for the benefit of the day students who didn't board there. Dr. Winthrop announced that study hall would also be cancelled for the night. The teachers were simultaneously happy and annoyed. No school meant no teaching, but it also meant that some shenanigans would probably go down. And, of course, they did.

Chase Alexander, a regular contributor to shenanigans at Ashford River, declared a continuation of the ongoing snowball war against the freshmen during dinner. The unanimous agreement was that the first shot would be fired at seven. The freshmen, being outnumbered, would defend the hill, and we would attack from below. Dinner was over, and most of the guys had run off to their rooms to outfit themselves in appropriate cold-weather battle armor. I was finishing a cup of hot chocolate in The Hampshire Room, still in my school clothes—halfway anyway: tie loose and my wrinkled shirt untucked. I was leaning against the French doors that led out onto the snow-covered terrace. The storm was picking up, and I could barely make out the forms of the freshmen who had begun building battlements between two large pines at the crest of the hill fifty feet from the window. The lampposts on the terrace cast orange light on the snow.

I could hear the teachers talking at the faculty table across the room, leaning in and trying to keep their voices down but occasionally bursting into laughter. I knew that half the time they were talking about us, but they didn't want to be overheard in the dining hall, so they always used these ridiculous tricks where they'd refer to kids by letters or some other code name and talked in vague sentences, like "Yeah, the same one that pulled it off last time...the RAS...I found him trying again on Tuesday, and I told him the consequences would probably be up to the Right Wing and they wouldn't be pretty." I figured out that RAS meant "Really Annoying Senior" and that the acronym referred to Jeremy Alters, who, to give the teachers their due, *was* a really annoying senior. The "Right Wing" was Dean Wagner.

I sipped the hot chocolate, hypnotized by snowflakes falling past the lampposts. The freshmen were stockpiling snowballs behind their ramparts, building an arsenal in preparation for our assault.

Trey walked in, pulled a chair across the floor to where I was standing, and collapsed into it. He punched me in the leg.

"We're gonna need you out there. That hill is killer." He zipped up the ski jacket he was wearing.

"I'm just finishing this." I sipped the hot chocolate. "That's a lot of snow. We might be off on Thursday, too."

"You think so? That would be really clutch 'cause I didn't even start that Dillon paper yet."

I wasn't really surprised by this. "This hot chocolate sucks."

"Hey, know what they're talking about over there now?" Trey nodded toward the teachers' table. "I do, and it's rich."

"No, what?"

Trey grinned and lowered his voice, leaning a little closer to me, keeping his eye on the teachers. He did the Trey-hand-on-your-shoulder thing before he started talking in his most conspiratorial *I've-got-a-great-little-story-to-tell-you* voice. "You know Mr. Novette, that bio teacher, the one that looks like he's still eighteen?"

"Yeah."

"Story is that he got completely plastered on Friday night and wound up in bed with Miss Parker, that college chick that helps coach the tennis team, and then she flipped her shit in the morning. I guess they were both so drunk they didn't remember what happened."

"Whoa." I formed a quick mental image of Miss Parker, her curly brunette hair all messed up and her eyes full of sleep, waking up in her bed with peach-colored sheets all tangled around her, looking confusedly at Mr. Novette lying next to her snoring away, with maybe his arm hanging over the side of the bed, a couple of empty wine bottles on the floor.

"Well, nobody really knows for a fact, but Chase and I heard some juniors in the gym. They were saying that Mike Turner, Steve Mallow, and some other guys snuck out to a Georgetown bar Friday night and—*Surprise!* Lucky them, a few teachers walked in. Mallow and the rest of them almost completely freaked out. They had to keep their heads down and sort of hide in a booth, because the whole goddamned math department was between them and the door. Belknap, DiVincenzo, MacPherson, Connelly, all of 'em. So they managed to hang in there for a half hour until the teachers finally took off and went to a different bar. Anyway, they heard Mr. Belknap say that Dave—that's gotta be Mr. Novette—was 'freaked about it' and wasn't sure if Claire was mad at him or what she was going to do about it. So then—"

"I didn't know her name is Claire." I upended the cup and swallowed the last of the hot chocolate.

"Umm, right. So then—and this is the good part—then Belknap says that it wouldn't be the first time that's happened with her and that 'the kid should calm down.' How friggin' funny is that?" Trey stood up quickly and grabbed my tie, pulling me from the wall. "So let's go, dude! There's a *war* about to start!"

I crumpled the Styrofoam cup and threw it into the trash bin on the way out of the dining hall. (We were not big on environmental initiatives in The Hampshire Room.) Trey headed outside, and I made my way upstairs to get changed. The more stories I heard about adults behaving badly, the more I realized that the admirable moral and ethical code preached at the Ashford River School was sometimes as permeable for them as it was for us teenage guys.

The terms of the snowball battles had been hammered out over the past two months, combining the rules of manhunt, hide-and-seek, and capture-the-flag. A campaign consisted of three consecutive thirty-minute battles, with alternating campaigns seeing different classes taking the defensive and offensive positions on the hill. The teams were officially made up of the freshman and sophomore houses, but sometimes, a senior with nothing else to do joined the freshmen or a junior would jump in with the sophomores.

With each consecutive battle, the rivalries got nastier and the strategies more complex. For the attacking team to win, a single flag held by no more than four defenders in "the Castle" had to be captured and returned to the Rear Attack Base, a snow fort built against the east wall of the boathouse near the pond a quarter mile away. The rest of the defenders couldn't go within fifty feet of the castle but could build little defensive bunkers anywhere on the hill. For the defenders to win, the flag needed to remain safe in the Castle for the half-hour duration of the battle. It hadn't really occurred to anyone that the job of the attacking team was about five thousand times harder than that of the defenders; however, nobody seemed to care because attacking was a lot more fun. You charged up the hill and then tried to hightail it back to the pond once you had the flag, which involved much more action than defending. Another problem was that the half-hour mark usually passed without anyone noticing, which technically violated the rules. The guy assigned as timekeeper and ref almost always got caught up in the battle and forgot to call time. But nobody cared. It was war, after all.

Both teams were assembled at Midway Point, a large pine tree half-way down the hill between the Castle and the Rear Attack Base. Dave Halsworth was a junior, but somehow he'd become the unofficial captain of the freshman team. He was standing on top of a rock and reviewing the terms of battle. He spoke with a deep Mississippi drawl.

"Right now, it's frosh one, sophs one, based on last night's battles. Winner of this one takes campaign [he said *kim-payne*] number three. As for campaigns, the freshmen got two, sophomores one so far." Dave gestured with his hand and held up fingers in case anyone was having trouble with the complex numbers. "In other words, the frosh are pretty much kickin' your soph-moron butts." Dave seemed to think this was a lot funnier than anyone else.

McNeal chimed in. "Listen! Don't forget the rule adjustment we made. If you get hit, you gotta put both arms in the air and walk twenty-five paces back toward your own base." He put his arms in the air. "*High* in the air, like this."

"Right. And they gotta be *slow* paces," added Halsworth, "and not bullshit little paces. You gotta take full steps, *Chase Alexander*."

Alexander gave him the finger. "I got it, Halsworthless." A round of laughter. "I got it. By the way, let's cut the shit and stop hitting guys with their arms up, you assholes."

We were about to head out when Trey shouted, "Hey, wait!" Everyone paused. "I got us a new flag." Trey pulled a bright-red bra from his jacket pocket. "Gentlemen, I present to you our new flag, courtesy of Secret Dave Halsworth's special friend!" He threw the bra at the group.

Even Halsworth was laughing at this one. "Screw you, Daniels," he said between laughs. "Screw you." Everyone had heard the story of how Dave had been caught sneaking Mary Ellen Timberlee from St. Amelia's up into his room. Mr. DiVincenzo got wind of some mischief and knocked on Dave's door. No one answered, but he heard a loud crash, so he keyed himself in. A lamp lay on the ground, the bulb shattered. Unfortunately, there was enough light from the hallway for him to see more than he wanted to. Halsworth was half naked, trying without much success to pull his boxers and pants on, a process complicated by the presence of a rather conspicuous state of arousal. While Dave froze, looking all deer-in-the-headlights, Mr. D. heard a noise in the closet, turned on the overhead light, and almost opened the door. Fortunately, he made a last-second judgment against opening the closet door, for if he had, he would have found himself in a pretty awkward predicament. Because he would have found Mary Ellen Timberlee standing there in nothing but bright-red Victoria's Secret panties, trying desperately to hook her bright-red bra behind her back, which was pretty much impossible in the tight confines of the closet. Instead, Mr. DiVincenzo escorted Dave (who had managed to get his pants and a shirt on) out of the room. A few moments later, Mary Ellen, now clothed, stuck her head out the door to face the music.

Once the fireworks calmed down in the week following, Dave—who just barely escaped expulsion based on his previous good behavior—became permanently (and pretty famously) known as Secret Dave, as in Victoria's Secret. Truth is, nothing too serious happened to Dave and all he had to do was rake leaves with the grounds crew for a few weeks. He didn't mind this one bit, of course, because every time the other guys saw him out there busting his ass on the leaves, they knew it was just because he'd been getting some. Mary Ellen Timberlee, on the other hand, had not been heard from since.

So the bra became the new flag, and Trey was officially the funniest guy around.

Twenty minutes later, battle raged on the grounds of the Ashford River School. Bloodcurdling shouts of agony and occasional obscenities followed hollered battle cries. The short-range attacks zipped from attacker to target like bullets, impacting hard, sometimes containing more ice than snow. Long-range defensive barrages from the top of the hill—eight or twelve coordinated snowballs thrown at once with military discipline by the freshmen—sailed in wide ballistic arcs across the night sky. They reached their zenith, seemed to pause at high altitude, and then gained speed and power as they screamed down from above, unleashing a tempest of splatter patterns upon our forward posts, freezing two or three advancing losers and sending them shuffling, pissed off and arms held high, back down the hill for the designated twenty-five paces before they could return to action. Of course, this part depended completely on the honor system, and there were quite a few lapses. Twenty-five paces turned into twenty-three, and soon to sixteen or seventeen, but no one really cared or counted.

Well, Eldrin probably would have, but he wasn't playing.

We were at the ten-minutes-to-go mark, and Trey and I had made it around the right flank and were only about twenty yards from the Castle, breathing hard from the uphill sprint and lying in the hollow under a large pine. Both of our hearts pounded from the exertion, and Trey spoke in short whispers, trying to catch his breath.

"I can't..." He coughed. "I can't believe we made it up here without those dipshits seeing us." He wiped some snot from his nose as he peered through the branches. "Looks like there's only two of them at the Castle."

I was just trying to catch my breath. "Yeah. We can get it. I can see it." The bra hung limply from a snow shovel sticking up from the ground behind the middle rampart of the castle.

"Just stay right behind me," he said. "That way, they can't knock us both out at the same time."

"Right."

Trey kept looking through the branches, waiting for the right time to move. "So whaddya think of the new flag?" He was grinning.

I shook my head. "Where'd you get it? It's not really Mary Ellen Timberlee's, is it?"

"No. I got it in the Bahamas, dude. It's Mandy's. Okay...let's go!"

In about two seconds, Trey was up and out of the hole, sprinting full speed toward the Castle. I jumped up and dug in hard, following in his path. I could hear the snow crunching beneath our feet as we sprinted closer. Secret Dave turned to grab a snowball from the almost-depleted reserves behind him and did a double take when he saw Trey, now only twenty feet from him and closing fast. He pitched the tightly packed snowball. Halsworth was a good shot—he should have been since he was the starting pitcher on the baseball team. It nailed Trey center-chest and almost knocked him over. Trey swore, stopped dead in his tracks, raised his arms overhead, and started walking down the hill, honorably counting out his twenty-five (or so) paces. Of course, Secret Dave hardly noticed this, because I was still running at him, ducking under the attacks coming from Jimmy Miller now too. I was only fifteen feet from the bra now, wincing as Dave wound up for another throw, when suddenly, a massive snowball from outside the Castle nailed Dave directly in the face and he hit the ground. A fraction of a second later, another snowball slammed into Jimmy Miller's shoulder, freezing him and leaving the flag defenseless for the next twenty seconds. I saw McNeal out of the corner of my eye and realized the covering fire was coming from him. I grabbed the bra, turned faster than I thought I could, almost slipped on the well-packed floor of the Castle, and began an all-out sprint down the hill.

I heard the shouts behind me and knew that snowballs had to be coming at me, but I kept going, half tripping down the hill, once actually falling and sliding for twenty odd feet before rolling back onto my feet and sprinting on. Two-thirds of the way down, a group of four sophomores joined up and formed a wall behind me, taking suicidal hits for the team as we all scrambled closer to the pond. My lungs were burning. I saw McNeal running toward me, waving frantically, shouting something. Suddenly, I felt an explosion of cold on the back of my neck, and a shout of *"Got him!"* echoed down the hill. I slid to a halt, swearing, arms raised, as McNeal sprinted past and grabbed the bra. If a freshman had managed to get to me first, I would have had to turn it over.

"I got it, Derby!" yelled Brian as he took off down the hill, three freshmen in hot pursuit.

A few feet later, Trey appeared next to him, grinning maniacally and leaping over mounds of snow as they continued running down the now-flattening slope. I could hear shouts from all directions now.

"You've got it!" I yelled, watching Brian sprint toward the base. "Go, go, go, go, go, go! Oh, *shit!*"

I saw the exposed root in front of McNeal a millisecond before he tripped over it, rolling his ankle and nailing the snow-covered ground like a sack of cement. The bright-red bra sailed through the air for half a second before Trey scooped it up and continued headlong down the hill. He roared with victory as he and a pack of sophomores crossed the line, winning the battle. Back on the ground, McNeal celebrated even as he writhed in pain, clutching his twisted ankle.

■ ■ ■

A half hour later, we were sitting in the common room. McNeal had his foot up on an ottoman as Brady wrapped his ankle. Trey, Halsworth, and Chase were there, too, all sprawled in various places on the furniture and drinking mugs of hot chocolate. We wore warm-ups and sweatshirts now, but our faces were still flushed from the cold and exertion.

"Lucky you didn't break this, you idiot," muttered Brady. "This is gonna keep you off your feet for a while. Why do you guys pull all this stuff on the nights I'm on duty?"

Trey jumped up from the couch. "Yeah, but, Coach, you shoulda seen it! This kid was *flyin'* down that hill, and then he hits the fuc-err—he hits the *darned* root and goes flying…Damn, you hit that ground hard!" The rest of us were laughing.

Brady put an ice pack on Brian's ankle. "Well, I'm glad you won. I have to hand it to you guys. You really go all out when you put your mind to something. Maybe I'll get in on the next snowball war. That is, if it won't kill me."

"Thanks. Yeah, you should do that," said Brian.

"Okay, you guys can hang in here and watch TV. Brian, keep that ankle up and keep the ice on it. I'm gonna go to my office for a minute."

Brady headed down the hall. Trey pulled the bra from the pocket of his sweatshirt, held it to his chest, and did a little dance, cracking up with laughter. He gave McNeal a high five and thrust the bra in his face.

"So how's the ankle?" Trey sat down on the ottoman and studied the injury.

"Hurts like hell."

"Here, you earned it." He flung the red bra at Brian. "Guess I'll have to find a new one for the next battle."

■ ■ ■

I often wondered why the memory of the snowball fight is so vivid. But eventually, it made sense. It was the last night things were normal that year at the Ashford River School. So much changed after the battle. And really, such enormous change hinged entirely on coincidence. If the faculty washing machine hadn't happened to short out that week, Mr. Paul DiVincenzo of the math department wouldn't have had to use the student laundry room on Monday night. And then Trey Daniels might have made it through sophomore year. He might not have been expelled, and he might not have pulled his father from a burning hotel room six years later.

# CHAPTER 26

I hated doing laundry. It wasn't a big deal at home, but at the Ashford River School, without fail, it was a major pain in the ass. The washers in the basement of MacKerry Hall worked okay, but the dryers took at least an hour to finish a load. This wouldn't have been such a huge problem if there were six or seven dryers, *"like every other decent boarding school,"* Rick Eldrin had declared during one of his dinnertime rants. Instead, there were only two, and of those two, only one actually worked. The other one, after catching fire and causing a midnight evacuation of the dorms, was declared out of order.

And this, for a number of reasons, sucked.

First off, there were two washers. With two working dryers, a natural, cyclical pattern existed. But in a dorm full of teenage guys, you can imagine the sort of chaos that was bound to happen when one of two dryers was down while two washers worked.

The last time I'd done laundry, I was lucky...at first. I got down to the basement early on a Sunday morning, found an empty washer, and dumped all my clothes in. (Nobody ever bothered separating lights and darks except for McNeal, but if you'll recall, this was the same kid who scheduled every aspect of his life.) I even had enough detergent left, surprisingly. Trey had made off with it the night before and returned it half empty, having lost most of the powder because he forgot to close the box before carrying it upstairs. My dirty clothes loaded, I added the soap, slammed the door shut, and set the dial for *Colors*. Forty minutes later, I came back, transferred the damp heap to the working dryer and started the one-hour cycle. I thought I was home free.

An hour later, after doing my Latin homework, I ambled into the dimly lit laundry room, muttering a series of verb endings. I was glad that for once I wouldn't be rushing to get dressed for Mass and that I'd have plenty of clean clothes to choose from.

This, however, was not the case. Instead, my clothes had been piled on top of the washer from which I'd taken them just an hour ago. They were still damp. The dryer was spinning a load of some unidentified origin, but I could make out a green-and-white-checkered shirt bearing a certain resemblance to one owned by Rick Eldrin. I stopped the dryer, took his clothes out, and left them in a heap on the floor, grumbling expletives. After putting my own clothes back in, I stood guard, leaning on the dryer, arms crossed and jaw set. For the next ten minutes, I thought of all the reasons why I despised Rick Eldrin, wondering just how much of an asshole one human boy could possibly become in less than sixteen years. What really made it bad, I decided, was that my clothes had needed only another ten minutes, but Rick obviously couldn't wait that long.

Being a decent human being and given that I was headed to Mass in fifteen minutes on this, the Lord's Day, I decided at this particular decision-making juncture to reload Eldrin's laundry and restart the dryer for him.

*Jerk.*

So that's the kind of crap that made doing laundry at the Ashford River School so much fun. Then there was the mysterious tendency on the part of the working dryer to devour socks. Of course, there were also the jerks who put their laundry in and forgot to start the machine and the jerks who didn't clean the lint filter, so their clothes never dried and they took up two cycles. But the worst were the jerks who "borrowed" your detergent, roommates occasionally excluded.

There were, I had decided, many kinds of jerks at the Ashford River School.

Anyway, the night after the snowball fight, I was standing in the doorway of the cramped room, waiting for Jimmy Speers to take his stuff out of the washer. The other one was full, with four minutes left in the spin cycle. Hasselwerdt played minigolf with a plastic whiffleball bat and a crumpled piece of paper on the ground, taking cues from Jimmy on how to fix his grip.

"Straighten out your thumb. Parallel to the club."

"Like this?"

"Nah, look." Jimmy stopped unloading clothes and fixed Mike's hand.

"Ah, come on, Speers!" I said, and kicked the crumpled ball of paper across the room. "Get your stuff out of there so I can put mine in. I've got a ton of geometry homework." I stood there, the mesh bag slung over my shoulder.

Jimmy looked up at me with a cool glare, his eyes narrowed. "Patience, Derby, is a virtue." He was wearing a threadbare blue tank top that said "BEWARE OF COX" in red block letters, a find from the rowing apparel stands at the Pittsburgh regatta.

"Christ, Speers. Come on."

"Okay, okay." Speers pulled the rest of the clothes out, and I began throwing dirty socks into the circular opening. Just then, Mr. DiVincenzo walked in, carrying an armful of whites.

"Hey, guys. Anything available? The faculty washer's broken again."

"Hey, Mr. D.," Mike said. "Check this out." He took a high swing, testing his new grip, and sent the crumpled ball of paper flying into the far corner of the small room.

"That's a good swing, Mike. So, any washers free?"

"That one's got one minute left," I told him, nodding at the second machine, which vibrated loudly as it spun, banging up and down rhythmically on the cement floor.

"Ah, okay. I'll wait for that one. Sounds like it's overloaded. And you guys wonder why these are always breaking down." The pounding halted, and we heard water draining as the washer hissed to a stop.

"This is definitely overloaded," said Mr. DiVincenzo, pulling a dense, wrinkled mass of khakis, shirts, warm-ups, and socks from the washer. "You guys know whose stuff this is?" An Ashford River crew jacket fell to the floor. It read, *"Daniels."*

"I should have known," he muttered, picking up the jacket and adding it to the massive pile. "Jesus, that kid must have two full loads in—" His speech stopped abruptly as a tiny object fell out from the pile. It landed on the floor with a singular, hollow *clink*, and rolled to a stop under the teacher's shoe.

Mr. DiVincenzo picked up Trey's favorite weed pipe, turning the enameled, dark-green ceramic piece slowly over in his hand. His eyebrows rose as he sniffed the bowl.

■ ■ ■

I took a shower early that night, thankful that there was no one there to ask me questions. There were times when I really didn't feel like talking to anyone, especially in the damned shower. Back in my room, I waited around for Trey, but he didn't come back before lights-out. I buried myself in my history book. McNeal appeared in the doorway, leaning on his crutches.

"Heard anything?"

"No." I didn't look up from the book.

Steve Mallow did bed check, because Mr. Brady was busy dealing with the situation. The last time I'd seen him, DiVincenzo was taking Trey to Mr. Wagner's office. It didn't take long for the news to spread through the hall. It was always the same whenever something scandalous went down. Conversations were lowered to conspiratorial whispers. Quiet bits of rumors passed in hushed voices, with looks over shoulders to see who might hear. The story was pieced together. Around me, guys dropped to an abrupt silence. Respect for the family of the deceased, so to speak. Speers and Hasselwerdt, the other two who were in the laundry room, were also treated with a sort of awestruck reverence. They were witnesses.

I lay on the top bunk, hands folded behind my head, and stared at the ceiling. It got quiet after lights-out, but the occasional fumbling noises of nervously awake classmates were audible through the walls. McNeal managed one after-hours visit, poking his head in. Before he could ask if I knew anything, I shot the answer across the room in a single, acidic syllable: "No." Brian let the door close softly and disappeared.

My mind raced through the conversations we'd had about smoking. I thought about all the times I knew about it. My face burned, when I thought about my role. My inaction. Did I do something? Was not doing something just as bad?

*You* are *your brother's keeper.*

*"I guess you're our guy."*

My face burned hotter as I thought about multiple deviations from the right and true path, following Trey in the wrong directions at various decision-making junctures. My stomach crunched into a tight knot as I thought about the Bahamas, the drinking, Laurie, the beach. The brief conversation with Dad on the way home from the airport. These things seemed to stack like bricks, one on top of the other, building a tower of guilt. And the weight of it was on my chest.

Then it occurred to me.

*He's gonna get expelled.*

The grades. The fight. The little chats.

For a second, my mind raced over the idea of getting kicked out myself. *I knew about it. Does that count?*

Then I issued myself a very hard mental kick to the ass. *How can you worry about yourself right now, you selfish little shit?*

*He's gonna get expelled.*

*But do they have the evidence they need?* I wondered. There weren't actually any drugs. Just the pipe.

*Right?*

But what about the weed?

*You keep it outside, right?*

*Under that rock along the running path.*

*The cigarettes are in the drawer, though.*

*Just cigarettes, please. Trey, you stupid bastard, you aren't stupid enough to keep your weed in the goddamned room are you, you stupid friggin' idiot?*

I climbed down from the bunk, switched my desk lamp on, and made for the drawer.

There was a soft knock on the door. I froze.

Brady. He looked tired. His tie was loosened, and he had dark circles under his eyes. "Hey, Matt."

"Hey." I wondered if I looked like I had just been running across the room. My face burned red hot. *Can he see it?*

"I need to talk to the whole floor, very briefly." His voice was soft, reserved. Gentle.

"Okay." I reached for a sweatshirt and pulled it on.

"Come on." He was holding the door, waiting. *Shit.* My heart pounded. *Please tell me you only have cigarettes in the drawer.*

I followed Brady to the small lounge at the end of the corridor. Most of the others were there already. All eyes were on me as I took a seat. Brady stood, leaning against the wall. He stared at the floor while he spoke.

"Gentlemen, I know the rumors are flying at the moment. So it's best that the truth of the situation be known, since rumors can do nasty things." He paused, rubbed his chin. I shot a look at Rick Eldrin, who was staring, disinterestedly, out the window.

"As you've probably heard, Trey is involved with a discipline issue regarding a marijuana pipe. There are other factors involved. I'm not going into the details with you right now, because the investigation is ongoing. I would ask you not to spread rumors or to make up any stories. Trey will be going before the disciplinary committee tomorrow." He didn't look up from the floor. "That's all. Please go to your rooms. I assure you that my tolerance for trouble is at a very low point at the moment. Please don't test me." His voice sounded different, quieter, strained.

The group started to get up. McNeal raised his hand. "Mr. Brady?" Everyone stopped.

"Not now." His voice was flat. Guys began filing back down the corridor, silently.

"Matt," said Mr. Brady, putting a hand on my shoulder as I turned to go.

"Yeah?"

"Have a seat a moment."

I sat down on the edge of the sofa, elbows on my knees. The teacher pulled a folding chair next to it and leaned in close. He whispered, since kids were still in the corridor. I could hear the fluorescent bulb buzzing above us. It needed to be replaced.

"You realize, I hope..."

I felt dizzy, and there was a hot, seething feeling under my arms, like a brush burn. My throat tightened, and my eyes were welling up. I tried to fight it.

"You realize that this puts you in a rough spot."

I nodded rapidly, wiping the snot from my nose. My neck was tense. It ached.

"Trey says you've never smoked weed."

I nodded.

Brady continued, "I believe him. He also says you *didn't* know about the marijuana in your room."

My mouth felt dry. I shook my head. *No.*

"Cigarettes. That's all he had in the room," I managed.

"No, Matt. He kept his weed in the base of the pencil sharpener."

"He *what?*"

"So you didn't know about that?"

"I knew about cigarettes," I said.

"Yes, we found those."

*Oh.*

"When?"

"Matt, we had to search the room immediately."

I chuckled nervously. "You did a good job. I...I couldn't tell."

"I know."

I was shaking.

*He's going to get expelled.*

Brady looked me in the eye. "Can you be honest with me?" he asked.

"Yes."

"As your coach, Matt."

"Yeah." I looked up.

"You didn't smoke any marijuana, Matt, did you?" It was less a question than a statement.

I stared him straight in the eye. "No." I wanted to blurt out everything. I wanted to break down about the girls in the pool, the Bahamas, drinking, Laurie, cheating on the test, everything. I thought of my mom. The tears came again. "No, I really didn't. Just a couple cigarettes once."

"You knew about this problem of his, though. You knew about this back when we talked in October, didn't you?"

"Sort of."

Brady nodded. "You're going to have to deal with that on your own."

I wiped my eyes with my sleeve. "What's gonna happen?"

"I don't know. He'll go before the disciplinary committee tomorrow. It's ultimately up to them and Dr. Winthrop."

"What do you..." I sniffled again, trying to regain my composure. *Grow up.* "What do you *think* will happen?"

"I think he'll be asked to leave the school. He's already on very thin ice."

"But what about everything he's done right? What about the kid he saved?"

"I know, Matt. He's a good kid. I don't think anyone on the faculty would disagree. But the school has strict rules about this type of thing. It has to stick to them, you know? Kids with drug habits just can't be a part of this community."

"But other kids…" I started, then stopped. I looked at him again. "It isn't that rare, Mr. Brady."

"I believe that. But we can only deal with the situations that crop up. This one cropped up. And to be honest with you, it's a little more than just some weed in your room. It seems like there was a fair amount of buying and selling, too. There's just no tolerance for that part of it, Matt. There can't be. Think about it."

I did think about this for a minute. And then, "What about me?" The words came out quicker than I had wanted them to. I looked at the floor, tensed my shoulders.

"You?"

"Yeah."

"Probably not much, Matt. Probably not much."

"I feel like—"

"I know."

"But I could have—"

"It's better in a lot of ways if we end this conversation here." Brady stood up.

*Huh?*

"Where's Trey?"

"He'll be staying in one of the guest rooms on the senior floor tonight. It's just policy with something like this, until we sort out the facts. He needs to stay isolated, so the facts don't get confused."

"Oh."

*Isolated.*

*That's the lamest fucking thing you've ever said, Coach.*

"Get some sleep, Derby. We'll talk more tomorrow."

# CHAPTER 27

The gears of discipline didn't always turn at Ashford River. But when they did, they turned fast. Trey wasn't in any classes the next day. I caught glimpses of him whenever I passed the dean's office. I could barely see him through the glare on the window. Every time I saw him, he was staring at the floor. Mr. Sharp, Mrs. Arena, Dr. Connelly, and Mr. Leavenworth, the faculty members on the disciplinary committee, were conspicuously absent from class that day, with substitutes assigned at the last minute. The story had flown through the school by the end of second period, and Dr. Winthrop, Mr. Wagner, and the other members of the committee could be seen huddled close together in The Hampshire Room during lunch, a buffer of empty tables around them. Even the other teachers kept their distance. At one point during Father Daley's Latin class, Mr. Wagner knocked on the door, and everyone immediately looked up as he pointed to Chase Alexander. Chase seemed to know he was defeated before the finger was pointed, and he shuffled to the front of the class, staring at the ground as he passed through the door, held open by the dean.

I ran upstairs to get changed for practice after school. No sign of Trey or Chase. Thank God we were going for a run and not working in the weight room. Too much talk down there. I ran hard and fast, out in front by myself. Even Rick Eldrin had the decency to leave me alone. The air was frozen and the sky gray. The snow-covered jogging path had been packed hard.

Halfway through practice, Mr. Brady waved me down. I jogged over to the boathouse. The teacher was standing in a dress coat and ski hat, holding his clipboard.

"You're getting faster." His breath was visible in the frigid air.

I coughed. "Thanks."

"Matt, Trey's leaving in about a half hour."

*A half hour?*

"He's what?"

"His mom wanted him on the first flight out."

"She's not even coming? Not his dad either?"

There are moments I can recall from those years when a white-hot, churning rage came on so quickly and so overwhelmingly that it frightened me. For whatever reason, the picture of Trey and his dad on the fishing trip surfaced in my mind and then shifted to the image of his dad with his head in his hands, Trey sprinting down the beach that night. And suddenly, I hated something, but I wasn't sure what, exactly.

Brady looked up at the gray sky. "No." He shook his head. "They...I was told they couldn't arrange it. They're both out of town. She's in San Francisco, and his dad's in New York." He was clenching and unclenching his jaw.

"Where is he?"

"Should just be coming out of a meeting with Dr. Winthrop in the MacKerry parlor."

"You mean he's already packed and everything?" The words were rushed. I couldn't believe Trey could possibly have packed up his massive collection of crap that quickly.

"Yeah, it didn't take long. He did it while you were running."

I shook my head, my mind spinning. I turned to sprint up the hill to MacKerry.

"Matt!" Brady shouted after me.

I skidded to a stop. "Huh?"

"I know he's a good friend. He's…he's a very good kid." He threw the clipboard on the bench next to him. It clattered noisily. He was shaking his head. "Too many things added up for him. Not the right place. It's…" I waited for him to finish his sentence, but he didn't. He just said, "I'm sorry." He shoved his hands deep in the pockets of the wool coat as I turned and headed up the hill.

*Sure you are, Coach.*

■ ■ ■

"You ever feel like you do stuff and you have no idea why?" Trey played with the short end of his tie, curling it around his thumb. He had buttoned his collar all the way to the top for his "departure interview" with Dr. Winthrop. Might have been the first time all year. "'Cause I don't really know why I do the stuff I do."

His voice was quiet and flat. We were sitting on a wooden bench on the terrace in front of MacKerry Hall, waiting for the airport taxi. Two large duffel bags filled with his stuff sat on the ground next to us. It was snowing, and I could feel the cold cement through my running shoes. I put the hood of my sweatshirt up and shivered.

An icicle fell from the gutter, landing in the bushes and spraying snow on the steps.

"How'd that meeting go?" I asked.

"Wasn't so bad. Winthrop was cool. Just said good luck, told me about transferring my transcript, and shook hands. At least he didn't try to blow a bunch of departing-wisdom sunshine up my ass."

I couldn't help laughing at this. "That's…that's good, I guess. I can't believe they're kicking you out."

"Eh, it was just a matter of time." He paused for a moment. "It wasn't just the pipe, man. I bought and sold. And there was the fight. And the grades. The grades, really, maybe more than anything. The weed was just the smoking gun they needed. Eldrin probably fed them some shit, too. I know for a fact he's the one who ratted out Chase. Winthrop said, 'it just isn't working out.'"

"I should have helped you more."

Trey shook his head. "Helped me? I wasn't helpless, Matt. Maybe I should have done my work. Maybe I shoulda not smoked up at school. Maybe I shoulda not gotten in that fight. Shoulda-coulda-woulda."

*You're pretty calm about this.*

"You don't really seem to care," I said.

"I'm not sure if I do," replied Trey. "To tell you the truth, I can't stand it here."

I paused for a few seconds. "Can you stand me?" My voice cracked.

Trey laughed and looked at me with narrowed eyes. "You're about the only thing I *can* stand around here, Derby."

Silence.

"Why the hell did you keep it in our room? I thought you always kept it outside."

"I usually did. It's just been so damned cold lately."

"Are you serious?" It almost seemed funny—that he'd take that sort of risk because it was cold outside. This from the kid who would row for two hours in a T-shirt in fifty-degree weather.

"Yeah," he said. "And I didn't tell you because…well, because I didn't want you to be responsible for it. Isn't it better that you *didn't* know?"

I didn't want to answer that question, because I knew he was right. "What about your parents?"

"It'll work out." He paused and nodded toward the yellow light spilling from the windows of The Hampshire Room. "You're missing dinner. Do you have any idea what you're *missing* in there? It's fried haddock night, Derby." Trey grinned. "Christ, I am *not* gonna miss fried haddock night."

I cleared my throat. "Do you know where you're gonna go?"

"Home."

"Where is home?"

Trey stopped playing with his tie and arched his back, fingers joined behind his head, stretching his chest. He smiled a little bit, but just for a second. "That sounds like one of those philosophical Father Daley questions. The ones that you don't really have to answer. Whaddya call 'em?" He stared up at the sky, still leaning back.

"Rhetorical."

"Yeah."

"So?"

"Well, I dunno where home is, buddy. My aunt lives in San Francisco, and I guess we're heading there for now. Mom says we might stay out west for good. She's been planning to sell the Georgetown place for a while now anyway. Now she has a real reason to. I'd be fine going back to Lake Placid, but she says she wants to move somewhere new. She was talking about Wyoming." He reached down and unclipped the shoulder strap from his duffel bag, examining the brass clip in his hands. "So I'll meet her in California, and we'll stay with my aunt for a while. Figure it out from there."

"What about school?"

"Not sure. Probably just a public school wherever we end up. I think my prep school days are over. This was my third one. Guess I'm not wired for this kind of place."

We both looked out, watching the snow. The flakes had gotten lighter, and they blew around in tiny swirls. The sky was gray with twilight.

"Trey."

"Huh?" He was back to playing with the tie.

"Never mind." I stared at my shoes.

"What?"

"Are you…mad about it?"

"Why should I be? It's my own fault." He managed a little laugh that came out like a snort. "Tough luck, really. And stupid."

"Yeah, but still, are you mad?"

"I guess I'd say I'm more disappointed than mad," he said.

"Now *you* sound like Daley."

"Nah, that's more like something Mr. Brady would say." Trey chuckled.

"No, then it would be, 'I'm more disappointed than mad, *chief*.'"

"Right." He smiled.

"You talk to him? I mean since Tuesday?" I asked.

"Brady? Don't really know what there is to talk about," he replied.

"He's pissed about it," I said.

"Of course he's pissed. It's his job to be pissed."

"Well, yeah, he's pissed at you. But I mean more at the whole situation. You leaving the team."

"Oh." Trey chipped a loose splinter from the bench with his thumbnail. "Well, at least Eldrin will shut the hell up now." We both laughed. Quick, stifled.

"Nah, he won't," I said.

It was getting dark, and the lamps flickered on.

Trey smiled. "You remember that storm when we hung out on the ledge?"

"First time I smoked a cigarette," I said.

"Yeah."

Large snowflakes kept falling. A loud peal of laughter and applause came from The Hampshire Room. Someone must have broken a glass. It was a tradition at the Ashford River School to applaud whenever someone broke a glass.

"I left the Bob Dylan poster for you."

"Thanks."

"And some other shit too. Stuff I couldn't fit."

"Thanks."

"No weed, though. Took all that with me. Along with the pencil sharpener." He grinned.

I looked at him, my brow furrowed, and then I smiled. "Yeah. Okay."

"You'll have the room to yourself now, right?" he asked.

"I guess. At least for a while."

"Well, that'll be a luxury, 'cause I left you some of the magazines." He laughed. "Try not to hurt yourself."

This made both of us laugh.

"Hey," I said.

"What?"

"Remember when you were sitting with that little kid in the back of the ambulance?"

"Yeah."

"What did you say to him?"

"I just said that everything was gonna be okay." Trey smiled and shook his head. "I guess that's bullshit, right? 'Cause it isn't always gonna be okay, is it?"

We both sat for a couple minutes, hands stuffed in pockets, watching the snowflakes. A pair of headlights heaved into view on the driveway. Trey tensed. I could feel it, and it was right then that something heavy and real and nauseating hit me, like I'd been punched in the stomach. My mouth went dry again. I felt sweat trickle down my back under the sweatshirt.

Trey stood up. "Airport limo. Only way to go." His voice wavered. His face was tense, the jaw clenching and unclenching. I stood up, too. I was starting to cry, and I fought it back hard. The black sedan pulled up, a loose engine belt or something making a screeching noise that faded as the car came to a stop. The white beams shone on the falling snow. The driver got out, opened up the trunk, and stepped to the terrace. "Thomas Daniels?"

"Yessir, that's me."

"This all the luggage you got, son?"

"Yessir."

"Reagan National, right?"

"Yessir."

The driver heaved the bags over his shoulder and clambered down the steps to the car where he fit them into the trunk. "Ready when you are. Traffic's heavy with this weather," he said and got back in the car.

Trey stood looking at the ground, his shoulders hunched in the cold, hands thrust deep in his pockets. He traced a line in the thin layer of snow with his shoe. He stuck out his hand. I gripped it.

"Well."

"Yeah. Stay...stay in touch." My voice cracked. I sniffled. More squeezing in my throat, burning. Vision a little blurry. Rapid wiping with the sleeve. Trey too.

A guy hug, simultaneous quick claps on the back.

Trey forced a smile. "This really sucks, huh?"

I laughed and took in one of those shaky, quick breaths that happen when you're sort of crying. "Yeah. But listen. Stay in touch. Really."

"No problem." Trey punched me in the shoulder. "Win some races." He headed down the steps, jumping the last one, ducked into the car, and slammed the door.

■ ■ ■

I was walking out of Latin class two days later when Father Daley stopped me.

"Matt."

"Father?"

"Come on over here and have a seat."

I looked at my watch, started to say something about my next class but then gave up on it and put my backpack on the floor and sat down.

"How are you holding up? I know you were close with Trey. It's hard when a roommate leaves. You look a little ragged around the edges."

"I'm doin' okay, I guess. I'm just—it's just weird not having him around."

"Are you staying in touch at all?"

"I gave him a call at his aunt's house in San Francisco, but he didn't call back."

Father Daley arranged some papers on the desk. "He might not, you know. For a while."

I looked at him. "Why wouldn't he?"

"Well, it's a shock to his system just like it's a shock to yours, Matt. There's a part of us that doesn't like change, and sometimes we try to ignore it."

"Whaddya mean?"

"I mean that the hardest part about leaving—for him—was probably saying good-bye to you."

"So?"

"So talking to you only makes it harder right now for him. Probably. And it might just be a while before he's ready to talk to you."

"I dunno, Father Daley. We were pretty tight. I think he'll give me a call. I might even go out there and visit him this summer."

The priest smiled and looked at the desk, nodding. I had the feeling—one I'd get often while I was growing up—that this man understood something I didn't, but he didn't want to say anything. "I assume you're aware of the problems Trey's parents were having."

"*Are* having, you mean. Yeah. Trey and me talked about it."

"Trey and I," he corrected, smiling a little.

"Trey and *I*," I repeated.

"Good. I'm glad you talked. But understand something. Sometimes when families are going through that type of thing they sort of lock up and don't talk to anyone. So it might be a while before he calls you. Don't let that upset you. But if and when he does, I think you'll continue to be an important guy for Trey in a lot of ways. There's a lot of instability in his life, and you're someone stable. He might depend on you just to be a listening ear, Matt. That might not be too easy, but it's important."

"Right."

"Well, I guess you better run. I don't want to make you late for your next class."

"Okay."

"Hang tight, Matt."

I hung tight. Days flowed into weeks and months. I tried writing a few times and left some messages through his dad's business numbers. But Trey never called or wrote back. I gave up by the end of the spring. As quickly as I'd made my first real friend, he disappeared, and for a long time, I hated him for it.

# PART II

# CHAPTER 28

A squeezing sensation in my ears woke me up, and I stretched in the cramped airplane seat. After a moment, the pilot's voice came over the speakers. "Folks, from the flight deck. We're beginning our final descent into the Jackson area. Estimate we'll be on the ground in about ten minutes. Keep an eye out the windows...Once we break cloud cover, y'all should have a great look at the Tetons as we make our approach. Cabin crew, please prepare the cabin for landing."

The mountains loomed into view as the plane made a wide, sweeping turn over the plateau. The Tetons were knife ridges, rising abruptly, shadow gray with thin veils of snow at the top. Thick pine forests clung to their shoulders, and streams cut through the valleys. The winding curves of the Snake River meandered through the flat land below. The mountains seemed to grow taller as we landed, forming a vertical wall of terrain that took up the entire view of the small window. The wheels touched down with a thud, and there was a loud roar as the engines slowed us to a smooth halt at the end of the runway.

"Ladies and Gentlemen, welcome to Jackson, Wyoming, where the local time is eleven thirty a.m. Please remain in your seat until we've come to a complete stop at the gate and the captain has turned off the fasten seat belt sign." The voice continued as I looked out at the tiny airport, the radar dish spinning on the tower.

It hit me pretty suddenly as we pulled into the gate that somewhere not far off, Andrew Daniels was lying in a hospital bed. And the guy who used to be my best friend had no idea I was coming to see him.

■ ■ ■

The noon sun glinted off the hood of the cab, and a warm breeze blew through the open windows. It was nothing like a city cab; instead, it was an ordinary Chevy Blazer with a taxi permit hanging from the mirror. The middle-aged driver wore jeans, a tank top, and a baseball cap. An empty soda can rattled in the cup holder. I asked him if he'd heard of Trey. He leaned over his shoulder, nearly yelling over the country music blaring from the radio.

"Trey Daniels? Yeah, that rings a bell. Help me out, though."

"The firefighter. Been in the news lately," I said.

"Oh yeah! Of course. The hotel fire and all."

"Yeah, that's right. You know him?" I asked.

The driver chuckled. "Sorry, buddy. It's a small town, but it ain't that small. Did see it on the news, of course. Heard they did a profile about him. Made national news, I think."

"Yeah, it did."

He glanced back at me, skeptically. "You a reporter or something?"

"No. Old friend. We went to high school together."

"Hmm. Well, speak of the devil, there's that hotel, or what's left of it." He pointed out the window at the charred remains of a two-story building a few hundred yards off the road. Bulldozers were at work clearing the site.

"Thing went up damned fast. Gas line, I think they said. Surprised your buddy managed to pull anyone outta there, it was burnin' so hot. Pretty ballsy move."

"Hmm."

"I'll just take you to the center of town. There's a few good motels there; shouldn't set ya back too much. Least-aways damn near not as much as during the winter. Ski season, sometimes ya can't find a place for under a buck fifty a night!" The driver seemed to say this with a hint of pride.

"Thanks." I was looking out the window. The Tetons rose steeply to my right, a broad flat plain to the left. The sky was immense.

"Ya know, come to think of it, I think that guy's mother owns a store in town. I remember hearing that on the news."

"Really?"

"Some kind of art store. Downtown. Ask around; you'll find it. There's a whole mess of 'em in one spot. Real touristy an' all."

"Thanks."

The driver pulled to a stop at a corner, in front of a small motel.

"This place is good. Decent rooms, decent rates," he said, changing the radio station.

"Thanks a lot. Hey, what do I owe you?"

"Ten bucks."

I paid him and reached across the seat to grab my duffel bag.

"Take it easy. Hope ya find yer pal." The Blazer pulled away.

I stepped inside the hotel's air-conditioned lobby. It was a small room with wood paneling on the walls and framed photos of mountain peaks and skiing scenes. I checked in and followed the number on the key to a room around the side of the building. After throwing my bag in the corner, I collapsed on the bed and rubbed my eyes. I called home to let mom know I was there, but she didn't pick up. I left a message, then turned on my side. Before long, I was asleep again. Flying always knocks me out.

273

I dreamt vividly of Lynn during that nap, so vividly that I was convinced, even after I awoke, that I would roll over and find her lying in the bed next to me. Instead, all I saw was the tiny red light on the smoke detector and the afternoon sunlight showing through the curtains.

In the dream, we were on a chairlift at a ski resort called Holiday Valley near the cottage in Ellicottville. The hill is called Tannenbaum, named for the thick stands of spruce pines that line the slope. It's a "green" hill, a gentle one, and that's the only type of skiing Lynn likes. Light snow was falling, and the sky had that sort of grayish haze that comes in early evening. I had my arm around her, holding her tightly against me, and I remember there were snowflakes landing on these bright-red mittens she wears. Yes, she even wore her real mittens in the dream. I was with her when she bought them at a consignment shop in Bethesda. I could smell her cocoa-butter lip balm. She was obsessed with the stuff. I turned to kiss her. She smiled and lifted her ski goggles, and I saw those green eyes. When I woke up, I think I said her name out loud.

# CHAPTER 29

I took a shower to wake myself up, then got dressed. I grabbed a sweat-shirt, thinking it might be cooler here in the evening. Stepping out of the hotel into the street, I began walking toward the center of town. The sky had cleared, and only a few light clouds huddled around the peaks. Otherwise, the sky was a light, late summer blue. The air was warm, but without the humidity I'd become so accustomed to in DC. This certainly was a tourist town, with wooden boardwalks lining the streets, and store-fronts resembling the sets of old Westerns. But even amidst the kitsch, there was a simple reality to the place, and I had the sense of a town full of residents whose ordinary, practical lives went on behind the Old West façades and expensive ski stores catering to tourists.

After a bit of asking around, I found Mrs. Daniels's shop without too much difficulty. I saw her through the window, talking on the phone. I stood outside for a minute, watching. She had car keys and a grocery bag in one arm, pen in hand, and the phone in the crook of her shoulder. A sign hung overhead, inlaid gold lettering on a varnished cedar panel that read:

## ALPINE HORIZONS

Brass bells tinkled as I pushed the door open and stepped into the air-conditioned shop. The hardwood floor creaked, and I could smell the scented candles lined up along the glass shelves to my left. Pine and something else, something sweeter. Tracy Daniels smiled quickly at me, obviously without recognition, and raised a "just a second" finger as she wrote something down. I stood there, shifting my weight, while she finished the conversation.

She hung up the phone.

"Hi." *Voice out of breath, lots on her mind.* "I'm afraid I'm just heading out and was going to close up. Are you looking for something specific?" The smile was weak and forced.

Hands in my pockets. "Mrs. Daniels?"

She looked up, her arms at her sides. "Yes? I mean, yes. Tracy Daniels." She narrowed her eyes. *Just like his.* "You look familiar."

"Matt Derby," I said, smiling. Her pupils shifted, the way people do to dig up old memories. "Ashford River School."

The narrowed eyes opened wider. She put the grocery bag down. "Matt Derby! Of course I remember. I...What are you doing all the way out here?"

I reached across the counter for a handshake. Instead, she pulled me into an awkward hug. I remembered the video games in the Georgetown townhouse. Lots of framed pictures. Trey on a fishing boat with his dad. "I, uh, saw the news about Trey and his father."

Her eyes darted to the counter, and she busied herself straightening some stuff. Her words were rapid. "I was just headed over to the hospital. You heard the news? And came out here? My God, you are so...wow, it's been a while." The lines on her face deepened.

"Almost six years."

"You must be...what? Finishing college?"

"It's my last year." I cleared my throat. "Mrs. Daniels, I came to see Trey. I-I haven't seen him since school. He doesn't know I'm here, because I couldn't find a listing for him. I was going to call you, but I thought that it might be hard—"

She put up her hand, smiling. "Matt. I'm glad you came. Trey will...
well, I don't know! What a surprise!"

"How is, err..." *Your husband?* "How is Mr. Daniels?"

The smile faded as her jaw tightened. "Andrew's out of the ICU, but
on a ventilator, still unconscious. He was in town visiting. We were trying
to...well..." She picked up the grocery bag and looked out the window.
"Things fell apart after Trey left Ashford, and sooner or later, Andrew and
I split up. We only saw each other sporadically after that. This time, it had
been two years. Anyway, he came out to visit, had just arrived, and then
this damned fire...Trey didn't even know he was coming and..." She shook
her head as if to clear it. "Sorry. That was a long answer to a short question. You asked me how he is. Not great. All I can say is, he's stable at the
moment."

I looked at the ground. "That's good, I guess."

"Well," she continued, "we have a great doctor taking care of him. Very
professional. Anyway, she's been good at helping Trey deal with it all. And
me." She let out what seemed like a forced little laugh.

"I'm sure that helps," I said.

"Yeah. Well, look, our buddy just got off work and was going to meet
me at the hospital. I can give you a lift over." She smiled again.

"Maybe I should call him first. Does he have a cell number?"

"Don't be silly. He'll be so happy to see you. This week's been full of
bad news. This will be a good thing, for a change."

■ ■ ■

The ride to the hospital was short. Our conversation in the car was a
little lighter and more casual after the awkwardness in the store. The windows were open, and the sun, though lower in the sky by now, still warmed
my arm. We talked about my flight, the airport, Georgetown. *Small talk.*
*This is easier.* The radio played low as we pulled into the parking lot. I could

smell new asphalt. As I closed the door, I realized Mrs. Daniels was driving a more modest sedan. *No more tank-sized Lexus.*

Inside the cool lobby, I followed her past the reception desk. She waved to the guard, and he gave her a sympathetic smile. We went down a corridor. *Hospital smell.* A heavyset nurse sat behind a counter in scrubs.

"Hello, Mrs. Daniels. Your husband is still sedated, but his pulse is a little more regular. Dr. Thornton is in there now if you'd like to go ahead in."

Tracy turned to me. "Matt, Trey's not here yet. He should be pulling in any minute. Why don't you wait for him in the lobby?" She squeezed my hand. "It's good to see you, really." She turned, began to walk, and then turned around again, looking at me with her eyes narrowed, her head cocked. "And, gees. I mean…thank you for coming. All that way! After all that time. Thank you." It sounded more like a question than a statement, as though she couldn't quite believe it.

■ ■ ■

I stared at the checker pattern on the cheap upholstered couches in the lobby. A large gas fireplace with a fake stone chimney stood in the center of the waiting room, lending the place an artificially rustic feel. Pages came over the public address system. A wheelchair van arrived. A UPS delivery. A family, including a little girl holding a foil *Get Well* balloon. I looked at the clock and counted minutes, my stomach churning. I remembered a snippet of that last conversation on the steps of MacKerry.

What had he said the night he left Ashford? *You're about the only thing I can stand here, Derby.* I remembered the airport limo pulling up, Trey closing the door. Snow falling. Going upstairs, not eating dinner, staring out the window for a long time. Crying that night, my face stuffed in the pillow so McNeal wouldn't hear me through the wall. Brady letting me come late to study hall, no questions asked, and ordering a pizza for me later, since I'd missed dinner.

I looked out the window in time to see a bright-red Toyota pickup pull into the lot. It had a light bar on top, gleaming blue in the sun and throwing little prisms of light onto the blacktop. The truck heaved into reverse and backed into a spot near the street. I stood up and walked to the double glass doors. The truck door opened.

It was Trey. Buzz cut, dark sunglasses, khaki utility pants, and a navy T-shirt with a white fire department seal. Block letters under the seal read "DANIELS." He had an air cast on his left wrist. He waited by the front of the car and waved to someone across the lot. It was a woman, who stepped out from her own car. She was tall and slender, wearing jeans, sandals, and a yellow blouse with a nametag. Her walk was full of energy as she approached him. A kiss, then they walked toward the hospital door, holding hands, chatting. Trey walked with a slight limp. He took off the glasses as they stepped inside and stopped in midsentence when he saw me. The eyes narrowed. There was a slight turn of the head.

*Caught off guard in English class. Quick on your feet. Think of something to say, even though you didn't read the book. You* never *read the book.*

Silence. The woman at his side, jolted to a stop by his hand, looked from Trey to me, smiling uncomfortably. "Honey?" The nametag read "SARAH" beneath *Teton Garden Center.*

The hospital was paging Dr. Nichols. A woman came through the door behind us, sending a wave of warm air into the air-conditioned cool of the lobby.

"Hi, Trey." My voice cracked when I said it, and somehow, the memories rushed in. *Voice cracked like it used to when you were my roommate do you remember the time your voice cracked at practice when you were yelling at Eldrin after Brady made us do that eight mile run God it was hot that day dude your hair is shorter who's the girl?*

The eyes stayed narrow, but the lines formed a smile, that signature grin. Trey extended a hand. "Matthew David Derby." His voice was lower, with more of a twang than I remembered. We held the handshake for a few seconds. Trey's mouth curved further into his smirk.

"I'm...I heard about your dad. I came to see you, man."

Trey still looked dazed, puzzled. "Jesus, what's it been?"

"Almost six years."

Trey shook his head, snapped out of something. He turned to the woman at his side, who still had a pretty confused look on her face. "Honey, this is Matt Derby from Buffalo. Remember, I mentioned him once when… Anyway, we, uh, went to school together back East for a year. Matt, this is my fiancée, Sarah."

Sarah extended a hand. I took it, my head feeling light. She was left-handed, and I saw the silver band around her finger, a tiny diamond perched on it. "Nice to meet you. Well," she said, eyebrows raised, "why don't I head in and find Tracy? You two can catch up."

Trey looked at her. A quick kiss on his cheek, and she headed down the corridor.

We stood in the lobby, arms hanging at our sides. We both spoke at once.

"You—"

"How did—"

"Jesus, man." He paused for a second, then gave me a huge hug. "Thank you."

We both sat down heavily on the couch. "I saw it on the news. Is he okay?" I asked.

Still a little dazed, he said, "The news? My dad? Right now he seems stable. But he'll be in the hospital for a while…He passed out in the room, took in a pretty solid amount of smoke. It'll take them a while to get him breathing right. His leg got burned pretty bad. Got infected. There's been some cardiac stuff, too."

"And how about you?" I nodded at the air cast on his wrist.

"Eh, this is nothing. Just a simple fracture. Don't even need the cast all the time. I'm limping a little on my ankle; no big deal. I was in the hospital for a couple of nights. They were scrubbing smoke outta my lungs, too."

"What are the chances? I mean your dad, in that hotel."

Trey looked out the window. "Yeah."

"You didn't know he was here?"

"He didn't tell me. I got a phone call from him a month ago. It was the first I'd heard from him in about two years. I told him I was engaged. But he never said anything about visiting."

"You pulled him out of there?"

"I was on deck that night; got the call. There were six of us that went in. I happened to bust into his room. He must have been passed out. He'd been drinking."

I shook my head, not sure what to say. I looked out the window. "Nice truck."

"Oh. Yeah. That's my toy. Just broke the bank on it."

*So the bank is broken.*

"When did you get engaged?"

"A while ago. Back in April. We're, uh, sealin' the deal in December."

*You're getting married, and I wouldn't even know if I didn't go to take a leak and see the TV at the cottage Wednesday night.*

"She's beautiful."

"She's perfect, Matt. She makes everything right."

"Where's the wedding?"

"Here."

"Hmm."

Trey brushed some lint off his pants and stood up. "I should go in to see him. Come along."

"Are you sure? I mean..."

"Yeah. Come on. I'm not just gonna leave you sitting out here."

■ ■ ■

The ventilator worked with a rhythmic hiss-click, and a quiet beeping metered out Andrew Daniels's pulse. The shades were drawn, and the room was filled with soft light from a single fluorescent tube on the wall. Tracy and Sarah were there, sitting on folding chairs. Dr. Thornton, a graying woman with her hair in a ponytail, made notes on a chart. I lingered in the corner. Mr. Daniels had a deep gash across his shoulder, which had been stitched over with tiny X's of black thread. His right leg was elevated and wrapped.

*Landing in the Bahamas in a single-engine plane. White linen shirt, gold chain, sun-bronzed skin. That drive in the Jeep. He said something about the sound shells make in the surf. Gave us a beer.*

Trey stood at the foot of the bed, his hands gripping the footboard. His voice was quiet, almost clinical. "Respiration any better? Pulse seems regular."

"It is," said Dr. Thornton, "and I imagine he'll be alert—if not entirely oriented—sometime within the next few days. He breathed in an awful lot of smoke, but that's not the main issue, actually. We're primarily concerned about secondary infections down the line, particularly some cellulitis from the leg injury and the burn. The beam that collapsed on him was dirty, so we'll be treating him with antibiotics for a while. At this stage of it, we'll be keeping him sedated, and that's why he needs help breathing." She read the numbers from one of the monitors and made another note. "Recovery's going to take a while."

Trey nodded.

Dr. Thornton felt Mr. Daniels's chin and around his neck. "He's going to have some fever along with the infections for some time to come. Tracy, I'm going to need to look over some paperwork with you if you have a moment." Before she left, she touched Trey's arm. "When he regains consciousness, I'll call you. He won't be talking for a while. But he should see you right away, if you're willing." She put her pen back in her lab coat pocket. "You know, things like this can make for a fresh start."

Tracy stood and rested her fingers on Mr. Daniels's hand for a moment and then followed the doctor out into the corridor. Sarah moved next to Trey and put her arm around him, thumb hooked in his waistband. He leaned his head, resting it on top of hers. The ventilator hissed.

# CHAPTER 30

The Caribou Lodge & Tavern was a couple miles outside of town. Trey had some paperwork to take care of back at the fire station before he could join us for dinner, so I rode with Sarah and together we waited for him at the restaurant. Just before we were seated, Trey called her to say he'd be a while and that we shouldn't wait for him to order dinner. He'd meet us for a drink afterward. Our booth was built right into the wall, with high-backed wooden benches and an oil lamp showing the old stains and scratches on the varnished pine table. A chandelier made out of a wagon wheel hung from the ceiling, and a giant moose head stared blankly from above a huge fireplace.

"So yeah, it's been quite a week for us," Sarah said, taking a sip of her Diet Coke and picking up where we had left off talking in the car. "Lots of surprises." Her voice tumbled easily, loosely, like water in a stream. She leaned in close, and I could smell…What was it? Something earthy, clean. Outdoors, like cut grass.

*The garden center, idiot.*

"I can imagine. I guess I'm just another surprise."

She laughed and put her hand on mine. I felt the ring brush my knuckle. Her hand was warm, the ring cool. "Oh, of course! But you're a good surprise, Matt." She took another sip, leaned back in the bench, and gave me a smile. "Okay, so, help me make sense of this."

"Make sense?"

"Of you two!"

"Oh!" I laughed. "Well, I'm trying to do the same myself, to be honest." The waitress came. Sarah ordered fried chicken, and I did the same. "Not really sure where to start." I took a sip of my beer.

"I'm sorry. I'm so rude." She held up her glass. "First of all, here's to you coming out here."

I tipped the glass, clinking it with hers. "To surprises."

She nodded and took a sip. Then she paused, looking quizzically at her glass. "Can you offer a toast with Diet Coke?"

"Sure." I smiled. "Not a beer drinker?"

"No, not really. So. Tell me about Trey in high school." She leaned in, elbows on the table, chin on her hands. Her eyes narrowed with intensity.

*Did she pick that up from him, the squinting bit?*

"We only knew each other for a few months, really. But we were roommates and teammates. You become friends fast in boarding school." I noticed the hair pushed over her left ear, but not the right. How one sleeve was crumpled up further than the other. Even her smile was a little crooked.

*Imperfect. And absolutely beautiful.*

I thought of Lynn. Thought about McNeal, the envious looks I used to get in the morning from him when she stayed over. *Tonight. Call her tonight. Tell her about all this.*

"He doesn't talk about high school very much," she said. "Come on; fill me in."

I watched the bubbles rise in my beer. "He seems so...put together now."

"Well, that's debatable." She smiled.

"See, when I met Trey back then, he was every kind of cool. At first, he just didn't seem to give a damn about anything. I didn't think anything could bother him."

She nodded, listening. Her blouse looked gold in the dim light. Her eyelashes were long.

"He was strong, smart, a good athlete. Didn't do a lot of work in school though."

"I can't even imagine him in a boarding school." She shook her head and made that little half smile. "Just the thought of him in a coat and tie is pretty funny."

"Well, he was in one, every day. At least sort of. He used to always have his shirt untucked and tie loose. Drove our housemaster, Mr. Brady, absolutely crazy, along with most of our teachers."

*The day of that English test stomach churning handing in those papers knocking them to the ground to mix them up what a stupid idea never did tell anyone...*

"Mr. Brady...He was the rowing coach, right?"

"Huh?" I snapped my attention back to her. Her brown eyes were kind, patient.

"You were saying something about Mr. Brady."

"Yeah, right. Trey told you about him?"

"Just in passing. It was probably in the same conversation when he mentioned you a year or so back. We were watching some footage from the Olympics and a rowing race came on."

"He mentioned me?"

"Yes. Because of the rowers. He told me he used to row at Ashford, and then he mentioned your name. You and Mr. Brady."

"Hmm."

"So he was a hell-raiser, huh?" she asked.

I wiped a line of sweat beads from the glass. "Yeah, he was trouble. We both were. We had some good times. Really good times." Suddenly, I thought of the night with the girls in the pool and almost spat out some beer, laughing.

"What is it?" Her eyebrows arched, eyes dancing.

"Nothing. Nothing, just…remembered something funny. So tell me about *you* guys. How did you meet?" I asked.

"I have a thing for firefighters."

"Big trucks and grimy faces, right?"

"No, seriously. My father is a captain over in Cheyenne, and that's where we met. Trey was there at a training conference about a year ago. I was volunteering, handing out water and sandwiches."

"Wow, just a year, and there's a wedding in the works." I shook my head.

"That surprises you?" Her mouth twisted into a grin.

"No. I just, well…I'm still in college. The idea of a wedding just seems…pretty *big* right now."

She nodded. "I can understand. I just finished my associate's at a community college here. When I told my parents about the wedding, they just about flipped." She smiled and looked down at the table. "How about you, Matt? Have a girlfriend?"

I hesitated. "No. I did last year, but, well…"

"Was it serious?"

*I don't know I thought it was it used to be…*

"I don't know." I rearranged the salt and pepper shakers.

"What does *that* mean?" she asked.

"It's probably not as serious as we thought it was." My jaw tightened.

"Hmm." Her voice was quiet. "Don't worry about it. If it's meant to work out, it will, right? If it's not, it won't." *Gentle, real, kind.*

I couldn't help smiling.

*"She makes everything right."*

The dinners came. She ate the fried chicken with her hands, wiping her face with a napkin. "Sorry. I'm so unladylike!"

*You are so…real.*

"When I met Trey," she gestured with a drumstick, "he was absolutely covered in ash from the practice fire they were on that day. He came over to the table where I was working to pick up water for his crew. I made some smartass remark about dirty firefighters, he flashed that grin of his, and it was all downhill from there."

"Well, he's a lucky guy."

"I'm the lucky girl. I've never met a guy like him. You should see the way he takes care of his mother."

"How's she doing?"

"This week? I've never seen her so mixed up. But in general, great. When Andrew left them, she took the money he gave her, which wasn't all that much, and opened that store. She's in love with it."

I shook my head. "I have to admit it's weird, you know. To see him so in control. Like you said, taking care of her. Carrying a pager. Talking about pulse and respiratory function. When I knew him, he was mostly just a loose cannon. A wild kid. And now he's getting married. Wow."

Her face turned more serious, and she looked at her plate. "I think a lot of things changed for Trey when his dad finally left, Matt. He told me that's when he decided not to go to college. He thought his mom would kill him. But he said it was like something snapped. All of the sudden, he stopped fooling around, took the test, joined the fire department, just...I don't know, got serious."

"It must have been rough."

"He said it was. But he says that's when he figured out what he was doing here. And the day he asked me to marry him, well, that's when I figured out what I was doing. You ever have one of those moments?"

"Sure. I think."

*Have I?* I decided to push the focus away from this annoyingly unanswerable question.

"Why'd he choose firefighting?"

"He said it was a real job. He was just so genuine. So generous. I think he just didn't want to be like his dad, no matter what it took. Maybe that's not fair, but he was really angry then."

*"We are the fucked-up rich people, Matt...I wish you were my brother."*

"So he really hasn't talked to his father since he left?"

"I guess they kept up on the phone, real sporadically. But other than that, no, not really. Especially not in the past two years."

"Does he talk about him at all?" I asked.

"Not much. Whenever I bring it up, he changes the subject. I don't blame him, of course, but he's been completely out of it this week since the fire. Really shook him up. You can't tell most of the time, but watch him closely. You'll see. It's definitely on his mind."

I ordered another beer.

"So the wedding's in December?"

"Around Christmas. It's a nice time out here." She was about to speak and then stopped and took a drink instead.

*You were about to invite me, weren't you? But you don't know if that's what he wants because you don't have any idea, really, who the hell I am, and I don't have any idea who you are or frankly what the hell I'm doing here.*

"He, uh, likes the job?"

"Firefighting? It's his life now."

"Lots of responsibility," I said, smirking. "Part of me wants to say I never would have guessed it, but in a way, it makes perfect sense. Did he ever tell you about the time he saved a kid when we were in high school?"

"He what? No! What happened?"

I recalled the story, including what Trey had told me about whispering in the kid's ear. "That kid—I think his name was Nick—is probably in high school now. Around the same age we were when Trey pulled him out from in front of that truck, actually. I wonder if he saw the same news report I did. That'd be weird, huh?"

"Too weird." She smiled. "Trey's a good man, Matt. I'm lucky. You guys should reconnect, really. He doesn't have too many close friends. I mean, he hangs out with a couple of guys in the department, of course. But he keeps to himself a lot, you know?"

"I do. It's funny. He was always the center of attention, but somehow, he was a loner, too."

"I see that," she said. "We live together now, so I see it more. I moved in to his place about six months ago, so we could save some money, pool some for the wedding and all. We had to argue about it for a while."

"Why?"

She laughed and rolled her eyes. "He didn't think it was right for me to move in until we were married."

I smiled. "Good Catholic boy."

"Yeah, I get that," she said. "I had my reservations, but it made sense for so many reasons." She looked deep in thought for a moment. Then her face lightened as Trey walked up to the table and sat down heavily.

"Hey, buddy." He shook my hand and smiled at Sarah, taking her hand in his as he sat down next to her.

*Gentle.*

*Kind.*

*Real.*

"Sorry I'm late," he said, raising his eyebrows. "Got tied up."

"What happened?" she asked.

Trey leaned back in the bench, stretching his arms. "I thought I was just going back to do some paperwork. Then we get this call for a broken hydrant that wouldn't go off. You shoulda seen it! Soaked this whole front yard, kids stompin' around in the mud."

"Sounds lively," said Sarah. "You hungry, hon?"

"What I really need is a beer." He waved to the waiter and ordered a Bud Light. "Gotta keep that gut off, right?"

Sarah poked him in the ribs. "Oh, stop. He's in such terrible shape, right, Matt?"

He laughed. "Speaking of being in shape, are you still rowing?" he asked.

"I am. About to start my last year at Georgetown."

Trey got his beer and shook his head at the glass the waiter offered, instead sipping it right from the bottle. "That's great, man. So hey, what are you doing next year?"

*Ha!*

"The million-dollar question," I said. "Thinking about law school. I'm a history major. But it's kind of up in the air. Let me tell you, if I could answer that question for my dad, there'd be more peace on earth."

Trey nodded, wiping his mouth with his sleeve. "How is your dad?"

"He's great. Mom too."

"You know, I remember that night they took us out to dinner after that race. What was the name of that place?"

"The Buffalo River Pub."

"Yeah." He turned to Sarah. "Hon, it was great. Such a down-to-earth place. After being cooped up in a boarding school for a few months, wow."

"Ah, The Hampshire Room," I said.

"The Hampshire Room! I can't believe they called the cafeteria 'The Hampshire Room.' Hey, how's McNeal and Speers and those guys?"

"McNeal and I are roommates at Georgetown. He's doin' great. Captain of the team, actually. Finance major. Speers, I don't see much; he's finishing up at Virginia. I think he's headed to medical school next year."

"Eldrin?" Trey grinned.

"Eldrin's living his Ivy League dream."

Trey shook his head. "That doesn't surprise me. Smart guy."

"He was a prick then, and he's a prick now," I said.

Sarah laughed at this. "A bit of bad history?"

Trey grinned. "Just some old school stories."

"Trey tried to kill him during study hall once." I thought back to the night of the fight.

*"My dad sends a damn fax, Matt."*

"I was such an asshole. I don't blame him. You remember that whole thing with the—"

Sarah nudged him in the thigh and said, "Okay, let me outta here. Time for you boys to catch up. I'm leaving before I hear more than I want to." Trey stood up to let her out of the booth. I stood, and she gave me a hug. "It was really great meeting you. I'm so glad you're out here. You two should plan a good day tomorrow. It'll give me some time to catch up with Tracy."

"I won't be late." Trey gave her a quick kiss on the cheek and a pinch on the butt, grinning. "Wait up for me." He winked at her as he sipped the beer.

*Real. They are real.*

290

"You won't be late? Bullshit. You meet up with a long-lost buddy at a bar, start trading war stories, and you won't be late?" She crossed her arms and raised an eyebrow.

He shrugged. "Nah, really. Just a couple drinks. I'm beat. Besides, I was thinking of taking Matt up the Cascade Trail tomorrow. We'll need an early start, so we'll have the whole day to catch up. My ankle's still a little rough, but I'll tape it up."

"Oh, that's a beautiful hike. Matt, you'll love it," she said, digging her car keys out of her purse. "Okay, hon. I'm heading home. See you soon."

"Careful driving."

She waved with her keys without turning around. We watched the door swing shut behind her, and then the air changed the way it does when someone leaves.

"So." Trey took a swig of his beer.

"So." I swirled the amber liquid around, watching the way the foam clung to the glass. "She's pretty amazing."

"You have no idea. What did you guys talk about before I got here?" he asked. "Sorry I left you hanging."

"Nah, it was good to talk to her. About you, mostly. Some high school stories. Don't worry. Nothing scandalous. I didn't tell her about your excessive collection of magazines."

He laughed. "She's got a way with people. Let me guess. You felt like you've known her for years."

I chuckled. "Yeah. You know, I did. She's really down-to-earth, Trey."

"When I met her, I was at this firefighting thing, and—"

"She told me."

"Oh. Yeah, I guess she would have. She loves to tell that story."

"I can't believe you guys are engaged. You only met her a year ago?"

"Best year of my life, man. No doubt in my mind about her. None. How about you? Any prospects?"

"Not at the moment. Broke up in the spring."

"Oh yeah?"

"Lynn. She's a great girl." I signaled the waiter for another beer. "It just...well..."

Trey nodded, listening. The intensity of his attention struck me, because when we were younger, I could rarely tell if he was actually listening or not. I continued, "I guess it wasn't what we thought it was."

"When it's real, you just *know* it, Matt. And if you don't know it, then it isn't real. There's no faking it."

I shifted in my seat. "So what's the update on your dad?"

Trey stiffened up, knuckles whitening around the bottle. He looked at a spot on the table. "About the same. The doctor says he needs to stay sedated for a while, but he'll probably be conscious in a few more days."

"Well, that's good."

"Yeah." He picked at the corner of his beer bottle label, staring absently at it for a few seconds. "Except."

"Except?"

"Except, what the hell am I supposed to say to him?" He shook his head. "Hi, Dad. Glad you're alive! By the way, I rescued you. So, are you here to stay this time or did you just stop by to fuck things up? You know, since it's been a while." He tipped the bottle, taking a long swig.

A group of teenagers crowded around the jukebox across the room, one putting in a quarter for a Springsteen song. There were six of them, moving with that ambling shuffle kids use, wearing jeans and T-shirts. There were high fives between two of the boys after a conspiratorial whisper. They nodded at one of the girls and shared a laugh.

"Well, I didn't really know what to say to *you* when I got here," I said. Trey's head snapped up. "Huh?"

"I said I didn't know what to say to you, either." The waiter brought my beer. "I didn't know what to say when I saw you and Sarah walk into the hospital. In fact, I was wondering what to say to you the whole way out here."

Trey went back to peeling the label on the beer. He squinted. "You know, I almost called you that night after I got kicked out. The flight got canceled because of the snow, and I had to spend the night at the

Georgetown condo." He cocked his head to the side. "But I couldn't, for whatever reason. I was sitting there in the living room and I was going to call you and say I was sorry or whatever. And then I almost called you the next day once I got out to California. But every time I thought about it, I just couldn't do it. And then it just got easier and easier to forget about everything and everyone. The school, the team, Brady, you, everybody."

"I guess that makes sense."

*Walking into study hall late that night everyone looking could they tell I'd been crying up in my room Brady let me sit in the corner table with my back to them...*

"Nothing makes sense when you're a teenager." He laughed.

I nodded. "You know, Father Daley pulled me aside about a week after you left, and—"

"Daley. I liked that guy. Our priest out here kind of reminds me of him."

"Yeah? Anyway, he pulled me aside and told me that I should stay in touch with you, not to lose contact, ya know?"

"Right."

"It didn't work so well." We both took a sip of beer. Springsteen crooned about his hometown.

After a while, he said, "It's good my dad's here, Matt."

"Is it?"

"Yeah. I mean not good that he's in the *hospital*, but you know what I mean. It's good he came back."

We watched the group of kids at the corner table; they were leaned in close in a huddle, one of them telling a story, waving his hands animatedly.

"Do you think he and your mom will put things together?" I asked.

"I dunno. They're gonna try. I mean we're both gonna try, me and my mom. Dad made the effort to come, so I assume he wants to try, too. Maybe he was gone long enough to figure some shit out."

"She knew he was here, right?" I asked.

"Yeah." He exhaled a long breath. "Actually, he'd been here for a day or two."

"They just didn't want to tell you?"

"She says they were waiting for the right time. He was gonna come to the station. I wish they'd just told me. They could have dispensed with all the cloak and dagger baloney."

"I guess that would have been easier," I said. "Maybe."

"I think it's really hard on her," he continued. "After I left Ashford, mom and I stayed out in San Francisco with my aunt for a couple weeks, but eventually we went back to Lake Placid and I went to the local public high school like a normal kid. Dad was usually in Manhattan or somewhere in Europe. Whenever he was home things were rough. Toward the end of my senior year, it got nasty. Violent. Never between the two of them, but God, we'd scream, the three of us. One night he said something to her after he'd had a few drinks, I said something back, then he took a swing at me. He missed, but I didn't. He left the house and wandered off to New York for few nights. Then he came back, and it all just stopped. I guess we just got tired, especially Mom and Dad. They made up their minds it wasn't gonna work. They both sat down at the dinner table one night, calm as hell, and told me he was leaving. Moving to the New York place for good. Just like that. It was probably the calmest I've ever seen them."

"What did you do?"

"Nothing, Matt. I didn't do a damned thing. I wanted him to go. And I didn't. Both at once. I think it was the same for Mom."

"It must have been hard for her."

"You'd be surprised. People can hurt with something for so long, eventually they stop feeling it. But I'm not sure if they *really* stop feeling it. We moved out here as soon as I graduated from high school. Wyoming was our fresh start, you know? I guess that's why it's so hard on her, him coming out here. It brings the past here. It's really hard on her."

"And on you," I said.

Trey stopped peeling the label and looked up at me. "Yeah."

"And his being in the hospital must make it harder."

"Right." He rolled the empty bottle back and forth on the table. "When he left, I stopped all that smoking shit. I didn't even drink. It was like something changed when it was just me and my mom."

"Just like that?"

"Just like that." He chuckled. "I mean you should've seen me. There I was, a senior in high school. Parties all over the place, right? But suddenly, I was straight-edged as a ruler. This girl I was dating dropped me like a lead balloon because she said I stopped being fun."

"That's hard to imagine." I laughed. "After the Bahamas, that is."

"God. What a shit show that was."

"Yes it was. Remember that girl, Laurie?"

"Yep. And I thought I was such hot shit the next morning after the night with what's-her-name...Mandy."

I smiled. "Me too. Just one small step for mankind, but a giant leap for Matt Derby."

"You never bragged about it," he said.

"I wasn't happy about it. It was stupid. Eventually, I spilled it in confession with Father Daley. No details, but he got the point. Good old Catholic guilt."

"Really?"

"Yep. Of course, being a Jesuit, he made me a great deal. Told me I'd burn in hell unless I got my Latin grade up past ninety-five, in which case the Almighty might see fit to redeem my wayward soul."

"So, *Latin* was the key to salvation all these years. Wish I'd known. Would have saved me some trouble." He laughed.

"Yeah. So what happened to all that? The island and everything?"

"It didn't last. Mom and I moved out of dad's cozy little nine-thousand-square-foot cabin in the woods, drove out here, and lived in a two-bedroom apartment above an antique shop. That giant house in Lake Placid? He either sold it or lost it or some combination of both, just like the rest of the stuff," he said. "Stuff. That's exactly what it was, and I think that's exactly what finally tore them apart. All the damned *stuff*. The houses, the cars, the boat, the island. His company went under with the tech bubble, and the stocks he had crashed. He went from millions to practically bankrupt in no time."

"My dad's software company took it hard, too."

"Ha. Yeah, but the difference, Matt…" He stopped rolling the beer and pointed it at me. "…is that your dad lived within his means. Realistic means." He set the bottle aside. "It took me a long time to understand what that meant after he left."

"I thought you'd be angrier at him."

"I was. Still am. But then I'm not. Shit. I just don't know. When I got kicked out of Ashford, my mom wasn't even mad at me. You know what she said?"

"Huh?"

"She told me I was acting just like him, and who could blame a son for acting like his father?"

I didn't know what to say to this.

He leaned back, looking up at the ceiling. "I don't know how you can be like that. In your forties, with a teenage kid, and still act like a teenager yourself. I mean, Jesus Christ. The Bahamas? What the hell *was* that? Who lets his teenager loose like that year after year? Your parents let you come down, but if they'd known what it was like down there, they never would have, right?" He tapped the bottle, hard, against the tabletop. "I'm surprised I lived to see twenty-one." Trey continued, shaking his head, "He was absolutely the best when it came to having a good time. A real pal. Problem is that I had pals already. Mostly the wrong ones, but I had pals already."

I finished my drink.

"Sorry. I didn't mean you," he said.

"I know."

Trey cracked his knuckles and took a deep breath. "I sure as hell got going on that. Talk about a long answer to a short question."

"You said something about some trail tomorrow?" I asked.

"Oh yeah. I was thinking, if you feel like doing a great hike, there's this trail called Cascade Canyon that's really incredible. Goes right up the center of the Teton Range to this glacial lake."

"You don't work tomorrow?"

"Tomorrow, no. Sunday, yeah. Somehow I got roped into speaking to a Boy Scout group in the morning. But tomorrow's completely free, and as long as you're out here, I think you should see why Wyoming is the most beautiful state in the Union. Besides, I wanna knock this ankle back into shape. Been babying it for a week."

"What about Sarah and your mom?"

"It'll be a good chance for them to hang out."

"Sounds great. I didn't really bring anything to hike in, though."

"Weather should be fine. You got sneakers and shorts?"

"Yeah."

"You're all set. I'll bring a jacket and hat for you. Cold on top. It's a long hike, but we'll have the whole day."

"Okay."

"Well." He stood up. "Oh. Shit. I almost forgot! Where the hell are you staying? Stay with us."

"Nah, I already checked into a motel in town. I already paid. It's no problem."

"Up to you. You leave Sunday morning, right?"

"Nine-thirty flight."

"Okay. Well, definitely plan on staying with us tomorrow night. The apartment is small, but there's a pullout bed in the living room. Save you paying for another night in the motel, right?"

"Are you sure?"

"Of course. Sarah will kill me if you don't. She'll want to make you dinner. Which, by the way, could be dangerous. Cooking is not exactly her strong suit. I worry for the future." He pulled out his wallet and counted some money for the bill.

"Let me get it."

Trey looked at me, eyebrows raised. "You're the starving college kid, buddy."

"Well…"

"Ah, shut up. I got it."

We walked outside. The air was cool and fresh. On the ride home, Trey lit a cigarette and offered one to me.

"No, thanks."

"It's one vice I haven't kicked. Sarah hates it, so I only do it when she's not around." He chuckled. "She says when the—" He paused and turned on the radio. "She says I have to quit." He looked distracted, glanced at the mirrors, and changed the station.

I felt the air rush by, my arm out the window. Stars poked out, and the knife-ridge of the mountains was dark against the blue sky. "You remember that night we smoked out on that fire escape?"

"Of course I remember that. It was raining like crazy."

"Sure was."

Another turn, and Trey brought the truck to a halt in front of the motel. "Listen, on a Saturday, and what with the good weather and all, the trail's gonna fill up pretty quick, so we should get there early to beat the crowds." He looked at his watch. "It's just ten now. Can I pick you up early?"

"Sure. I'm used to it from rowing. You know that. What's early?" I asked.

"Six."

"Wow, things have changed," I said. "You never liked getting up early at school." I opened the door and climbed out.

Trey laughed. "Right. Let's call it seven. I'll see you then." He leaned across and held out his hand through the window. We shook hands.

"Night, man. Good to see you."

"Night. Hey. Thanks for coming out here," he said.

"Sure."

"Seven."

"Yeah."

■ ■ ■

Inside, I flipped on the light and threw my wallet and room key on the table. The room had that hard-to-nail-down hotel smell, like stale cigarettes and carpet cleaner.

I called home again, told them I was fine and that yes, Trey and I had met up and it was going okay. Then I read free-trade policy. Ten pages of it.

I picked up the cell phone again and scrolled down to Lynn's number. And set it down on the table.

*When it's real, you just know it, Matt.*

*There's no faking it.*

*Shit.*

I set my alarm. It took a while to fall asleep. I lay in bed thinking about Lynn and whether or not what we had was "real." I reached for the phone again around midnight.

I almost called.

But I didn't.

# CHAPTER 31

The morning was cool, and a thin layer of fog rested on the blue-black surface of Jenny Lake. We wore windbreakers for the first couple miles, an easy stroll around the southern perimeter from the parking area to where the trail began to climb. The quiet reminded me of early mornings spent fishing at the cottage, when all I could hear was wind as it rustled through the trees. We passed a boulder field where Trey pointed out the detritus and scattered, car-sized boulders deposited by an immense landslide. Then we began to climb more steadily past a couple of glistening waterfalls, the sound deafening after the near silence of the lake. Mist rose from the stream as it fell into churning pools, tumbling over slick rocks on its way to the lake below. The air smelled of pine.

As we began to ascend, the sun peeked out and felt warm on my neck and legs. The jackets came off, and we settled into a rhythm, climbing higher, able to hear the sounds of our breathing and footfalls. Trey's limp became less pronounced as he went on. He wore the air cast on his wrist, which he had in a sling across his chest. After almost an hour, the path leveled out to a rocky terrace with a view of the entire Teton Valley. The sky was pale blue and cloudless. Hundreds of feet below and far across the lake, I could see the parking area beginning to fill. The first of the water taxis that allowed less ambitious hikers to skip the lakeside part of the trail began its trek across the expanse of blue. The engine made a barely audible, high-pitched buzz and left a V-shaped wake behind.

"Inspiration Point," said Trey, noticeably winded from the climb and pointing at a wooden sign. He put down his backpack and fished out a water bottle. "It's a good view, eh?" He rubbed his ankle.

"It's incredible."

"By ten o'clock this place will be mobbed with families. Hey, check that out." He nodded toward a large boulder, on top of which sat a chipmunk, upright, looking intently at me. "Little kids feed them here all the time, so they're absolutely fearless. Watch this."

He pulled a cracker from a plastic bag inside his backpack. He squatted down, holding it out in the palm of his hand. The chipmunk looked from Trey to me, then back at him, and finally set its unblinking gaze on the tiny white speck in Trey's hand. In a flash, it scampered down the side of the rock to within a foot of the prize, where it froze, muscles tense and whiskers twitching. Trey grinned, motionless. After another moment, the animal hurried forward, snatched the cracker from his hand, and bounded off to the shadow of the boulder, where it sat up on its haunches, nibbling away.

"It's the little kids that feed them, eh?" I smiled.

"Shut up. You should see when it gets crowded. There's dozens of 'em. Park service doesn't know what to do about it. If we stick around, all his buddies will be here in a few minutes."

The path rose steadily into Cascade Canyon, winding for a bit and then meandering roughly parallel to a stream, which I guessed was the source of Lower Cascade Falls, which we crossed on the way up. It was shallow in some places, with the water forming gentle rapids over the rocky bed. In other spots, the surfaces of deep pools were nearly flat, just little whirls and eddies betraying the current. On either side, the slopes of the mountains rose steeply, canyon walls hundreds of feet high, lined with vast boulder fields and stands of tall pines dotted with yellow and white flowers. I shielded my eyes from the glare as I craned my neck to look around. The tops of the ridges were ash-gray against the deep-blue sky.

Trey raised a hand to signal a stop and then put a finger to his lips before pointing out into the stream. It took me a moment to see where he was pointing.

"There," he whispered. "About fifty feet from the far bank. In that deeper spot where the water looks black."

I squinted across the distance and realized why it was so hard to see. The moose was the same color as the water, a dark molasses brown. It stood nearly motionless, perpendicular to us, a single large black eye trained, it seemed, on the two of us.

"He's lookin' right back at us, wondering, 'What are they up to?'" Trey smiled, his voice low, eyes never wavering from the moose. "Sarah has a thing for them. She loves moose everything. She has this moose apron, moose-shaped soap in the shower, moose pillows on the couch, moose stencils in our bedroom."

*You've become a pillar of domesticity. Who is this guy?*

I laughed out loud.

"What?" Trey threw me a look.

"Nothing, man. Nothing."

We watched the moose for a while in silence. We both seemed to appreciate the stillness of the morning, and we felt no need to disturb it with much conversation. From there, we walked for nearly two hours without a word and encountered no one aside from a group of three other hikers, obviously coming off of a multiday trip judging by their heavy, full-size packs and mud-splashed legs. The respect for silence must be universal, I thought, because these other hikers simply nodded and smiled as they passed. The path continued gently uphill through the valley, passing through wide expanses of grass alternating with dense forest, always running alongside the river. Finally, we reached a junction in the stream where it joined another, and a solidly built wooden bridge bore to the right over a thunderous cascade. A sign read,

## NORTH FORK—LAKE SOLITUDE—2.7 MILES

We sat down on a log, both winded. My T-shirt was soaked in sweat. It was almost noon, and the sun was hot now. Trey took a sip from his water bottle and passed it to me. The water was cold. A mosquito landed on my leg. I swatted it.

"How you feelin'?" Trey elbowed me in the side. "All that college partyin' got you tired?"

"I'm the one still rowing, buddy. I feel fine. It's you I'm worried about, still smoking your cancer sticks."

"I like the taste of smoke. Call it a job skill." Trey smiled, swirling the water around in the plastic bottle. "Well, believe it or not, that was more than six miles we just did."

"Really? It doesn't seem like it."

"It never does here. You kinda get lost in the scenery. Of course, we aren't carrying much of anything. And the weather's been good. It goes fast, doesn't it?"

"It does," I replied. "How's that ankle?"

"It's okay. I'm gonna rewrap it, though." He set to work taking his boot off and gingerly removed the elastic wrap. The ankle was bruised and still a bit swollen.

"Doesn't look great."

"It's no big deal. I twisted it in the fire." He wrapped it again, using an intricate, slow motion process that began midsole and continued to just below his calf. "So, you've been pretty quiet. What's on your mind?"

Thoughts raced. *Oh not too much, buddy, just the fact that I don't know how I found myself here and how you found yourself here—but then you* did *find yourself here, didn't you?*

"Nothing, man. Really. I'm just…I'm just taking it all in, you know?"

He nodded. "I think I know what you mean."

A breeze moved the branches overhead. The waterfall thundered. Trey started with a laugh. "Do you remember the day Brady made us do two of those goddamned Ashford River runs back-to-back?"

"Jesus, yeah."

"That must have been nine miles."

"Closer to ten."

"That guy was a maniac. You stay in touch with him?"

*"I guess you're our guy."*

"I see him sometimes. He comes down to the boathouse for the Potomac regattas, likes to keep up with the Georgetown coaches. He's married now, you know. Got married the year after you left."

"Do he and his wife still live in MacKerry with the sophomores?"

I chuckled. "No, he moved to one of the separate apartments in the senior house. I don't think his wife could take sophomores. They got Dr. Connolly's place when he retired."

"Brady was a good guy. I should have left things on better terms with him."

"He was upset when you left. I think it hit him pretty hard."

"Really?" He took another swig of the water, offering it to me afterward.

"Yeah. We stayed pretty tight my next two years there. I had him in junior year for English. Really good teacher. You should look him up. Get some advice from the old married man."

"Maybe I will," he said, putting the bottle back in his bag.

"Seriously. I'm sure he'd like to hear from you."

"I've thought about that before. Him and Father Daley. Catching up with them." He paused and looked at me. "And you."

"Yeah. Well, one down, two to go, right?"

"Sure. We should get going. This lake is incredible, and I want you to see it before any weather comes in. Clouds can roll in fast in the afternoon."

We stood up, and Trey shouldered the backpack. "Hey."

"Huh?"

"Brady. Does he have any kids?" he asked.

"Two. They had a daughter over Christmas break my senior year. Guy was beaming the whole spring semester. Practices were a lot easier, actually. Then they had a boy about a year ago."

Trey nodded and started across the bridge. "Just wondering."

The 2.7 mile distance to Lake Solitude was deceptive. The trail was steep and rough in places, making it seem much longer. It took us almost an hour and a half of steady climbing to get there, but it was worth it. As we neared the lake, the path ambled over a long series of man-made steps, clearly designed to blend in with the natural surroundings. As we reached the top of the valley, Lake Solitude stretched out below and ahead of us, a deep-blue teardrop in the valley. We followed the path as it swung around the right shore and then took a side path leading to a rocky peninsula. We sat there, motionless. The surface was flat calm. Bright overhead sun illuminated the shallower sections, revealing how clear the water was, a blend of turquoise, gray, and green around the glacial rocks that protruded near the shore. A large rounded boulder formed an island directly in front of us twenty feet out, with a single, tiny pine tree growing from a fissure. The breeze was cooler up there, and I imagined that the water must still be ice cold, even in late August. The lake sat in a glacial amphitheater, surrounded on three sides by sharply rising cliffs hundreds of feet high. Snowpack hugged the granite walls and extended, in narrow tendrils, down through stream-carved canyons. Above, the sky was a blue panorama dotted with puffy white clouds, and a sliver of moon was still visible. I could smell pine, and the only sound was of water falling, as those far-off tendrils of snow formed tiny cascades across the lake. To our left, the Grand Teton clawed at the sky, gray and majestic, a slab of blue-white snow and ice capped on its shoulder. I heard a hawk cry, the sound echoing for a moment before it faded. On the far side of the lake, a small collection of tents marked a camping area. The tiny forms of other hikers moved about, busily setting up for the evening.

Trey pointed behind us and up. A barely perceptible pattern of switchbacks marked the continuing trail. "It comes from the other direction up there, over that pass. It's called Paintbrush Divide." He handed me the water bottle.

"Thanks."

"Me and a buddy climbed it in June, which was stupid. Covered in snow."

"Looks like there's still some snow up there now."

"In places that don't get much sun, yeah." He nodded at the lake. "The rangers call this Lake Plentitude, 'cause it gets so crowded sometimes."

"Doesn't look bad now."

"It'll fill up in a few hours with people on overnights. Some of them are coming over the pass, but you'll see lots coming up the way we did when we go back down."

"Good place to camp. You stayed here in June?"

"Yeah. Froze our asses off. But the stars. You should see the stars up here at night, man."

"I can imagine."

"You should come out sometime next summer when you have more time. It's probably gonna get snowed in over the next month, but it's pretty nice at the end of July. Sarah and I came up and spent two nights then."

We sat down on the rocks, which were warm from the sun despite the chilly air. Lunch was a box of Triscuit crackers, a stick of pepperoni that Trey began cutting into slices with his pocketknife, and some cheddar cheese. I was surprised by how hungry I was.

"Anything's good when you've been hiking all day."

"Not bad."

Trey squinted, looking out over the lake. "So, tell me about Lynn."

I sort of laughed. "That's hard."

"It's like that, eh?"

"It's like that."

We sat for a few moments, eating. I picked some mud off my sneaker. He smirked and handed me another cracker. "Okay, pal. I know it's been six years, but I used to be your roommate, remember? There wasn't much we didn't know about each other for a while there. So quit dodging my question. Tell me about Lynn."

I looked at him and rolled my eyes. "I just don't know. It was happening, and then it wasn't. It's like we were crazy about each other, but we drove each other nuts at the same time."

"Hmm. Sounds familiar. Ever occur to you that most relationships are like that?"

"I dunno," I replied. "Are they?"

"Sarah drives me crazy all the time, and I do the same to her. And we're getting married. I'm not so sure craziness and love are mutually exclusive."

I changed course. "I think it has something to do with both of us graduating this year. Different paths, ya know?"

"Geography and all, eh?"

*Distance and circumstance.*

"Yeah. Geography. I mean, who knows where we'll be in a year?" I said.

"Does that bother her as much as it bothers you?" He brushed some dirt off a piece of cheese and ate it.

"I don't know. I just think that's what it might be about."

"So you know you're graduating and part of you wants to end it now instead of later, when it would probably hurt even more." He stuffed a cracker into his mouth.

*Trey Daniels: Firefighter, Hometown Hero, and Doctor of Love.*

"Something like that. Actually, yeah, a lot like that."

"And she probably feels the same way, right?" he asked.

"Probably," I said. "Maybe. I dunno, actually."

"Got a picture of her?"

"In my wallet. It's in your backpack." He tossed the bag to me, and I dug out the photo and handed it to him.

"I'd do her." He grinned.

"Go to hell. You're getting married."

"Just kidding, Matty. Relax." He laughed. "When's the last time you went out with her?"

"While ago."

"When's the last time you *talked* with her?" he asked.

"While ago," I repeated.

"Maybe that's the problem." He handed me a piece of cheddar on a cracker.

"They teach you psychology in firefighting school?" I asked, eyebrows raised.

He laughed. "No, buddy. But my family's messed up, remember? And I live with a woman. Both of these things equip me with, basically, the same qualifications as a psychology degree."

"Right." I chuckled and ate the cracker.

"Seriously, you haven't talked to her in a while?" he asked.

"Nah."

"Call her."

I stared at the ground. "Yeah. I almost did yesterday."

"No, really. Call her. You've gotta communicate. You obviously still have feelings for her. You can't just hide."

I played with my shoelace.

He changed the subject. "So...law school, huh?"

I continued staring at the ground. "I really don't know, Trey."

He took his shoe off and shook a stone out of it, inspecting the ankle wrap. "I've gotta tell you, for a senior at Georgetown, you don't really know much."

"What the hell is that supposed to mean?" I shot back.

"Your answer to everything I've asked has been, 'I don't know.'" He raised his eyebrows.

"So? I'm just being honest with you. I really don't know. You want me to make something up?" I was getting frustrated, speaking rapidly.

"No, I don't want you to make something up. Because the problem isn't that you don't know," he said, cutting another slice of pepperoni and then gesturing with the knife. "It's that you haven't made any decisions."

I gave him a look. "Of course I've made decisions. You think you can get through three years of college without making any decisions?"

He put the knife down and stared, thoughtfully it seemed, at the slice of pepperoni he'd just cut. "Well, I wouldn't know about that, would I? I just mean..."

"You just mean what?"

"I just mean that maybe you haven't had to." He squinted.

"That I haven't had to *what?*"

"Make decisions," he said, calmly.

"I've course I've made decisions!" I shot back, not calmly at all.

"But you haven't *had to*. Push hasn't come to shove up till now. And now it has, Matt." He ate the pepperoni and looked out over the lake. "So now that you have to, it's hard. Takes some balls."

I paused for a few seconds and then asked, "Hold on. Are we talking about my balls—or the apparent lack thereof—in the context of Lynn or law school?"

"I don't know. You tell me. They're your balls." He grinned and shrugged his shoulders.

"Oh, Christ."

"It just seems to me that—"

I cut him off. This was getting not so funny now. "It seems to you. Come on, Trey, you haven't seen me in almost six years! That's almost a third of our lives! What the hell do you know about me?"

He folded the pocketknife and leaned back, looking up at the sky.

I stared at the ground again. "Sorry."

He looked at me and spoke quietly. "You're the one who flew out here, remember?"

I looked back at him. "I know."

"I don't think you flew all the way across the country just to see me. I mean I get the loyalty thing, and the long-lost friend bit. And I appreciate it. I really do. But it's not just that, and you know it. You came here to run away."

"Run away? From what?" My voice was starting to quaver.

"Decisions."

"Oh, for God's sake. Back to this? Jesus, you sound exactly like my father."

"Is that a bad thing?" he asked.

"No. I just…Oh, I don't know."

"Come on. You've made investments. You've poured yourself into some things, but now you're afraid to move on to what's next."

I shook my head. "If you're talking about law school, I just don't know. Do you realize what that involves? I mean, it's three years, a ton of money, and I don't even know if I want it."

He rolled his eyes. "Bullshit."

"Bullshit?"

"Yeah, that's right. Bullshit. You're gonna graduate from Georgetown with an honors degree; you can probably go to any law school you want. You've studied this stuff for three years, and you've been talking about it since you were fifteen. Now you're 'not sure about it?' I say bullshit."

I stood up. My chest was pounding. My voice came out louder than I meant it to. "This, coming from you? The guy who defied all expectations and escaped his trust-fund destiny to pursue a clean, honest, blue-collar living, up here in the mountains? You're just as smart as I am, Trey, probably smarter! You could've gone to Harvard for God's sake! But instead you're up here driving a pickup and wearing flannel shirts! You're a goddamned Bruce Springsteen song! Why the hell don't *you* go to law school?"

His voice was very quiet. He looked me in the eye. "Because I don't want to go to law school. But you do." He paused. "Don't you?"

I didn't answer, but something inside me shifted right then. It was a small, barely discernible shift, but I felt it for sure, the same way you know when someone walks into a room behind you. I sank back to the rock.

"I've thought about teaching instead."

"Teaching?"

"Yeah."

"You'd be good at it. What? History?"

"Yep. High school."

"Really? High school? Don't you remember what a pain in the ass we were at that age?" He chuckled.

"I remember. I've talked to Brady a couple of times about it. He thinks they'd hire me back at Ashford. He wants to give up coaching, and they'd need a replacement."

"What goes around comes around, huh?" He smiled. "You know they'd terrorize you. Little demons."

"Kinda like we did, right?"

"Yeah, kinda like we did."

"It wouldn't pay much," I said. "Not compared to a law career."

"Neither does firefighting, pal." He smiled.

We sat there and looked out at the lake. We didn't talk for a while. I lay down on my back and gazed up at the pine branches silhouetted against the sky. Occasionally, a low rumble would echo across the water, followed by a splash as more of the snowpack tumbled off the rock face. The sun felt warm. A half hour or so passed, and Trey stood up, shouldered his backpack, and offered me a hand. I reached up, and he pulled me to my feet.

"You know, I really appreciate you flying out here. I mean that."

"Guess I sort of needed to," I said. "You were right about that."

"You remember how Father Daley used to talk about stuff happening for a reason?" he asked.

"I do remember. He mentioned it again at graduation. It was corny."

He tightened the shoulder straps of his backpack. "I was thinking about that with everything that's happened."

I looked at him. "So you think stuff like this happens for a reason, or is it just coincidence?"

"Maybe it's both." He started walking back down the path. "Okay. Let's go. If Sarah sets the house on fire making dinner, I want to be there to help put it out."

# CHAPTER 32

It was almost six by the time we got back to the parking lot. Trey was right about the hikers heading into the park for the night. We passed fifteen or twenty people with heavy backpacks, all headed for the lake campsites. It must turn into a tent city at night, I thought as they passed. We opted for the water taxi on the way back, enjoying the warmth as we lay on the benches in the stern, the sky bright and the spray flying over us. Trey struck up a conversation with the driver, who turned out to be the little brother of a guy in the fire department.

The sun was low and hidden behind the mountains to the west as we drove home. The sky was soft indigo and still completely cloudless. A few stars were visible, white and sharp. We turned down a side road, passing some kids playing street hockey, and then made our way up a small, one-way avenue that climbed a hill. Streetlamps began to blink on as dusk fell.

Trey's apartment complex was a converted ski lodge, the original guest suites made into twelve small, one-bedroom units. The developer tried hard to modernize it, but the original dated design was hard to hide. The bedroom upstairs was built into a small loft overlooking the living room, which opened onto a deck through sliding glass doors.

I was amused to see the table set when we walked in, three places meticulously arranged with bright-blue dishes, silverware, and artfully folded napkins. In the center of it all—next to a flickering trio of candles—sat four cartons of Chinese takeout, steaming, each with its own serving fork. Sarah was drying her hands with a towel when we walked in. Country music blared on the stereo.

She paused, a surprised look on her face. She glanced quickly at the table and then at Trey. Trey's hand went to his face, and I could tell he was making a valiant effort to hold back laughter. Sarah put the towel down on the counter, her smile broadening. "Lo mein by candlelight, honey."

He laughed and hugged her. She looked over his shoulder back at me and raised her eyebrows.

"Tracy and I were out later than we thought. We got talking," she said after he let her go. She handed Trey and me bottles of beer and opened a can of Diet Coke for herself. "So I had to improvise."

The conversation wandered freely during dinner. We talked about Sarah's job at the garden center and the nearly deaf old man who owned it, country music, the rowing scene at Georgetown, memories of practicing and races at Ashford, various hiking routes in the Tetons, quality skiing at Jackson Hole, leasing the apartment versus buying a house, some technicalities of firefighting, and even a little free-trade policy.

We made quick work washing the dishes. I insisted on helping. Sarah sprayed Trey with water from the sink, and soon he held her upside down, slung over his shoulder with his good arm. She squealed and whacked him in the leg with her dishtowel. As he swung her around to put her down, her foot caught the ice-cream carton, splattering the far wall and my hair with Neapolitan. The three of us laughed for a good five minutes.

■ ■ ■

A little while and one shower later (both to clean up from the hike and to get the ice cream out of my hair), I was sitting on the deck with Trey, wearing a borrowed Jackson Hole Fire sweatshirt and sipping a beer. The sky, speckled with stars, was pure velvet. The mountains loomed like shadows, patches of ice-blue snow hugging the peaks and extending down into the valleys like fingers.

I heard the *whoosh* of the sliding door behind us, and we turned to see Sarah standing just inside, leaning out through the opening. She was wearing a terrycloth bathrobe. Her hair was still damp and hung straight down, neatly combed, and her face glowed with the flush of a warm bath.

"Hey, you guys."

Trey smiled. "Come on out and sit with us."

"No! It's cold out. I'm going upstairs to read. Matt, I'll see you in the morning." She smiled. "Come over here, and give me a hug."

I did. She smelled clean. Her hair was soft and full where it touched my ear. I put my hands quickly in my pockets. "Thanks so much for dinner. I haven't laughed that much in a while."

"Neither have we," she replied. "Well, you guys chat it up. I'm whipped."

Trey leaned around in his chair, squeezed her hand, and pulled her toward him for a kiss. "Good night."

Once inside, she closed the door and then opened it a few inches to say, "By the way, breakfast will be *real* tomorrow. No takeout." She gave a tiny wave through the glass and then turned out the kitchen light and went upstairs.

Trey stretched his arms. "I love her."

"She's something."

We listened to silence for a while, watching the moon heave into view. Lynn. It was Saturday night. Were would she be? Out with friends? Maybe with a guy. No, more than likely home in her apartment, reading a book and getting ready for the start of classes. I thought about all that Trey had said on the mountain. About my not making decisions, about not communicating. I sipped my beer.

After a few minutes, Trey said, in what was almost a whisper, "I want to go see my dad." He set the bottle on the ground, shivered a little bit, and hugged himself in the sweater. "I want to go see him right now."

■ ■ ■

The hospital room was still, and Andrew Daniels was motionless except for the subtle rise and fall of his chest. The room was lit in strange, pale colors by the various computer readouts, and the workings of the ventilator seemed slower and shallower than before.

Trey stood at the foot of the bed, leaning his weight on the frame, forearms tensed. I lingered by the door, halfway in the room. Down the darkened corridor, a nurse sat in a pool of light working a crossword puzzle, occasionally sipping from a mug of steaming coffee. I could hear the scratch of her pencil on the newspaper. A quiet, monotonous beeping came from a room across the hall.

When I looked back at Trey, I saw that he'd moved to the chair by the bed. His eyes were closed, and he leaned forward, elbows on his knees. His hand gripped his father's, which hung limply over the edge of the mattress. I could sense a shift in the air then, something barely felt, like that subtle tremor of change I'd felt earlier that day. It was a dull sort of weight that pulled on the shadows in the tiny hospital room, drawing them down and closing in. At first, it was silent, a slight shudder in Trey's shoulders, but soon, quiet sobs racked his body as he wept, just like he'd wept on the beach when we were kids, drawing deep breaths, tears flowing freely. I moved to his side and put a hand on his shoulder until the shaking subsided. My own eyes stung as we walked outside into the cool air of the parking lot.

■ ■ ■

"Sarah's pregnant." The words hung in the air like snowflakes, suspended for a moment, and then quietly settled on the darkened asphalt.

We both halted at the words. I repeated them in my mind to be sure I'd heard them right. Trey sat down on the rear bumper of his truck, hands in his pockets. The lamp cast a whitish glow that made everything look flat. A column of mosquitoes and moths buzzed above us near the bulb. "No one else knows," he murmured.

*Why tell me?*

"No one?"

"No one."

*Why me?*

I sat down next to him and stared at a bottle cap on the ground. "When is she due?"

"Early March."

"She doesn't show at all."

"She's not that far along. Hides it well."

"You haven't told your mom?"

"You're the only person I've told, Matt. Sarah hasn't told anyone at all." He turned and faced me. "It's a boy."

"That's...that's big news."

"It is."

I turned to Trey, throwing him a punch to the shoulder and smiling as the initial shock of the surprise subsided. "Hey! That's really *great* news, Trey!"

The grin came slowly. "Yeah. Yeah, it is, isn't it?"

"Have a name yet?"

"No idea. She likes Patrick."

"Patrick Daniels," I said. "That sounds good."

"Yeah."

Trey reached down, picked up a bottle cap, and turned it over in his hand. "I used to collect these. Had a huge jar full of 'em. Guess I left it in the old house in Lake Placid. I wonder if dad saved them."

"You know, I was wondering. How did you recognize your dad? I mean, in the fire?"

"I didn't. Not until we got outside. It was that stupid bathrobe. And the scar from the fight."

"He got a scar from your punch? Must have been a hell of a hit."

"Well, yeah, it was. But the scar isn't from the punch itself. I wasn't that strong. It's because his face hit the corner of the kitchen table on the way to the floor. I only knocked him off his feet because he was drunk." He exhaled loudly. "The last time I had a conversation with my dad was two years ago, Matt. On the phone. And the last thing I said was, 'Go to hell.' After that, I hung up on him."

I pondered this for a moment. "Are you going to tell him about the baby?"

Trey turned the cap around slowly, watching the lamplight glimmer on the scratched blue metal before putting it in his pocket. "Yeah. As soon as he's conscious. He's a grandfather now. I guess that'll wake him up, huh?"

# CHAPTER 33

Breakfast the next morning was simple but thorough, and Sarah woke me up at five thirty with noise in the kitchen. I sat up on the sofa, stretched, and walked over to a mug of coffee already poured and waiting on the counter. Sure enough, the mug had the silhouette of a moose on it. Sarah put on Tim McGraw just loud enough to wake Trey up, and he waved silently to us from the loft as he trudged from his bedroom into the bathroom. I read the paper and sipped coffee, trading small talk with Sarah until Trey came downstairs, dressed in his utility uniform, pager on his belt. He had his duffel bag packed, as he'd be on duty overnight at the fire station.

After breakfast, I said good-bye to Sarah and assured her that we'd see each other soon and stay in touch. She gave me a hug before I threw my backpack in the truck bed and climbed in. There was no talk among us of the baby.

The morning news droned from the radio while we drove, but I barely heard it. The windows were wide open, and the breeze carried pine and cedar. The sun, just climbing into view, illuminated the gray east face of the mountains with a soft glow as we drove toward town. We turned down a side road near the hospital, and Trey parked in front of the fire station. We got out, and he locked up his truck.

"Just be a minute. Using the department's truck today. I gotta get the keys from inside."

I leaned against the tailgate and waited. He came out in a few minutes and nodded toward a yellow-green Suburban marked "JACKSON HOLE FIRE/EMS—PREVENTION & INVESTIGATION." The back was full of fire and medical gear, and a red, white, and blue light bar was mounted on top. "Gotta pick up a few guys at another station after I drop you off. We're supposed to visit some Boy Scout career fair. Talk to them about firefighting and all. Chief's idea. Of course, Chief's on vacation this weekend, so the local hero gets to do it."

"Lucky you," I said.

"Lucky me." He chuckled.

We drove without talking for a while, the scanner squawking with occasional chatter. Trey turned the volume down.

"So you gotta tell me what you decide," he said.

"Whaddya mean?"

"I mean what we talked about. School. Lynn. Life."

"Yeah."

He adjusted a vent on the dashboard. I watched the digital readout on the scanner. He lit a cigarette and turned on the radio. We rode quietly and I watched the mountains.

After a little while, we turned off the highway onto the airport road. Trey pulled the truck around to the passenger drop-off. He put it in park alongside the curb.

"So you got a full shift after the Boy Scout thing?" I asked.

"Shift and a half, man. Overnight. Gonna be a long one."

"Hope it's quiet for you."

"Never is." He smiled. "But that's what keeps it interesting." He gazed at the steering wheel; I stared at the dashboard. We could hear the whine of a warming jet engine across the tarmac.

He looked up. "Well, hey, it was good to see you. I—"

Trey's pager beeped loudly, and he looked down at it. A dispatcher squawked an EMS alert and a Jackson address over the scanner. "Hmm. Kicking in early today. Guess the Boy Scouts have to wait." He held out his hand, and I gripped it. I pulled my backpack from the rear seat, climbed out, and closed the door.

"Matt." He leaned over to see me through the window.

"Hmm?"

Trey turned the volume down on the scanner, relegating the radio chatter to the background. "Come to the wedding."

"I'll be there."

Trey reached up and flipped a switch. The light bar above the cab spun up with a whirring noise as the pager beeped again. He gave a nod and a smile as he put the truck in gear, and I watched as my friend drove off, lights flashing like beacons.

# CHAPTER 34

It was only last night when I landed at Reagan to return to school. Between the time difference and a long delay on the connecting flight, I got in pretty late. It was a clear night with a full moon, and as we neared the runway, I looked out on the tidal basin and the white granite monuments beyond. The obelisks and rounded edifices glowed brightly, bathed in floodlights. The noise and commotion of the terminal and metro station jolted me. After the relative quiet of Wyoming, the nation's capital hummed with an agitated, powerful energy.

When I got back to the apartment, a note from McNeal said that he was out with the rest of the crew team ringing in the new academic year down on M Street. For a moment, I thought of joining them, but it would have taken a second wind that I just didn't have. So instead, I stood in my bedroom, the duffel bag hanging from my shoulder, and stared at the wall for a while. I looked around at the scattered books, papers, and laundry. An empty beer bottle sat on the windowsill, looking dejected with its brown glass and peeling label. I put the bag down on my bed and emptied my pockets, throwing stuff in a pile on the desk. Wallet, keys, loose change, and the boarding pass I carried, now creased and dog-eared. I looked at the photo of Lynn and me.

As tired as I was from traveling, I couldn't sleep. So I went outside and sat on the front steps, watched the traffic, and sipped on a beer. I'm not sure how many times the light changed or how many cars went by. It was still warm—the end of summer in DC always is—and I sat out there for the better part of an hour, just thinking. McNeal came stumbling home sometime around one or two to pick up his cell phone but then went back out, mumbling incoherently and giving me a high five on his way down the steps. In the houses on either side of ours, college rocked on.

Images of Lake Solitude surfaced, and I thought about a documentary I'd once seen about glaciers. I remembered the British narrator rambling on, describing the movement of an immense mass of ice somewhere in Argentina or Chile. "The glacier moves only inches each year," he'd said. Steady, slow movement, hardly detectable. But this movement was periodically accelerated by tumultuous change, when the forces were just right, and a huge slab of blue-white ice would fall away with a thunderous crash, reshaping the entire thing. It could be a tiny seismic tremor that began the chain of events, a particularly stubborn granite ridge deep beneath the surface, or even the transmitted force of the slightest movement of another glacier miles away. Whatever it was, it would be enough to send a hairline fracture ricocheting through the mass, and that, in turn, was enough to tip the balance between friction and gravity. Inertia gave way to momentum, and within moments, a new, shimmering face of mirror-smooth ice basked in sunlight for the first time.

Something became clear in the darkness last night. I felt peaceful and warm. Come to think of it, it was the same warmth I used to feel as a boy, when despite all the confusion of growing up, the company of a friend could make everything okay. I didn't figure out the rest of my life sitting out on those steps watching a traffic light. Lots of things are up in the air. I guess they probably should be at twenty-one. Like my dad always says, things happen on their own time, and you figure things out when you figure them out. But I did make two decisions before I went to sleep. And as the sun shines through the window this morning, they're even clearer in my mind.

■ ■ ■

I'm going to see Lynn today.
And I'm not going to law school.

# ACKNOWLEDGMENTS

*The trouble with acknowledgments is that despite an author's best efforts, it is nearly impossible to acknowledge everyone deserving. I began writing this book more than ten years before I published it, and a story grows up quite a bit over the course of a decade. The inspiration for that growth has come from too many people and experiences to recall. All the same, I think some specific words of thanks are due, foremost to my parents. Next are my four brothers, who were my first friends and my companions in so many adventures as a kid. Thank you to my grandparents, who set the stage in many ways for the experiences we had together, and to a lovely woman named Helene "Granny" Smith, who was like another grandparent and certainly helped to foster my love of books. And to the core group of pals from high school, who taught me what friendship was about and so, I suppose, provided the foundation for this story, especially Scott, Brian, Nate, John, and Pete. Thanks to Mr. Frank Tudini, who first taught me how to read a book the right way in eleventh grade, and Dr. Bob Butler, who helped me get better at it in college. Dr. Mick Cochrane taught me how to write a story. Dr. Jim Power took a chance on me and got me started in my teaching career at the tender age of twenty-two. Every student I've taught at Georgetown Prep and Canisius, and every rower and swimmer I've coached, deserves my gratitude. I suppose these characters and their stories find their roots in the many years of laughter and challenge that have come with trying to educate kids in the classroom, in dormitories, on the water, in the water, and in faraway places. The Amigos and Compañeros (both young and old, "gringo," Dominican, and Nicaraguan alike) who have worked so hard at my side in rugged places off the beaten track have been a great inspiration. Jeff Keitzmann, Daniel DeKay, and the Wilderness Medicine Institute of the National Outdoor Leadership School (NOLS) gave me a new appreciation for firefighters and EMS providers during my EMT training. My professors and classmates at the great University of Saint Andrews across the pond—especially Max Adler, Brent Bonds, Dr. Douglas Dunn and Ms. Meagan Delahunt—lent me a generous year of patient reading and feedback during grad school. This story took shape in that ancient, beautiful town atop the craggy Scottish shore of the North Sea. I owe much to my colleagues in teaching and coaching, especially Ben Williams, Joe Powers, Trevor Bonat, Greg Eck, Jeff Jones, Steve Ochs, Adam Baber, Ron Ahrens, Tom Flaherty, and Jack Hailand. And, of course, to the Jesuits, especially Father Jim Van Dyke, Father Fred Betti, and Father Rich Zanoni...thanks for teaching me how to make decisions. Thank you to my early draft readers. If I try to mention you all, I will certainly miss someone. Know that each of you played a role in helping me. But a special thanks to Amy Kimmel, whose thorough final spot-check helped put my editing saga to rest. Thanks to the town of Jackson, the village of Lake Placid, the city of Buffalo, and the Capital Region.*

*David, thank you for taking the time to read the book, custom-design a fantastic cover, and accommodate my numerous adjustments. That was a hell of a nice thing to do for your big brother. I owe you a lot of drinks.*

*Of course, my wife Megan should know that she is the truest inspiration and my single favorite muse. And finally, Matthew, you're only a few months old at the time of publication, but I want you to know that you're the guy who finally convinced your old man to get this thing in print after ten years of "editing," otherwise known as "stalling."*

# ABOUT THE AUTHOR

Paul Cumbo is an English teacher, rowing coach, and director of domestic and international service-learning programs at Canisius, a Jesuit high school for boys in Buffalo, New York. He began his career in September 2001 at Georgetown Prep, a Jesuit boarding school in Bethesda, Maryland, where he served on the residential faculty and taught English for three years. He lived in Scotland while earning a postgraduate degree in creative writing and fiction at the University of St. Andrews before returning to Buffalo in 2005, where he lives with his wife and son.

Visit www.paulcumbo.com to learn more about the author and other works.
Follow the author on Twitter at @PaulCumbo.
One Lane Bridge Publications is a self-publishing imprint.
Cover and interior art: David M. Cumbo.
Author photo by John Anderson. Glenn Pass, Sequoia-King's Canyon National Park. August 2010.